GALVESTON: 1900
INDIGNITIES

Book 1
The Arrival

N.E. BROWN
S.L. JENKINS

MINDSTIR MEDIA

Galveston: 1900 – Indignities
Book 1: The Arrival
Copyright © 2013 by N. E. Brown and S.L. Jenkins. All rights reserved.

Published by Mindstir Media
1931 Woodbury Ave. #182 | Portsmouth, NH 03801 | USA
1.800.767.0531 | www.mindstirmedia.com

Printed in the United States of America

ISBN-13: 978-0-9894748-8-7

Library of Congress Control Number: 2013945716

The Arrival

CHAPTER 1

Catherine Grace Eastman was gazing out the window of St. Mary's Orphan's Home as she had done on numerous occasions. It was peaceful watching the sea of waves crash on the rocks as the evening tide began its nightly ritual of dancing over the sandy beaches and seashells, each time inching a little closer to the shoreline. The seagulls were still filling their bellies with the evening catch of the day and she could see the dim lights of a ship that looked to be miles away at sea. Was it coming or going, she thought to herself. Catherine began to fight back the tears that were filling her eyes. Why, after all this time did it still hurt so much? Catherine cried to herself. She was fifteen years old when she left her home in Sandgate, England on July 7, 1898, and traveled to America with her mother, Anne Eastman. Her younger sister, Whitney, had died six months earlier from the fever. Prior to that her father, Adam Eastman, and older brother, Henry, had died in a horrible accident. It was all behind her now and she needed to prepare herself for her future outside the orphanage. At least that is what Sister Maria DePaul kept reminding her. Catherine was going to be sixteen on her next birthday in February and there were choices she would have to make. Choices that would affect the rest of her life.

Catherine stopped daydreaming and looked around the small room filled with baskets of children's clothing that had been donated by the church's parishioners and other baskets with clothing in need of repair or to be remade into clothing for the smaller children. She liked sewing. Her mother had been a seamstress and it was one way Catherine could feel close to her mother. When she was growing up in Sandgate she would often watch her mother sew, and after her studies and lesson plans were completed, she helped her mother with cutting the fabric and pinning the seams together. The Singer sewing machine that Catherine was using now was the same one that accompanied her and her mother on their journey to America. Her father had bought the sewing machine for his wife from a down-on-his luck sailor who was a drinking buddy of Adam's. The sailor's mother had apparently passed away suddenly and the sailor was getting rid of anything he could sell in order to raise money for his own family. Sewing machines in the small village were hard to come by, and Adam didn't mind using his weekly wages to buy it for Anne. The sewing machine would help Anne sew clothing more quickly so they could be sold to the local merchants.

Sandgate was a small fishing village in England and ships would stop there on the way to other destinations. Clothing was much in demand and on many occasions the ships' captains would place orders with Anne to sew clothing for their wives or mistresses, whichever was the case. In any event, it provided Catherine's family with extra money to live on. Some of the money went into a small tin canister that her mother kept in the kitchen cupboard.

"We are going to America someday," said Anne.

"We will get a new start there. More opportunity for your father to find work and I can sell my clothing for more money there," she told Catherine.

If only they had stayed in Sandgate, thought Catherine. Those were happier times and now she had to look to the future.

Sandgate spanned almost three kilometres of the Kent coastline between Folkston and Hyde and fringed the English Channel. The quaint little village the Eastmans called home was clustered atop steep rocky slopes and overlooked the English Channel. It was on one of these steep slopes that Adam and Catherine's older brother, Jacob, had fallen to their deaths on October 10, 1897. That morning, Adam and Jacob had left home early hoping to reset the fishing nets before sunrise. The heavy rains the night before had weakened the winding road over the cliffs at Lizard Point. The early morning was just waking up as the sun began to sneak over the horizon. Large puddles of water and early morning fog gave little indication that a small curve in the road had been washed away and danger was ahead. With no warning in sight, Jacob, Adam, and the family horse, Jess Belle, tumbled down the rocky slope along with the sulky they were riding on, falling onto the rocks below just above the Lizard Peninsula.

They were supposed to be home early afternoon and by evening Anne began to fear the worst. She left a lantern on in the front window and she held her Bible in her hand as she began to pray. Anne tried to hide her anxiety from Catherine and Whitney, and told them that the men had probably found shelter at a friend's home near the fishing pier. Anne sent her daughters to bed that evening after a quiet dinner and she finally fell asleep in her rocking chair. The next morning Amos Slaughter, the lighthouse keeper, woke Anne by pounding his fist on the door. He was very sorry to disturb her at this early hour, but as he was making his morning rounds, he noticed a pile of rubble at the bottom of the cliff. He originally thought that it was something that had been a part of a boat that had washed up on the rocks, but after a closer inspection he discovered the wooden planks of the sulky and tack that was still attached to the horse. Jacob's body was discovered several feet away, sprawling over the rocks and seaweed. Adam's body was found lifeless on a small boulder ten feet above his son.

Catherine never quite understood why her mother wanted to leave Sandgate. Perhaps there were too many memories there. It was always her father who had dreamed of going to America. She had overheard her parents discussing some of the events regarding the Boer War and that they should leave England before her father was forced to join the English Navy. Catherine and her younger sister, Whitney, were happy in Sandgate. They loved the townspeople, and although they had no close relatives that she knew of, this little village was her home. But home or not, the cottage was just too much for the Eastman girls to keep up. Without the extra income Adam and Jacob had brought in from their fishing business, Anne was falling behind in their mortgage to the bank. To make matters worse, Whitney began to run a fever and needed constant care. Catherine tried to help her mother keep up with the sewing, but customers became disgruntled and began to take their business elsewhere.

"We need to sell the cottage," said Anne.

"But mother, where will we go?" asked Catherine.

After a thoughtful moment Anne replied, "America…we will go to America."

Selling the cottage was the least of Anne's worries. Whitney's health began to fail. After several days, she was not getting any better and Anne worried that the trip to America would be too hard for her. The doctor told Anne that Whitney most likely would not be able to survive the trip and that she would not be able to get a clean health card, which was required of all passengers making the trip abroad. That evening Whitney died in her sleep as Anne was reading Whitney's favorite story to her. She was only nine years old. Catherine and her mother wept in each other's arms. That night Catherine slept in her mother's bed and wondered what life was going to be like in America. She loved her sister and couldn't imagine their life without her.

"We cannot question God's will. We must find strength in everything and move forward," Anne said to Catherine.

Whitney was buried alongside her father, brother, and her mother's parents in the family plot at Lowery Cemetery outside of Sandgate. The ride home in their neighbor's buggy seemed endless. When they reached the cottage, their neighbors, John and Celia Emory, asked if they could come in to discuss the possibility of buying the Eastman's cottage. Anne was surprised at their request as they had never mentioned their interest in the cottage before now.

"We know ye have suffered great loss and our timing is not the best," said Mr. Emory, "but we would fancy making you an offer on your cottage. I took it upon myself to speak with your banker and he told me what a fair price would be. I am prepared to offer thou more than that as my brub's family is moving here next month from Ecosse and we would fancy for 'em to be close by. I understand that ye are planning to move to the colonies, and with the wedge I am prepared to pay ye, after ye pay off your loan to the bank, there would be a fair wedge for ye and Catherine to begin a new life there," Mr. Emory continued. "Ye don't have to give me an answer right now, but I would need an answer within a day or two so my blud can make his arrangements…please, do speak with Edward Herring at the bank."

The next day Anne and Catherine went to see Edward Herring at the bank. He informed Anne that Mr. Emory's offer was more than generous and if, indeed, it were her desire to sell the house, she most likely couldn't do better. She was only past due two months, but if she did not sell soon, the bank could foreclose. She really did not have any other choices. The deal was made with Mr. and Mrs. Emory, and the Emory's gave Anne and Catherine two weeks to move out.

Anne had been an only child and had gone to the Princess Helena Boarding School outside of London when she was growing up and she spent her summers learning the fine art of tailoring from her father. Anne and Adam had grown up together and had known each other since they were small children. Everyone said that Anne could have had her pick of any of the young men from London to Liverpool because of her striking good looks. She had thick, wavy, raven hair, high cheekbones, piercing hazel eyes, and her smile was electrifying. She was well educated, smart, and loved her family.

Catherine had also attended the Princess Helena Boarding School, but because of the economic conditions in their small village she had to complete her education at home, and she loved her mother's tutorials. She also liked the freedom that came with it. She would often roam the countryside exploring the butterfly fields and throwing rocks from the cliffs with the local boys. She was carefree, and like her mother, exceptionally pretty, and she liked flirting with the boys. Catherine was a bit precocious and curious about everything and it often got her into trouble when her father would find her roaming the countryside past dinner time. She had a striking resemblance to her mother and she was favored by all the young men.

Anne had sold most of the furniture and the equipment in the barn to Mr. Emory for his brother. It was difficult trying to decide what personal possessions she wanted to take. Pictures of her parents and family along with a few pieces of jewelry that had belonged to her mother, her family Bible, and Adam's gold wedding band and watch, were all she intended to take. With Catherine's help, they selected their lightest clothing and began sewing hidden pockets in their slips and undergarments where they could hide money and the jewelry. Their birth certificates and health cards were placed in protective bags and also sewn into the clothing they were going to wear.

"It is not safe to carry anything that pickpockets or thieves can grab," cautioned Mr. Emory. "Thou need to travel light."

After they had carefully selected their garments, they packed up one small trunk along with her sewing machine to be transported to the train station. Anne and Catherine carefully dressed layering two dresses each over their slips and corsets and topping it off with a light jacket and hat.

"We won't need too many things for our trip," said Anne to Catherine. "After we get settled there, we can sew whatever we need."

The Emory's had been Anne's neighbors for almost fifteen years and Mr. Emory had admired Anne for some time. He had tried to flirt with her when the occasion permitted, but Anne always politely put him in his place. He was hopeful that his eagerness to help Anne plan her trip to America would make him more attractive to her, but Anne ignored his advances.

Mr. Emory had been a business man in the shipping industry and he spent several nights mapping out the itinerary for them. "I think it best you take the route to America aboard the Liverpool & Texas

Steamship Co. Line and sail from Liverpool to Galveston, Texas," said Mr. Emory. "New York has been inundated with immigrants and I fear it is taking days to get through customs," he continued. "Your birth certificates and health cards should be all ye need to complete a quick walk through at customs in Galveston."

The day of departure was difficult for both of them. Anne was actually having second thoughts, but she felt that America would offer a better life for Catherine, and she felt there was nothing left for her in Sandgate. London and Liverpool were too expensive and from everything she had read, America promised them more than what they could find in England.

Mr. Emory offered to take Anne and Catherine to the train station for their trip to Liverpool. Along the way, Anne asked Mr. Emory if he wouldn't mind stopping at the cemetery for a brief moment so they could say their last good-byes to their family. Catherine and her mother knelt quietly by each of the graves and said their farewells in a final prayer. As they joined Mr. Emory in the buggy, Anne turned and looked back. She knew this would probably be the last time she would visit their graves and she felt a sorrowful emptiness in her heart. Anne asked Mr. Emory if he would please make sure the caretaker looked after the graves and he agreed. It was a short trip to the train station and they said their good-byes to Mr. Emory.

Anne and Catherine arrived at the train station two hours before the train was scheduled to leave and take them to London and then on to Liverpool. The train from London to Liverpool would leave at 7:00 o'clock that evening and they would travel overnight to Liverpool making only four stops. They had booked a small compartment with two sleeping bunks and a bench so that they would be more comfortable. They both watched out the window absorbing the beautiful English countryside that had been their home for so many years. The meadows were filled with the splendour of summer flowers and they drank in its beauty.

When they arrived in London, Anne and Catherine decided to

walk to a nearby park and eat from a basket of food that Mrs. Emory had prepared for their trip. The biscuits, pear preserves, cheeses and cookies were a delightful treat and they devoured all of it. Both women had been to London many times and they had little time to see the sites so they decided to return to the station and wait for their train.

The train ride to Liverpool was very loud and bumpy but Anne and Catherine managed to get a few hours' sleep. They read and did needle point and talked about happier times and tried to envision what their new life would be like in another country. Anne looked younger than her 32 years and she had a natural beauty that made her stand out in a crowd. Not only could she speak English beautifully, but she was fluent in French, German and Italian. She had made sure that Catherine was also well versed in these languages. Sandgate had been a melting pot of people from all over the world and they often had to address them in other languages when they were around them at the local markets and when the travelers were being fitted for new clothing. Anne prided herself in the fact that she never met a stranger and that language was not a barrier. Mr. Emory had warned her, though, that she should be cautious speaking to strangers on their trip and the more she and Catherine kept to themselves the better off they would be.

CHAPTER 2

They arrived in Liverpool early on Friday morning. Their ship would sail at 5:00 o'clock sharp that afternoon and they needed to be at port by 10:00 a.m. in order to clear customs and check their luggage. Mr. Emory had told Anne that there would be long lines and that she should not waste any time. They had already purchased their tickets for their trip from a ticket agent in London that Mr. Emory had referred her to. Mr. Emory had also seen to it that a horse and buggy were waiting upon their arrival after they stepped off the train. Anne asked the porter to take them directly to the passenger area at the ship yards so she could be close to the front of the line when they began boarding the passengers. As they began to get closer, Catherine asked the porter why so many people were standing around.

He replied, "Many questions to answer, documents to look at and everyone these days want to go to America."

Each passenger had to answer a long questionnaire before boarding the ship. Some of the questions included, among others, their name, age, sex, marital status, occupation, nationality, race, physical and mental health, where their last residence was and the country, and the name and address of the nearest relative or friend in the immigrant's country of origin. Anne answered each one and then moved on to the next line with Catherine staying close by. Both she and Catherine had received shots and a medical card from her local doctor before they left home so they passed quickly through the line that required a doc-

tor's examination and shots if they had no health card. Finally, with all
of the questions answered and medical cards examined, they were led
to their accommodations. Anne had been warned by Mr. Emory that
she should purchase second class tickets so she and Catherine would
not have to endure the overcrowded steerage passenger areas which
were located on the lower decks of the ships and had limited access to
food, toilets and fresh air. Their small inside cabin was on the second
deck just below the stairs and was only a few feet away from the community bathrooms and toilets. They both gave a sigh of relief as they
stored their travel bags under their bunks. The trip was going to take
eight to nine days depending on the weather and they were going to
have to make the best of it considering the cramped quarters and foul
smells.

Mr. Emory had also arranged for Anne and Catherine to eat in
the steward's cafeteria. It was well worth the additional cost as it served
a lot of the same food that the first class passengers were eating in the
dining rooms. It mostly fed the ship's crew, but there was a small dining room adjacent to the open area of long tables where limited seating
allowed second class passengers to gather and have their meals separate
from the crew. So far, Anne was pleased that they had made it this far
and that everything was falling into place. It was just her and Catherine
now, and in eight days they would be in America. The last year had
been a time of despair and terrible loss but she could not allow herself
to be sad. She had to be strong for Catherine and she was going to see
to it that Catherine would have all the advantages she never had. Yes,
they were going to the promised land, she thought, and all would be
well.

The ship pulled away from its pier at half past five in the afternoon and headed in a westerly direction. Once it was out in the Irish
Sea, it would head south around the lower part of Ireland into the Atlantic Ocean. After a light dinner in the cafeteria, Anne and Catherine
decided they had plenty of time to explore the ship the next day. There
was a bathroom two doors down from their cabin, which they were told

would be shared between four cabins. The door was unlocked so they decided to stop in and wash up before going to their room. The bathroom consisted of a water closet and two sinks and a salt water shower.

"Not the best accommodations but it will have to do," Anne said to Catherine.

Catherine replied, "It's not so bad, mama, we won't be spending that much time in here."

They both chuckled and went back across the hall to their cabin. They were delighted to remove the bulky layers of clothing that they had been wearing the past two days.

The small cabin was musty and cramped and allowed very little room to move around, but Anne and Catherine were glad to have their privacy and knew they had to make the best of it for the duration of their trip. They hung their clothes in the tiny closet and placed the remainder of their personal things in the four drawers that were built into the wall. Just above the drawers there was a pull-down canvas sleeping area which Catherine said she could take leaving the sofa/daybed for her mother. They found two pillows and some blankets on a top shelf in the closet and they prepared both beds for sleeping. Anne and Catherine hugged each other tightly and said their prayers before falling asleep.

As the steamship left the waters of the English Channel the waves soared and pounded against the bowels of the ship causing an enormous rocking motion from side to side. The room was dark black and Catherine called out to her mother.

"I'm afraid I'm going to roll off my bed."

Anne got up and lit the lantern, falling against the wall and to the floor when the ship made a severe rocking motion. Catherine jumped down and helped her get back up.

"Get your pillow and lie with me. There is room for both of us," Anne said.

By midnight the ocean had calmed and so had the noises that had accompanied the thrashing of the ship. There had been screams throughout the night and they had been difficult to ignore. Several times there were giant thuds that sounded like barrels rolling and hitting the inside of the ship's metal walls. Anne was hopeful that this was not going to be an everyday occurrence.

The next morning at breakfast Anne and Catherine learned that the steerage passengers slept, ate, and socialized in the same spaces. They had to bring their own bedding and although food was provided, passengers had to cook it themselves in a small community kitchen. On rough crossings, steerage passengers often had little time in the fresh air on the upper deck. If the passengers did not fill steerage, the space often held cargo. The vast majority of the passengers, usually immigrants, bought bunks in steerage, also called the "tween deck" for its position between the cabins and the hold. There was a steward assigned to each section of the ship and a young steward by the name of Matthew Fletcher took a fancy to Anne. He had been a steward for three years and the fact that he was ten years younger than Anne did not stop him from thinking he might get her to have a drink with him during one of his breaks. He looked older than his twenty-two years and he considered himself a ladies' man. He wasn't handsome but he had an appealing face and an outgoing personality.

Matthew knocked on Anne's door and warned her that as they got farther out to sea, the water could be very rough. He said that the previous night was a good example of what it would be like and they needed to be careful. As a rule, passengers were not permitted on the upper deck when it was dark or during bad weather.

"It was not safe," he said. "People have fallen to their death because they could not hold on." He also warned them that many of the people suffered from sea sickness and if they needed a doctor, one was available to assist them. He said that he wasn't trying to scare them; he just wanted them to feel safe.

Ann thanked him and asked him to give her directions to the community room for the cabin passengers, which she understood housed a small library. Matthew took out a small piece of paper that looked like a small map with small rooms printed on it and a different diagram of each of the ship's decks. He warned her again not to go below the second deck and circled the room with his finger indicating the community room, and then pointed to a room.

"This is where we are now; you may keep this so you won't get lost," Matthew said.

Anne thanked him and he dipped his head saying, "Anytime, ma'am."

Catherine and Anne made their way down the stairs and down the long corridor to a door with a sign that read *Community Room, Second Class Passengers Only.* There was a matron at the door to check their passes and allowed them to come in. They were delighted with the openness of the room and the walls of library books that were secured behind wood slats so they wouldn't fall out on rough waters. There were a half-dozen small tables with chairs and a seating area that had cushioned, upholstered chairs fastened securely to the floor. On one side there were windows that allowed sunlight to fill the room on a sunny day and on the other wall, groupings of pictures of various sailing vessels and a map showing the route of their crossing. Catherine was particularly interested in the map, as it would allow her to see the progress of each day of their voyage. She had studied the maps of the Atlantic Ocean prior to her trip and was intrigued by the fact that she was physically sailing on a ship that was sailing to America.

Catherine selected two books to read from the library. One was a history book on the United States and the other a smaller book simply called *Texas.* She decided to read about Texas first, as Galveston was going to be their new home. Anne, on the other hand, decided to read something more current and picked up several *Galveston Gazette* newspapers and a *New York Times* magazine. The newspapers were a couple of weeks old and the magazine was a month old.

"Well, at least I can get an idea of what people are doing in America and what the fashions are like," Anne told Catherine.

They returned to their room and settled in to explore their books and newspapers. Catherine looked in the index and found a list of the cities mentioned in the book and found that Galveston had several chapters dedicated to its heritage. "Galveston is a small sand island and is parallel with the southeast coast of the State of Texas. The main business district of the city itself is located on the east end of the island. There is a causeway that links the island with the mainland via a wagon bridge," she read...

Wow, she thought. It's just as remote as Sandgate is to the rest of England

"At the end of the 19th century, the city of Galveston is expected to have a population of 38,000. It is the center of trade in Texas, and one of the largest cotton ports in the nation, in competition with New Orleans."

Excitement grew in Catherine and she closed her book and repeated everything she read to her mother.

"Galveston is going to be wonderful," Catherine said to her mother, "and I can't wait to get there."

Anne read an article from the *Galveston Daily News* out loud to Catherine:

"Galveston has a large European population and the social calendar is filled with opportunities for fancy dress." She continued reading, "Galas and opening night at the Opera House will be dazzling with magnificent costumes and dress."

Oh, Catherine, the opportunities will be endless for me," said Anne.

After talking and reading for a while they both put their reading material away and went to sleep. The next morning when they got up, they noticed the ship was heaving back and forth at a much greater force. They made their way to the toilet areas and found it very difficult to stay balanced. They met one of the matrons in the hall and she told them that they had just sailed into a horrible storm. She suggested that they go to the cafeteria and pick up some food for the day and then stay in their room. They took their jug with them to get some fresh water for their room and then made their way to the cafeteria. The ship was rocking back and forth so badly that Matthew stopped them and told them to go back to their room.

"I will get you both something to eat and will fill your water jug for you," he said.

It seemed liked hours had passed and Anne checked her small gold watch to see what time it was. It was half past one in the afternoon and they had had nothing to eat all day. Finally, there was a tap, tap on their door.

Anne asked, "Who is it?"

"It's me, Matthew," said the steward. "I have your food and water."

Anne slowly opened the door and Matthew was balancing himself on the wall and holding a small tray.

"Sorry it has taken me so long, but I had to take trays of food to everyone on this deck and it is difficult to move very fast. The good news is that the storm is about to pass and we are expecting nicer weather over the next few days."

Anne thanked him and took the tray.

"You best stay confined to your room the remainder of the day and night. This should be enough food to tide you over," he said.

After he left, Anne and Catherine removed the covered top of the tray. Bread, cheese, fruit and pastries greeted their hungry appetites. There were also a few slices of beef. The food on the ship was not great but at that moment they were delighted that they had anything at all. There was also plenty of it so they set half of the food aside to eat later in the day. They read, did some hand sewing and played a few games of cribbage. By evening time, Anne was feeling a bit woozy and didn't feel like eating. Catherine snacked on some of the leftovers before going to bed.

On the fourth day, Anne woke up with a splitting headache and nausea. The ship's movement was not as shaky and rough as the day before, but Anne did not feel well enough to go to breakfast.

"I'll go to the cafeteria and get you some food, mama," said Catherine. "I know the way and I will hurry back."

Anne really did not want Catherine to go alone but she felt too sick to argue. When the door closed behind her Catherine skipped down the long corridor and bumped into a very large man and woman as she turned the corner.

"Look out little one," the man said. "Hold your horses. Where is your mother?" he asked her.

"Ummm, she isn't feeling very well so I am going to get her some soup," said Catherine.

She had recognized the couple from dinner a few nights earlier. They had introduced themselves as Mr. and Mrs. Tucker from Liverpool.

"Why don't you come and eat breakfast with us and then you can take your mother back something when you are through?" asked Mrs. Tucker.

Catherine was starving and was glad she did not have to eat alone. She enjoyed listening to the Tuckers talk about their travels and was glad to be out of the tight cabin. Catherine was gone for almost an hour when Matthew approached Catherine and told her that her mother had stopped him outside their cabin and asked him to look for her.

"Oh my," she said, "I better get back now."

"I will bring your mother some soup," Matthew said.

When Catherine returned to the cabin she could see that her mother was worried. "I'm so sorry, Mum," said Catherine. "I sat with the Tuckers at breakfast and they were telling stories...I promise I won't ..."

Anne had put up her hand to silence Catherine. "I am relieved that you are alright, my darling," and she hugged her. Anne knew Catherine had learned her lesson and there was no need to get her upset too.

Later that day, Mrs. Tucker stopped by Anne's cabin and asked if they would like to go to the upper deck for some fresh air and then have dinner with them. Anne still felt a bit under the weather but she told Catherine she could go. After collecting her bonnet and shawl, Catherine joined the Tuckers and they made their way to the upper deck. Once outside, they noticed a small crowd in the corner of the ship and a man addressing them in German. Catherine strained to see what was going on and noticed a small oblong box made out of old wooden planks. The sides of the box had small holes cut in it. Mrs. Tucker whispered to Catherine, "I think it must be a funeral for a young boy who just passed."

A moment later several men picked up the box and threw it overboard. Catherine stood motionless as the crowd broke out into a song which they were singing in German. Catherine watched as the box danced along the movement of the water. She stood motionless and fixated as it slowly drifted away. It seemed to take forever to sink, but a small wave finally engulfed the tiny box and it was gone forever.

"Come, my child," said Mrs. Tucker. "We need to walk around and enjoy the fresh air."

During dinner, it was difficult for Catherine to concentrate on the conversation. She kept seeing visions of the tiny box in the water and she was having flashbacks from her own family's funerals. At last they were through and the Tuckers walked Catherine back to her cabin. Catherine said nothing about the little boy's funeral to her mother because she did not want to upset her. Best to just keep it to herself, she thought.

Anne and Catherine passed the next few days in their cabin, sewing, reading and talking about old times and what their new lives were going to be like in Galveston. Catherine was getting restless and asked her mother if she could go to the community room and return the book she had read. The community room was on the same deck but located on the opposite end of the ship.

"Are you sure you know your way there?" asked Anne.

"Yes, Mum, I'm sure I can find it," answered Catherine.

Catherine knew there were three turns and that the room would be on the right. As she walked down the corridor she made one turn, walked a little further and made another turn. Nothing looked familiar. She turned to go back and became confused. All the halls and doorways looked the same. She decided once she reached a set of stairs she would go up to the main deck and get her bearings.

Catherine was almost to the stairway when all of a sudden someone grabbed her by her arm and pulled her underneath the stairs. It was dark and she couldn't quite make out his face. It was a man with a beard, someone she had not seen before and he smelled of whiskey and sweat. The man pushed her down on the floor and said, "Don't make a sound or I will kill you." Catherine was terrified and wanted to scream but something inside her said to do as he said.

"Please don't hurt me," Catherine begged.

He began lifting up her skirt and pulling her pantalets down. "Be quite, now," he said, and he began touching her and moving his hand up between her legs.

Catherine was scared and horrified. The man began unbuttoning his pants while holding Catherine's arms above her head. Catherine looked around for someone or something to help her, and she realized she was still holding the book in her hand. With all her strength she managed to get her arm away and she hit him on the head with her book. It stunned him and he released his grip on her. Catherine freed one of her legs and she kicked him so hard in the groin that he fell backwards. Catherine jumped up quickly, jerking her pantalets back up, and began running as fast as she could. She was running so fast that she was hyperventilating and had to stop to catch her breath. Catherine saw a ship's matron standing outside a bathroom and she went in. She turned the water tap on and splashed the salt water on her face. It stung a bit so she took a towel and dried it off. Never in her life had she been so afraid. The matron came in and asked if Catherine was alright.

Catherine did not answer her at first but then said, "I was returning a book to the community library and I got lost. Could you show me the way?"

"Certainly, follow me," said the matron.

Catherine walked close behind the matron and the matron said,

"Why don't you go in and return the book, I'll wait here and then see you to your cabin." The matron sensed that Catherine was upset by something or someone.

Catherine quickly went in, returned the book and when she came out the two began walking back to Catherine's cabin.

"You know," said the matron. "It's not really safe for a young girl to be alone on this ship. Terrible things could happen to you."

When Catherine walked back into her cabin she was relieved that her mother had fallen asleep. She didn't want to share the details of what had happed just now and decided to keep the incident to herself. Catherine never left their cabin again unless Anne accompanied her.

On the eighth day they were told at breakfast that they had picked up wind and that they would be arriving in Galveston mid afternoon. Matthew handed out a leaflet that had information on it explaining the disembark process along with pictures for those who were unable to read. Anne was given a landing card which Matthew told her to pin on her dress so she could move through the Money Exchange line more quickly. There were several cashiers exchanging gold, silver and paper money, from countries all over Europe, for American dollars, which was based on the day's official rates. The rates were posted on a blackboard by the exchange windows. All that remained was to make arrangements for their trunks, which had been stored in the baggage compartment of the ship. Each newcomer was also given a tag with his or her manifest number from the steamship and it was to be matched up with their luggage once they were off the ship. Everyone had to be checked by a medical officer and an immigration inspector reviewed their papers. It took a few hours to get through the lines and many people lost their patience, but finally Anne and Catherine were allowed to leave the ship and claim their luggage. Matthew waved to them as he saw them leaving and regretted that he never had the opportunity to have that drink with Anne.

CHAPTER 3

It was, Thursday, July 15 1898, when they first set foot on Galveston's wharf. It was a hot steamy day and the sun was brilliantly cascading rich colors of gold and orange behind the clouds. After being in an enclosed cabin for so long they had to wait a few minutes for their eyes to adjust. Anne and Catherine couldn't believe that they were actually on American soil and even though there were crowds of people everywhere their excitement began to grow. They followed the crowds a bit until they found a colored man with a horse drawn buggy to take them to a hotel.

"Everyone calls me Joseph," he said; "Joseph March. If you don't have a place to stay let me suggest the Tremont Hotel at Church St. & Twenty-fourth St. It's very nice. I checked with them earlier and they said they have some rooms available. If they are already taken, Galveston has twenty hotels and I am sure we will find something for you," he continued.

Joseph was a large black man with a shaved head and a low husky voice. He had come to Galveston eight years earlier from Africa as a stowaway on a cargo ship. He had earned enough money doing odd jobs to buy his own buggy and had won his horse in a back street poker game. He had done well for himself, he thought.

"Yes, that would be fine" said Anne.

Joseph took them through some of the back streets to avoid some of the traffic, stopping several times to allow the street cars to pass. The city began to take on a new energy. The streets were bustling with activity as they approached the downtown area. They passed by beautiful large Gothic and Victorian houses, fancy shops and restaurants and the scenery was absolutely mesmerizing.

It only took about twenty minutes to arrive at the Tremont Hotel. It was considered one of the finest hotels of its time west of the Mississippi towering over five stories high. Joseph suggested that they stay in the buggy while he checked to see if a room was available. He was gone only a few minutes when he returned with a big grin on his face.

"Yes ma'am," he said. "There is one on the second floor. You can go on in and I'll see that the bellman brings your luggage in." Anne paid Joseph his ten cent fee and tipped him a few pennies more.

"Bless you," he said.

Anne and Catherine waited for the bellman to gather their luggage and they entered the hotel. The main room of the Tremont Hotel mirrored the beauty of a European Hotel and an atmosphere of elegance. The spacious lobby towered up several stories and a beautiful winding staircase led to an open veranda and sitting areas. The room that was available was a dollar-fifty a night which was more than Anne wanted to pay but it was for just for one night and the room did have an adjoining bath. Anne was hoping they could move to more permanent accommodations the next day. The receptionist at the hotel registry suggested that she leave the large trunk and box downstairs in the holding room and she gave Anne a receipt. A bellman picked up their small bags and escorted the two women up a beautiful winding staircase to the second level, down a hallway and then stopped in front of a door with the scrolled numbers "222".

It was getting late and although room service was more expensive, Anne asked the desk clerk to send up some soup and finger sandwiches so they would not have to leave their room. Tired, exhausted and relieved to be at their final destinations, Anne and Catherine began removing the layer of clothing that had been their constant companions for the last eight days. Both Catherine and Anne slipped on their robes and waited for room service. By now they were both really hungry and when the food arrived they indulged themselves with everything on the plate and talked about the events of the day and their new journey.

Catherine began making a list of everything that they needed to take care of first as she and her mother talked. The bellman had given them a map of the city and told them that they could walk most places and that the street cars were very handy and only cost five cents. They went to sleep early as they knew that they had to complete several of their tasks before the end of the next day, which was Friday.

After a light breakfast Anne and Catherine set out for their five-block walk to the Galveston Island Community Bank where Anne would open an account and arrange for the remainder of her money to be wired from Sandgate to Galveston. She also needed a safe deposit box for her valuables. Anne wanted Catherine to be a co-signer on everything. She was actually following the instructions that her banker in Sandgate,

Mr. Herring had given her. "It's time for Catherine to learn responsibility. If you became sick or unable to transact business yourself, Catherine would be able to step in and take over." Mr Herring had told her.

When Catherine and Anne arrived at the Bank they were introduced to a gentleman named, John Merit, who was the new accounts manager. Anne couldn't help but notice how attractive he was and he looked to be in his later twenties. He was clean shaven with sandy colored hair and a tall muscular frame. He introduced himself as the new accounts manager for the bank. He noticed Anne was wearing a wedding ring and asked Anne if she was opening up a joint account.

"No, it will only be in my name at this time," she said. "However, she continued. "I want my daughter, Catherine, to be a co-signer. I am not sure when my husband will be joining us."

"Alright then," said John.

He was smitten with her beauty and was secretly hoping that

she was a widow. John had lost his wife two years earlier when she died during child birth. The baby was too pre-mature and had also died. He mostly stayed to himself since then and he was not in any hurry to find a new wife. However, there was something about Anne that appealed to him. She had a subtle beauty and quiet demeanour about her, and he thought she was the most beautiful woman he had ever seen. John didn't want Anne to leave, so he took his time and even gave Anne the wrong form to complete just so it would take a little longer.

"Mr. Merit," Anne said. "We don't have a lot of time as it is Friday and many businesses will be closed tomorrow. We have a lot of things we must take care of today."

John flushed with embarrassment as he completed the process. After everything was signed and attended to, John led them to the safe deposit box area and gave Anne her new key. It only took a few minutes for Anne and Catherine to place their prized possessions in the safe deposit box. Some old letters that Adam had written her, birth and death certificates, her jewelry, and hidden under all of it was a letter to Catherine that she had written on the ship and placed in a blank envelope simply marked: To Catherine, my beautiful daughter.

Before they left the bank, John gave Anne his calling card.

"Please let me know if I can assist you in any way. The wire should not take more than a week, but you have brought ample funds to tide you over for a while. Please stop back in once you have settled on a permanent address."

Anne thanked Mr. Merit and she and Catherine set out to explore the city and find a new home.

John followed them out the door of the bank, "Please check back with me later next week so that I can give you an update on the wire." John said. He wanted to make sure he saw Anne again. He did not want to leave anything to fate. Even though Anne had said something about her husband joining them later, there was something about her story that did not ring true. John watched Anne and Catherine as they disappeared into the crowd. He was lost in the moment.

"Mr. Merit, Mr. Merit," said a young woman's voice. "Your next customer is waiting."

Anne and Catherine had just turned the corner when they looked up and saw Joseph in his buggy. "Morning ladies, need a ride someplace?" He asked.

Anne was glad to see a familiar face even if it was just Joseph. There was a gentleness in Joseph's eyes but she could tell he had a troubled past. Even so, she needed to heed Mr. Emory's warning and be wary of people who might try and take advantage of her. After all, Joseph was black. She wondered if he had been a slave. She had read about slavery in America in the history books but even if he was free now, black people in America were considered lowlifes and criminals. She did not see that in Joseph. After all, he owned his own horse and buggy and seemed to be tolerated on the streets along with everyone else.

"Actually," said Anne, "we don't mind walking but could you tell us how far it is to 16th street and Avenue H?"

"Hop on," Joseph said. "I'm going right past there. My horse, Lucy, here, needs a rest and some water and I'm on my way to the stables."

"Thank you," said Anne as Joseph got down and put a stool on the ground for them to step on.

"Giddy up, Lucy," said Joseph as they lunged forward. "Sorry for that quick start, ma'am, Lucy gets excited here when she knows it's time to head back to the stables."

They had traveled several blocks when they finally turned down 16th Street. They were trying to get their bearings and were looking at their map when Joseph said "It's just down here on the corner, ma'am."

There were rows of lovely one and two story Victorian and Gothic style homes. They pulled up in front of a two-story Victorian styled house and saw a sign that read "Room for Rent. No Colored Folk." Anne breathed a sigh of relief. She had seen an ad in the local paper she had picked up at the hotel and was not sure there was still a vacancy. Anne took out some money to pay Joseph.

"No need, ma'am," said Joseph. "Like I said, it's on my way to the stables.

"At least let me give you a tip," Anne said.

"Another time," said Joseph. "Maybe I can stop back here in a half hour on my way back into town and pick you up. You'll need to get your things and bring them back here." He said.

"Yes," said Anne. "That would be very kind of you."

Joseph pulled away and drove Lucy around the corner and stopped. He got out and took an empty can from under his wagon seat. He walked over to a cistern in back of a church and filled up his bucket. He only told a little white lie. It was time for Lucy to be watered but there were no stables. At least none he paid to use. Joseph looked around to be sure no one was watching. The white folks didn't take too kindly to colored people taking their water, he thought.

Joseph wasn't his real name. When he arrived in Galveston he knew just enough English to get by and he wanted to have an American name. He had overheard two ladies on the ship he was traveling on discussing a story about Mary and Joseph and a little baby named Jesus. He liked the story and decided his new name would be Joseph. It was March 1st when he got off the ship, so he took March as his last name. He slept in vacant buildings until he became familiar with the city and made the decision to stay in Galveston. The climate agreed with him. Now Joseph stayed most nights at the far west end of the beach behind an abandoned overgrown cotton gin. The heirs were still squabbling over whose it was so it had been closed down and left to the rats and varmints to take over. Joseph was allowed to stay there by the family to be the caretaker at no cost to him and he kept his personal things in an old leather suitcase that he had bought at a church thrift store. There was a large opening in a barn-like structure that he used as Lucy's stable and an adjoining small room that used to be an office. He had lived in these small quarters for over a year now. Sleep was not always easy, especially in the summertime and during school breaks. Teenagers often migrated to the far west end of the beach to build camp fires and to party. It was his job to run them off. There were posted signs everywhere, saying "Keep out, Private property." Damn kids, he thought, might as well say come on in. Joseph had privileges most of the coloured didn't have. He had earned respect in the community when he had saved the lives of two children who had gone too far out into the bay.

One day as Joseph was traveling down Seawall Boulevard and he heard schemes coming from the beach. He stopped his buggy and ran to the mother. "My babies, my babies," she cried as she pointed to the two screaming children.

Joseph kicked off his shoes and dove into the gushing waves. One of the children had gone under and Joseph dove under until he caught the hair of a little girl. They emerged into open air and pulling the little girl as he swam, caught up with the little boy. Joseph was strong but swimming with two small children under his arms while keeping their heads out of water was no small task. Gently, he calmed the crying children and told them they needed to float on their backs while he put his arms around their bodies. Joseph was tall and was able to plant his feet on the sand and jumped each wave as it threatening to knock them over, Joseph held onto the children tightly until they made it to shore. By now a large crowd had gathered waiting for the children's return. No one else had gone in to assist Joseph in recovering the two children.

"They're gonna be fine ma'am," Joseph said. "They are just shook up a bit."

Joseph turned back to walk up the sandy slope to his buggy but before he could get to the wooden steps he fell to the sand and put his head between his legs. He rested for a moment, overcome by the fact that he too had almost drowned, and then raised his head up. Glaring into the sun with squinted eyes, he said, "Lord thank you for this blessing,"

"Amen" the crowd shouted.

He did not realize that a group of people had gathered around him and began thanking him for his kind deed. That was how Joseph had earned his place in Galveston's community. Now he had nobody. Not the right color to fit into Galveston's pompous and rich society and now even his own coloured people rejected him because he was treated better by the white people because of his good deed.

CHAPTER 4

The boarding house was located on a corner and had a large porch that wrapped around the side of the house. It had originally been painted white with green shutters and now, after years of high humidity and hot afternoons in the summer, the paint was peeling off like bad sunburn. Still the blemishes of time did not detour from the architect's intended design. It was like an old lady who had aged gracefully. Her character was still there but her original beauty had declined over time. It sat about eight feet off the ground on stilts and facia board trim nailed around the sides to give it a more finished look. It looked weathered as it had survived several major storms.

Anne and Catherine walked up the eight steps and stopped to ring the doorbell. They were greeted by a middle-aged woman with wiry grey hair and a mole on the crease of her nose.

"Hello, my name is Anne Eastman and this is my daughter, Catherine," said Anne. "We are here to inquire about a room."

The inn keeper introduced herself as Minnie Wyman. She had a German accent and mumbled something in German to herself about not wanting to rent to children.

"Oh," Anne said. She is not a child. She is a young woman."

Minnie was surprised that Anne had understood her. Anne had a British accent but German was a second language to both her and Catherine. A bit embarrassed, Minnie invited the two Eastman women into her parlor.

"The room only has one bed and it might be a bit cramped," said Minnie.

"May we take a look at it?" asked Anne. Minnie showed them up the stairs and down a corridor. When they opened the door they were met by a warm glow of sunlight coming through one of the windows. Anne walked over to the window and was amazed that they could actually see parts of the Galveston Bay.

"There is a small area over here that used to be a closet and now it is set up with a small ice box and hot plate, plus a sink. My deceased husband, Zackary, fixed it up that way when the children left so we could have boarders. There is also a small private water closet," said Minnie. The living area had a sofa, a small table and two chairs plus two other chairs, side table and a reading lamp. It was an L-shaped room and at the back of the "L" was the bedroom area with a double bed, small closet and a dresser.

"It will do just fine," said Anne. "How much is it?"

"Its five dollars a week paid in advance," said Minnie.

"Perfect." said Anne.

"If you want supper included, dinner is at 6:00 p.m. sharp and is an additional fifty cents for each of you. I supply a full set of sheets and towels every other week, but it's up to you to change them." continued Minnie.

"You are most kind," said Anne. "There is an eight dollar deposit and rent is due every Friday," said Minnie.

Minnie preferred to rent to men and was reluctant to rent the room to the two women and thought the extra deposit would scare them away.

"It will do just fine," said Anne and she took the money out of her purse and gave her the exact amount.

They proceeded downstairs into the parlour where Minnie gave them a quick tour of the dining room and kitchen area.

After getting the key to the front door, Catherine and Anne went outside just as Joseph was pulling up in his buggy. After they had left,

Minnie pulled one of the curtains aside and watched them leave. The fact that Anne spoke German and seemed to have the means, she assumed that it was a good risk. She preferred to rent to men only as they kept to themselves more, but it would be nice to have a female companion, especially someone who could speak her own language. Since her husband, Zachary, had passed, she rarely spoke German to anyone except the local butcher and her priest.

Anne and Catherine checked out of the Tremont hotel and Joseph loaded their belongings onto his buggy. He liked the two women. They didn't look down their noses at him like most people did. They were warm and friendly towards him and didn't order him around like a servant. He hoped that he would see more of them. They also needed someone to look after their welfare. They were two young women in a new country, starting a new life -- and where was her husband? He thought to himself. Whatever the situation, if he could help them in any way, he would be there for them.

It was half past 1:00 in the afternoon when they arrived at the boarding house. Joseph hauled all of their things upstairs and congratulated her on her new home. Anne followed him back downstairs and paid him.

"Thank you so much, Joseph," she said. "You have been such a big help and I pray that God will bless you for your good deeds."

There was something about Anne Eastman, Joseph thought. For the first time in his entire life he wished he were white. At forty-two years old, Joseph had never married. Yes, he had had a few lovers and more than his share of whores but he wondered what life would be like if he met someone like Anne Eastman who was of his own color.

There was a soft knock on the door and Minnie said, "Uhh, I thought you might be hungry so I have made you some sandwiches,"

Catherine opened the door and invited Minnie in.

"Mother is freshening up in the water closet and will be out in a few minutes," said Catherine. "You are so kind, Mrs. Wyman." said Catherine as she took the plate of sandwiches.

Minnie went on to say that she had left a quart of milk and some scones in the ice box for them and also a slab of ice.

"The iceman and milkman deliver every Monday, Wednesday and Friday. You can place an order for the next week yourself. It will be up to you and your mother to pay for that. Just leave the empty milk bottle with a note inside with your order." Minnie said. "See you at supper....6:00 p.m. sharp." Minnie said and left closing the door behind her.

Catherine wondered if Mrs. Wyman did not like them or if she was just a rude person. It didn't matter, she thought. It could just be her temperament and Catherine would do everything she could to make Mrs. Wyman like them.

Anne and Catherine were eager to go downstairs to meet some of the other boarders and strolled downstairs to the parlour at 5:45. They decided to sit on the sofa until dinner and quietly chatted about the days events when a grey haired gentleman holding a cane approached them from the hall.

"Good evening, ladies." he said. "My name is Professor Edward Gorman and you must be the new boarders.""

"Yes, I am Anne Eastman and this is my daughter, Catherine." Anne said.

The professor told them that he had been living at the boarding house for the past year and that he taught math at Scherer's Business College. Prior to that he had been living in San Antonio, Texas, where he had also been a professor.

"Dinner is ready," announced Minnie.

They all gathered around the table in the dining room and took their places. Minnie had prepared meatloaf, mashed potatoes and gravy, peas and cornbread. It was all served family style and Minnie seemed to take great pride in her efforts.

"I see you have introduced yourselves to each other," said Minnie. "Professor Gorman lives in the room at the back of the house with a separate entrance. I have another boarder who is also a widower, who lives in the carriage house around back. His name is Bryan Wheat. Mr. Wheat travels a lot and does not take dinner with us except on special occasions like Thanksgiving or Christmas. He has a full kitchen in his apartment so he prepares his own meals when he is in town," added Minnie.

"Your food is wonderful," said Catherine.

"Yes," said Anne. "It has been weeks since we have had a home cooked meal."

"What are your plans here in Galveston?" asked Professor Gorman.

"Catherine will register in school in the fall and I am hoping to seek employment in the field of fashion," answered Anne. "I design and sew clothing." Anne continued.

"You shouldn't have any problem," said Minnie. "The ladies of society in Galveston spare no money on beautiful dresses and costumes." She continued, "There are parties almost every week and the new opera house on Post Office Street is a haven for high society to dress up to the nines."

"Oh, I hope you are right," said Anne. "I would like to find a job right away."

Minnie dominated the conversation during the remainder of dinner and finally left to clear the table and serve desert.

"Lass mich dir helfen," (let me help you) said Catherine in German as she got up to take things to the kitchen.

Minnie was surprised that Catherine also spoke German and was glad for the help. She hoped Catherine would take it upon herself to help do the dishes also. Dessert was hot apple pie with a scoop of vanilla ice cream.

When dinner was finished, Catherine asked Mrs. Wyman if she could help with the dishes and Minnie was delighted to let her help. Professor Gorman excused himself and said he had some lesson plans to do as he was also teaching a summer school program for the high school. Anne also excused herself and went upstairs leaving Catherine and Minnie to get better acquainted. They chatted in German and Mrs. Wyman's attitude slowly changed as they got acquainted.

It was Saturday, July 21, 1897, and Galveston was waking up to another hot, steamy day. The heat was going to be something Anne and Catherine would have to get used to and their clothing was much too heavy for Galveston's humid climate. Sandgate was usually dry during the summer and rainy in the winter time, with an average summer day in Sandgate being more tolerable. They decided to go to the dry goods store to find some light-weight fabric and made some purchases at the 5 & 10 cent store. It was a beautiful morning despite the ninety-degree weather and they walked the eight blocks to the dry goods store. They stopped at the local drug emporium and ate lunch at the food counter, then jumped on a trolley so they could explore the city. Beautiful homes, some on stilts, were surrounded by lush landscaping graced with oleanders and palms that had been imported from the West Indies. As they traveled from one end of the strand to the other they saw many horse drawn carriages and for the first time, they saw an automobile. There were many saloons and restaurants bustling with activity and beautiful hotels. The smell of the salt water and the flying seagulls reminded them of their home in England. Not being used to the ninety-five-degree temperature and high humidity, they returned to their new home to rest and spend the rest of the day sorting out their purchases and cutting out new dresses for each of them to sew.

Anne had gotten permission to use the sewing machine in the day time but she had to be finished by 8:00 p.m. so as not to disturb Minnie's sleep. They spent most of Sunday sewing their new dresses and making plans for Monday. Anne was planning to visit some of the local tailors and dress stores in hopes of finding a job while Catherine stayed home and sewed. At half past nine on Sunday evening Anne had put the finishing touches on her new dress. It was a light blue cotton dress with buttons up the front, short sleeves and a white lace color. The skirt was slightly gathered at the waist and flowed just below her ankles. A darker blue sash finished off the waist and Anne stood in front of her mirror to see the finished product.

"You look beautiful, Mummy, Catherine said.

Anne's reflection embraced a slender young woman staring back at her and she was pleased with the results.

Anne had seen an ad in the paper for H. Koch – Merchant Tailor on Post Office Street. It stated that they made costumes for balls and theatricals. She decided that would be her first stop. When she entered the store she was approached by a distinguished young man who introduced himself as the manager of the store.

"I would like to speak to Mr. Koch," Anne said. "If he is not available right now, perhaps I could make an appointment?" she continued.

"Mr. Koch is a very busy man," said the manager. "Might I ask what the nature of your business might be?"

"I have just arrived in the states from England where I, too, was a tailor, and I wanted to inquire about a job," said Anne.

'Well that is my department," said the manager… and we are not hiring right now. You see, "he continued, "we have a very large Chinese population in Galveston and they are very cheap labor. You just simply would not fit in."

He showed Anne to the door and she was outside before she could say anything else. Anne stopped at several department stores and inquired about employment. She stopped at two more tailor shops and they all said the same thing; they were not hiring at this time.

Anne was walking past the Galveston Island Community Bank when she decided to stop in and give John Merit her new address. He was out of the bank so she gave her information to his secretary. As she was leaving Anne almost ran into John Merit coming into the bank.

"'Mrs. Eastman," said John. "What a surprise. I did not expect to see you until later in the week."

John invited her to come into his office so they could visit in private. He could tell Anne seemed to be upset about something.

"I don't mean to pry, but is something wrong?" asked John.

Anne was silent for a few minutes and took in a deep breath before she began telling John about all the snobbish people she had encountered.

"Some of them were just so rude to me," said Anne. "I didn't think it would be this hard." She was trying to hold back her tears and her nerves were beginning to get the best of her as she continued saying, "I'm sorry; I shouldn't burden you with my problems."

"It's all right," said John. He was glad that Anne was sharing her problems with him. "This is only your first day out looking for a job. Sometimes it takes a few weeks." He continued. "I heard from a friend that The Grande Opera House is looking for an alterations person. I know you are more qualified than that, but maybe you could look into it, if you can't find anything else," John said.

Anne thought for a moment and said, "Thank you, John. You are right. It's only my first day and I usually don't give up so easily. I think the heat might be getting to me," replied Anne as she got up to leave. "I have left my new address with your secretary and will check back with you at the end of the week ....and thank you for being such a gentleman and allowing me to unload my burdens on you," Anne said to John and then left his office.

John stared and watched her leave. She was so beautiful, he thought. Even in distress she held her head high and projected an elegant air about her. He had to find a way to see her again and hoped it would be soon. He decided to write a letter to Anne's banker in Sandgate. Just doing a background check, he thought to himself.

After Anne left the bank, she was feeling a bit uncomfortable about unloading her problems on John. He was such a gentleman and he tried to be so helpful. It was nice of him to tell her about the alterations job that was available at the Grande Opera House but she was not just a seamstress, she created her own designs and sewed beautifully. She might check it out though, she thought. It couldn't hurt anything to inquire.

The Grand was located at Post Office Street and 21st Street and only a few blocks from where she was, so she decided to walk there even though it was terribly hot. It was 4:00 o'clock in the afternoon and when she arrived there was no one at the ticket counter and the door was locked. Anne looked at the sign and noticed that the next production did not start until Saturday, August 25, 1897. She turned to leave and noticed a man unlocking a door on the side. She called to him and he turned around.

"Excuse me," said Anne. "Do you work here at the Grande Opera House?"

The man stopped and looked at Anne for a moment and said, "Yes ma'am, I do.....are you here for tryouts in the next opera?"

"Oh no," said Anne, "I had heard that there might be an opening for an alterations person."

"My name is David Brooks" he said. "I'm a stage hand and do most of the behind the scenes work." "Excuse me for staring," said David, "but you are much too beautiful not to be in the theatre. You could be an actress."

"That's very kind of you," said Anne feeling apprehensive and uncomfortable with the way the stranger was looking at her. "I'm actually a dress designer and am having a bit of trouble finding employment. Someone told me that you might need a seamstress," she said.

"I'm the only one here today," said David. "Everyone else has left for the day. Come back tomorrow morning around 11:00 o'clock and I will tell the boss about you." David continued. "By the way, what's your name?"

"Anne, Anne Eastman," she replied. "And thank you for setting up the appointment for me," said Anne and she turned and left.

Other than seeing a couple of operas in London several years ago Anne knew nothing about the people who worked behind the scenes and she hoped they would not all be like him. For some reason she felt uneasy around David Brooks and she wasn't sure why.

CHAPTER 5

David Brooks had been working for the Grande Opera House for eight months. He had grown up working in the Ringling Brothers Circus because his mother was one of the striptease ladies in the side show. She had joined the circus when David was five years old and his mother told him she did not know who his father was. They lived on the circus train and traveled from city to city setting up tents and entertaining the locals. His mother would frequently have men spend the night in her room while she made David hide in the closet. It was a ritual he hated. One night he coughed and the man she was entertaining took David out of the closet and abused him and he hated his mother for it. She just sat there and watched. He cried when it was over and his mother scolded him for being a sissy and told him that it was time he grew up. His mother often watched as strange men violated and abused David. When he was twelve, he had had enough and he took the few things he had and jumped off the train. He was tall and looked older than his twelve years so he picked up a few odd jobs in the local town, sleeping anywhere he could find a dry place to sleep.

After two months he saw a notice on a store window that said the Barnum & Bailey Greatest Show on Earth was coming through and would stop for a one day show. He waited until the train was unloaded and he began helping the men put up the tents and take care of the animals. No one knew where he came from but he was strong and he seemed to know the ropes so they let him stay. His only pay was a place to sleep, free food and all the women he wanted. He was passed around by all the ladies who educated him on the pleasures of the body. At that time in his life it was more than he could hope for. For the next ten years he traveled with the circus and one day after getting into a fight outside a bar in St Louis, he killed a man. David jumped on the first train he could find and didn't stop until he got to New York. He liked show business and did some odd jobs in the theatre.

David was tall and good looking and tried out for a few parts but he was told that acting was just not his thing. His temper usually got the best of him, especially when he drank and he was always getting into trouble. His mood swings were unpredictable but always escalated when he hit the whiskey bottle. One night after an all-night poker game he followed an attractive woman down the street and cornered her in an alley. Forcing her down to the ground, he choked her and raped her as he saw flash-backs of his mother. The woman died in his arms and he felt redemption. David ran when he heard voices coming and he disappeared into the streets.

David never stayed in one place very long and decided he might try Houston. It's close to the Mexican border in case he needs to make another run for it, he thought. He had trouble finding a job and had heard from a buddy that Galveston had opened up a new opera house and they were hiring stage hands so he jumped a train and came to Galveston. David liked Galveston and decided he was going to clean up his act so he cut back on his drinking, but he couldn't give up on his smokes. He was 30 years old now and he was tired of running.

David stood and watched Anne walk down the block. She was everything he had never had -- class, beauty, and an alluring English accent. He had never been with a classy lady and decided Anne would be his first. He had noticed the wedding ring on her finger and decided he would take his time with this one. David decided to catch up with Anne and when he did it startled her.

"You gave me a fright," Anne said

"Sorry about that, but I figured as long as you were going my way, I'd walked with you, David replied.

Anne really didn't know what to say so she started walking with David beside her.

They were still about eight blocks from the boarding house when they heard a carriage come up beside them and stop.

She was exhausted and she was glad when she looked up and saw Joseph.

"Afternoon, Mrs. Eastman." said Joseph. "You need a ride?"

"Oh, thank goodness, yes." She said. "I don't think I could walk another step in this heat."

"I'm sorry, David, but it's been a really long day and I'm much too tired to walk any farther," Anne told David.

David helped Anne get in the carriage and his hand lingered on her hand making her feel uncomfortable. They said good-bye to each other and Anne breathed a sigh of relief.

"Galveston can take some getting used to," said Joseph. He pulled out an umbrella from under his seat, opened it and gave it to Anne as he smiled at her.

"You really know how to treat a lady," said Anne. Yes I do, Joseph thought to himself, Yes I do.

It was 5:45 p.m. when Anne made it home to the boarding house. She was exhausted and asked Catherine to bring her a plate of food upstairs after Catherine had finished with her dinner. Anne told Catherine she needed to soak in the bathtub and knew Mrs. Wyman would be upset if she was late for dinner.

"Sure mama," said Catherine.

"I am sure Mrs. Wyman will understand."

After dinner Catherine prepared a plate of food for her mother and took it upstairs. Catherine had spent all day sewing a new dress for her mother and was anxious to show it to her. When she walked into the bedroom Anne was in her robe fast asleep on the bed. Catherine placed the food on the table and went back into the living area. She sat in a chair and watched her mother sleep for awhile. Catherine loved her mother so much and couldn't imagine what life would be like without her.

They had been through a lot and she prayed that their new home in Galveston would be everything they hoped it would be. There was a fan on the dresser that Anne had turned on to comfort her from the heat and she slept until the next morning.

The next day Anne woke up early and was surprised to see her new dress spread out on the sofa.

"Do you like it, Mama?" Catherine asked.

"Oh Catherine, it's beautiful. You must have spent the whole day yesterday sewing it…I love it. Thank you so much," Anne said, as she hugged Catherine.

Anne changed into a cotton slip and put the dress over her head. It was a simple straight orchid coloured dress that flared just below her hips and had three-quarter length sleeves. It had a simple neckline and a button at the neck in the back.

"I left the neckline plain, Mama," said Catherine. "Your necklace with the locket will be the perfect accessory."

Anne was overwhelmed and kissed Catherine on the cheek.

"You are truly my best gift," Anne said.

Anne and Catherine had milk and toast for breakfast and Anne told Catherine about yesterday's events.

"I am going back to the opera house at 11:00 o'clock this morning," Anne said. "If they will hire me, I could continue to seek a job elsewhere and have income coming in for us."

"I wish I were older," said Catherine. "Then maybe I could work, too."

"No, my sweet daughter, I want you to go to school and get your diploma so you can enrol in college someday," replied Anne.

There was no further discussion. Catherine was going to be sixteen on her next birthday in January and she knew her mother was right.

Anne left at 10:30 a.m. to walk the twelve blocks to the opera house. There was a slight breeze and the town was bustling with morning walkers and people on bicycles. She was nervous and excited and she practiced what she might say to the manager. Upon arrival at the opera house, David was outside smoking a cigarette he had rolled.

"Morning Mrs. Eastman," He said. "My boss isn't here yet but you can come in and I'll show you around the place." David said.

Anne looked around and saw two young women go in the side door and she was glad she would not be alone in the building with David.

They entered the marbled foyer and were greeted by a grand staircase. The wood on the elegant parquet floors had been imported from Europe. It was magnificent and the most beautiful room Anne had ever seen. The architects had constructed all of the walls in the auditorium without a square corner to prevent echoes, and the seats were arranged in a curve to allow better viewing by the audience.

"It's more than I could have imagined," said Anne to David.

"Yep, they spent a ton of money on this place," said David. "The manager's name is Tom Gregory." David continued, "And I think he is in his office by now. You can wait outside his office while I go in and tell him about you."

David was gone for fifteen minutes before he came back and escorted Anne into Tom's office.

The door closed behind Anne and David listened with his ear up to the door while Anne and Tom talked. Anne was in Tom's office for about twenty minutes.

"The job is yours, if you want it," Tom said as he opened the door and Anne walked out.

"I appreciate your time, Mr. Gregory," Anne said. "May I think about it overnight and get back with you tomorrow?" asked Anne.

"Sure thing," said Tom. "If I'm not here David can show you where you will be set up in the garment room. You can start next Monday, if that works for you."

Anne walked outside with David following behind her.

"What do you think?" asked David.

"I am not sure," said Anne. "The pay is much less than I had hoped for but perhaps I could work my way up the ladder to costume designer."

"Sure could," said David, "but I wouldn't wait too long as I know he has a few more ladies eyeing the job."

David lied about that but hoped it would encourage Anne to say yes.

"In that case," said Anne, "Tell him I will be here Monday morning at 9:00 sharp."

"Great," said David. "Rehearsals start at 10:00 a.m. Plan to stay late. Crazy director doesn't know what an eight-hour day is." David snickered.

Anne left the Grande with mixed emotions. Late hours and low pay means low self-esteem, thought Anne. Oh well, it's a start. The ten dollars a week pay would just barely cover their food and rent with a little left over for necessaries. If she had any free time at all she might be able to pick up a few odd jobs. She still had a few days before she began her new job and she needed to use her time wisely. Anne stopped again at the dry goods store and purchased some more material, thread and buttons. She stopped at a thrift store and purchased another dress for herself and bought Catherine some shoes and a new dress. Her last stop was at the local grocer where she purchased bread, bagels, honey, tea bags, and a few other items that would feed them for a few days. Anne was loaded down with shopping bags and tried to balance it all in her arms when David walked up.

"Need a hand?" David asked.

"Anne blushed and said, "I thought I could handle it but a little help would be appreciated. I'm just a few blocks from my home."

"Not a problem," said David. "I have the time. It's always a little slow between shows and I was just running an errand myself."

They both turned the corner and walked to Anne's boarding house.

"So this is where you live," said David.

"Yes, said Anne. "At least it's in walking distance to the Grande." Anne continued.

"It might be alright in the daytime, but I would be careful if I were you at night." David said. "There's a lot of gambling and prostitution taking place down towards the end of Post Office Street. It might not be safe for a lady to be alone." David continued.

Anne looked worried but didn't say anything. She hadn't thought about the shows ending late in the evenings and she would have to be there.

"I live a block or two past your street….maybe I could walk you home on those late nights," David said.

"I'll manage, but thank you," said Anne just as they arrived at her home. Anne didn't want to impose on David and she didn't have a good feeling about him. He seemed nice enough but she sensed that he had not had an easy life. He had a hard look about him and she didn't want to give him any encouragement that she needed or wanted his help. I'll figure something else out, she thought. David set the packages on a chair on the porch and nodded his head at her. David could tell he might have come on to too strong and decided to back off. He turned and walked down the steps.

"David," said Anne. "I didn't mean to offend you and I really appreciate your help. Thanks for carrying my packages."

"My pleasure," said David and he walked back in the direction he had come from. He had sensed her apprehension and knew it would take some time, but he was certainly willing to wait.

David frequently walked Post Office Street and sometimes the Strand where he would pick up prostitutes. His favorite pick up place was between 28th Street & 29th Street called Fat Alley. It was a sleazy place crawling with opium addicts, gamblers and prostitutes and there was one in particular he liked.

"Hey David." called out one of the hookers. "You looking for good time?" She asked. The hooker called herself Wanda. It probably wasn't her real name but she was his favorite. They were all the same, thought David. Give them a few dimes and they will do anything. David nodded his head toward the lower end of the alley where there was an old, abandoned building. The door was partially ajar and he pushed it open. There wasn't a lot of activity during the day. At night though, finding a little privacy in the neighborhood was tough. That's why David always took his lunch break when the streets weren't so crowded. Wanda followed David through the door and David grabbed her pulling her up to him.

"No, David," Wanda said. "You know I need the money first."

The interior of the building was in poor condition with exposed nails sticking out and part of the ceiling coming down. David pushed Wanda up against a partially fallen wooden door and she felt her wrist hit one of the nails. She cried out in pain but David ignored her cry. It was over in a matter of minutes and David pushed her to the floor, buttoned his pants, and left. David threw her a dollar and was out the door before Wanda could say anything. She sat up on the floor and felt the blood trickling down her hand from a cut by the rusty nail that scratched her wrist. She dabbed it with her skirt.

Wanda liked David a lot and let him do things to her she wouldn't let anyone else do unless they paid good money for it. They were two of a kind, she thought. They were two losers just looking for a little gratification. Wanda picked up the dollar and tore off a bottom of her petticoat to wrap around her bleeding wrist.

Wanda's story wasn't a whole lot different than David's. She didn't know who her white daddy was and her Negro mother left her when she was thirteen years old. She went to live with an aunt and uncle where her uncle abused her every chance he got. He threatened to kill her if she told anyone. When she got pregnant at fifteen her uncle took her to a back street doctor who did a botched abortion. Her uncle gave Wanda two dollars to buy a train ticket and get out of town.

"And I don't ever want to see your face again," said her uncle.

Wanda was scared to death of her uncle and was glad to leave.

The train ticket from Houston to Galveston was one dollar and twenty-five cents. When she got off the train she found her way to the strand and walked until she saw a sign in a café that read, "Dish Washer Wanted." She was hired on the spot. Wanda told them she was sixteen and lived across town. There was a store room behind the café and she asked if she could sleep there for awhile until she could find a place to stay. "My daddy threw me out of the house because he was drinking and didn't want me around." Wanda told the owner.

Wanda worked at the café for two months and slept in the storage building at nights on a homemade bed made out of cardboard boxes and straw. One night the owner followed her into the storage building after closing and he raped her. Afterwards, she threw the few possessions she had into a feed sack and left. She slept on the streets, in alleys and storage buildings and finally made her way down Post Office Street. She watched the other ladies of the night working the street and being paid for sex. Why not, she thought, I might as well get paid for it.

Life got a little easier for Wanda once she learned the trade but after a couple of months she found herself pregnant. She worked the streets like a professional but had to quit when she began showing. She had saved enough money to take care of herself but she knew the streets were not a place to raise a child. Another prostitute helped her deliver her baby. It was a tiny little girl and she named her Sadie. She nursed it for a week but she was low on funds so she put it in a large shoebox and left it at the orphanage early one morning with a note pinned to it: My name is Sadie. Please take good care of me.

After several years Wanda had regular customers and a room she rented above a feed store not far from the action. Sometimes she would take men to her room, but the owner didn't like it until he started taking Wanda's rent out in trade. She still didn't want the men knowing where she lived for fear they would come knocking on her door at all hours of the night. David Brooks was the exception. One night after a late night poker game David followed Wanda home after she had finished with her last customer and pushed his way into her room.

"I'm done for the night," she had said.

"What will it cost for me to spend the rest of the night with you?" said David.

"Depends on what you want," Wanda said. David grinned and flashed her a two dollar bill he had won in an alley poker game. Wanda let him come in and he stayed the night. David was nicer to her then. Now his drinking and gambling was getting the better of him and sometimes he would become abusive. She quietly moved to another place several blocks away, which made David really mad. She told him that her landlord evicted her because of too much noise. She knew it was only a matter of time before David found out where she lived, and he did. She was making a good enough living on the streets and she didn't want to leave Galveston. Besides, most of her customers were pretty nice to her except for David, and she knew she was his favorite girl on the streets. He was always seeking her out.

CHAPTER 6

Together, Anne and Catherine took turns using the sewing machine. By Thursday they had completed two new dresses, two bloomers with an over blouse for swimming and a knapsack that Catherine would carry her books in when she would go to the library.

Anne had made a larger one so that she could use it if she had to bring items home for alterations or repairs. The knapsacks were made out of leftover material, some old tassels they had found at a thrift store, and buttons. There were two outside pockets in corresponding fabric and they looked like something they had purchased at a store.

Friday was going to be Anne's and Catherine's errand day and they were both excited to be outside and decided to walk the fourteen blocks to The Galveston Island Bank. They took a detour down Broadway to see the homes of the wealthy residents.

"Wow," said Catherine. "What do you think these people do to make all this money?" she continued.

Anne replied, "I read that Galveston is one of the richest cities of its size on the continent and the third richest city in the United States. I think a lot of them came with their own money and made even more. Some are in shipping business, banking, the railroads, cotton and others just own the land, I guess. America is the land of opportunity," Anne told Catherine. Their first stop was the bank.

Anne looked stunning in one of her new dresses and John Merit was really happy to see the Eastman girls.

"I am so pleased to see you both and I hope you are enjoying the Galveston scenery," said John. "I have your receipt for the wire transfer. I put half of it in a savings account where you could draw interest and the remainder is in a checking account where you can draw money anytime you need it." John continued, "I will need you to sign here and Catherine will sign on this line as the co-signer."

They finished the paperwork and Anne told John that she was going to begin her new job at the Grande Opera on Monday. John already knew this as Tom Gregory, the manager, had told him about Anne and how much he liked her but John pretended not to know.

"I really appreciate your opinion and help in directing me to them," said Anne. "Maybe I will see you at one of the operas," Anne remarked.

"I have season tickets," said John. "I usually go with my sister or a customer of the bank," John added. They said their good-byes and Anne and Catherine left the bank.

"I think he likes you, Mama. He looks at you the way Daddy used to look at you," said Catherine.

"Catherine," said Anne. "You have such a wild imagination. What have you been reading in those books you got from the library?

They laughed, talked and giggled all the way to the mercantile. "Let's see if we can find some of that imported French fabric," said Anne.

They browsed through yards and yards of fabric and finally settled on some imported silk that had been shipped from England. The French textiles were too expensive, but they loved feeling and touching them. They picked up a few more sewing items, miscellaneous trim, some less expensive fabric and a couple of new patterns. Anne knew how to sew without the patterns, but Catherine still needed some guidelines. Catherine needed new clothes for school and Anne would teach her how to take a basic pattern, make some adjustments, and create whatever design she wanted. They really enjoyed sewing together and for now, they were happy with their new life.

Saturday was going to be their last day to have fun for a while, so Anne and Catherine decided to pack a lunch, gathered up their new swimming suits and a towel and go to the beach.

"Finally," said Catherine. "Now we can act like tourists." She joked and began tickling her mother. They both laughed and chased each other, screaming and playing around the room. Realizing they were making too much noise, they waited a few moments to see if they could hear Mrs. Wyman's footsteps. Sure enough, there was a knock on the door.

"Are you two okay in there?" said Mrs. Wyman.

Anne opened the door and apologized and said they were just playing around.

"Well," said Mrs. Wyman. "Try and keep your voices down. Loud noises make me nervous." When Mrs. Wyman turned and went downstairs Anne closed the door and put her hand over her mouth as she muffled her laughter.

"I hope she doesn't evict us," laughed Catherine in a whisper.

They got off the trolley a block away from Murdoch's Bath House where they would change into their new swimming garments and walked down the beach. There was a certain mystique about the whole island. The smells, the seagulls, the people, all had made a lasting impression on almost everyone who visited there. It was a perfect day and the two Eastman girls had made up their minds to indulge in the fun. Anne had made a solution of olive oil and iodine that they both rubbed all over each other. Even so, the sun began to take its toll on their pale skin after a while. They were having so much fun running into the water and bouncing in the waves they forgot about the heat of the sun. After they ate their lunch Anne could see that Catherine's face was turning a bright red. They had both worn bonnets but the sun somehow seemed to glare into their happy faces. Disappointed, they decided to leave and they walked up the steps to the street and over to the waiting area for the trolley. On their way over to the trolley a lady stopped and asked them where they had bought their knapsacks.

"Oh, we made them," said Catherine.

"Well," said the tourist. "You could make a lot of money selling those bags on the beach. I'd sure buy one." The lady turned and went back to the beach.

A few minutes passed and Joseph pulled up and said hello. "I be happy to take you home."

Anne and Catherine walked over to the buggy and Joseph helped them get in.

"I didn't realize the sun could be so brutal," said Anne. "I am afraid we stayed too long in the sun."

Joseph opened up his umbrella and handed it to Anne.

"Thank you Joseph, we are so glad you came by," said Anne. When they turned up 16th Street, Joseph pulled up in front of an old wooden boarded up house. Without saying anything he jumped off the buggy and went around to the back of the house. A few minutes later he came back and handed Anne a paper bag.

"There's an Aloe Vera plant inside the bag," said Joseph, "its juices will soothe your skin and help cool down the sunburn."

Anne was speechless. After a few moments she said, "You seem to know everything, Joseph. It was our lucky day when you came along."

"I left enough dirt in the bag for it to stay fresh for a few weeks. Just put the bag in a bowl, cut away the excess paper at the top and keep it lightly watered. That way it'll keep," Joseph said.

When they reached the boarding house, Anne paid the fare and then quickly went upstairs with Catherine. They felt as if their skin was on fire. Anne took the bag and placed it in a bowl and followed Joseph's instructions. She broke off several of the plants leaves and squeezed the pulp into a bowl. She added a few drops of water and after doing this several times, she rubbed the mixture over both of their faces, necks, arms and the tops of their feet. They decided to lie down for a while and let the mixture rest on their bodies. When they woke up it was 5:00 o'clock in the afternoon; their skin had cooled down a great deal. They took turns in the bathroom carefully washing off the sand on their legs and feet before they bathed in some cool water. They dressed and began feeling better. Their faces still showed evidence of a day in the sun, but Joseph's magic potion improved the pain greatly. They were hoping that the bright red would fade to a soft pink the next day.

At dinner, Mrs. Wyman scolded them both for not checking with her regarding the havoc of Galveston's sun at the beach.

"The water acts as a magnifying glass by reflecting every angle of the sun on your open skin," she said. "I'm sure you have learned your lesson." she chirped.

Anne changed the subject and asked Mrs. Wyman about the closest Catholic Church.

"Every good Catholic goes to St. Mary's Cathedral." It's located at Church and 21st Street and is just a short walk from here." Minnie continued. "There is a mass every two hours, starting at 7:00, 9:00 and 11:00 every Sunday. Confession starts at 10:00 a.m. each Saturday and they hear confessions all day until 7:00 p.m. They stay late on Saturdays for those who have to work," she said. "Professor Gordon and I like to go to the 7:00 o'clock mass so we can get on with our day," Minnie added.

"That won't be us," said Catherine. "We will probably go to the later one so we can be lazy in the morning."

Minnie looked at Catherine with disapproval.

They slept in a bit on Sunday morning and after a light breakfast of milk and toast Anne and Catherine dressed for mass. Their skin felt a lot better but still showed the effects of the sun on their faces.

St. Mary's Cathedral was the first Roman Catholic cathedral in Texas, having been built in 1847. The bricks for the church had been shipped from Belgium to Galveston. It was a Victorian Gothic castle-like structure with three towers. Atop the middle tower was a statue of Mary, Star of the Sea, positioned to look out over the island as its protector. Catherine and Anne were enamoured by its beauty and couldn't wait to go inside. Almost all of the pews were filled and it looked like everyone in Galveston was going to Mass. Galveston's large German population favored St. Mary's because the 11:00 service was said in German rather than Latin. Anne and Catherine were kneeling in prayer and Anne happened to look up just as John Merit walked past her. Their eyes caught for a second and she noticed a slight smile on his face when he saw her. After the service was over John waited outside the door and approached Anne and Catherine with a smile.

"I wanted to say hello and how nice it is to see you both again."

Anne smiled and said how glad she was to see him, too. John was planning to ask the ladies to lunch, but before he could, the priest approached them. John introduced Father Jonathan and explained that he and the Father had known each other for many years. Father Jonathan expressed his delight to have Anne and Catherine attend St. Mary's mass and he looked forward to seeing more of them. Afterwards, Father Jonathan excused himself to visit with his other parishioners.

"I would be most pleased if you and Catherine could join me for lunch," John said to Anne.

"That sounds wonderful," Anne replied. "We were just thinking of having lunch somewhere."

"There is a small seafood restaurant about four blocks away," John Said. "It's a beautiful day if you don't mind walking."

Catherine looked at her mother and winked. Anne took John's arm when he offered it and Catherine took his other arm. They visited on the way and talked about the beauty of the city and how glad Catherine and Anne were that they had chosen Galveston as their new home.

John Merit could not have been happier. He had no idea that Anne and Catherine were Catholic. Both of the ladies were really attractive and they made him feel very comfortable and relaxed. He couldn't help but notice that in comparison, they favored each other a lot, both in looks and their actions. Anne didn't look a whole lot older than Catherine and he figured that she must have married and given birth at a very young age.

It was almost 2:30 p.m. when John told Anne that he need to get home to his sister, Amelia. He had told her about Amelia's accident and that he looked after her since his parent's had died and that they lived in his parent's house. Anne was touched by his affections for his sister and the need to care for her. It said a lot about his character, she thought. John walked them to the trolley stop and he waited until their trolley arrived and they got on, before he caught another trolley to his home. John was totally infatuated with Anne and Catherine and he was going to make sure that he saw them again.

That evening at dinner Anne told Mrs. Wyman about her new job and asked if it would be all right if Catherine could bring Anne's plate upstairs after dinner and save it in the ice box until Anne got home from her job.

"I'm not sure what time exactly or what my hours are going to be. I expect that for the first few weeks I will be home before dark. However, once the play opens I will be expected to stay through the third act. There is one other seamstress and we might be able to switch off nights," Anne said.

"Well, certainly," said Mrs. Wyman. "I will look after Catherine…I have taken quite a shine to this little girl."

Catherine smiled. Professor Gordon smiled too, and congratulated Anne.

"You'll get to see all the operas free," said the professor. "I hope it all works out to your liking. I must say, though, I like my sleep and I wouldn't want to stay up until 10:30 or 11:00 o'clock every night."

On Monday, Anne woke early so she could have breakfast and visit with Catherine before she left for the Grande. Catherine could tell her mother was nervous and tried to take her mother's mind off the new job by chatting about the fun day they had at the beach. While Anne dressed, Catherine prepared a lunch for her mother of bagel and cheese and wrapped it up. Money would be tight and they could not afford to eat out every day. Catherine didn't mind staying at home by herself. She was anxious to sew her new dresses and she also had a library book she wanted to finish reading. School would be starting in a month and she wanted to learn everything she could about American History and the Indians. Catherine had loved their first two weeks in Galveston. She and her mother had always been close, but they had created a special kind of bond now. They had been through a lot together and she prayed her mother's new job wouldn't be too stressful.

Anne arrived at the Grande a little early and she waited outside because the door was still locked. She walked to the corner and noticed people going in a side door so she asked if they were cast members.

They greeted her and then someone said, "You must be the new girl who's going to keep us in our costumes." And they all laughed.

"At least she is a looker," said another voice in the crowd.

"Come on in and get acquainted. You are going to see us all half necked anyway," a female voice said.

Anne couldn't help but laugh herself at their enthusiasm. She walked down a hall and went through a door leading to a room with rows and rows of costumes lining the walls, and she walked to the back where there were two sewing machines. They appeared to be brand new and she was excited to try one of them out.

"The one on the right is mine," said a lady with a deep voice. You may use the one on the left. By the way, my name is Helga."

Anne introduced herself and told her either one was fine with her.

"The other seamstress was fired last week because she was slow and she kept making mistakes," said Helga. "We have a lot of sewing to do so let's get started." Helga handed Anne a sketch of a dress and asked if Anne could make it.

"Yes," said Anne, "but I thought we only did alterations."

"The main stars and cast members come with the troupe and they bring their own costumes. The rest of the cast consists of local talent. We have some costumes, but they all need alterations and we are short three. We will need to do some fittings and take measurements."

Everything seemed to be happening in double time. Cast members came in and out getting fitted, pinned and measured. Several hours passed when David stuck his head inside the door and asked how things were going. Helga was busy sewing and Anne was busy fitting a half-naked female cast member who was one of the dancers. It didn't seem to bother the dancer that David was staring at her half-dressed body. Anne flushed with embarrassment.

"It's no big deal," said the actress. "You can't be modest around here and David's like one of the cast members. He sees us half-naked a lot," she bragged and giggled.

David slapped her on her buttock as he walked past and out the door.

"You'll get used to it, said Helga. It's just one big happy family around here."

Anne went back to pinning the costume and didn't say anything. What have I gotten myself into? Anne thought to herself.

It was almost 2:00 p.m. when Anne finished pinning the last dancer. Helga had already left for lunch and Anne was alone. She made some room on the side of her work table and picked up her bag of food that Catherine had prepared for her. Before she could take her first bite, the door opened and David came in. He walked over to her table and picked up half of her bagel and a piece of cheese and began eating it.

"You know," David said, "actors and actresses are a breed of their own. They demand a lot of attention and modesty just isn't in their makeup. You looked shocked when I slapped Angela on her bottom. The ladies all like it when I pay attention to them. It's part of my job to see they get all the attention they want."

Anne didn't answer him because she really didn't know what to say.

"You need to lighten up a little bit, Anne. Have a little

fun...you're too stiff."

He put the half eaten bagel back on Anne's table and left. Anne's eyes filled with tears and she sat motionless for a few minutes. She wanted to run but she needed her job. She grabbed up the food and threw all of it in the trash. She had her back to the door when it opened again and she pretended to be sorting through some costumes. She wasn't sure who came in and she didn't want to turn around for fear they could read her face.

Helga came in and asked if everything was all right.

Anne tried to compose herself and gave a half-smile to Helga. "It's all right," said Anne. "Just a little misunderstanding, that's all."

The two ladies worked in silence the rest of the day. Before Helga left she turned to Anne and said, "It took me a while to get used to how things work around here. They are all different from us, Anne. You'll get used to it."

"Thanks, Helga," said Anne, "I'm sure you're right. I'll see you tomorrow."

CHAPTER 7

Another week went by and everything settled into a routine for Anne and Catherine. Anne was often home by 7:00 in the evening and she often brought costumes home to work on so she wouldn't have to stay so late. Anne knew that in a few weeks when the opera opened she would have to stay until the final curtain which could be as late as 10:30 or 11:00 p.m. She had Mondays off and she vowed that would be her day with Catherine. Friday was usually payday so she would have to keep her check until Monday when she and Catherine could take it to the bank and cash it. Anne took out the cash to pay her room and board, she kept a little so she and Catherine would have some spending money and the rest went into her tin canister to save. There were only a few dimes and nickels left each week, but every little bit added up. Catherine had begun making knapsacks out of the leftover materials. She made all sizes and put them in a pile in the corner of the closet. Day by day, the stack grew, and after she made a dozen or so, Catherine showed them to her mother.

"We can go to the beach on Monday and sell them to the tourist," Catherine told her mother. Anne was surprised that Catherine had made so many.

"All right," said Anne, "but when school starts in a few weeks I want you to concentrate on your studies."

The next Monday Catherine and Anne neatly folded the knapsacks and tied them in colorful ribbons. They dressed appropriately this time and wore large straw hats to prevent their faces from getting sunburned again. They both carried the two knapsacks they had made two weeks earlier so they could show them off. They sold the knapsacks for twenty cents each and in less than an hour Catherine had made two dollars and forty cents. As they were leaving, a tourist came up and asked to purchase the one Catherine was carrying. She sold that one for twenty-five cents, giving her a total of two dollars and sixty-five cents to put away. Anne was greatly impressed with Catherine's initiative and told her that there were lots of scraps that they threw away at the Grande and that she would bring them home for Catherine to use.

John Merit had just come out of a meeting when his secretary put his mail on his desk. There was an overseas letter from England. John opened it first. The letter was from the Bank of Sandgate, England, and signed John Herring, President.

Dear Mr. Merit:

I was pleased to hear that Anne Eastman and her daughter, Catherine, are now settled in Galveston and that Mrs. Eastman has found employment. One of your questions was regarding the marital status of Mrs. Eastman. While I feel it is not my place to give you that information, I can only say that I do not expect her husband will be joining her in the future.

Perhaps it best that you ask Mrs. Eastman the question regarding her marital status yourself. I can only say that I have the utmost respect for her and her daughter and that if I were not married myself, I would not let the ring on her left hand discourage me from pursuing her friendship as a gentleman.

Kindest Regards,
Edward Herring, President

John read and reread the letter several times. He understood that Mr. Herring would not betray Anne's confidence. In a few weeks, Catherine would be starting school, which meant that Anne would be taking care of her banking by herself on her day off. He would be patient and wait to ask her to lunch when the time was right.

David Brooks felt intimidated by Anne. It was clear she wasn't going to make it easy for him to bed her. She barely looked at him when they passed in the hallway even though she would say hello and acknowledge his presence. She was not at all like any woman he had ever been around before. Even though she wore a wedding ring, he didn't think for a minute that she was really married. If she wasn't married, he wondered if she ever had any sexual fantasies about being with a real man. He decided he would try another approach the next day and ask her to go to lunch with him.

Helga always took a bathroom break around 10:00 o'clock in the morning so David waited until Helga came out and went down the hall. David went in and saw Anne busy with some handwork.

"So, how's it going so far?" asked David.

Anne looked up and then back down and said, "Everything is great, thank you for asking."

"How about having lunch with me today and I will bring you up to date on the new schedule once we open," David asked.

"Can't you tell me here while I am working?" asked Anne.

"I'm on my way to a meeting with Tom. I'll meet you outside the side door at 11:45," said David, as he walked out and closed the door behind him.

Anne had mixed emotions about having lunch with David and she told herself that it was going to be all right. She was a little afraid of David but since he was such a good friend of Tom's, she thought it best to try and make amends with him.

When Anne left at 11:45, she told Helga that she had an errand to run. David was standing outside smoking a cigarette. He threw it down on the sidewalk and stepped on it and grabbed Anne under her arm.

"There's a diner a couple of blocks down the street that serves great food. I think you will like it," said David.

They walked the two blocks in silence. When they went in, the waitress smiled at David and told him his usual table at the back was available and he could seat himself. There were two menus on the table and Anne was glad to have something to do that would occupy them for a few minutes.

The waitress brought water to their table and took their orders. David ordered the daily special of meatloaf and mashed potatoes and Anne ordered a grilled cheese sandwich. David was staring at Anne when she finally looked up.

"What was it you were going to tell me?" asked Anne.

David smiled. "Nothing you don't already know. It's just that I felt we got off to a bad start the other day and I just wanted to clear the air. You are really a classy lady and I wanted to apologize to you for being such an idiot."

Anne smiled and said, "Apology accepted, although it wasn't necessary."

"Maybe not," said David, "but how about we start over and see if we can just be friends. Tell me," David continued, "what kind of husband would let his wife and their daughter sail half-way around the world by themselves?"

Anne replied, "Life isn't always an open book, David, and if you don't mind I would like to keep our relationship on a business level."

David wasn't pleased that Anne was making it so hard for him and decided to change the direction of the conversation and began telling Anne about the new opera and what to expect opening night. There would be a party afterward for the cast and crew members and he hoped she would be able to stay for it.

"I'll look forward to it," said Anne.

David paid the check after they finished eating and they walked back to the Grande. All in all, David was pleased with the way things ended up with Anne. She still intimidated him though, and he wasn't used to women getting the better of him. Most of the ladies fell all over themselves to get David's attention.

When David and Anne reached the Grande, David said that he had an errand to run. Anne thanked him for lunch and went back to work. David headed down to Fat Alley to find Wanda. None of the other girls had seen Wanda that morning so David headed to Wanda's new place and banged on the door.

"Go away," said Wanda. "I'm off today."

"The heck you are….open up Wanda, it's me, David." Wanda opened the door a crack and David pushed his way in.

"Come on, David, I don't feel so good today. Please leave," Wanda pleaded. David saw her bandaged wrist and asked if she had gotten into a fight.

"No, you did that to me the other day in the storeroom when you pushed me up against the wall. There was a nail and it scratched me really bad. I've been sick ever since," Wanda said.

Anne's rejection of David made him angry and he needed to relieve his stress. Wanda didn't look well, and if she had a fever he didn't want to get sick too. David left and closed the door. He knew he didn't have a lot of time and he finally found a young black prostitute coming down an outside stairway. She stopped halfway down when she saw him and she motioned for him to come up. David followed her back into the room. He was on his way back to the Grande twenty minutes later.

It was half after two when David walked back to the Grande and slipped in without being seen. Maybe Tom hadn't come looking for him, David hoped. He and Tom got along pretty well but Tom was always on his back about being late and holding up rehearsals. Time was on David's side this time, the director had just gotten back himself and the afternoon rehearsals were just beginning.

By the next morning, Wanda's fever had gotten worse. Her symptoms for the tetanus disease had started with a bad headache. The wound wouldn't heal and as each day went by she developed a fever and her jaw and neck began stiffening. Wanda forced herself to get up out of bed so she could get dressed. She needed to go see Doc Griffin. The Doc, as they all referred to him, took care of the girls and was really nice to them. He didn't demand any favors and accepted whatever they could pay him. Wanda struggled to keep her balance. The sun was not up yet when she went outside. She had no idea what time it was and hoped she might see one of her friends on her way home from a late night so they could go get the Doc. Wanda sat down on the top stairs and tried to scoot down on her bottom but her legs didn't seem to want to move either. She had only slid down a couple of steps before she passed out. It was noon before someone found her.

Galveston was growing faster than any other city in the United States. Thousands of immigrants arrived every week and what the ships didn't bring in, the railroad did. William Morgan was the chief of police and another dead hooker was not at the top of his priority list. The chief was struggling to keep up with the daily drunks, prostitutes, gamblers, opium addicts and murderers. He spent most of his time trying to identify the stowaways, the drunks and the dead. Prostitutes and hookers were low on the totem pole. Besides, several of Galveston's elite, including a judge, frequented the brothels. If he had to arrest one of them, he would have to arrest them all.

"Looks like she might have died from natural causes," said one of the policemen to the Chief as they took turns on the steps looking at Wanda.

"It appears like the wound on her wrist is about a week old....time enough for tetanus to set in," the Chief said. "Send her over to the colored funeral home and let them identify her. Being a hooker she probably has no kin, at least none here. Word will get out. Someone will know her."

The chief walked back down the stairs, mounted his horse and walked it down Fat Alley. No telling what went on here last night, Chief Morgan thought to himself. The Chief took his job seriously but he knew that one more deceased hooker wouldn't make the newspapers. He would be up for re-election again in November and he was pretty sure he would get re-elected.

That week the Galveston newspaper featured opera singer, Sarah Everhart, on the front page of its newspaper. She had taken her own traveling company on a worldwide tour that included the far reaches of Europe, Australia, Canada and the United States. She was an international star and would be performing *La Tosca* at the Grande Opera House on August 25th, 1897 and the show would run for three days. The socialites were frantically spending enormous amounts of money on elaborate costumes, jewelry and false hair. Parties were being planned by Galveston's elite and all the prestigious hotels and restaurants were getting booked up. The city couldn't get enough of all the excitement; and lines formed outside the Grande Opera house with people hoping to buy general admission tickets to *La Tosca*. The season ticket holders had no intention of selling their tickets and the general admission tickets sold out the first hour.

Anne knew the opera, *La Tosca*, was the one they were making the costumes for but she had only found out recently that Sarah Everhart would be playing the lead role. Anne was familiar with the opera, as she had heard about it when it played in London, but she never in her wildest dream thought she would be a part of it. Anne was told that Mrs. Everhart would be arriving two days earlier for dress rehearsals and that everything had to be finished by then. Anne was almost through with the new costume she had made from the earlier sketch and wondered if it was for Sarah. She was nervous and excited at the same time and knew it would be impossible to get a ticket for Catherine, but she hoped she could talk Tom Gregory into allowing Catherine to watch a dress rehearsal. Anne decided to wait and talk to Tom before she told Catherine because she did not want her to be disappointed if Tom did not want her to come.

Things were beginning to heat up for David, and Tom was demanding more and more from him. The director wanted everyone to know their routines before Sarah Everhart and her troupe got there and the lighting had to be just right. It was David's job to see to that. It was hard for him to get away for any length of time during the day, so when they finished early one night he went looking for Wanda.

"She's dead...died from the fever," one of the prostitutes told David.

David was stunned. He had no idea Wanda was that sick and he was glad he hadn't stayed around that day she told him she was sick.

"I'll be your come-to girl," the hooker said. "I can do anything she did and I can do it better."

It had been more than a week since David was with a woman, so he followed her down the street and they stopped in an opening between two buildings.

"Here," David said as he pulled down the ladder to a fire escape and motioned her to crawl up it. They climbed to the third story of the building and David pushed a window up to see if it would open. "My lucky day," David said as he handed her a dollar bill and they crawled in. Before he closed the window David looked out to make sure no one had seen them.

"My name is Sheila," said the hooker.

"Shut up and take your clothes off," said David.

David was anxious and he didn't want to talk. Sheila wouldn't stop talking so he slammed his fist into her mouth before she could finish. She whirled around and fell, catching a rope that was hanging by the side of the wall. The curtain attached to the rope fell and David picked up the rope and wrapped it around Sheila's neck tightening it so she couldn't talk or scream. Sheila struggled but she was no match for David and she finally blacked out. After he raped her, he tried to wake Sheila up. He hadn't intended to kill her, but she wouldn't shut up. He didn't know what had come over him. Maybe Wanda's death triggered something in his head, he thought, and then he saw the image of his mother's face and he felt the need for a cigarette. David took out a cigarette he had rolled earlier and lit it. The glow from the match reflected on Sheila's face and her open eyes staring back at him. There was no doubt in his mind she was dead. David walked over to the window and looked down on the dimly lit street. He didn't see anyone so he opened the window and crawled out. When he climbed down the ladder he pushed it back up and left. He walked down between the buildings toward the opposite end of the street they came in on. Seeing no one, he made a quick exit.

CHAPTER 8

The next day Chief Morgan and one of his sergeants, Edward Husky, were standing in an alley between 28th and 29th Street a few blocks from Fat Alley looking up at a window on the third floor.

"They must have pulled the ladder down to the fire escape and crawled up it to gain access through the window," the sergeant said. "Two hookers in one week," he said, "now ain't that a coincidence."

"Yeah," said the chief, "except this one didn't die of natural causes. Who did you say reported it?" asked the chief.

"The owner did. Said he smelled a dead rat upstairs and went up to take a look. He used the third floor to store his records in so he didn't come up here much," the sergeant continued.

Chief Morgan pulled the ladder down to the fire escape and stood looking up. He crawled up the ladder and Sergeant Husky followed him. They stood on the landing of the third floor and "Husk" as his friends called him, opened the window. Once they were inside they pulled all the curtains aside to let the light in. They put their handkerchiefs over their noses and opened all the windows so they could breathe. They had smelled death before but the odor from the decomposing body was overwhelming.

"Looked like he had a smoke," said Husk, as he picked up a cigarette butt and a box of matches.

Chief Morgan took the matches and looked at it. "Grande Opera House" was printed on the front of the match box.

Husk asked, "What do you think?

"They could belong to anybody. We will keep it in the evidence drawer," the Chief said. "Meanwhile call the funeral home that
handles the pauper's graves and have them pick her up. I'm going to
get some fresh air."

When they crawled back down the ladder, the Chief made some
notes in his notebook and left. It bothered him that this particular crime
might never be solved and that there was a murderer on the streets. If
another one happened anytime soon he might have take a closer look.

Back at the police station, Chief Morgan was finishing up his
notes when Mayor Raymond Dooley came in. Dooley carried a holster
and gun on his hip and paid little attention to city management. He
liked throwing his weight around and Morgan always got the brunt of
it.

"I hear we had a murder down in the red light district," said the
mayor.

"Yeah," said the chief. "A young prostitute, maybe eighteen or
twenty years old. Hard to say cause she's been dead at least two days."

"Got any suspects?" asked the mayor.

"No, said Chief Morgan, "didn't find much evidence."

"Wasn't there another death in the same area last week?" asked
the mayor.

"Yes, but that one was natural causes."

"You know," said the mayor, "the people around here don't pay
too much attention about another dead hooker but we better keep our
eyes and ears open. The next time it could be one of our own. I don't
like murderers on our streets," the mayor said in a sombre voice.

"Neither do I, "said Chief Morgan, "but when you have a part
of your town infested with dead beats, opium addicts and prostitutes
anything can happen. Just give me the word and I'll clear the scum
out."

"Not so fast," said Mayor Dooley. "I'm just suggesting that we
keep our ear to the ground and ask a few questions and act like we give

a darn. The owner of the building the girl was murdered in is a friend of mine. You're not doing an autopsy are you?" Dooley asked.

"We're over budget, as you know, and this being an election year we need to cut out some of our spending," Dooley said as he tipped his hat and left.

Chief Morgan was agitated that the mayor was always trying to tell him how to do his job. Autopsy, thought Morgan, she had a rope wrapped around her neck, why waste money on an autopsy? The Mayor didn't really care what happed in that part of town. But many of the Mayor's buddies hung out at the Artillery Club not too far from the red light district and one of Galveston's most exclusive whorehouses. Husky came in and asked what the Mayor had to say.

"He was uneasy about the murder being too close to their playground at the Artillery Club," said Morgan. "Head on over to the Grande and check with Tom Gregory, see if he has heard of any riff-raff or has a problem with any of his people," Morgan ordered.

Husky thought it was a waste of time but knew that Morgan was under a lot of pressure from the mayor so he left and headed over to the Grande.

"Let me guess," said Gregory to Sergeant Husky. "You want a couple of tickets to our new opera."

"That'd be nice," said Husky, "but that's not why I'm here. A couple of days ago a young woman of the streets was murdered and we found one of your advertising match boxes next to her dead body." Husky continued, "Just checking to see if you might have any thoughts on that?"

Gregory laughed and said, "I bet if you check the pockets of all the men who frequent the Artillery Club that many of them will have our matches in their pockets."

"I know that," said Husky, "but the mayor wanted us to check it out anyway." "The mayor?" said Gregory. "Doesn't he have enough to do without getting into your business?"

"My sentiments exactly," said Husky, "but the owner of the

building the deceased was found in belongs to a good friend of his. We're just pursuing all of the evidence, what little we have," Husky said.

"Sorry I can't help you," Gregory commented.

David watched from the corner when Sergeant Husky left out the door. Tom Gregory came out of his office and David asked what the detective wanted.

"He was just following up on a murder in the red light district. Seems a prostitute was murdered a couple of days ago," Tom said.

"What's he doing here?" asked David.

"They found one of our match boxes next to her dead body. I guess he must have been in a hurry and dropped it," said Tom.

David excused himself and said he had to check on something. It bothered David that he had dropped those matches when he lit his cigarette but half of the men who attend the opera have those matches. It could be any one of them. He needed to be more careful, he thought.

Anne and Catherine decided to spend one last day at the beach on Monday before the Grand's opening of the opera. Catherine would be starting school the next week, so they wanted to make a day of it. Catherine had made some more of her knapsacks and this group of bags was even prettier than the first ones as she used a lot of the leftover trim and fabric Anne brought home from work. All of the pieces she used were small and she had sewed them together like a patchwork quilt. When they got to the beach, several tourists were waiting for them and one person bought three. Catherine had brought ten and this time charged twenty-five cents for each of them. Again, they were sold out in an hour.

"You are so clever," said Anne to Catherine.

"Let's go get changed into our swimming clothes," Catherine said and they took off running towards the beach house.

They decided to rent a beach umbrella this time and took special precautions not to stay so long in the sun. It was a beautiful day and there was a slight breeze blowing off the Gulf. They had both brought a book to read and they relaxed under their umbrella, only going out to the water for short periods of time. Anne still had the aloe vera plant that Joseph had given them just in case they misjudged the penetration of the sun's rays. They had brought some crackers, cheese and apples that they snacked on.

"This is one of the most wonderful days of my life," Catherine told her mother.

"Hello, ladies," David Brooks was standing over both of them.

They exchanged greetings and David said, "I thought I might take in a little sun myself before the play starts."

Actually, David hated the beach and he only decided to go after he overheard Anne telling Helga what she was going to do on her day off. David had a towel hung around his neck and he took it off and shook it out, laying it on the ground beside Anne and Catherine.

"You don't mind if I join you, do you?" asked David.

"We were actually going to be leaving soon," Anne said.

"Oh, I'm sorry to hear that," David replied. "This must be your beautiful daughter I have heard so much about," said David.
"This is Catherine," Anne said as she got up and began gathering up their things. "We still have a number of errands to run and I'm afraid the day is getting away from us.""Enjoy the day," Anne continued and the two Eastman girls started walking towards the beach house to wash off the sand.

"Who was that man?" asked Catherine.

"Oh, he is one of the workers at the opera house. I really don't know him that well," answered Anne.

Catherine could sense that her mother was afraid of him but decided not to ask any more questions.

David was angry as he watched the two girls walk up the beach. He got up and walked toward the incoming waves and then dove into the biggest one. Anne was making his skin crawl with desire and he hoped the water would deflate his arousal. He swam out about thirty feet before he decided to turn around and come back. Damn her, he thought, after the show ends I'll show her what she is missing. David didn't like rejection from any woman… no exceptions!

David dried off with his towel and put on his shirt and sandals and then took the next trolley that was headed towards his one bedroom garage apartment. It was still early in the day and he had a little cash, so after he cleaned up in his apartment, he decided to head up to Fat Alley. There were a couple of new girls on the corner, both giving him the eye. "Haven't seen you two before," said David. They giggled and said they were from Houston and that they had heard business was really booming in Galveston.

"Well which one do I choose?" asked David?

"It's been pretty slow today so how about the two of us for a dollar-fifty," said the taller girl.

David smiled.

"Why don't you take us to your place?" asked the other hooker.

David stopped and picked up some whiskey and they all headed to his apartment, with the girls walking a good ten feet behind him.

"Just don't want to call attention to what's going on," said David.

After the door closed behind them, David went to get three glasses from the kitchenette area. When he returned, the freckle-faced red haired girl was already standing buck naked by David's bed. The tall one had her top off and took one of the glasses. They all took a few drinks and the girls began undressing David.

"I could get used to this," he said.

"We hope so," said one of the hookers, and they pleasured him for several hours. Afterwards David had fallen asleep, the two girls emptied his pockets, taking the twelve dollars he had left over after he had cashed his pay check. When David finally woke up and saw they had left, he knew he had been set up. Wait till I get my hands on those two girls, he thought to himself. David looked around the room to see if anything else was missing and figured they just wanted the cash.

David dressed and went looking for them and when he couldn't find them, he figured they had caught the next train back to Houston.

Anne and Catherine decided to walk back down Seawall Boulevard towards Sixteenth Street, laughing and talking about the excited tourist and their successful day selling the knapsacks. They saw Joseph letting some bathers off at a crosswalk and he waved to them.

"You ladies want a ride?" asked Joseph.

"Why not?" said Anne. Joseph got down and helped them get in the buggy.

"Any particular place you want to go, or just home?" asked Joseph.

"Actually," said Anne. We were going to stop at the snow cone stand a few blocks down and then go home."

"I can do that," said Joseph.

When they got to the snow cone stand Joseph waited while they went to buy the snow cones. Catherine came back with two snow cones one in each hand.

"I sure hope you like cherry, Mr. Joseph," laughed Catherine.

Joseph reached out and took the snow cone.

"Why thank you, Miss Catherine, Cherry is my favorite."

Joseph had really grown fond of Anne and Catherine and he always enjoyed giving them a ride.

When they reached the boarding house Anne told Catherine she needed to ask Joseph a question and that she would come in shortly. Anne turned to Joseph.

"I am glad you came by today. Opening night is Friday night and the show will run through next Tuesday. The show should be over around 10:30 p.m. each night. I am not real comfortable walking home by myself that late at night, and wondered if I could arrange for you to pick me up at the side door and see that I get home. I'll be glad to pay you whatever the fare is."

"That would be my pleasure, Mrs. Eastman," said Joseph. "I'll be there Friday night at 10:30. Just look for me as there will be a long line of buggies and a few of those new fangled automobiles lined up around the corner."

"I'll find you Joseph," Anne answered back and went into the boarding house.

CHAPTER 9

The famous opera singer, Sarah Everhart, and her troupe were arriving on Tuesday on the 10:00 a.m. train from Houston. Everything was happening in double time. Anne and Helga had spent the better part of the morning straightening up the garment room and sweeping up the remnants of fabric and thread that had fallen to the floor. The cast members had sandwiches awaiting them at the Grande Hotel next door, but Tom Gregory and the Mayor were taking Sara Everhart to the Tremont for lunch. Rehearsals were to begin with the entire cast at 2:00 p.m. Trunks and props began coming in and David was showing the workers where everything was to be put. Most of the set had already been built according to Mrs. Everhart's specifications but she still liked to have some of her personal things put in the set, especially the silver chalice that the pope had given her.

Anne had brought her lunch and decided she had better eat it before the cast arrived. It was going to be a long day. Fortunately, the days were longer and it didn't get dark until 9:00 p.m. She hoped the rehearsals would be finished by then.

Anne heard some loud talking coming her way and looked up just as Sarah Everhart walked into the costume area. She knew immediately who it was and stood up. Helga jumped up too and walked up to Mrs. Everhart and said, "I'm Helga, the head seamstress here, and I'll be happy to help you with your costumes."

Anne smiled at Mrs. Everhart and didn't say anything. Sarah

walked over to a costume that was hanging up and looked at it very carefully.

"Is this the costume made from the sketch I sent?" asked Sarah.

Anne said, "Yes."

"Did you make the dress yourself?" asked Sarah as she turned to Anne.

"Yes ma'am," answered Anne.

"Your stitching is beautiful, my dear, and I love how you added the trim. It looks wonderful. My seamstress could not accompany me to Galveston due to illness and she had to stay in Houston," Sarah told them. "Mrs. Helga," Sarah continued, "Since you are the head seamstress here, you may look after my troop's needs and this young woman can take care of me and my costumes." Sarah addressed Anne and said, "Would you be so kind as to show me to my dressing room?"

"Yes ma'am, I would be happy to," replied Anne.

"You're English... from where did you come?" asked Sarah.

"I lived in Sandgate, England, most of my life," replied Anne, as she showed Mrs. Everhart to her dressing room.

The trunks had already arrived and Sarah pointed to two of the larger trunks. "Those are my costumes. Would you please unpack them and hang them up? A couple of them need attention as I happened to have stepped on one of them making my exit in the last show, and tore the hem."

"Certainly," replied Anne.

Anne began the tedious task of taking the heavy costumes out of the trunks and hanging them up. She commented on the beautiful beading and said the fabrics were the most beautiful she had ever seen.

"All of the fabric was imported from Italy and France, and of course, the beautiful fur accents came from Russia," replied Sarah.

Someone knocked on the door. "Rehearsal's in five minutes, Mrs. Everhart."

Sara left for rehearsals, leaving Anne alone. Anne never expected she would be working so close with Mrs. Everhart. After she had hung everything up, she noticed a playbill at the bottom of the trunk and next to each scene in writing was a description of the costume she would be wearing. Anne began sorting each costume, placing it in the order she would be wearing it. When she hung up the last one, she checked the hem where it needed to be mended. Anne took her needle and thread and made the repair. Next, Anne picked up Sarah's train case and began placing the items on the dressing table. After she had finished organizing everything she was planning to leave, but David walked in.

"Well I hear that you will be Mrs. Everhart's personal dresser," said David. "You can expect a nice big tip from her at the end of the show. Usually that tip would go to Helga, so I hope she will be talking to you at the end of the show," David smirked.

"I did not solicit anything," answered Anne. "In fact, I had nothing to say about it. Helga did all of the talking." Anne was angry that David would think she purposely took something she shouldn't have.

"Are you trying to make me feel guilty?" asked Anne.

"Hardly," said David. "I'm just giving you a head's up that Helga will not be happy."

"Well, I get the message, loud and clear," Anne replied. Just then, Sarah came into her dressing room and David walked out the door.

"Is everything all right?" asked Sarah.

"Everything is fine," answered Anne.

It was close to 6:00 p.m. and Anne excused herself.

"If you don't need me anymore today, I will say good-bye now and I'll see you tomorrow," replied Anne.

It was the final day of rehearsals and all the costumes had to be finalized. There would be two rehearsals, one in the morning and a final dress rehearsal at 2:00 p.m. that day. The day before, Anne had asked Tom if Catherine could attend the afternoon rehearsal. He said "No. I have a ticket for Catherine for opening night."

Anne was very appreciative and told Tom that Catherine would be ecstatic.

The morning rehearsals went really well but Anne was nervous about the dress rehearsals. She would have to help Sarah in and out of all of her costumes and there were ten costume changes. The costume that Anne had made from Sarah's sketch fit Sarah perfectly. Anne had been given all the necessary measurements and Sarah was amazed that no adjustments had to be made. Helga had been a bit cool to Anne but she never said anything. Perhaps it was just Anne's imagination. The afternoon rehearsals went according to plan and the director congratulated everyone on their excellent acting and singing and the excitement began to grow.

The next day, the city began to explode with anticipation. All the hotels and restaurants were booked up and every conversation included talk about what everyone was wearing to the opera. It was not every day that a renowned actress of Sarah Everhart's caliber came to Galveston. It was going to be the biggest social event of the year with a reception after lunch at the Tremont Hotel. Beautiful carriages and white horses arrived on the morning train from Houston. It was rumored that President William McKinley was even coming to the opening but it was just that, a rumor. It was planned that Mrs. Everhart and some of the cast members would participate in a small parade down the strand. One of the bank presidents had rented a carriage and white horses for Mrs. Everhart to ride in. Many of Galveston's city officials and dignitaries, including the mayor, also rode in the parade. It was obvious that Galveston was the third richest city in the United States and the Galvestonians loved to show off their wealth.

While everyone was at the parade, David stayed behind at the opera house. He had seen more than his share of parades when he worked at the circus. Anne did not go either, as she still had some mending to do on some of Sarah's costumes. Some of them were not in the best condition and she noticed that several of the seams had been ripped and sewed poorly back together. David knocked on the door and went in. He acted surprised to see Anne working and said that he needed to adjust the ceiling fan. He was carrying a ladder and although Anne acknowledged him, she did not want to carry on a conversation with him. David fumbled around getting up on the ladder and coming down, picking up different tools and pretending to work. Anne was getting nervous and excused herself to go to the powder room. David knew she would be gone at least five minutes because she always preferred to use the nicer bathrooms in the adjoining hotel.

As soon as she was gone David began rummaging through her purse, which was stuffed inside her knapsack along with her personal sewing kit. He carefully opened her small purse and found a small velvet bag with a gold watch inside it. He hastily put everything back the way he found it, putting the watch and its velvet bag in his own pocket. He picked up his tools and carried his ladder and tool box out the door, meeting Anne in the hallway.

"All done," smiled David.

Anne was relieved and went back in to finish her sewing. It was now lunch time and Anne needed to get some water in her pitcher so she left for a short while. When she came back, Helga was standing at the door waiting for her. They greeted each other and then went into Sarah's dressing room.

"I understand that you think I am upset by the fact that Mrs. Everhart chose you over me, and that is not so. I really don't like working with the stars as it makes me very nervous," said Helga. "Most of them are very demanding and it makes me nervous."

"I'm glad to hear that," said Anne, "and thank you for coming in."

David left for an early lunch and headed out the door. He stopped on his the way and took out his tobacco pouch and a thin paper. He lightly tapped the tobacco into the paper and then rolled it up and licked it slowly, all the while picturing Anne searching for the watch. After he lit his cigarette, he started walking to the diner and fingered the gold watch in his pocket. Earlier that morning David had encouraged Helga to talk to Anne at her first opportunity about Sarah choosing Anne over her.

"Why it never crossed my mind," said Helga. "Anne is a wonderful seamstress, and much better than I am. Yes, I will speak to her," Helga assured David.

So far, David's plan was working perfectly. Anne would now assume that Helga took the watch and he would be in the clear. David had finished eating his food and looked around the diner to see if anyone was looking his way. He slowly took the watch out of his pocket, keeping his hands under the table. He took the watch out of the velvet bag and clicked it open. At closer look he read the inscription inside it. So, her husband's name was Adam, he thought. He closed it and looked up to see the waitress coming with the coffee pot.

"Just the check, please," David said.

Anne had made arrangements for Catherine to attend the opera with Minnie and Professor Gordon and instructed Catherine to wait next door in the lobby of the Grande Hotel afterwards until Anne could meet her and have Joseph take them home.

That evening the common people began lining the streets at 6:00 p.m. in anticipation of the evening's events. Watching the island's wealthy and affluent socialites arriving in their impressive carriages pulled by beautiful stallions was one of the highlights of the evening. Many of the women attending the evening's events were dressed in avant-garde-style costumes and the men wore lavish top hats and tuxedos. It was a memorable evening for everyone.

It was almost 7:00 p.m. and Anne was waiting for Mrs. Everhart to arrive and begin putting on her stage makeup. Anne was also a bit nervous and decided to check her time piece. She pulled out her small purse from her knapsack and took out her small mirror, a handkerchief and her coin purse. The watch was not there. She picked up her knapsack and began taking everything out. There was a knot in Anne's stomach. The watch had belonged to her father and when she married Adam she had given it to him as a gift. She had taken it to a jeweler who engraved an inscription on the inside of the case, "To Adam, the love of my life. Anne." She searched the floor around her sewing table and confirmed what she already knew. Had she taken it out at home and left it? She wondered. Oh my goodness, did Helga take it? Anne thought. Helga had admired it earlier and commented on it. She heard the door open and Sarah walked in.

"Oh, what a day I have had, would you please help me with my makeup?" Sarah asked Anne.

CHAPTER 10

Sara Everhart's magnificent performance in *La Tosca* was a sensational success with six standing ovations. The audience seemed a bit horrified by the play's sexual themes and grotesque use of torture, murder, and suicide, but they were all positively overwhelmed by Sarah's splendid performance. It was everything the Galvestonians had expected it to be. Both Sarah and Anne were exhausted but pleased that there were no mishaps and very little downtime during Sarah's changes.

Anne finished hanging up the last of Sarah's costumes and then left to find her daughter. Catherine, Minnie and the Professor were waiting for Anne at the Grande Hotel and congratulated her on her part in the production. John Merit was also there and introduced his sister, Amelia, to them. John had offered to buy them all a drink at the hotel bar but everyone thanked him and said it was past their bedtime. John looked especially nice, thought Anne, as he was wearing a tuxedo and had a top hat in his hand. She didn't tell him that as she would feel embarrassed in front of everyone and she decided she must remember to tell him how dashing he looked the next time she saw him. Anne's group walked outside to find Joseph and he was not far away. They all managed to fit in Joseph's buggy, but the Professor had to sit up front with Joseph, which he did not mind as he really did not want to walk back to the boarding house so late at night.

David watched Anne leave with her party. He guessed that

since her daughter was with her she needed to see her home. Perhaps she forgot about the party afterwards. In any event she was gone and so was David's opportunity to possibly be alone with her.

David went inside to where the cast was drinking and his eyes connected with one of the girls from Sarah's troupe. She really wasn't that attractive but she had a fabulous voice and a very sexy scene in the opera. David had noticed her the day before when they ran into each behind the stage. A few minutes later she was standing in front of David with a drink in her hand.

"My name is Esther," she said. "And I know your name, David."

David smiled and thought, "What the heck, he'd play along for a while and see where it went.

They began talking about the opera and then Esther asked if David were married. David replied, "No, or you?"

She told him she was divorced and had joined Sarah's company in New York.
"It was my big break and I've been with the troupe every since," said Esther.

They made small talk and had a couple more drinks. "Let's get out of this boring place," Esther told David.

She grabbed his hand and led him out the door and up the stairs to the third floor of the Grande Hotel. For some reason David didn't seem aroused by the fact that she was throwing herself at him. He just couldn't seem to get Anne out of his head. When they got to Esther's room he saw two suitcases and shoes and clothes thrown all over the place.

"Another girl sharing your room?" asked David.
"Yeah," she answered, "but don't worry about her; she likes to stay out late."

Esther came over and started unbuttoning David's shirt. She started kissing his neck and then undid his belt. David wasn't ready yet so he grabbed her and pushed her on the bed. He started taking off her clothes and after she was naked he pulled off his pants and underwear and crawled in bed with her. They were lost in the sensual gratification of each other's company and pleasured each other for over an hour.

"Why don't you stay the night?" asked Esther.

"No, I better go before your roommate decides to come home," said David.

"Ahh, that's too bad," she said. "Maybe we can get together again tomorrow night."

"Maybe," said David and he left.

For some reason David was finding it harder and harder to get excited by anyone other than Anne. She was on his mind constantly. On David's way to his apartment he walked by Anne's boarding house and saw the light was still on. David walked across the street and down the side of a house, hiding behind some foliage and watched. He saw movement behind the curtains and wondered what Anne might be doing. He wanted to go to her but thought better of it, so he went home.

Anne waited until Catherine was asleep before she started searching for her watch. She did not want to worry Catherine and knew it was only a matter of time before Catherine asked her about it. They had a clock beside the bed but Anne preferred to take the watch out of her purse to check the time. Catherine often watched as her mother took the watch and opened it, smiling as though it were talking to her. Anne finally sat down on a chair, frustrated, and wanting to cry. She found it hard to believe there was a thief at the opera house. Anne finally crawled into bed and tried to go to sleep. Hundreds of thoughts went through her head, reliving the whole day over and over. At 2:30 a.m. Anne finally fell asleep. Catherine woke Anne at 7:45 a.m. and set some hot tea on the side table.

"Mama, the opera was the most unbelievable and amazing thing I have ever seen. There were some things in it I am not sure I understand, and I was wondering if you might be able to explain them to me?" Catherine asked.

Anne jumped up and said they would talk later as she would be late to work. Catherine was disappointed but knew her mother was right. Anne hurriedly dressed and kissed Catherine on the forehead.

"My little darling," said Anne. "I am not sure I understand the whole thing either. Monday will be totally your day and we will figure it out together."

Catherine smiled and kissed her mother back.

Anne had never been late before and she was out of breath when she finally arrived at the Grande. She went in the side door and was surprised that there was no one around. She went into the theatre and looked around and opened some of the dressing room doors and found the rooms empty. It was almost 9:00 a.m. and she decided she would go back to Sarah's dressing room to work. On her way, she ran into David.

Where is everyone?" asked Anne.

"Big party last night. They usually don't meander in until noon. What happened to you?" asked David.

"I had to see my daughter, Catherine, home," said Anne. "I was tired from the long day so I decided to stay home." Anne picked up her knapsack and started to leave.

"Where are you going?" asked David.

"I have some business I need to take care of," Anne said.

Anne did not want to be alone with David, so she left and started to walk toward town. She wasn't sure where she was going but she knew she did not want to stay there by herself with David breathing down her neck.

When Anne had walked several blocks she found herself standing at the front of the bank and decided to go in. John Merit noticed her immediately and motioned to her to come back to his office.

"What a pleasant surprise," John smiled and said.

"I wondered if I might impose on you once more, as I have a small problem," said Anne.

John asked if Anne had had breakfast and suggested that they go across the street to the drug store coffee shop where they could find a table in the back. John ordered for both of them. "They make great coffee cake here, and the best coffee in town," said John. Anne looked up at John and tried to smile.

"What's wrong Anne? The opera was a big success and the costumes were beautiful," John said.

"Before I tell you my dilemma, I wanted to tell you how nice you looked last night and I so enjoyed meeting your sister," Anne said and then paused. "What I have to tell you should be kept in the strictest confidence as I am not sure what I should do."

"Of course," replied John.

Anne told John the story about her missing watch and finished her story by saying, "The watch belonged to my father and I gave it to my late husband as a wedding...."

Anne stopped herself and realized what she had said.

"I'm sorry I lied to you," said Anne, and she was actually relieved. John smiled and told her he had secretly hoped that she wasn't married and briefly told her about his late wife and child. John put his hand on top of Anne's hand.

"I'm sure the watch will show up. Give it a few days, maybe whoever took it will have second thoughts and return it." He continued, saying, "Do you think it possible that someone in Sarah's troupe could be a thief?"

Anne answered, "I rarely leave without taking my purse with me except the day it went missing. There were two people in the room while I was gone, Helga Smith and David Brooks," Anne told John. "Helga is a strong Christian woman and I can't believe she would be that vindictive," Anne said.

"So what about David Brooks?" John asked.

"I'm not sure," Anne said.

"Would you like me to talk with Tom Gregory?" John asked.

"No, I don't know," Anne said holding back her tears.

John waited a few moments and smiled at Anne and said: "It distresses me to see you so upset, Anne, and I want to help you."

"I know you do," said Anne, "but I think you are right about waiting a few days."

"Would it be possible for us to maybe see each other again outside the bank?" asked John.

"Yes," said Anne, "I would like that. The opera ends its tour Sunday night and I promised to spend the day with Catherine on Monday; perhaps we could have dinner Monday evening," Anne continued.

"Great, I'll look forward to it, but promise me that if anything else happens you will come to me immediately," John said.

"I promise," answered Anne.

"There is one more thing, John," Anne went on to say, "If anything happens to me I have left a letter for Catherine in the bottom of our safety deposit box and I want to be sure she reads it. Also, I would like for you to see that my account is well taken care of."

"Of course, I would," said John, "However I am sure nothing is going to happen to you."

Anne thanked John and left to go back to the Grande.

CHAPTER 11

The streets continued to be crowded with onlookers every evening before the opera and it opened to record breaking crowds every night. Anne and Sarah Everhart worked very closely together and Sarah was extremely happy that Anne was so meticulous in her work. Sarah loved Anne's quiet demeanour and before the last show Sarah made Anne a proposal.

"Why don't you come and work for me? All your expenses will be paid for and you will travel as my head dresser and companion, "Sarah said.

Anne was taken by surprise. "I...I have a fifteen year old daughter and she will be starting school in a few weeks," said Anne. "I moved here to provide some stability in her life and make sure she gets a good education," continued Anne. "I appreciate your offer but I am afraid I must decline."

Sarah smiled and took out a piece of paper. She wrote down her permanent address and gave it to Anne. "If you change your mind, here is my address, I have someone who checks my mail for me and we talk frequently. All you have to do is write to me and I will send for you," Sarah said.

"You are very kind and I appreciate your offer," Anne replied.

"After the show tonight we will be packing up and leaving on a midnight train," said Sarah. "It will be hectic and we won't get a chance to talk but I want you to know I greatly appreciate all of your help and I couldn't have done it without you," Sarah said with sincerity.

Anne thanked Sarah and told her she would never forget her kindness. Sarah gave Anne a sealed envelope and told her she could open it later. Anne folded it and put it in her pocket.

The final performance was as great as the ones before, except this one had nine standing ovations. After each costume change Anne would neatly fold each costume and place it in Sarah's trunk, so that at the end of each performance, every costume was in place and ready to go. When Sarah left her dressing room for the final act, Anne began packing up all of the stage makeup. The set and personal items would get packed up the next day and sent on the afternoon train that would take it to Houston and then Denver, Colorado, where her next performance would be. Afterwards Sarah came to the dressing room and changed, and kissed Anne on the cheek good-bye. Sarah had asked Anne to stay and make sure her trunks were picked up and taken to the train station as she never traveled without her costumes. Anne waited patiently as the time ticked by. She decided to go outside and tell Joseph she would be late but he was nowhere to be found.

Earlier during the final song, David went out to the street and saw Joseph waiting five carriages back. David smiled as he walked up to Joseph and said,

"Miss Anne sent me out here to tell you that she has to stay late and won't need you tonight. She said you should pick up another fare."

David went back inside, pleased with himself that everything seemed to be falling into place. The trunks were finally picked up and Anne followed them out to the street. She saw the clock on the building across the street and it said 11:05. She looked up and down the street and did not see Joseph. Just as she turned around she came face to face with David.

"I think your buggy driver got tired of waiting and I saw him pick up a couple after the opera was over. I heard them give him an address clear across town so it will be a while if he returns at all," said

David. Anne went in to get her knapsack and David followed her.

"Listen," he said. "I will be happy to walk you home. My place is just past yours a bit."

Anne wasn't sure which was worse, walking home alone or letting David see her home.

Anne hesitated and then said," Thank you that would be nice."

David told Anne to go ahead and he would catch up with her at the end of the block. He told her he needed to get something. Actually David did not want anyone to see them leave together. Anne had walked almost two blocks when David seemed to appear out of nowhere.

"Why don't we stop up here a bit and let me buy you a drink?" asked David.

"I'm really tired and just want to go home," Anne told David.

"You know, Anne, if you would just take some time and get to know me; I think you would enjoy my company," David said.

"I'm sorry, David, but with raising my daughter and work, I really don't have a lot of extra time," Anne said.

David took Anne's arm and put his arm around hers and they walked a little further until they came to a dimly lit alley. David pulled Anne into the alley so fast that she dropped her knapsack on the sidewalk. Anne started to scream but David cupped his hand over her mouth pushing her up against a brick wall so hard that the impact stunned her for a moment. He began kissing her forcefully on the mouth, cupping his hand under her jaw, and pulling one of her arms behind her, holding her so tight she could hardly move. Anne was terrified and mad at the same time. She couldn't scream and she struggled, but David was much stronger than she was.

"Just relax, Anne, I'm not going to hurt you," David said in a whisper.

"Please let me go...I won't scream... I just want to go home," she pleaded.

Anne had remembered that she had stuck some straight pins in her dress as she always did when she was sewing. When David did not release her, Anne freed her right hand and pulled out one of the pins and stuck it in David's hand. David jerked away angrily and then hit her in the jaw with his fist. Anne was stunned and tried to run away, but David grabbed her hair and pulled her back. He hit her again and the blow so hard it knocked her several feet and thrust her head against a pipe protruding from a building. The pain was excruciating and Anne fell to the ground. Anne rolled over on her back and she could feel the blood trickling down her forehead. At first she had no idea where she was and when she looked up everything was a blur. Memories of her past began flashing in her head and she faded in and out of consciousness.

David heard the galloping of a horse and buggy, picked up a pipe from the ground and then hid in a door way. There was just enough moonlight for Joseph to see something on the ground and he stopped. It was Anne's knapsack. He got out and went over to pick it up and heard a noise. Joseph walked a few steps down the alley and saw someone lying on the ground.

"Oh no," said Joseph as he bent over Anne crying, "Miss Anne, wake up. Please God, don't let her be dead."

A moment later David struck Joseph on the head with the pipe he had picked up. David took Anne's envelope from her pocket and put it in his own pocket. Then he left running down the street screaming, "Help, help, we've been attacked."

Joseph had been knocked out for a few minutes and when he came too he heard police whistles and running in the background.

"It's him," said David. "We were just walking home and he attacked us with that pipe."

Joseph slowly began to regain consciousness and he tried to get up. There were two policemen now and they began beating Joseph with clubs. When he succumbed to the beating he was put in shackles and taken away.

One the officers checked Anne's pulse and said, "She's still alive."

Anne's last thoughts before she passed out were of Catherine. She couldn't leave her alone and she had to get away from this evil man. Anne thought she had been asleep and at times she could hear strange voices but she couldn't recognize them. She didn't know where she was and she slowly drifted into darkness. By the time they placed Anne on a stretcher it had been over an hour. It took awhile for the ambulance wagon to make its way to the hospital and by the time it arrived, it was too late. Anne had died a violent and tragic death.

David sat down on the curb and put his head in his hand and moaned. Thirty minutes later Chief Morgan and Detective Husky showed up at the murder scene.

"Can you tell us what happened?" the chief asked.

"Well it all happened so fast," said David. "I was escorting Mrs. Eastman home from the opera and out of nowhere this Negro grabs her purse, pulling her into the alley. He hit her first with the pipe and then tried to hit me. I ducked and knocked the pipe out of his hand. I got to the pipe first, picked it up and then hit him. That's when I ran to get help," said David.

The chief just shook his head and commented on the blood he noticed on a protruding pipe and said, "When he hit her with the pipe it must have knocked her up against that pipe so hard it broke her neck."

The detective asked David if he had been drinking and he lied and told them no. He said that he and Anne had worked late at the Grande and he was walking her to her boarding house.

Husky asked David, "You say her name is Anne Eastman?"

"Yes," said David.

The chief told Husky to get David's and the victim's home address and told David he could go home after that.

"I'm going back to the jail to talk to the Negro," said Chief Morgan.

"Looks like it's gonna be a long night," said Husky.

David was worried that if Anne woke up she might remember

what happened, so he went to the hospital emergency room to check on her condition. He was told she had died in route to the hospital. If only she hadn't rejected him, David thought. He took out the envelope he had found in Anne's pocket. There was a twenty dollar bill in it. It didn't make him feel any better; he would rather have had Anne. At least now that she was dead, she wouldn't be tormenting him anymore. When David got back to his apartment he found a bottle of whiskey, drank two-thirds of the bottle, and then passed out.

When Chief Morgan got back to the city jail they told him that the murderer was not awake yet. He was relieved because he still had to gather his thoughts about what had actually happened. He looked at the time and it was after midnight. One good thing, he thought to himself, at least the newspaper presses were already running off the next day's newspaper and it wouldn't be reported until the day after.

The phone rang at the police station and Husky told Morgan that Mrs Eastman had died in route to the hospital. Now Morgan would have to notify the next of kin, if there was any. He did notice the woman had a wedding band on, but a lot of women wore them. They figured it would keep them safer. He knew the mayor would be happy that they caught the murderer who had been doing the killings in the red light district; at least that was how he saw it. Chief Morgan told one of the guards to grab a bucket of water and meet him at the cell Joseph was passed out in. Morgan poured the bucket of water on Joseph's head and Joseph began coughing and sat up.

"Where am I?" asked Joseph.

"You're in the city jail," said Morgan, "and you are in a lot of trouble. What's your name?" he asked.

"My name is Joseph, Joseph March," he said.

The guards pulled Joseph up and walked him down to one of the interrogation rooms. Morgan walked in and closed the door behind him.

"I ain't done anything," said Joseph.

"You assaulted and killed a woman last night off Post Office

Street and almost killed the man she was with," said Morgan. Joseph was stunned and tried to remember where he was the night before. His head was hurting really bad and he put his head in his hands. The chief struck the table with his club and Joseph jerked up.

"I didn't kill anyone," Joseph said.

The chief struck Joseph on the back of his shoulder really hard and Joseph groaned.

"We have a typed confession here saying you killed a whore two weeks ago and then murdered a woman last night who worked at the Grande.

"All you need to do is sign it and we'll go easy on you," said the chief.

"You got it all wrong," said Joseph. "That man she was with did it. I was trying to stop him," Joseph continued.

The chief and guard laughed and the club hit him even harder on his other shoulder. The beatings continued for another hour until Joseph passed out and they dragged him back to his cell. Before they had finished with him though, they had put a pen in his hand and forced him to sign the confession. They didn't know Joseph didn't know how to write. The chief went back to his office and fell asleep in his chair until one of the guards woke him in the morning and said there were a young girl and old lady here and that the young girl's mother did not come home last night.

CHAPTER 12

Catherine had awakened earlier than usual and noticed the bed was smooth and had not been slept in. She called out thinking that maybe she had fallen asleep on the sofa, but the room was empty. She hurriedly dressed and went downstairs. She heard Minnie in the kitchen humming to herself.

"Mummy didn't come home last night," said Catherine.

Minnie looked puzzled.

"She always comes home. We have to go look for her," Catherine said.

Minnie was wearing a house dress and grabbed an old, worn sweater and a handkerchief for her head and she followed Catherine out the front door. Minnie tried her best to keep up with Catherine but followed several steps behind. They stopped at the Grande Opera House, but all the doors were locked and the lights were off in the ticket area. They went next door to the Grande Hotel and inquired if anyone had seen her mother last night. No one remembered seeing her. Minnie suggested they go to the police station.

"Hello, I'm Chief Morgan, please come into my office," said the chief.

Chief Morgan invited them into his office and they sat down.

"My name is Catherine Eastman and this is Minnie Wyman, my friend," said Catherine.

"Morgan guessed the young girl couldn't be more than fifteen years old.

"My mother, Anne Eastman, works at the Grande Opera House. She had made arrangements for a colored man and his buggy to bring her home every night, except last night she did not come home," said Catherine.

"Do you know the name of this colored man?" asked Morgan.

"Yes," she said, "his name is Joseph March."

The chief was not accustomed to talking to young girls and wasn't quite sure how to approach Catherine. Morgan turned to Minnie and asked if she was related to the family. Minnie replied that she owned the boarding house that Catherine and her mother lived in.

Chief Morgan asked Catherine to wait outside for a minute and when she walked out she sat in a chair not far away. The chief closed the door.

"Ma'am," he said to Minnie, "Mrs. Eastman was killed last night on her way home from work. Do you know of any other next of kin?" asked the chief.

"No, they don't have any," said Minnie. "Mrs. Eastman had confided in me that her husband was deceased. Oh my, they have only been in the states for a month," Minnie cried.

"Then the kid will have to go to the orphanage," said the chief. "Do you want to tell her, or do you want me to?" asked Morgan.

Catherine sat quietly in the chief's office while he tried to delicately tell her about her mother. Tears filled her eyes as she stared out the window at the street.

"Do you know who did it?" asked Catherine in a shaky voice.

"Yes, he is in jail now. His name is Joseph March," said the chief.

"That's not possible," said Catherine. "He would never do anything to hurt me or my mother. I want to talk to him."

"We can't allow that. Besides, he signed a confession and the evidence leads to him. We also have an eye witness, David Brooks," Morgan told her.

Catherine stared at Minnie and fought the tears consuming her eyes. She felt as though someone had stabbed her in her heart. She wanted to run, scream and most of all she wanted to die, too. She was in shock and Minnie put her arms around her and led her out of Chief Morgan's office. Before they left, Morgan said that they should have the funeral home check with the hospital and make arrangements for her burial.

Minnie was as much in shock as Catherine and they began walking back home. John Merit was on his way to work when he saw them from across the street. He called out to them and began criss-crossing in the middle of the street, trying to avoid the carriages and automobiles, and made his way up to them. He saw Catherine's face first and then looked at Minnie.

Before he could say anything Minnie said, "Anne's dead."

John looked as though he had seen a ghost, and said, "Oh my God! How can I help?"

"The police chief told us that we needed to have a funeral home pick up Anne's body this afternoon from St. Mary's hospital," said Minnie.

"You let me take care of everything," John said. "I'll go to the police station and make the arrangements. You need to take Catherine home and I'll be over later to see her," John continued.

John rushed into the police station and went directly to the chief's office.

"What the hell is going on Chief Morgan? I just heard the news that Anne Eastman is dead."

"What's it to you, Merit?" asked the chief.

"I met them when they first arrived in Galveston and she opened an account at the bank," Merit paused. "We had developed a relationship and I was dating her," Merit lied.

"Well I'm sorry about that," said the chief.

Morgan told John about the events the night before; that Anne had been taken to the hospital and had died before she got there. John was surprised when David Brooks' name came up.

"Brooks gave us the impression that he was dating her, too," said Morgan.

John knew Anne would never date David Brooks; she really did not like him.

"The Negro signed a confession and was caught red-handed," The chief went on to say.

John left and went back to the bank. He called Morris Brothers Funeral Home from one of the two phones that were in the bank and asked them to pick up Anne's body from the hospital and that the family would be back in touch with them. He told them he would incur all the expenses. After he hung up the phone, John told his secretary he was leaving for the day.

John headed over to the Grande and walked into Tom Gregory's office. David Brooks was also there and it made John even angrier.

"Why couldn't you have protected her?" John asked.

"I almost got killed myself," said David.

"I want to hear what happened and I want you to tell me everything," John demanded.

"What's it to you?" David asked.

"I really cared about her and Catherine."

"So did I," said David.

Tom stood up and tried to calm them both down. "Why don't we all sit down and David can tell both of us what happened," Tom said.

David began telling his version of what happened the night before, making himself out to be the hero because he knocked the murderer out. John didn't believe a word David said and he told him so.

"Look John," said Gregory, "You need to leave and try to settle down, and David, you have been through enough....go home and get some sleep."

David stormed out the door and John stayed behind to talk to Tom Gregory.

"Anne and I had become very close friends and she was afraid of David," John said.

John filled Gregory in on what happened to Anne's watch and how David was always bothering her.

"David may be a ladies' man and I know he drinks a lot, but he is not a murderer, "Gregory said.

John didn't reply and he got up and left.

Chief Morgan was at his desk when the mayor came in. "So I hear you caught the man who was responsible for those murders. Shame he had to kill someone else before we caught him," said the mayor. "Poor woman," he continued. "I understand she had only been here a month and was working at the Grande Opera House."

"That's correct," said the chief.

"Well, you know what to do," the mayor said. "We don't want to waste the taxpayer's money on a trial for a Negro. Make it look like an accident."

The mayor walked out the door and the chief shook his head.

When David left the opera house he was really anxious and needed a drink. He walked down Post Office Street till he came to the White Horse Saloon. He ordered two shots of whiskey and downed them immediately. One of the ladies from the brothel upstairs came over and began flirting with him.

"You're too rich for my blood," said David.

"What if I said it was half price? I've noticed you before and a couple of the girls told me you were nice," said the hooker.

"That right?" said David as he motioned to the bartender for another shot. David told the hooker he had an appointment and that he would be back later, and then he downed his drink and left. That was the first time that David could remember he had ever turned down sex. David went around to the back of the alley and threw up.

John Merit walked over to the alley where Anne was killed. He saw the blood on the pipe and on the ground where she had laid. His eyes began tearing up. He just couldn't imagine what her last thoughts might have been. He turned and left the alley and headed towards Anne's boarding house.

Mrs. Wyman opened the door and invited John in. Catherine was in the parlor and so were Father Jonathon Cain and a nun by the name of Sister Margaret. John greeted everyone and made his way to an empty chair. They all waited for John to speak first.

"I've contacted Morris Brothers Funeral Home and asked them to take special care of your mother, Catherine," John said. "If it is all right with you, perhaps Father Jonathon could do a graveside eulogy for your mother tomorrow afternoon at Calvary Cemetery."

Catherine nodded her head yes and looked down.

"There is another matter we need to address," said Father Jonathan. "Catherine has no other living relatives and since she is under eighteen she has now become a ward of the state. She will need to come with us to the orphanage."

Catherine jumped up and ran upstairs.

"Poor child," said Mrs. Wyman.

"May I make a suggestion," asked John. "If it is alright with you Mrs. Wyman, why not let Catherine stay here until after the funeral tomorrow. That will give her some time to pack and prepare herself for the move."

"Why of course," Mrs. Wyman said.

"I'll only come on one condition," said Catherine, who was now standing at the bottom of the stairs.

All eyes turned in her direction.

"I want to put my mother's things in storage and I want to bring her sewing machine with me."

"Why, I think that can be arranged," said Father Jonathan.

"I'll be happy to store your mother's trunk in my closet until you come for it," said Mrs. Wyman.

John walked over to Catherine and sat on the stairs next to her.

"Catherine," John said. "You and your mother were very special to me, and I want you to know that I will take good care of her trust fund. You may stop in anytime and see me, and if you need anything, I will be there for you."

John then turned to Father Jonathan and asked, "Could you give me permission to visit Catherine at the orphanage and maybe take her from the orphanage for a few hours on the weekend, that is, if Catherine would allow me?"

"I believe that can be arranged," answered Father Jonathan.

Catherine nodded her head yes and then said, "It would please me for you to visit."

As John started to leave, Catherine asked, "What's going to happen to Joseph March, Mr. Merit?"

"There will be a trial and he will most likely go to prison," John said.

John knew Joseph would most likely be hanged but he couldn't bring himself to tell her that. He also decided to wait until after the funeral to tell Catherine about the letter her mother had left for her.

John walked back downtown to the jail. The chief was giving some instructions to one of the guards when John came in.

"I'd like to see the prisoner," said John.

"What on earth for?" asked Chief Morgan. "Anne's daughter wanted me to give him a message," John lied.

"Well you can just tell me and I will deliver it," said Morgan.

"No," said John, "I want to tell him myself."

"I'll give you five minutes," said the chief.

John followed the guard to the back and down a corridor and stopped at a locked door. The guard unlocked it and they went in to a group of jail cells. Joseph was lying on a cot with his back to them. John waited until the guard went back out and called to Joseph. Joseph looked over his shoulder at John Merit and asked what he wanted. John was astonished when he saw Joseph and gasped at the condition of his face.

"Catherine and I don't think you killed Mrs. Eastman....I wanted to hear the real story from you," John said.

Joseph turned slowly and tried to get up but fell back down on the cot. He was bloody all over and his clothing had been badly torn. It was hard for John to look at him. Joseph finally hobbled over to where John was standing outside the cell.

"Mrs. Eastman and her daughter Catherine were really nice to me. I cared for them a lot and worried about their safety. That night I was supposed to take Mrs. Eastman home like I did every night. That man, David Brooks, came outside to where I was waiting and told me that Mrs. Eastman was working late and that I should pick up another fare, so I did. I took those folks to their house and I came back to the Grande and waited a while for Mrs. Eastman. When she didn't come out I decided to go looking for her."

Joseph stopped and wheezed, finding it hard to breathe.

"When I came to that alley, I thought I heard a scream and I saw her knapsack on the sidewalk. I got down and picked it up and then heard her moaning so I walked down the alley and found her on the ground. Then something hit my head and I blacked out. When I woke up the police were there and they started hitting me," Joseph said, and he had tears in his eyes.

"Your five minutes are up," yelled the guard.

Before John left, Joseph said, "I ain't afraid of dying, Mr. Merit, but her killer's still out there and he's gonna get away with it."

That evening, Chief Morgan and three of his deputies unlocked Joseph's cell and told Joseph they were moving him to another cell. One of the guards had to help Joseph walk the twenty steps to the other cell. When they got to the cell, Joseph saw a chair in the middle of the floor. He looked up and saw a noose hanging down. Joseph shook his head like he understood and the guards helped him get up on the chair. Joseph knew he had already been tried and convicted and there was nothing he could do. They tied his hands behind his back and once the noose was secured around his neck, they kicked the chair out from under him. Joseph's body swung from the ceiling. He kicked a few times and then urinated.

"Clean it up," said Chief Morgan and he left.

The next morning on page three of the *Galveston Gazette* newspaper there was an article that read:

MURDERER COMMITS SUICIDE

The article went on to tell the story of how Joseph had killed Anne Eastman, signed a confession, and then hung himself in his jail cell with his belt. Joseph was buried in the pauper's cemetery next to Wanda's and Sheila's graves.

CHAPTER 13

Catherine got little sleep the evening after her mother died. She had terrible dreams and pictured her mother swimming after the floating casket that was sinking in the ocean. She also woke up terrified when she saw the man with the beard trying to rape her under the stairway. It was 6:00 in the morning and she got up out of bed so she would not be subjected to any more bad dreams. Alright, Catherine, she thought to herself. You've got to take control. There are too many things to do. Catherine forced herself to begin the long tedious task of packing and sorting through things. She pulled the large trunk out of the closet and opened it. Catherine looked inside the trunk and thought she should just crawl inside and die. All of a sudden she heard her mother's voice inside her head, "We must find strength in everything and move forward." Catherine looked around the room and seeing no one, she sat on the floor and cried. She must have fallen asleep again because now she and her mother were running on the beach into the waves, laughing and splashing each other. They were having such a great time and they were happy.

Catherine woke to a knock on her door. She opened it and Minnie came in with a tray of milk, scrambled eggs and a biscuit.

"Good morning, my dear," said Minnie. "You need to eat something. Afterwards, I'll help you pack."

Catherine didn't want to eat and she wasn't sure she could handle the endless chatter of Minnie while she was trying to sort through everything. Catherine didn't say anything and knew if her mother were there she would tell Catherine to be compliant and not hurt Minnie's feelings. Catherine began eating the eggs and biscuit and had no idea she was so hungry. She couldn't remember when she had last eaten. Had she skipped a whole day? She wondered. Yesterday seemed like a bad dream and she forced herself not to think about it for fear she would break down again. Minnie was very helpful assisting Catherine pack up her mother's personal belongings.

"Don't you worry about this trunk. I'll take good care of it for you," she said.

"I have a large closet off the back porch and it's almost empty, so I can have someone put it in there for me," suggested Minnie.

"Thank you," said Catherine. "I am very grateful to you."

Catherine opened her mother's closet and began carefully folding her clothes. She tried to distance herself from the moment but she broke down again.

Minnie handed her a handkerchief and said, "I'll fold these things for you, dear."

Catherine stood looking out the window and then heard Minnie say, "Oh," in a tender voice.

When she turned and looked, Minnie had just taken Anne's wedding dress from the closet. Catherine walked over and touched it.

"I didn't know my mum brought this," and she took it from Minnie. She held it close to her body and then laid it on the bed so she could carefully fold the layers of the silk organza and lace dress. She placed it in the trunk along with a small box that said, "Wedding veil," in her mother's handwriting. She would look inside it another time. It was painful to look now.

After they had put the last of Anne's personal effects in the trunk, Catherine began packing her things. With all the packing complete, Catherine dressed in one of the dresses her mother had made for her.

"I need to go to the bank now," Catherine said.

"What on earth for?" asked Minnie.

Catherine went into the closet and picked up a tin off the top shelf and then proceeded into the bedroom and took a small shoebox off the floor. She opened the shoebox and put the tin inside.

"I need to put some money in the bank and put these personal items of my mother's into the safe deposit box," said Catherine as she took a small key out of the box.

"Alright then," said Minnie, "I'll get my purse and go with you."

When they got to the bank, John came out and greeted them.

"May I speak with you, Mr. Merit, in private?" asked Catherine.

Without saying anything John put his arm around Catherine and led her into his office, closing the door behind them.

"I'm not sure how this works," said Catherine, "but my mother and I have saved a little money and I wanted to put it in a safe place. Also, I need to put some other personal items into the safe deposit box. The priest told me I could bring my mother's sewing machine and the necessary things for it, but that other than my shoes, socks, underwear and two dresses, I would not be able to bring anything else because I would be in a room with twenty other girls and there was only a small box for each of us."

John was taken aback by Catherine's maturity. She reminded him so much of Anne, that he was awestruck. He genuinely felt sorrow for Catherine. They had only been here less than two months and now she was alone. It saddened him and he wanted to protect her.

After a pause, John explained to Catherine that the money currently in her mother's account was well over twelve thousand, three hundred twenty-five dollars and that all of the funds would be held in trust for her until she was eighteen years old. John and Catherine counted the money in the tin and altogether there was fourteen dollars and fifty cents. John suggested she put the tin of money and the personal items in the safety deposit box. He explained that if she ever needed cash, she could get it out of the tin. In order for her to get any of the money from her mother's estate, a letter of request would have to be submitted to the bank's trust department.

"I think I understand," said Catherine, "and that is what I'll do." John took Catherine into the safe deposit box room. He was relieved when she came out with an empty box and asked to place it in his trash can. He probably should had told her about the letter her mother had left, but he thought he should read it first and it would give him a reason to visit Catherine at the orphanage later on.

"There is one more thing," said Catherine. "What do you think happened to my mother's knapsack? She always kept my father's gold watch in her purse and it meant a lot to her..."

John couldn't bring himself to tell Catherine what had happened to the missing watch because apparently Anne didn't want Catherine to know.

"I'll be happy to look into it for you," said John.

Catherine thanked him and said, "You told me that you might visit me at the orphanage and I hope you do."

"I promise, and I will see you soon," John said and he meant it. John felt a strong connection to Catherine and he wasn't sure why he was so drawn to her. Catherine said good-bye and left with Minnie to go to St. Mary's Catholic Church to light a candle for her mother and to say the rosary. When they had finished, Father Jonathan was waiting at the back of the church for them.

"I have a carriage waiting to take us to the cemetery," he said.

He helped Catherine and Mrs. Wyman get in and he sat up front with the driver. It was another hot, humid day but the sky was overcast. They rode in silence to the cemetery. Following behind them appeared another carriage that stopped and John Merit and his sister stepped out of it. Catherine looked back at the gate they had come through and saw several people walking up from the street. The trolley had let them off several blocks away. With Catherine leading the way, they all walked over to a recently dug grave where Anne's pale white casket sat, covered in beautiful colors of fresh cut flowers. They all formed a circle and Catherine couldn't help but look up. Helga, some of the local musicians, actors, and actresses from the Grande, Tom Gregory and a sombre looking David Brooks were all in attendance.

Father Jonathan gave the last rites and nodded to one of the musicians, who walked forward with his violin and played "Amazing Grace." When he had finished, Father Jonathan nodded to Catherine who walked slowly over to her mother's casket, turned around and addressed the bystanders, saying, "My mum had a favorite passage from the Bible that she loved and lived by. I want to read it for her.

'Strengthen the weak hands, and make firm the feeble knees. Say to those who are fearful-hearted, Be strong, do not fear! Behold your God will come with vengeance, with divine retribution; he will come to save you.' Isaiah 35:3-4"

"My mother is in heaven now, and I take comfort in the fact that she is with the Lord."

When Catherine looked up everyone's eyes were on her. David Brooks was staring also. He was mesmerized by her astonishing likeness to Anne. He hadn't paid much attention to her before. As he stared, he fumbled with the watch in his pocket. Catherine waited while the grave diggers lowered the casket into the ground and then she stooped down and picked up some dirt and let it slowly fall onto the lowered casket. She said a silent prayer and when she was through John Merit came over and kissed her on the forehead.

"I'll come see you soon," said John.

"Thank you, I'd like that," said Catherine. "The service and my mother's casket were beautiful and I know I have you to thank for that."

John smiled at her and then escorted his sister to their waiting carriage. Everyone left and Mrs. Wyman took Catherine's hand and started walking over to where the priest was waiting by their carriage. David Brooks stepped in front of them and Catherine almost ran into him.

"I just wanted to give my condolences, Catherine. Your mother and I were very close and I will miss her terribly," David said.

Catherine grew tense as she looked at him and mumbled a polite thank you. He had his hand on her arm and Catherine jerked it away. John was already leaving when he saw Catherine jerk her arm away and it made him angry. It was too late for him to intervene.

The ride back seemed to take forever and Catherine noticed they were not going back the way they came. They were headed west down the road that ran alongside the beach. There was a slight breeze coming off the Gulf and it dried the tears that were left on her cheeks. They pulled up in front of two very large, wooden buildings that sat back from the road. There was a sign that read St. Mary's Orphanage. Oh no, we're already here....not now, it can't be, thought Catherine and a flood of tears filled her eyes.

St. Mary's Orphanage was located three miles west of town on some property originally known as Green Bayou Place, which was formerly owned by Captain Farnifalia Green. There were two large, two-storey wooden dormitories just off the beach behind a row of tall sand dunes that were supported by salt cedar trees. The buildings each had balconies that faced the Gulf. One building was exclusively for the girls and the older building, known as the Green Bayou residence, was used by the boys. The rule was to keep the girls until they were adopted or became eighteen years of age. The boys were only kept at the Green Bayou residence until the age of fourteen. After that they were sent to St. Mary's College to continue their educations.

David Brooks watched as Catherine left and wondered if they were taking her to the orphanage. He decided to put it in the back of his mind. Right now he needed to get away. The trauma of Anne's death affected him more than it should have. Now that the stupid Negro was dead, no one would ever know the real truth, he thought to himself. David told Tom Gregory he was still shaken up over the whole ordeal and asked if he could leave work. He said he needed to get away for a day or two and would be back to work on Monday. Tom felt bad for him and, since they were in between shows, Tom didn't see it as a problem.

David stopped at his apartment and picked up a clean shirt, some underwear and a bottle of whiskey. He stuffed it into a pillow case, tied it up and walked to the train station. David pulled out a twenty dollar bill and bought a one-way ticket to Houston. He was planning to come back to Galveston, but he didn't want to hang on to a return trip ticket that he might lose. It felt good to get out of town, he thought. He had gotten into a rut, one he wasn't happy with, and he thought a trip out of town might change his luck. David pulled out the gold watch that he had tucked in his pocket and opened it. The inscription was staring back at him. "To Adam, the love of my life, Anne." David shut it quickly.

The thought of Anne was still eating away at him. Yes, he had killed before. But they were people he didn't really care about. He had an unrealistic perception about Anne, that she was some kind of goddess, and it grew out of proportion. She was the woman of every man's dreams and he had caused her death. David wondered if Catherine were like her mother. He liked that Catherine was so young and probably a virgin. It made him excited to think about her. David untied his sack and pulled out his bottle of whiskey and took a couple of swigs. The train wasn't full and he was glad. The last thing he wanted to do was carry on a conversation with some stranger. David must have fallen asleep because the next thing he remembered was the porter yelling, "Houston, next stop."

Catherine stood looking up at the dormitory. Minnie got down saying good-bye. "They are going to come and pick up your bag and the sewing marching tomorrow, dear," said Minnie, "and I'll try my best to come visit you from time to time. It's a long way down here and too far for me to walk but I'll stay in touch."

Minnie got back in the carriage and left. A few minutes later a nun walked out on the porch and motioned for Catherine to come upstairs. She greeted Catherine and said,

"My name is Sister Maria and I am assigned to the girl's dormitory. Come and I'll show you around." Sister Maria was of Spanish descent and couldn't have been more than twenty-five years old.

"My name is Catherine Eastman," answered Catherine.

"Yes, I know, and I am so sorry to learn of your mother's recent passing," Sister Maria said. "I know today is a difficult day for you, but all of the children here have also lost their parents. If you must cry, I suggest you do it in private. We have strict rules here and you must learn them and abide by them," continued Sister Maria.

Catherine didn't answer. Actually, she didn't know what to say. Sister Maria showed Catherine the dining hall, some classrooms and finally the dorm rooms where the girls slept.

"This will be your bed," said Sister Maria. "It is your responsibility to make it up every morning before breakfast and change your own sheets. Breakfast is at 7:00 a.m., lunch at 11:30 a.m. and supper at 5:00 p.m. Every girl is assigned a chore and I understand that you sew and will be bringing your sewing machine," she continued, "so that will be your chore; sewing and mending. I have to go now," said Sister Maria.

She turned and walked out the door. Catherine walked out on the balcony and looked out at the beach. She saw several young girls playing with a ball and they stopped and looked up.

"Look," said one of the girls, "another new one."

John took his sister back to the house they shared on Avenue M Street. His older sister, Amelia, had almost died in a riding accident when she was thrown from a horse at the age of twelve. The fact that she walked with a slight limp and was frequently in pain made her terribly self-conscious, so she never married.

"Catherine is a lovely young girl and I hate to think of her growing up in an orphanage," said Amelia.

"I know," said John. "I did speak to the bank's lawyer about Catherine to see if there was any way she might be able to move in with us," John continued.

"What did he say?" asked Amelia.

"He told me to wait until she turns sixteen and then marry her," answered John. Amelia was speechless. John thought it was a bit unusual, but the legal age for marriage was sixteen. At first he laughed but the more he thought about it, the more it became fixed in his mind. No, he thought, I'm too old for her, or was he?

David got off the train and started walking in the direction of Houston's red light district called The Hollow, which David was very familiar with. The Hollow was located in the Fourth Ward and bordered by Milam, Louisiana, Capitol and Prairie Avenue and was home to a number of boarding houses and brothels. One in particular belonged to a colored woman named Josie Jackson who rented the rooms in her house to white women. She let David stay there a few years earlier when he was looking for a place to live. David stopped and lit one of his cigarettes and then jumped on a cable car on Main Street. When he got to the Fourth Ward, David got off and headed in the direction of Louisiana Street. He cut through an alley and then jolted up a back stairway to the second floor. He went in, walked down the hall and knocked on Josie's door.

"Well, I declare," said Josie. "If it ain't the infamous David Brooks."

David picked Josie up and swung her around. Josie was a little thing and probably didn't weigh more than one hundred pounds but she swore like a sailor and carried a thirty-eight-caliber pistol in her high top boots. Josie didn't take shit from anyone and she ran a tight ship. Some of the girls she rented rooms to worked for her and she got a piece of their action.

"What brings you to Houston?" asked Josie.

"I needed a little rest and relaxation," said David.

"Well, you came to the right place," replied Josie.

"Do you know a freckled faced red haired hooker about twenty? I think her name is Rosie," David asked.

"I seen some that look like that but not my girls," Josie answered. "Why is she so special?" Josie asked.

"She visited in Houston a while back and I liked her style," answered David.

"Well, if you don't find her, I got plenty of girls with style," replied Josie.

David laughed and asked Josie if he could leave his bag of stuff there while he went out.

"As long as there ain't no drugs in there. You know I don't allow it," Josie said.

David ate some beans and cornbread Josie had cooking on the stove, left his bag and walked over to Capitol Street. He nestled himself inside a boarded up doorway, lit a cigarette and waited. It was dusk now and the whores were marking their territories like a dog leaves its scent. David had been in the doorway about thirty minutes when he saw her across the street. He decided to wait and let her pick up a john. It wasn't long before a young white kid about seventeen came by and the two of them walked up Capitol Street, down an alley and in through a door. David was close enough behind them that as soon as the door closed he opened it, watched them go down the hall and into a room.

David tried the door and it wasn't locked, so he went in. The young kid already had his pants unzipped. "Who are you?" asked the kid. Rosie started to scream but didn't when she recognized David.

"Vamoose, out!" said David.

"What about my money?" said the kid.

David acted like he had a gun in his pocket and the kid ran out the door.

"I think you still owe me a couple of free nights," said David, grinning at her.

Rosie smiled back and patted the bed. David took off his shirt and began undressing Rosie. Rosie was afraid at first thinking David might be angry because she and Darlene took all his money when they were in Galveston, but David seem different. David was different. He was stone cold sober. They had sex several times during the night and

David made Rosie get up and get him some whiskey. Rosie did as she was told and David drank it quickly. Rosie wanted David to leave but she was afraid of him. He knew where she lived now and if she didn't do as he said she was afraid he might come back and hurt her. It was 4:00 in the morning and David got up, rolled a cigarette and smoked it. Rosie asked David if he had had enough. David blew out a puff of smoke in her face.

"The way I see it, Rosie, at a dollar a lay, you still owe me six more," said David.

"What about Darlene? She was in on it, too," said Rosie.

"Then, why don't you tell me where she lives?" asked David.

Rosie would have done anything to get rid of David. She wasn't making any money as long as he stayed there. Besides, Darlene got half the money they stole from David so she should be the one paying her half back. Rosie told David where Darlene's boarding house was and gave him explicit directions.

David smiled at Rosie and said, "Good girl."

Rosie started to get out of bed and put her clothes on but David stopped her.

"One more for the road," David said.

David put out his cigarette and crawled on top of her, holding her arms over her head. It was over in a matter of minutes. Rosie couldn't move but relaxed thinking he would leave now. David put both of his hands around her neck and squeezed; Rosie tried to hit him with her fist, but to no avail. He held her in that position, squeezing, squeezing, and squeezing until he had ended her life.

David dressed and quietly took eight dollars out of Rosie's purse and walked out the door when no one was looking. Busy place, David thought. David showed no remorse for what he had just done and figured she wouldn't be missed until he was well on his way back to Galveston. David walked through the dark alley with his head down and his hands in his pocket so no one paid attention to him. Before he left, he had picked up his cooled cigarette butt and matches and put them in his pocket, planning to thrown the butt away at the end of the alley. He didn't want to make that mistake again. When he got to Louisiana Street he saw an all night diner open and he went in. Darn, he was hungry, he thought.

David sat at the counter and ordered. He didn't want to sit in a booth because it would be open territory for another prostitute to try and pick up another john. It didn't make any difference though, once his scrambled eggs and bacon arrived there was a young hooker sitting next to him ordering coffee. She didn't say anything at first and when David began eating she watched him. David didn't want to fall into her trap and start a conversation. Right now all he wanted was to eat and find a place to sleep.

"You been up all night working?" she asked. David didn't answer and kept on eating. She couldn't have been more than sixteen.

No," said David. "Came in on the midnight train and I'm looking for a cheap place to sleep," he continued.

"You can sleep at my place, I'm on my way home," she said. David didn't answer and kept eating.

When he finished he got up and paid for his breakfast and her coffee, looked at her and said, "Let's go."

CHAPTER 14

The sun was just coming up and Catherine heard noises around her. She sat up in her bed and looked around, trying to get her thoughts together and then remembered where she was. All the girls in the room were putting on their clothes and making their beds.

"You better get dressed," said one of the girls. "Sister Margaret gets really mad if we are late for breakfast," she snapped at Catherine.

Catherine jumped out of bed and dressed as fast as she could. She started to leave with all the other girls when one of the girls looked over her head and said, "Don't forget to make your bed."

Catherine stopped and went back and quickly made her bed. She ran down the hall and down the stairs getting to the dining hall just when Sister Margaret told the girls to bow their heads for prayer. Sister Margaret saw Catherine out of the corner of her eye and motioned for Catherine to walk to the front where Sister Margaret was pointing to a chair. Catherine sat down in an empty chair in front of a long table and also bowed her head.

After the prayer, Sister Margaret said, "Children, we have a new arrival, and her name is Catherine Eastman."

In unison, they all said, "Welcome Catherine," and then they all began to eat. Catherine ate the oatmeal and drank the glass of milk in front of her. She thought it strange that everyone ate in silence. When she looked up, she noticed several of the girls staring at her, which made her feel very uncomfortable. One of the girls smiled at her and rolled her eyes towards Sister Margaret, who was eating at another table with some other nuns. Catherine smiled back at her. A few minutes later one of the nuns stood up and said, "You're dismissed."

Catherine got up and followed the older girls out and down the hall where they stopped and used the bathroom. Everyone was quiet and Catherine was afraid to speak. She wasn't sure if that was one of the rules and she sure didn't want to make any mistakes. She saw her reflection in the mirror and thought at first it was her mother. But when she looked around her mother wasn't there. When she looked back at her reflection, it was the first time she realized she was the spitting image of her mother, Anne Eastman. Someone behind her pushed her out the door.

"Come on," she whispered, "we don't want to be late."

The new school year had just begun. Reading, penmanship, history, English and basic math was their curriculum. Higher math and science was only offered to the boys. There were about twenty girls in her group which ranged in ages of twelve to eighteen except she didn't think any of the girls in her class were much older than sixteen. At lunch time, Catherine followed the girls into the dining hall, again in silence, and they were served soup, a hard roll and water. Afterward she followed the girls again to the bathroom and then back to the classroom where they would be taught catechism and the laws of the Catholic Church.

Class was dismissed at 3:00 p.m. and when Catherine walked out the door, Sister Maria told her to follow her and she would show her where she would be doing her chores. Catherine followed behind Sister Maria in silence, since that seemed to be the proper thing to do. They arrived at a door bearing a sign that said: Laundry. Sister Maria opened the door and they both walked in. There was a colored lady washing clothes by hand in a large oversized wash tub. After she washed them, she rung them out with her hands and put them in another large tub of clean water. Sloshing them around, she wrung the clothes out again and then put them in a basket where she would later hang them on a clothes line.

"This is Miss Lillie Mae," said Sister Maria to Catherine. "She does the laundry here every day except Sunday. There is a basket over here with clothing in it that needs to be mended. Your sewing machine was dropped off this morning and I had them put it over here by the window to give you ample light. Your chore will be attending to the garments. You will check them and replace any missing buttons and sew up any tears you find. Is that clear?" she asked.

"Yes, ma'am," answered Catherine.

"When you hear the dinner bell at 5:00 p.m., put your things away and come to dinner," Sister Maria said as she walked out the door.

Catherine walked over to Lillie Mae and said, "My name is Catherine Eastman and it's a pleasure to meet you."

She walked over to the sewing machine and opened the accompanying sewing box that contained the thread, bobbins and scissors. She had begun the task of threading the needle on the sewing machine when she heard voices coming from outside the open window.

"The little kids get to play outside on the beach in the summer time. They don't get assigned chores until they is twelve," said Lillie Mae. "That sure is a nice machine you got there," Lillie Mae said with admiration. "You bring that with you?" she asked.

"Yes ma'am," answered Catherine. "It belonged to my mother. Her funeral was yesterday," she said sadly.

Lillie Mae stayed silent, picked up the basket of wet clothes and walked outside to hang them on the clothesline. Catherine busied herself sewing on buttons and sewing up the torn seams, placing the boys' clothes in one basket and the girls' in another when she was finished with each one. It was 5:00 before she realized it, and she jumped when she heard the dinner bell. Catherine started putting everything away when Lillie Mae said, "There ain't time for that, you better git out of here and head to the dining hall."

Catherine got up and ran falling into line with the other girls as they moved forward toward the dining hall. After dinner they were dismissed to go to the main hall to study or read, or in the summer time they could take their studies outside on the balcony off their rooms. Catherine had kept two books that belonged to her mother. One was her mother's Bible and the other was the book of poems by John Greenleaf Whittier. She took the book of poems out to the balcony, sat in a chair and opened the book. Catherine was mesmerized by Whittier's beautiful poems and thought what a brilliant man he was to have such an understanding of life. His writings comforted her and she closed her eyes and imagined her mother reading the poems to her. Catherine heard giggling and she opened her eyes. There were two girls around the same age as she standing over her and they introduced themselves.

"Hi, I'm Katy," said one girl.

"And I'm Erica." They were smiling at her.

"Will we get in trouble for talking?" asked Catherine, and the two girls laughed.

"Not if we don't get caught," Katy said.

The two girls found a chair and opened their books. They pretended to be reading and were mouthing things to each other and giggling. They seemed to have a language of their own. Catherine tried to block them out and went back to her reading. After a while they began talking with Catherine and including her in their conversation. Katy and Erika seemed to like Catherine. She was pleasant to be around and fit into their little group quite well. Before it was time to turn out the lights, the three girls sat chatting outside on the balcony.

Catherine woke up early on Saturday and wondered what the day would bring. Katy had told her the night before that after breakfast there was an hour of catechism and then they would say the rosary. She understood that Father Jonathan often came and heard confession and then gave communion to the sisters and older girls. Sometimes, he would stay and visit with the girls who were preparing for their first communion. She expected she would be in this group. The Catholic Church was a little different in Sandgate. They were not quite as strict since it was a fishing village and a lot of the children worked with their parents to survive. There was no catechism and the priest gave communion to anyone who went to confession. It was up to the children's parents to give them the proper training in learning the rosary and the prayers that were necessary to receive the Lord's blessing. Catherine knew them all and had been receiving communion since she was thirteen.

After breakfast, the younger girls went to arts and crafts and the girls over twelve attended the catechism just as Katy had said. Father Jonathan was running late so the older girls were dismissed to either finish their homework or do additional chores. Sister Margaret stopped Catherine and asked her to come into the rectory. She offered Catherine a chair and Catherine sat down, unsure why she was there. Katy had told her that the only time you ever went to the rectory to see either Sister Margaret or Father Jonathan was if you were in serious trouble.

"Am I in trouble?" asked Catherine?

"Oh no," answered Sister Margaret. "I just wanted to visit with you to ask you some questions and answer any you might have." Catherine gave a slight smile and sat back in her chair.

"Tell me your story, for instance where you came from and some history about your family," asked Sister Margaret. Catherine proceeded to give brief details about her life in Sandgate and how she and her mother came to Galveston. Catherine found it hard not to cry, but willed herself to be strong and brave.

"That's quite a story," said Sister Margaret. "I have already heard about your mother and I give you my deepest sympathy."

Catherine was relieved. She had managed to hold back the flood of tears, but knew if she had to talk about her mother she would have to give in and let the tears flow.

"I'm sure you have figured out that all of the girls and boys here at the orphanage have similar stories, some even more tragic than yours," said Sister Margaret. "Here at the orphanage," she continued, "we strive to keep harmony amongst all the children and ask that if you feel the need to feel sorry for yourself and need to talk to someone, that you consult your counselor, which in your case is Sister Maria."

Catherine looked down at her sweaty hands and said, "Yes, Sister Margaret."

The Sister took Catherine over to a smaller desk and gave her a pencil and a questionnaire to fill out. She told Catherine that she should answer honestly. There were twenty questions which included her nationality, languages she spoke, books she had read, what her talents were and what her future ambitions might be. There was a signature line at the bottom. Catherine signed when she was finished, and then handed the questionnaire back to Sister Margaret. Sister Margaret excused her and told her to wait outside until the lunch bell rang. Catherine did as she was told and sat on a long bench in the hall. It was 11:45 a.m. which meant she had to sit alone for fifteen minutes and wait. She felt awkward and alone.

The first thing Sister Margaret noticed on the questionnaire was Catherine's beautiful penmanship. She spoke three languages and Catherine listed ten books: The Bible first, World, American and Texas History, Shakespeare, Whittier and several others. Catherine's ambitions were just as impressive.

"I want to finish high school and go to college," Catherine wrote. "I want to be the person my mother taught me to be: independent, caring and most of all to be a godly woman."

Sister Margaret thought carefully and decided she needed to do some more advance testing on Catherine before she placed her in any category. It was obvious Catherine was extremely bright and had many talents. Perhaps Catherine could help her in her office, not every day, but maybe one or two days a week. She would have to discuss it with Father Jonathan.

On Sunday, after attending a small mass in the chapel and then choir, the older girls were free to participate in games, arts and crafts. Erika had already told Catherine about the adoption process. One Sunday a month, families from all over would come to the orphanage and visit with the younger children in hopes of adopting one. The children lined up and walked by each family and introduced themselves. Boys were more in demand because they were needed to work on the families' cotton and sugar cane farms and dairies. She explained that there were usually five to fifteen families that came and that they all would select a child, sometimes two, and take them back to their respective homes. Not every child was available for adoption. Only the ones that had no family members at all like Catherine. Wow, thought Catherine, I'm not sure I want to go live with a strange family and be forced to do manual labor.

After lunch, Catherine was told by Sister Maria to sit outside the rectory because she had a visitor. Catherine did as she was told and thought it was probably Minnie Wyman. After all, she had told Catherine she would try to come and visit her. Sister Margaret's door opened and John Merit walked over to Catherine, smiled and took her hand. Catherine stood up, surprised to see him.

"I thought I might take you for a little ride, if that is alright with you?" John asked.

"If that's OK with Sister Margaret," Catherine replied. Sister Margaret had already been informed by Father Jonathan that John Merit could take Catherine from the orphanage for a couple of hours on Sunday. She nodded her head yes and smiled. John led Catherine outside and to a waiting buggy. He helped Catherine up on to the seat and then got in after her. There were flowers lying on the seat and Catherine had to pick them up so she didn't sit on them. She looked up at John who was smiling at her.

"I thought you might like to visit your mother's grave; the flowers are for her," he said.

Catherine smiled and was surprised at how glad she was to see him. John had a sweet tenderness about him and he reminded Catherine of her own father. They had similar qualities and she could understand why her mother found him so attractive. When they got to the cemetery John escorted Catherine over to her mother's grave. They both stood there looking down at the loosely spread soil and decaying flowers that were once so beautiful on her casket.

Catherine stooped down and picked up the wilted flowers and put them off to the side. She arranged the new bouquet of flowers at the head of the grave and then knelt down and said a prayer. She fought back the tears she felt coming, and stooped to pick up a lone flower out of the decaying bouquet from Anne's grave.

"I'm going to press this one and keep it in my mum's Bible," Catherine told John. They stood there together in silence and then turned and walked back to the buggy. When they returned to the orphanage, Catherine asked if John could stay a little longer, as she wanted to talk to him. John said, of course, and then went over and sat on the steps beside Catherine.

"I was wondering if you had found out about my mum's watch that she carried in her purse."

John thought for a moment and said, "When you first asked about the watch, I thought it best to wait for a better time to give you the answer. That is one reason why I came to see you today," John continued. John quietly and gently explained to Catherine about his meeting with her mother before she died.

"She did not want to tell you, Catherine, because she had hoped that whoever may have taken it might have remorse and return it. I'm afraid it has not shown up yet. I spoke to Tom Gregory and asked him to keep his eyes and ears open in case anyone said anything. I picked up your mother's knapsack and purse from the police station and took it over to Mrs. Wyman's so she could put it with the rest of your mother's things."

"You have been so helpful, Mr. Merit," said Catherine. "I know my mother would be pleased by your kindness. I suppose she too didn't want to tell me because she knew it would upset me. That also may explain why she seemed so nervous and out of sorts the last few days before she died."

There was a tear falling on Catherine's cheek and John handed

Catherine his handkerchief. Catherine got up and hugged John's neck and asked, "Will you come see me again?"

"Of course," said John, "I'll see you soon."

John climbed up onto the buggy and left. His anger had returned, thinking of Anne's death and the hardships Catherine would now be facing. It's hard enough to live in a corrupt world with your own family, much less facing it alone. He realized he forgot to tell Catherine about the letter in the safe deposit box and decided it best left for another time.

CHAPTER 15

It was early Saturday morning and the sun was beginning to come up. David and Vickie walked several blocks until they were almost out of the Fourth Ward. They were in a residential neighborhood when Vickie took out a key and unlocked the front door.

"Look!" she said. "My mother is dead and my daddy works down on the shipping docks.

He works four days on and three days off. So he sleeps down there, too, 'cause it's kind of far away. He's at work now and won't be home for two more days. I'll let you crash here if you promise not to steal anything or beat me up."

Darn, David thought, this was his lucky day.

"You are a hooker, aren't you?" David asked.

"Not like those other girls," she replied. "I'm very selective. I only do it during the summer when I'm not in school because my dad won't buy me anything or give me any money. He drinks a lot when he is home so I try to stay out of his way. I'm home at night because I have to cook for him and he would beat the tar out of me if he had a clue what I was doing," Vickie said.

Vickie stopped talking and walked over to David and put her arms around him and began purring like a cat. She pushed him back just enough that he fell on the sofa and she straddled him.

"I really was serious when I told you I just needed a place to sleep," David teased.

She started kissing him and she seemed older than her sixteen years. David took his time with her on the sofa and Vickie reciprocated by stroking him and fulfilling his needs. Afterwards they both fell asleep on the sofa.

David woke up and Vickie was lying beside him facing the sofa. David was on the outside and it was easy for him to slide off. He dressed and stood there looking at her naked body and really kind of felt sorry for her. They had talked a while before going to sleep together. She told him that after her mother died, her stepfather started coming into her room and abusing her when she was twelve. David took out two dollars, put it on the side table and left.

David walked back over to the Fourth Ward, down Louisiana Street and upstairs to Josie's boarding house. When David knocked, Josie came to the door and opened it.

"My stars," said Josie. "Where have you been? Did you find your lady friend?"

It was 11:00 in the morning and David walked over to the stove where Josie had put on chicken and dumplings.

"You are the best cook in the south," said David as he filled his plate and began to eat. David asked Josie if he could shower and change clothes and Josie said yes. He put on a clean shirt and underwear and got back into the same faded jeans he had worn from Galveston. David kissed Josie on the forehead and gave her a great big grin.

"You're the best," he said.

"You leavin?" asked Josie.

"Yeah, I'll be back in a couple of weeks though. Would it be too much for you to wash my shirt and underwear and keep it here so I won't have to worry about it?" Josie agreed and David gave her a dollar. As long as David was good to Josie, she would be good to him.

David walked the three blocks back over to Capitol Street and tucked himself back in the doorway. A couple of hookers came by and asked if he wanted anything and David said no. He didn't want to ask for Darlene by name in case the cops came looking for snitches after she disappeared. He was playing it over and over in his mind what he was going to do to her. Just thinking about her punishment made him excited. After an hour and a half he was beginning to get tired of waiting and figured she was probably on another street. David walked down to the end of the street and over to another but he did not see her. David found himself in front of the diner he had breakfast in the night before and decided to go in to get some coffee. This time he sat in a booth looking out the window hoping Darlene would show up on the corner. Another hour passed and the waitress came by and asked if he was waiting for someone.

"Yes," said David, "but I guess I'm being stood up."

David ordered another cup of coffee. When he had finished, he paid his check and decided to take a walk. Darlene was very tall with long legs and dark hair. It was hard to tell if she was Mexican or just had a dark complexion. Her face was ingrained in his thoughts and he was getting anxious now.

"Looking for a place to sleep?" Vickie said coming up from behind him.

David smiled at her and said, "Maybe."

Vickie tucked her arm through David's and began walking with him, giving him a big smile. David's patience was wearing thin and he decided Darlene could wait. Vickie was young and submissive and he knew he could probably talk her into doing just about anything.

Vickie unlocked the front door and she and David went into her house.

"When did you say your old man was coming back?" David asked.

"He usually gets off at 2:00 p.m. and it takes about forty-five minutes for him to get home. I'd said between 2:00 and 3:00 tomorrow."

"Good!" David said. "I need to take the 2:00 o'clock train back to Galveston tomorrow and I'll be long gone. Got any whiskey?"

"Sure, I sometimes hide it so my daddy can't find it....I'll get it for you," said Vickie.

She went to a tall shelf on the back porch and pulled out some canned goods and reached for the whiskey. She got two glasses out of the kitchen cabinet and walked back into the living room. David wasn't there but a few minutes when he came out of the bathroom, picked up Vickie in his arms and carried her up the upstairs.

"Which one is yours?" David asked.

Vickie still had the glasses and whiskey in her arms and used her index finger to point to a closed door at the end of the hall. David opened it still holding onto Vickie and stopped when he saw the bed. It was a four poster double bed and tied around each post were pieces of rope. David sat Vickie down on the bed and took the whiskey and two glasses from her. He poured himself a full glass and Vickie a half and then he took a big slug.

"What's the rope for?" asked David.

"It's punishment," said Vickie. "My daddy gets mad at me sometimes when I won't do what he wants."

"How often does he tie you up?" asked David.

"Just about every time he comes home, depends if he's already drunk," Vickie replied.

"Why do you stay?" asked David.

"I've left a couple of times but I don't have any where to go and he always finds me. Then he beats me up really bad and ties me to the bed. He told me if I left again, that when he found me he was gonna take me over to colored town and sell me to some Negro pimp. I guess I figured the latter was worse than him," Vickie said.

Vickie took a big gulp of the whiskey and made a face. She looked up at David and grabbed his shirt, pulling his face down to hers. She got on her knees so she was eye level with David. She kissed him tenderly on the neck and David kissed her back, as he pushed her on the bed. Before he could undress her, they heard the door downstairs slam shut.

"Oh no!" said Vickie. "He's back early, quick get in the closet."

David grabbed his glass and the bottle of whiskey and Vickie opened the door to the closet. David eased in so he wouldn't spill his drink. Vickie ran out of her room and met her father at the top of the stairs.

"Where the heck are you going in that get up? You're dressed like those cheap whores on Louisiana Street," said her father.

Vickie stuttered a bit and said, "I'm just playing dress up, daddy, like I always do. I'm not going anywhere."

Her father grabbed her by the hair and pulled her, screaming, towards his room. "You whore," her father shouted at her. "You want to play dress up, I'll show you."

David quietly walked out of Vickie's room and up to the door of the bedroom and watched as Vickie's father abused her. Her old man was as big as a bear with tattoos up and down both of his arms. He must have weighed 270 pounds, David thought. David wanted to help Vickie, but knew he would be no match against this giant. David quietly left, taking the whiskey with him and thought to himself, I have my own agenda.

David walked back over to Capitol Street where the place was beginning to crawl with the night people. He leaned up against a dark corner, sipped on his bottle of booze and waited. Fifteen minutes later Darlene finally showed up. She was with another hooker, named Barbara. Barbara saw David looking at them and walked over and asked David if he wanted some fun.

David did not look up, but said, "No, but I'd like to talk to your friend. Tell her to come over."

Barbara walked back to the corner where Darlene was waiting and said something to her. Darlene grinned and walked toward David. By now, David had drifted back a bit into a darker area of the building. He didn't want Darlene to recognize him and say something to her friend.

Before she got to him, he turned and said, "This way."

She followed a few feet behind him and figured he was staying at one of the local hotels in the red light district. She still hadn't seen David's face. They walked half way down the block and David turned down an alley.

The alley was dark and empty. When Darlene caught up with David he grabbed her arm and pulled her into a darker area of the alley. Darlene stumbled and swore. When she looked up she saw David's face and before she could scream, David popped her in the mouth with his fist and she fell backwards hitting the ground. He quickly pulled out a piece of the rope he had taken off Vickie's bed and wrapped it around Darlene's throat, pulling it tight. Darlene tried to say something but she blacked out. David continued tightening the rope and she went limp. David looked down at her face and she was staring back at him, blood coming out of her mouth, lifeless. David took the rope from her neck, curled it up and stuck it in his pocket and then rummaged through her purse till he found six dollars. He made his exit at the opposite end of the alley and walked over to Louisiana Street to catch the trolley. David was pleased with himself. He had dreamed about how he was going to pay back the two girls and it had all fallen into place. He looked at his gold watch and thought, plenty of time to make the 11:00 p.m. train back to Galveston.

The trolley was just stopping to pick up passengers and David ran to catch up with it and jumped on. He found an empty seat at the back and sat down by himself. He put his head back and visions of Vickie tied to the bed filled his head. He really hated it for Vickie, so young, so innocent, and it was hard for him to believe her own father would violate her like that. He was glad he didn't have any kids and figured he probably never would. David opened his eyes when someone pulled the lever for a stop. He looked out and realized he had missed his own stop, so he jumped off, too, and started heading back the other way. When he got to the corner he realized that he overshot his exit by four streets and thought he might save some time by cutting through a few alleys. He had a good sense of direction and knew his way around enough that when he reached the end of the alley, he could cut up another back street and be at the train station in less than ten minutes. David heard some footsteps behind him and realized he had left himself vulnerable by cutting through the dark alley. He picked up his pace and another man appeared in front of him from out of no-where.

David felt a gun at his chest and he threw up his hands.

"Look, I ain't got anything," David said, as he heard the other men from behind coming up.

He knew if he wanted to get out alive he better take his chances with the one. David brought his arm down and tried to knock the gun out of his hand. The perpetrator struck David in his gut, knocking the wind out of him, and then struck David up against the side of his jaw, knocking him to the ground. The other two men caught up with them and began kicking him and pounding him with their fists.

David was no match for the three men and he blacked out from the pain. He lay unconscious on the filthy ground for several hours and when he woke up he could only see clearly out of one of his eyes. He reached in his back pocket and got out his handkerchief to wipe his eyes. He checked his other pockets and they were empty. He grimaced in pain as he tried to get up. His money and Anne's watch were gone. David crawled over to a large trash container in the alley and used it to pull himself up. Once he was up every bone in his body ached and hurt with every step. It must have taken him over an hour to make his way over to Josie's place. He managed to crawl up the stairs on all fours. Several men came out of different rooms and walked past him on the stairs and acted like he wasn't there. When he got to the floor where Josie's room was, he pulled himself up by the banister and hobbled to the door.

It was after midnight when Josie slowly pulled David from the floor into her living room. It was difficult dragging David's 180-pound body into her living room, but she couldn't leave him out in the hall. She dragged him inside until she fell on the floor from exhaustion. She got up and felt his pulse and was glad he was still alive. She didn't want to have to deal with a dead body. Josie boiled some water and threw some herbs and soothing oils in it and while it simmered she collected some rags from the closet. She heard David moan so she opened his mouth and poured a few drops of whiskey in it. The stinging from the alcohol brought David around and he opened his one good eye and saw Josie.

"What the hell happened to you?" Josie asked.

"I got robbed," David answered in a low, hoarse voice.

Josie got up and went over to the potion simmering on the stove. She put three rags in it and stirred it around. After draining the rags, she put them in a large strainer and mashed the excess water out. The rags were steaming and condensation filled the air as she took them over to David.

"Lie still," Josie said. She pulled one of the rags out with some wooden tongs and waved it around in the air to cool before she gently wrapped it around David's swollen head leaving openings for his nostrils so he could breath. David screamed in pain and attempted to pull the rags off but Josie grabbed his hands.

"Leave it, you'll feel better in a little bit," Josie said as she walked over to her ice box and chipped off a piece of ice and wrapped it in a clean rag.

When the rag on David's face cooled, Josie gently began cleaning off the dried blood on his face. When she finished, she told David to hold the ice bandage over his eye to reduce the swelling.

"Whiskey," David whispered.

Josie put the bottle of whiskey up to David's lips and lifted his head up so he could take a few sips. He passed out again, and Josie got a pillow to put under David's head. Josie unbuttoned his shirt to see if there were any open wounds. There were numerous bruises on his body but fortunately no knife wounds. At best, David had a few fractured ribs but it was his head injuries she was worried about. Josie slept on the sofa to be close to David in case he woke up and needed something. She woke up several times during the night and checked his breathing.

David slept until noon the next day. Josie put some clean bandages on his face and brought him some soup. David was awake and alert but felt like hell.

"I need to get back to Galveston," David said.

"You're not going anywhere for a day or two," replied Josie.

On Tuesday morning Josie loaned David a couple of dollars so he could buy a train ticket back to Galveston. He was feeling better but still looked awful.

"Thanks, Josie," David said. "I don't think I could have made it without you. I'll pay you back for everything next time I come to Houston," he promised.

CHAPTER 16

It was suppertime when Catherine got back from the cemetery with John Merit. She loved being with John and didn't want the afternoon to end. Later, she tried to remember if her mother had said anything about the disappearance of her father's watch. She had a lump in her throat and found it hard to eat.

"You better clean your plate, or you will get in trouble," said Katy.

"If you don't want your cornbread, I'll eat it," said Erika. Catherine handed the piece of cornbread to Erika and tried to eat the rest of the beans. Sunday night was a free night and Katy, Erika and Catherine walked out on the balcony off their rooms to talk. Katy and Erika were asking Catherine all kinds of questions about her family, and Catherine tried to explain to them that it really hurt to talk about them right now but that in time she might be more open to their questions.

"Well, then," said Erika, "tell us who the attractive young man was that you went out with today?"

"He works with one of the banks," explained Catherine. "I don't know a whole lot about him; except that he seems very nice and helped make the arrangements for my mum's funeral." Catherine changed the subject and asked Katy what had happened to her parents.

"Dead," she said. "Daddy was killed in an accident on the wharf when a chain carrying a large container of sugar cane broke and fell on him. Momma died a year later, they say of a broken heart, but she had a lot of health problems. She was always sick," said Katy. "I've been at the orphanage for four years now and I'll be fourteen next month."

Catherine looked at Erika who told a similar story except that her mother was pregnant when her father died and that both her mother and the baby died during childbirth.

"I went to live with my aunt and uncle on their farm, but they had eight children of their own and just couldn't find the means to support another kid. I was sick a lot when I was little and they said I was too much trouble and dropped me off at the orphanage a year later. I was six then," Erika continued, "and I've been here ever since."

The girls were still talking about where they had come from when a young, dark skinned girl around eight years old walked up.

"Hi, my name is Sadie," she said. The girls stopped talking and looked up. "I came here in a shoe box," she said proudly. "I think the store sent me and they made a wrong delivery."
The girls laughed. "Wow," said Catherine, "that's quite a story. How old are you?"

"I'm gonna be nine in a few weeks," and she turned and left.

"Everyone says she is a mixed breed," said Erika.

"What is that?" Catherine asked.

"It means her mother was black and her dad was white, or could be the other way around," answered Katy. "That's why she will never get adopted."

"Oh," said Catherine, "that's too bad. She's really cute."

David got back to the Galveston train station at 11:00 a.m. on Tuesday and walked over to the Grand. He knocked on Tom's door and went in. Tom gasped and said, "What happened to you?"

"I got beat up and robbed," said David.

"Well, when you didn't show up for work yesterday I thought you might have decided to stay in Houston," Tom replied,

"Nope," said David. "I was just minding my own business the other evening and while walking back to my hotel three guys came out

of nowhere. They pulled me into a dark alley, beat the living hell out
of me, took my money and left me for dead." David wanted Tom to
feel sorry for him and hoped he might hand him a little cash, but he
didn't. David really didn't want to ask for an advance on his pay, but
he did.

Tom took out a ten dollar bill and handed it to David and said,
"Pay it back when you can. Go home and get some rest now and come
back in the morning."

David thanked Tom and left. He his rib cage was still really
sore so he headed over to Fat Alley and into his favorite saloon.

"Whiskey," David ordered. He gulped it down, paid his tab,
and left.

David was still tired so he headed to his apartment, grimacing
as he stepped in potholes and had to adjust his footing. Every inch of
his body ached, so he changed direction and headed over to one of the
brothels where he could get a hot bath and soothe his aching muscles.
One of the madams greeted David and could tell by the way he looked
that he was hurting.

"Just a hot bath," said David. The madam took David down to
a small room where he was introduced to a girl by the name of Ginger.

She walked him over to a bench and helped him undress. Ginger helped David into a soothing metal tub of water that was so hot it
took a few minutes for him to ooze down into it. She couldn't help but
notice the bruises on his chest but kept silent. Ginger picked up a large
sponge and poured some warm, soapy oil on it and began stroking David, cleaning off some of the leftover dried blood. David asked her to
take off the robe she was wearing and she did. He pulled her closer to
him and tried to kiss her.

"It'll cost you extra," said Ginger, smiling. David backed
down. He couldn't afford to use his last five dollars so foolishly. His
rib cage was still hurting and after the bath he just wanted to go home
and sleep.

John Merit arrived for work at 8:30 a.m. and went into his office. The bank owner and president, Steven Mitchell, saw him come in and walked into John Merit's office. Steven sat down in one of John's empty chairs.

"You've been working at the bank now for a couple of years and I just wanted you to know you have impressed me and the board of directors. As you know, we are growing by leaps and bounds and now find that our needs are also growing. We think it necessary to expand and integrate a trust department to satisfy the needs of the widows and children who have money in our bank. You are already fulfilling this need for several of our customers and we would like to give you a more private office and make you a vice-president and trust officer of the trust department of our bank," continued Steven. "Of course, you will also receive a small raise along with your title."

John sat up straight in his chair and listened intently. "Why, I would be delighted, Mr. Mitchell," John said.

"There is one more thing," said Mitchell. "There is a seminar in Houston exclusively for employees in the trust department, and I have arranged for you to intern at one of Houston's larger banks for a couple of days. All in all, you will be gone about a week and you will need to leave on Sunday as the class begins at 9:00 a.m. sharp on Monday," Mitchell said.

John was silent for a few minutes. "As you know," said John softly, "I take care of my sister, who has some health issues and I need to make some arrangements."

"I need to know as soon as you can arrange it, as I have another gentleman we are looking to hire to take your place as the new accounts manager," Mitchell answered back.

John worked through lunch and then left at 1:00 p.m. He had sitters before for Amelia, but this was different. He would be gone six days and nights. There was no way he could leave Amelia alone. She would forget to take her medicine and probably get scared at night. He thought about Minnie Wyman and decided to take a detour over to her place. The sign was back out on the street. "Room for rent, No colored folk." Minnie answered the door and invited John in. She was delighted to see him and they sat in the parlor and talked. After John had told Minnie about his visit with Catherine on Sunday, he told her about the promotion at the bank. He went on to tell her about his dilemma regarding Amelia's condition and that he did not want to leave her unattended.

She pretty much takes care of herself, but I need someone to make sure she eats three times a day and takes her medication," John explained.

Minnie had met Amelia before and really liked her.

I would be willing to pay you well if she could stay in Anne and Catherine's old room for a week. All you would have to do is prepare her meals and make sure she takes her medication," John repeated.

"Would fifteen dollars be too much?" Asked Minnie. John smiled with relief and said that was more than fair.

After mass on Sunday, John and Amelia rode over to Minnie's boarding house so John could help Amelia get settled. He picked up her bag from the buggy and helped Amelia slowly walk up the stairs. John knew the stairs might be an obstacle for her, but she assured him that she could do it twice a day if Minnie could just walk beside her to keep her steady. Once John helped Amelia get settled, he had the buggy driver take him to the train station where he bought a round trip ticket to Houston and boarded the 2:00 p.m. train.

John couldn't help but be nervous about Amelia. He had never left her overnight before, but Minnie had the information for the hotel where John was staying and promised she would send a wire if anything happened. John took out his newspaper and tried to read, but his thoughts were on Catherine. He had wanted to go see her today and tell her about the letter her mother left and wondered what she was doing. He also thought back to the conversation he had with the attorney about waiting until Catherine turned sixteen to marry her. The attorney also told him that marriage was also possible if the girl was fourteen and had parental consent. There were no parents where Catherine was concerned and John wondered if he might talk to Father Jonathan about having the church give consent. John was a good ten years older than Catherine, but it wouldn't be a conventional marriage, he thought. He wouldn't require Catherine to do the usual things a wife does and, when she turned eighteen, if she wanted to have it annulled, he would arrange it. He just couldn't stand the thought of her spending the next four years at the orphanage.

Catherine's first week at the orphanage went rather quickly. The sewing and mending kept her very busy when she wasn't studying. The sisters insisted all of the older girls needed to earn their keep and if they were found idle with nothing to do, there was always another chore. Catherine settled into her daily routine and enjoyed developing her friendship with Katy and Erika. They were funny and made Catherine laugh. On Sunday, Catherine spent a few extra minutes getting ready for the day. She was hoping that John Merit would come again. After all, he did say he would be back soon. After lunch Catherine went out on the front porch and sat in one of the chairs.

She had taken one of the books from the orphanage library and decided she would stay there for awhile and read. She found it difficult to concentrate on her book and kept looking up to see if she could see John. By mid-afternoon she closed her book and went inside.

How foolish of her to think that John actually cared about her and would come again so soon, Catherine thought. She tried to will herself not to think of him and decided to go inside and find Katy and Erika.

It was a long week for everyone. Amelia had difficulty managing the stairs, so Minnie took all of the meals up to her. At lunch time, Minnie would take her lunch upstairs, too, and they would visit for several hours. They enjoyed each other's company but Minnie could tell that Amelia really missed John and was counting the days until he came home. Amelia never complained, even on the days when her pain was worse than usual.

John's days were filled with seminars and round-table discussion with other bankers. There were probably fifty other men in attendance and once the three-day seminar was over, he would spend two days in the trust department at The Bank of Houston. Although John enjoyed learning everything he could about investing other people's money and the importance of a trust department, he continually worried about Amelia and Catherine. When John had finished his internship at the bank on Friday, he decided to check out of the hotel and take a late train back to Galveston. John arrived back in Galveston at 11:30 p.m. and knew it was much too late to pick up Amelia so he went home and tried to sleep.

The next morning John woke up early and went directly to St. Mary's Catholic Church. He saw another priest go into one of the confessional booths and was hoping Father Jonathan was still in his office. John knew Father Jonathan fairly well, as he and his sister had been members for over ten years, and Father Jonathan had married John and his first wife.

"Come in, my friend," said Father Jonathan. "What can I do for you today?"

John explained to Father Jonathan about his first meeting with Catherine and Anne Eastman and that they had developed a very close friendship. He told the priest about his discussion with the bank's lawyer and was wondering if it might be possible for him to marry Catherine. He also assured the priest that his motives were honorable, and she would have her own room and live in the same house with him and his sister. While a divorce would not be possible, if the marriage were not consummated then they could have it annulled if Catherine wanted it when she reached the age of eighteen.

"Have you spoken with Catherine about this?" asked Father Jonathan. John explained to him that he did not want to get Catherine's hopes up.

"I will need to talk with the bishop, and it may take some time," said Father Jonathan. John felt encouraged by Father Jonathan's comments; he thanked him for his time and left.

Catherine's week was exasperating for her. She didn't mind having chores to do, but she liked being creative and found the daily task of sewing and mending everyone's clothing a bit monotonous. Because a number of the girls in her class were younger, the material they were covering in class was things she had already learned. She was several years ahead in reading, penmanship and history. She made 100's on all of her homework and tests. The library housed only a small number of books and often times the good ones were already checked out. She tried to fight off her depression and Erika and Katy were always trying to lift her spirits. Catherine began eating less and less and by the end of the week, she fainted in class. The sisters managed to get Catherine into her bed and they had the colored caretaker take the wagon and summon the doctor.

The doctor arrived an hour later and gave Catherine an examination.

"Fortunately," he said, "she is not running a fever; but she appears to be extremely dehydrated and is in need of fluids. I suggest we wrap her in a blanket and take her in the wagon to the hospital so we can monitor her for a day or two."

John Merit had just gotten back home after picking up Amelia from the boarding house. They were having tea in the kitchen and John was filling her in on his trip when the doorbell rang.

"A letter for you, sir; from Father Jonathan," said the messenger. John took the letter into the kitchen and opened it.

Dear John,

While making my rounds at the hospital this morning I was told by one of the sisters that one of the girls from the orphanage had taken ill and was being treated here at the hospital. Upon further investigation, I learned that the young girl is Catherine Eastman. She is being well taken care of, but I thought you might want to come visit her, as her spirits are very low.

Cordially, Father Jonathan

John read the letter out loud to Amelia and she encouraged him to leave immediately. She would be fine by herself for a while.

John pulled his old bicycle out of the garage and jumped on it. One of the tires was a bit low, but John figured it would make it just fine to the hospital. It was certainly faster than he could run and he had already missed the trolley. He was there in ten minutes. Catherine was on the third floor in a ward with twelve beds and drawn curtains in between. John picked up an empty chair and sat it down beside Catherine's bed. She was asleep, so John sat in the chair and watched her for a while. He was amazed at how much she looked like Anne and how her skin looked like a china doll. Catherine stirred and opened her eyes.

"Am I dreaming, or are you really here?" she asked. John smiled down at her and took her hand and they talked for an hour. He told her about his promotion and his trip to Houston and then listened as Catherine shared her week with him. A nurse brought in a tray of food for Catherine.

"I'm not leaving until you eat all of it," said John.

"Then I'm going to take my time," giggled Catherine.

"I can't even begin to imagine how it feels to be in your shoes. But I do know this.....your mother loved you very much and she would be very upset if she knew you were not taking care of yourself. You haven't been eating and you're dehydrated and only you can change that. I really care about you, and it hurts me that you want to give up."

Catherine squeezed his hand and looked up at him. "I know, you're right, and I will try harder, I promise."

They continued talking and Catherine ate most of everything on her plate. "I really am stuffed," said Catherine as she smiled up at John.

The doctor came in and told Catherine that if she continued to improve, she could go back to the orphanage on Sunday. John told the doctor that he would get permission from Father Jonathan to take Catherine back to the orphanage after mass on Sunday.

CHAPTER 17

Catherine seemed shy when John came to pick her up. She had already had lunch and was dressed and waiting for him.

"Would it be possible to stop by my mum's grave on the way to the orphanage?" asked Catherine.

John smiled and said, "Of course."

This time John had brought three red roses to place on Anne's grave and Catherine smiled when he gave them to her. They were at the cemetery just a short while and when Catherine got up to leave, she stumbled. John caught her before she hit the ground and he lost his footing. John fell first and then Catherine on top of him. It was the first time Catherine had laughed since the death of her mother and it felt good. John joined in on the laughter and apologized that he fell, too. When they stood up, Catherine put her arms around his waist and hugged him.

"Thank you, again, Mr. Merit," said Catherine. "You seem to always come to my rescue."

On the ride home, John felt Catherine was feeling a bit low, so he promised he would come see her the next Sunday and it seemed to make her feel better. Catherine enjoyed John's company and she hated that she had to wait another week to see him. She had felt her heart beating fast when she hugged him and she didn't think it was because of the fall. They said their good-byes and Catherine watched as John's buggy turned at the end of the street.

Before, John did not have the authority to access Anne's safe deposit box, but now that he was the vice-president in charge of the trust department, he had the authority to retrieve the letter from Anne's box. He wanted to read it before he took it to Catherine.

My darling Catherine,

I wanted to write this letter to you in case something should happened to me. I don't really know why we have had so much tragedy in our lives, but God has blessed us in so many other ways. God led us to America and I pray you make this your permanent home. Know that I will always be with you and I need you to be strong no matter what. Live life, Catherine, go to school, get married and have children or have your own career. You must be in charge of your own destiny.

My love forever,
Your Mother.

John was deeply touched by Anne's letter and knew that it would give Catherine encouragement. He folded the letter and put it inside his suit pocket so he could give it to her on Sunday.

During the next week, Sister Maria monitored Catherine more closely and made more time for her during off periods and after chores. Catherine didn't notice it, but Sister Maria also watched more closely to see that Catherine was eating and taking better care of herself. By Saturday, Catherine's spirits were much better and she told Sister Maria all about John and how she was looking forward to his visit. Sister Maria was sceptical about John Merit, and told Catherine she should not get her hopes up since John was not a relative and she hadn't know him very long. However, she had told Catherine that Father Jonathan had approved of Mr. Merit and thought he seemed to be a fine, upstanding man with good intentions.

John rode up to the dormitories in his buggy after lunch on Sunday and Catherine was outside waiting for him. After signing her out for a few hours, John and Catherine made their way to the cemetery first. Before they got out, though, John told Catherine her mother had written her a letter and had placed it in their safe deposit box and that he had retrieved it once he became head of the department. He also told Catherine he had read it because he was concerned about her welfare and wasn't sure what the letter might say. He helped Catherine down off the buggy and handed her the letter. She walked slowly over to Anne's grave and slowly opened and read the letter. She turned to John who was still waiting by the buggy and motioned him to come join her. She took John's hand and pulled it up to her face slowly grazing her cheek and then kissed his hand.

"Thank you, John. I don't know what I would have done without you."

They were standing very close together and John had to fight the urge to kiss her. Surprising him, she stood up on her tiptoes and kissed his cheek. He held her close, looking into her eyes, and then he reached down and kissed her on the lips. It all seemed so natural, but John immediately pulled away and apologized.

"I should not have done that, Catherine," said John. "I don't know what came over me and it won't happen again."

Catherine couldn't understand why he was apologizing and asked, "Why was it so wrong? Is it because you are much older than me?"

John looked down at the ground and answered, "Yes."

"Don't worry," Catherine said, I'm not going to tell anyone."

"I know that, but you are still a child, Catherine, and you have your whole life ahead of you," answered John.

"I'll be sixteen on my next birthday and two years after that I'll be considered an adult. Besides that," Catherine continued, "my mum and dad married when she was sixteen and he was twenty-one."

John smiled at her and shook his head. "Let's go take a ride," he said. He was totally fascinated with Catherine and knew deep down this was what he wanted, too.

They rode over to John's house so that he could check on Amelia. On the way there, John told Catherine about his first wife and the loss of his child and that now he took care of Amelia because of her failing health. If John and Catherine had any kind of future together, John wanted Catherine to know everything.

Amelia, John, and Catherine sat around the kitchen table drinking tea and talking about everything from the weather to the local gossip. Catherine laughed at all John's jokes and she fell in love with Amelia. It was an absolutely beautiful day and Catherine hated to see it end. They had to be back at the orphanage by 4:00 p.m. and when they left, Catherine invited Amelia to join them.

"I think I need to rest," said Amelia. "John can see you back by himself," she teased.

The ride back to the orphanage was bumpy and Catherine put her arm through John's arm and gripped it tightly. She smiled up at him as if to say it's all right and she so didn't want the day to end. "This has been the best day I've had in a long time," she told him as they rode up to the orphanage. She kissed him on the cheek and jumped down off the buggy like a school girl and waved as she went inside.

John was thinking about the events of the day and thought it crazy that just a few weeks earlier he was trying to court Catherine's mother. Now, for reasons he could not understand, he had similar feelings for Catherine. Anne and Catherine were so much alike, he thought. Anne was much more reserved and Catherine was more outgoing and inquisitive. Perhaps that was because she was only fifteen. Now he was smitten with Catherine, and he hoped his plans for her future would bring a whole new outlook to his life. She made him feel young again.

David Brooks found it hard to keep his mind focused on his job at the Grande. Tom was giving him more and more things to do and his lunch breaks were getting shorter and shorter and his evenings longer. By the end of the day, he was too exhausted to do anything except buy some booze and go home. He still didn't feel too good and it was taking longer than he thought to recover from his injuries.

Lying in his bed at night, David's mind kept going back to the night Vickie's father came home and beat her up. He could relate to Vickie's trauma because he, too, had suffered as a young boy the perils of an unloving parent. He wanted to go see her again but knew he had to let some time go by before he showed up in Houston again. David had bought a couple of Houston newspapers after he had gotten home but didn't see any write ups about any hookers getting murdered in the Fourth Ward. Still, he needed to wait a few weeks just to be sure. Maybe by then his pain would be gone and he would have more stamina.

Since John's promotion at the bank, his work seemed endless. There were lots of meetings, and in between trying to do his own job he had to train a new employee named Edgar Whiting to take over his old job. He was busy and glad of it because at every turn he could see Catherine's face looking up at him. If only he could see her. It was just before noon on Thursday when Father Jonathan walked into the bank.

"How would you like to buy me some lunch?" asked Father Jonathan. John laughed and said he would love to. The two men walked down to the Tremont Hotel and they were given a table out on the veranda.

"When I asked you to buy my lunch, I thought we might get a burger at the drug store," said Father Jonathan. John laughed and told him he deserved better than that, and besides he needed someone to help him celebrate his new promotion. They both ordered steaks and a glass of wine.

The two men sat visiting for awhile and then Father Jonathan said to John, "I met with the bishop about your intentions for Catherine Eastman and, while we both agreed it was a highly unusual request, we think that under the circumstances it would be in her best interest -- if she agreed, of course -- for you to marry her. There are some stipulations, though," Father Jonathan continued. "First, you must wait until her sixteenth birthday in January and secondly, you cannot ask her until two weeks before. We want you to be discrete about this and not say anything to anyone until that time. We feel it is in the best interest of the orphanage for this to be handled quietly so as not to disrupt the everyday functions of the orphanage. I will visit with Sister Margaret and let her know that you may continue your Sunday visits."

John was almost speechless and asked if he could buy Father Jonathan another glass of wine.

"I think I need to stop at just one glass, but I may take you up on it another time," said Father Jonathan. It was obvious that John was delighted by the good news and he told Father Jonathan that he would certainly keep it a secret.

When John picked Catherine up the next Sunday, it was hard to hide his excitement. He decided to plan something different and knew, from his previous talks with Catherine, that she grew up going out on her father's fishing boat and she seemed to have a real love for it.

When he picked her up, Catherine couldn't help but notice the two life vests under their seats.

"Have you recently been boating?" asked Catherine.

"Not yet," said John. Catherine looked at him, puzzled.

"I have a friend with a small boat that he is loaning to me this afternoon."

Catherine's whole face lit up and she exclaimed, "You're taking me out on a boat today?"

John smiled and said, "Yes."

Catherine could hardly believe it, and told him so.

They rode through town and over to the wharf area past several of the large sailing vessels. The longshoremen were busy at the docks loading cotton bales onto ships for exporting to other countries. They finally entered an area where there were smaller boats tied to a longer pier.

John helped Catherine out of the buggy, fetched the two life vests, and stopped at a twenty-one-foot, small sailing boat. After helping Catherine into hers, John put his vest on and went aboard. He introduced her to the captain who happened to be an old college buddy of John's and after untying the boat, the two men got busy getting the boat ready to go out.

Catherine watched them using the paddles to jockey their way around the other boats and when they finally were out about two hundred yards, they began to set the sails. There was a wonderful breeze that bowed the sail and the boat immediately took off around the east side of the island. John came back over to where Catherine was sitting and she grabbed his hand and smiled up at him.

"You are spoiling me, John Merit," she said. John smiled back.

The scenery was breathtaking and the sky was smouldering in colors of blue with intermittent white clouds. The sun was peering through the clusters of clouds and John handed her a jar of cream to put on her face. Catherine was wearing her bonnet and a dress with three-quarter length sleeves, so she put some on her arms, too. She reached up and put a dab on John's nose and laughed.

"Miss Eastman," John said, "now you have to rub it in." Catherine beamed and smoothed the cream around John's eyes, chin and forehead. She laughed when some got caught in his moustache, and tried to get it out.

They sailed around the island for two hours and it was smooth sailing all the way. Catherine and John were in a world all their own and hardly noticed the captain, who was busy guiding and maneuvering the vessel out into the bay. John watched the captain from the corner of his eye and always seemed to know when to get up and assist when it was necessary.

The trip ended all too soon, Catherine thought, and she was delighted when the captain asked her to take the wheel and guide the boat into dock as they paddled their way in and stopped at the pier. She wasn't sure if it was the breeze on her face, the floating motion over the water or just being with John Merit, but she had never felt more alive than she did at this moment. When they got to the buggy and took off their vests, Catherine threw her arms around John's neck and kissed him.

"Thank you, Mr. Merit," she said.

"My pleasure, Miss Eastman," John replied as he held her in his arms and grinned.

They drove through the business district of Galveston on their way back to the orphanage, unaware that David Brooks was standing outside a saloon watching them. David thought it odd that they seemed so cozy, and wondered why she was with Merit. Tom Gregory had told David that Catherine was living at the orphanage now. He decided to check into the matter when he had a chance.

CHAPTER 18

It took almost four weeks before David Brooks began to feel human again. He was beginning to get his libido back and his manly urges were becoming more frequent. He had been stopping at the brothel once a week for a hot bath and salts which relieved his pain substantially, but what he really wanted now wasn't an occasionally hooker. He thought back to when he last saw Catherine and then to Vickie and the night her father punished her.

It was Friday afternoon around three o'clock when they finished up rehearsals for the next opera. The director had a death in his family and had to go out of town for a funeral and wouldn't be back until the next Tuesday. David left and took a trolley over to the train station and waited for the 6:00 whistle to blow that indicated the incoming train. He was beginning to get excited and was proud of himself for saving up a little money for the trip. He hadn't felt like gambling and had cut down on his drinking, so getting away from the grind of his job gave him an anticipated pleasure knowing what might be ahead of him. He wasn't going to make the same mistake as last time. He had bought a good sharp knife and ankle holster and strapped it around his ankle underneath his pants. David smiled and thought, I'll be ready this time.

The trip to Houston took a little over two hours as it was not an express train. David slept most of the way except for the occasional stops and people getting off and on the train. When he got to Houston, he decided to bypass Rosie's place and go straight to the Fourth Ward.

David hadn't eaten all day so he made his way over to the familiar diner where he had met Vickie. He ordered the special, which was fried chicken, mashed potatoes, peas and cornbread. He finished it off with his favorite dessert, apple pie, paid the ticket, and left. He walked down a few blocks and saw a young girl who looked like Vickie, talking to two other girls. She saw him and turned and walked away. David had to run to catch up with her and when he did, Vickie turned and put her hand up to stop him.

"Leave me alone," she said.

David looked puzzled.

"How could you just stand there and watch what he did to me?" Vickie asked.

"What could I have done?" asked David. "Your father is as big as a giant and if he had known I was there he would probably have killed us both. Come on, baby, I came all this way just to see you."

"You did?" asked Vickie.

David smiled, took her hand and kissed it. "Is your daddy home?" he asked. Vickie smiled and shook her head no.

On their way back to Vickie's house, David stopped and bought some whiskey for him and tequila for Vickie. When they got to Vickie's house, David poured her a shot of tequila. Vickie downed her drink in one gulp and David poured another. She gulped it down equally as fast and began unbuttoning David's shirt. They took turns taking their clothes off of each other. David put his drink down and crawled up on the bed. He started kissing Vickie's neck and she kissed him back.

They passionately pleased each other for over an hour. David reached over and chugalugged his whiskey, then handed Vickie her glass of tequila, which she also chugalugged. They both lay back down on the bed and fell asleep in each other's arms.

It was early morning when they woke up. Vickie put her head on David's shoulder and said, "Take me back to Galveston with you. I hate it here."

"What about your daddy?" David asked.

"He's not my real father. My real dad never married my momma and I don't know who he was. Ivan, my step-dad, married my momma when I was two. He used to beat her all the time. I think he killed her, but I'm not sure," Vickie answered.

David thought a few moments and then said, "I know it's tough for you here, but I have my own baggage to contend with. I wouldn't make a good companion for you."

"Please just think about it. You're the only man who has been nice to me. I have no friends and I'm afraid my daddy is going to kill me."

"It's out of the question," David said as he got out of bed and began putting on his pants.

"Oh, please don't go. Make love to me again." Vickie was pleading with him now.

"I have to take care of some business," David said as he grabbed his shirt and left.

David's adrenalin was rushing through his body and he needed air. Outside, he put his hands in his pockets and walked back over to the diner. He needed some coffee to clear his head and he was hungry, too. Why are they always so clingy? he thought.

They had a good thing going and taking her back to Galveston would just be out of the question. That old feeling of wanting to kill was throbbing inside his gut again, and Houston was probably a safe haven for him to do his hunting. He knew too many people in Galveston and there were more choices here. He just had to keep Vickie at a distance.

It was 3:00 a.m. when David decided to head over to Prairie Avenue. It was not as crowded as some of the other streets in the Fourth Ward but there were a couple of girls standing on the corner. On his way over, David kept his eyes open for a dimly lit area of an alley where he could take his victim, and he made sure there weren't a lot of stray men around. He stopped across the street just outside the

0 The Arrival

gleaming light of the street lamp so his face was unnoticeable. A couple of minutes later one of the girls strolled across the street to make contact.

"Are you interested in a night of pleasure?" she asked.

David sized her up real fast. She was probably twenty, had knowledge of the streets and knew her way around.

"Not now." David said and turned and walked to the opposite end of the street. He wanted to stay away from the seasoned prostitutes and preferred to play it safe.

On his way, a younger girl, maybe sixteen or younger, stepped out of a doorway. She was short, maybe five feet and probably only 100 pounds or less. David looked back over his shoulder to see if anyone was watching and it was clear.

"Hey," she said as she walked faster to catch up with David. "What's your hurry?"

David kept on walking toward the alley he had checked out earlier. "This way," David said. The young prostitute followed behind him.

"When they reached the alley it was dimly lit and he didn't see anyone else, so he stopped behind a large wooden container underneath a pull-down stairway. David could feel the rush, the exhilaration and his breathing grew heavy. It only took a couple of minutes for David to end the young prostitute's life. She had a small neck and David could hear her larynx crush under the pressure of his strong hands. He placed her body between the container and the wall of the building and threw some trash over her. He looked around, bent down and took the money from her hand and began buttoning his pants as he walked down the alley to the next street.

David just made it to the station before the train pulled away. He sat in the back and tried to make himself disappear into the seat. The train was mostly empty because it was still early in the morning and after it left, he breathed a sigh of relief. His thoughts bounced from Anne, to Catherine, to Vickie and his need to kill. He needed more and his anxiety was making him crazy.

It was Monday again, and David stopped to buy a Houston newspaper on his way to work. He left early so he could have a cup of coffee and read the paper before work. David glanced over the headlines on each page and on the third page at the bottom, a headline caught his eye.

"STEP-FATHER KILLS TEENAGE DAUGHTER

Ivan Polanski murdered his teenage step-daughter early Sunday morning by hanging her from a homemade guillotine in the girl's bedroom. Polanski said he came home at noon and found his step-daughter, Vickie Ryder, dead and claimed she committed suicide but evidence of bruising and lacerations all over her body indicate foul play. Polanski has been jailed pending further investigation."

David read and reread the short article. Did her father really kill her, or did she actually commit suicide, David wondered. He thought back to Saturday night when they were together. He usually had no remorse for another dead hooker, but Vickie was a lot like him. He had left his past behind but she was still living hers. There was no way he could have brought Vickie back to Galveston. In the long run, Vickie wasn't what he wanted anyway, but there was something about her he liked. He hoped they would hang Polanski for what he had done to her. Even if it were a suicide, her old man drove her to it, David thought.

CHAPTER 19

Catherine began adjusting to her new life at the orphanage. Sister Margaret had given her some additional duties in the library along with her other chores of mending and sewing. She loved working in the library and she gave Sister Margaret the names of several other books she thought the girls might enjoy reading. All the girls really respected her, especially the girls who were fluent in German and Italian. They were always speaking to Catherine in their native tongues. Catherine especially looked forward to Sunday when John would come and pick her up. He always brought flowers for her to put on her mother's grave. She had grown quite fond of him and hoped he would not grow tired of her. After all, she was just a child in his eyes and he probably had a girlfriend. She decided to ask him the next time she saw him.

On Thanksgiving weekend, John Merit had spoken with Sister Margaret in advance about the possibility of Catherine staying with him and his sister over the four-day weekend. Father Jonathan had already spoken to Sister Margaret about their impending marriage and she reluctantly said yes.

When John picked up Catherine after breakfast, they went back to John's house, picked up Amelia, and went to mass at St. Mary's Cathedral. John had invited Mrs. Wyman and Father Jonathan to join them for a Thanksgiving meal at the Tremont where he had made reservations for later that afternoon. They were seated at a table on the veranda and shortly after their meal had been served, John noticed Tom Gregory and his wife and son, David Brooks, and two other people he did not know. Tom got up and walked over to John's table with David following behind him. They greeted one another and Tom acknowledged Catherine, saying, "It's good to see you looking so well, Miss Eastman."

Catherine blushed and said thank you. David couldn't keep his eyes off Catherine and stared long and hard at her. John noticed and asked David if something was wrong.

David replied, "It's just that Miss Eastman looks so much like her beautiful mother."

John was not amused at David's gawking and said it was nice to see them and sat back down to eat. David and Tom went back to their table. David made the comment to Tom that he had seen Catherine and John Merit together on several occasions and wondered how John was able to do that.

"I think John handles her mother's trust fund. Other than that, I'm not sure," Tom said.

David smiled to himself. So, she has money, too, he thought.

Catherine had carefully packed a small bag and was excited to be getting away from the orphanage for a few days. She was most excited about being with John for four full days and nights. Their Thanksgiving meal was delicious and very tasty and the day ended well. After dropping off Mrs. Wyman at the boarding house, John, Catherine, and Amelia headed home. Father Jonathan preferred to walk and said he needed the exercise after eating so much.

It was 4:30 p.m. when they got home and John asked Catherine what she wanted to do the over the next couple of days.

"Could we go to the beach tomorrow? Winter has not quite set in and I'd love to walk in the sand if it doesn't rain," Catherine answered.

"Sounds like fun to me," John replied.

Amelia said she was not up to it and that the two should go

without her. John took Catherine and her bag upstairs to show her where she would be staying.

"This was Amelia's room, and mine is down the hall. When my folks died I moved Amelia into their old room since it was downstairs," John commented. "The bathroom is across the hall."

Amelia's old bedroom was bright and cheerful and decorated in pale and dark pink floral wallpaper. There were corresponding lace curtains with pink tiebacks and the double bed had a pink and green bedspread with a folded up quilt lying at the foot of the bed.

"It's lovely," said Catherine as she smiled back at John. Catherine felt awkward and John sensed her uneasiness.

"Why don't you take a few minutes and put your things away and I'll meet you downstairs when you feel like coming down," he said.

Catherine was glad to have a few minutes to herself. This was all so strange to her. John was so nice to her and she couldn't tell if he was trying to be a father figure to her or if he actually had other feelings for her. She had flirted with some boys at school when she was living in Sandgate, but they were just boys she had grown up with. She had never been kissed before John. He did kiss her first, she thought. She had made up her mind and decided to speak to Amelia and find out if John had committed himself to someone else.

Catherine arranged her things and went downstairs. Amelia was sitting at the kitchen table and offered Catherine some hot tea. Amelia told Catherine that John had left for a short while and would be back soon. They visited for a while before Catherine got the courage to ask Amelia if John had any other female friends.

Amelia laughed and said, "No, I'm afraid John is such a good brother that he finds it hard to leave me alone. I have encouraged him to do things outside of work and home, but he always finds an excuse not to go unless he can bring me along."

Amelia asked Catherine if she had a boyfriend back in England. Catherine laughed and told her that most of the boys she knew liked to fish and hunt and she mostly did things with her family.

"Thank you for sharing John with me. He loves you so much," Catherine said to Amelia.

Just then John came in the side kitchen door with a box of muffins in one of his hands. "The grocery store was still open so I picked these muffins up for breakfast," John said. "And I got these flowers for my two favorite girls," he said as he held out the flowers to them. They both laughed at him and Amelia pointed to a vase on the buffet.

Catherine went over and picked up the vase and took it over to the sink, filling it with water. She smelled the flowers and rolled her eyes, indicating her pleasure.

The next morning, John and Catherine walked over to the trolley station and caught a ride over to the beach. It was an unusually warm, sunny day and there were people everywhere milling around. They walked over to Murdock's bathhouse and John led her over to the long pier that extended out over the bay. There were rows and rows of fishermen throwing their lines out into the water, and the smell of raw fish filled the air. It reminded Catherine of home, and she smiled at the thought. John returned the smile and when he looked into her eyes he knew at that moment he was smitten with her and was looking forward to getting to know her better.

John liked that Catherine was outgoing and seemed to enjoy the simple things in life. She had an aura of mystery about her which he liked. She was unpredictable at times and she amused him with her flirtatious attitude. She was much more mature than her fifteen years and their age difference did not seem to bother her at all. It was almost lunch time, so John suggested they have lunch at the Beach House Hotel.

"I've only seen it from a distance," said Catherine, "and I've always wanted to see the inside of it."

The Beach House Hotel was an impressive three-story, 200-room hotel on Galveston's beach with many of the rooms overlooking the bay. The interior boasted high ceilings, a veranda, and many open galleries where the Gulf breeze would fill the open air markets. There was an octagonal dome at the top that seemed to be influenced by an Elizabethan church. It was flanked by two Victorian style attached buildings with wraparound porches and walls of windows. It was truly one of the most beautiful buildings Catherine had seen since arriving in Galveston.

John and Catherine walked through the lobby, stopping from time to time to look at some of the art work and lavish mouldings, and they made their way to the back part of the hotel to find the restaurant. John asked to be seated by a window overlooking the Gulf and the maître-d' showed them to a small table by a picturesque window with a panoramic view of the water. John and Catherine ordered lemonade and the waiter gave them a description of the daily specials. They took their time with their meal and enjoyed their time together. Catherine felt more at ease with John knowing that he did not have a girlfriend, and she finally got up the nerve to ask John if he thought he might get married again someday. John was surprised by Catherine's question and almost choked before he answered.

"I must say I haven't given it much thought, but I suppose someday I would like to have a family of my own. What about you?" he asked.

Catherine was also surprised that he would ask her that question. "I haven't given it much thought myself, but I suppose I would like to get my high school education behind me first and then possibly go to college or maybe medical school."

"That's very forward thinking and I hope it will happen for you," John said. "Your trust fund certainly has enough money in it for you to go to college anywhere you choose."

"I haven't thought that far ahead," answered Catherine, "but I'd like to stay in Galveston and complete my education here."

When they finished their lunch, John and Catherine explored the rest of the hotel and then set out for their walk on the beach. They took off their shoes and Catherine tucked them inside the knapsack she was carrying. The water felt cool on their feet and John would occasionally bend down to pick up a sand dollar that had washed up. They had walked awhile before John grabbed her hand and held it. She felt her heart skip a beat and she smiled to herself. John was the sweetest, most generous man and yes, she had thought about marriage. She wanted to someday be John's wife.

They found a place on the beach where they spread out a small blanket. Catherine sat down and John offered to go over to the snow cone stand and get them a treat. It was about fifty yards down the beach and just as he left, a man came up to Catherine.

"Small world, finding you here, Miss Eastman."

Catherine looked up and saw David Brooks standing over her.

"So why are you spending so much time with John Merit now...are you living with him?"

Catherine was stunned by his abruptness and wasn't sure how to answer him. "I live at St. Mary's Orphanage. Sometimes Mr. Merit and his sister invite me to do things with them," Catherine answered.

"Well, I'd be happy to pick you up sometimes, too, and show you around Galveston. Your mother was a good friend of mine. I know I could show you a good time."

John walked up before Catherine could say anything.

"Hello, David," John said. "Can I help you with something?"

"Actually, I was just leaving," answered David as he turned and winked at Catherine.

John looked at Catherine and could tell she was upset. He was angry also and he asked her what David had said. She relayed David's communication to John, who found it hard to hide his anger.

"That son ..." John stopped himself and said, "That's not very gentlemanly of him and I'm sorry it happened. I won't leave you alone again."

They finished eating their snow cones in silence. It was obvious David had scared Catherine and John wasn't quite sure what he was going to do about it. When Catherine finished her snow cone, she turned to John and told him about the encounter she had had with the strange man on the ship and that she had never told her mother because her mother had taken sick. She felt tears coming down her cheeks.

John wanted to hug her but felt this was not the time or the place to do it. "I think it's time to head back," he said.

"You're not mad at me, are you?" Catherine asked.

John took her hands in his and looked in her eyes. "Catherine, I don't think I could ever be mad at you. You are so brave and I admire you for who you are," he said. "I truly care for you and I am angry that there are men in this world like David Brooks and the man on the ship."

When they got to the sidewalk they dusted off their feet and put their shoes back on. They made their way to the trolley and then back to John's house.

David had been standing by a small wooden structure and ducked when they passed by him. He had seen them get on the trolley earlier and he jumped on it at the last minute and followed them to the beach. He smirked, thinking about the fact that they had no idea he was following them.

John was beginning to have second thoughts himself. Catherine was so vulnerable and he began to beat himself up thinking that he might be just as bad, wanting and desiring Catherine the way he did. When they returned to John's house, Catherine went upstairs without a word.

Amelia came into the living room and saw John was sitting in his chair just staring into space.

"What has happened?" she asked.

John slowly turned to look at her and his face was ashen. He told Amelia everything that had happened and that now he must re-evaluate his feelings for Catherine.

"I must admit, at first I presumed it was the best thing for her, but I never stopped to consider what she wanted. I know I am probably much too old for her, but the problem is that now I have fallen in love with her," John said. "When I look at her I don't see a fifteen-year-old girl. I see a young woman who I want to spend the rest of my life with. I'm planning to return her to the orphanage tomorrow."

"What will you tell her?" asked Amelia.

"I'll just say I had some business come up and I won't be able to look after her," John answered. "She is a strong, intelligent girl and I'm sure she will understand."

Catherine had started down the stairs when she heard the last part of the conversation between John and Amelia in which John said he was planning to take Catherine back to the orphanage the next morning. She turned and went back to Amelia's room and fell on the bed fighting back tears. She didn't know what she had done to make John so angry that he wanted her to leave so she replayed all the day's events in her head, finally deciding it was really her fault. She was just a child in John's eyes and he probably didn't want the responsibility of looking after her. After all, Amelia took a lot of his time. She had to be strong and understanding.

Just then there was a tap on her door and John said, "Amelia has made some soup and wants you to join us,"

"I'll be right down," answered Catherine.

Catherine splashed some cold water on her face and came downstairs. She put on a fake smile and told Amelia how much fun she had had at the beach. She rambled on and on about the hotel and some of the more pleasing events of the day. John stared admiringly at her and embraced her every word.

After dinner they went into the living room and when they sat down, Catherine asked, "Mr. Merit, would you mind taking me back to the orphanage in the morning? One of my friends there is having a birthday and I'd like to be there to help keep her spirits up."

John was surprised but assured her he was happy to do it.

Catherine was dressed and waiting in the living room when John came downstairs the next morning. She smiled and said, "This has been a wonderful Thanksgiving and yesterday was great, but I think you have spoiled me too much."

John looked at her and said, "Catherine, I like spoiling you. I have also enjoyed it." There was an awkward silence and Catherine walked to the door. John followed her and opened it.

"Let me leave a note on the table for Amelia, and I'll be right there," John said. He left a note telling Amelia he would return shortly and went outside where Catherine was waiting. They walked over to catch a trolley to the stables where John kept his horse and buggy. Without saying anything, John stopped at the cemetery. He helped Catherine down from the buggy and waited while she walked over to Anne's grave. Five minutes later she walked back to the buggy and they returned to the orphanage. Catherine had mixed emotions about the way things were left. She really cared for John and was discouraged when he often treated her like a child.

CHAPTER 20

Catherine was greatly disappointed when John did not to return the next Sunday. It upset her that John did not feel the same way she did. She waited a while and then decided she would just leave and go the cemetery by herself. No one would notice she had left alone, she thought. She knew the way and she hoped the walk would clear her head. She figured the sisters would think she was with John and right now, she really didn't care. She just wanted to get away. It was father than she had remembered and the road to the cemetery was really eerie. Catherine was surprised that she had not noticed how remote it was. Her common sense told her to turn back, but she felt that since she was already there, she might as well visit her mother's grave.

Catherine noticed a Negro grave digger watching her and she felt uneasy so she decided she better leave. She walked back to the road and for some reason she was confused as to whether to take a right or left. The sun was behind her, it was beginning to get cool, and there were shadows everywhere. She was sure the road to the left would take her to the main road and then back to the orphanage. She was growing tense and a little scared as she had never just walked away before.

John had brought some work home from the bank and spent most of Sunday working on books and going through some of his customer files. He felt miserable and found it hard to concentrate, but willed himself not to think about Catherine. There was a knock on the door and he walked over to answer it. The Negro caretaker from the orphanage asked if Catherine was with him.

"No, why would you think that? Is she not at the orphanage?" asked John.

"No sir," said the caretaker. "She been gone a few hours and no one checked her out. Sister Margaret sent me to look for her, but to come here first."

"Wait for me a moment," said John. "I'll go with you. I think I might know where she might be."

John told Amelia about Catherine's leaving the orphanage and that he was going to look for her. John and the caretaker pulled onto the main road to the cemetery and drove through the area, but didn't see Catherine. John saw a man tending a grave and got off the buggy and walked over to him. "Good afternoon," he said. "Did you see a young woman earlier today at the cemetery?"

"Yes sir, but she left on foot 'bout an hour ago," he said.

John thanked him and got back in the buggy. The two men rode back to the main road.

"Before we head back to the orphanage, let's go left and see if maybe she took a wrong turn," John said.

Catherine had walked almost a half mile before she realized she was lost. She was cold and scared and she wanted crying. She had never felt so alone and she was angry with herself for leaving. Catherine saw a buggy coming and stood on the side of the road while she waited to see who it was. She recognized John immediately and started waving.

When they got close, John jumped off the buggy and ran to her. "What on earth were you thinking, Catherine? You have had us all scared to death and worried about you."

Catherine had never seen John angry and she was embarrassed that she was so careless.

"Who cares, anyway?" she cried.

"I care!" John said. "Please don't ever do that again."

John wanted to kiss Catherine but thought better of it as the caretaker was watching.

"Catherine, I'm sorry I didn't come today. I should have at least let you know. I don't know what I would have done if anything had happened to you."

Catherine hugged his neck and John put his arms around her.

"We need to get you back," he said.

When they got back in the buggy John told the caretaker to drop him off at the south end trolley stop.

"You're not coming back with us?" Catherine asked.

"No, I'm not, Catherine. You did this on your own and you need to take whatever punishment they decide to give you," John said.

They rode over to the trolley stop in silence. Catherine knew John was angry with her and she didn't quite know how to make it right. She knew she acted foolishly and regretted what she had done.

"Good-bye, Catherine," was all John said, and Catherine looked away. She did not want him to see her cry.

Catherine waited outside Sister Margaret's office for fifteen minutes before she was called in.

"Your actions today have given us all a fright, Catherine. What do you have to say for yourself?" asked Sister Margaret.

Catherine took a deep breath and said, "I'm very sorry for what I did and I don't have a good reason, other than I wanted to visit my mum's grave. I wasn't thinking and I did not mean to cause concern. I can assure you I will never do it again. I am prepared to accept whatever punishment you give me."

"I appreciate the fact that you are taking total responsibility, but you have to understand that you are not the only girl here, and that rules are meant to be followed," Sister Margaret said. "Your punishment is as follows: starting now, you are to go into the chapel and say the complete rosary. You will not be permitted to visit with the other girls, and you will spend all your spare time in the laundry room where you will be mending and sewing. Every evening after dinner you will continue to say the rosary in the chapel and continue with you chores until bedtime. Your punishment will end on Friday of this week. That is all."

"Thank you, Sister Margaret," Catherine said and left to get her rosary.

John couldn't help but wonder what would have made Catherine do such a reckless thing, and he was worried that he might have been part of the reason. He thought about talking to Father Jonathan, but decided not to. If Father Jonathan suspected he was having second thoughts, he might not allow the marriage to go forward. John realized he had inadvertently been trying to court Catherine and make her dependent on him because he wanted her. It was not right, and he knew it. He would put some space between them and allow Catherine time to make the right decision.

Catherine accepted her punishment, and in a way she was glad she didn't have to talk to the other girls. She was still a little embarrassed that she had disobeyed the rules and her worst fear was that she may have lost John. She could still see his angry face when he got off the wagon and she longed to beg his forgiveness.

Catherine had finished her chores early on Friday afternoon and was gazing out the window towards the Gulf. It had rained most of the day and she missed hearing the laughter of the younger children who played outside her window. Christmas was only a few days away, and the halls in the orphanage were filled with pictures the children had colored in honor of Jesus' birthday. Lilly Mae had to hang the laundry up inside the laundry room on a clothesline she had rigged up with the help of the caretaker.

Catherine liked Lilly Mae a lot; sometimes Lilly Mae would give her pep talks about life. Lilly Mae had five children she was raising, and from what she said, they all had to help around the house and do their homework. Her children were enrolled in the black school and she walked them eight blocks to school before she caught the trolley to come to her job here at the orphanage. Catherine decided to ask Lilly Mae why men were so complicated.

"They don't think with their heads, child," she told Catherine.

"Once their manly genitals reach the age of fourteen they start looking at girls differently. Do you know what sex is?" Lilly Mae asked.

"I think so," said Catherine. "My mum said that when a man and woman get married, they discover each other's bodies in a loving way and that the man is more aggressive and the woman is submissive and that whatever he wants to do, you have to go along with it. She also told me that sometimes it might hurt."

Lilly Mae smiled and said, "That right? Well, that's all well and good in a make-believe world, but not all men think you have to be married."

"I know," Catherine said. "I discovered that when a man tried to rape me on the ship when we came to America, but I got away."

Lillie Mae smiled and said, "I think you have it all figured out now. Hopefully, you will find yourself a good man who will love you and take care of you some day."

Catherine smiled to herself and thought, I already have.

Catherine longed to see John. He had only come once since Thanksgiving to see her and they had sat on the porch at the orphanage and talked for a while. Nothing was really said though, and it was awkward. John told Catherine he was giving Amelia a new walking cane for Christmas. She had admired it in a catalogue they had gotten in the mail. He also told her that he was enormously busy at the bank and brought work home on the weekends just to get caught up. She really missed him and wanted to tell him so, but she didn't. John hadn't said anything about seeing her on Christmas. It was going to be just a normal day at the orphanage. There would be a mass, and they would sing Christmas carols. Some of the children made things in arts and crafts to give each other, but no one really said anything about gifts. Catherine had kept a book of poems that belonged to her mother and wrapped it in some plain brown paper she found in the trash. She was going to give it to John for Christmas if he came to see her. On Friday evening, Christmas Eve, one of the sisters read the story about how baby Jesus was born and what the true meaning of Christmas really was. She could only imagine what Mary must have felt when he was born. Catherine admired Joseph, too, and smiled to herself when she remembered how Joseph March told them about his name.

CHAPTER 21

Christmas day arrived, and there was a small amount of excitement in the air. This was going to be Catherine's first Christmas without any of her family, and she promised herself that no matter what, she would not cry. A visiting priest by the name of Father Mark Andrews said mass and at the end, they sang Christmas carols and a special song called "Queen of the Waves." The song was special because it was introduced to St. Mary's infirmary by three sisters who came from France to Galveston, Texas, in the year 1866. Two of the sisters had later died in a deadly yellow fever epidemic that struck Galveston in 1867. It's a song about gathering strength in a time of need and was written to lift one's spirit. The words were easy to learn and Catherine learned it the first week she arrived at the orphanage.

The girls had free time after lunch and the clock in the library reminded Catherine that it was already 2:00 p.m. and John Merit had not come. She went upstairs and tore the paper off the book she had wrapped to give John and put the book away. She was devastated and never felt so alone. Katy came upstairs and told Catherine that Sister Margaret needed to see her and Catherine went to her office. Catherine knocked on Sister Margaret's door and went in. "A letter came by messenger for you," Sister Margaret said as she handed Catherine the letter.

Catherine smiled and thanked her. When she got out in the hall, she looked at it and saw it was from John. She wanted someplace to be alone so she walked down to the laundry room and tried the door. It was unlocked so she opened the door and went in. She walked back to her sewing machine and sat down, looking at the letter. She opened it with her scissors and quietly read the letter.

My dearest Catherine,

I was in hopes that you would be able to spend Christmas with Amelia and me but I am afraid she is not well. She is having chest pains and trouble breathing. The doctor just left and has put Amelia to bed for a few days. I will be staying close by her side and won't be able to leave the house for any length of time. I will have to find someone to look after her next week because I have to work. I am so sorry you have to spend Christmas alone, and I do miss you and hope you are well.

Fondly,
John Merit

Catherine put the letter back in the envelope and went to find Sister Margaret.

She gave the letter to Sister Margaret to read and said, "I would like to help Mr. Merit look after his sister. Would it be possible for me to stay with them for a few days and attend to her needs?"

Sister Margaret did not like giving special privileges to any of the girls, but she had to comply with Father Jonathan's request to allow her to visit John and his sister, when it was requested. She knew Catherine was very concerned about John's sister and told her she could go, but if she found out that Amelia was contagious with something that might make her sick, she should return immediately. Catherine assured her she would and went upstairs to pack her bag. The caretaker picked up Catherine in the food wagon and took her over to John's house. He had been given strict instructions to wait until Catherine found out if

Amelia had a contagious disease. John answered the door and was surprised to see Catherine. They talked outside for a few minutes and then
Catherine went back to let the caretaker know Amelia was not contagious. She went in and told John that she wanted to help him with
Amelia and there was no need to find anyone else. Her only condition
was that she get messages back to Sister Margaret with Amelia's progress. John looked relieved, but more than anything he was grateful to
see Catherine and hugged her tightly.

"Thank you," John whispered. "I've missed you terribly."

Catherine smiled and hugged him back reluctantly. "What do
we need to do to help Amelia?" she asked.

John showed Catherine into the kitchen where he had several
pots of boiling water. "Her airway gets clogged up and the mist from
the water helps to open it. I was going to bring her into the kitchen and
try and make her comfortable here," John said.

"My mum used to do that for my sister when she had trouble
breathing. I noticed you have a eucalyptus tree by the side of the
house. I'll get some clippings from the tree and put it in the water. The
oils will help her breathing."

Catherine looked in the cabinets and found some rosemary
leaves to add to the boiling pot. She took a knife from the kitchen
drawer and went outside to cut some small clippings from the eucalyptus tree, then put them in the boiling water. John came back in the
kitchen carrying Amelia and put her in a chair beside the stove. Catherine leaned over and kissed Amelia on the check and bent down beside
her.

"I used to help my mum take care of my sister, Whitney, when
she had asthma. This should make you feel a lot better in a few hours.
I'm going to make you some hot tea with honey and lemon and that
will also make you feel a lot better," Catherine said. John stood watching Catherine take over the kitchen and was amused that she looked
right at home. "And you, Mr. Merit, look like you haven't slept in
days. Go lie down on the sofa. I'll look after Amelia."

John didn't argue. She was right. He had been up all night with Amelia and was glad to take a break. While Amelia sat by the stove breathing in the mist, Catherine found some chicken in the ice box, along with some vegetables, and took them out. She cleaned and cut up the chicken and put it in another pot to stew along with the vegetables. Catherine attended to Amelia while the soup cooked and encouraged her to take deep breaths. She made Amelia another cup of hot tea and also made herself one. Amelia grabbed her hand and thanked her for coming.

"We've both missed seeing you, Catherine. I hope that whatever has come between you and John can be mended. He really cares for you," Amelia said.

Catherine smiled and said, "Right now I just want you to get better."

Amelia's breathing improved and they both sat at the table eating a bowl of soup and crackers. It was nearly 8:00 p.m. when John came into the kitchen to check on them. He was surprised to see Amelia looking so well. Catherine got up to get another bowl and put a large ladle of soup in it.

"Umm, this smells wonderful; did you make it?" John asked, looking at Catherine. She smiled and shook her head yes.

The next afternoon, Father Jonathan stopped by to visit Amelia. Sister Margaret had informed him about Catherine leaving the orphanage to care for Amelia. John went to the door and showed Father Jonathan into the kitchen. He told Father Jonathan that Amelia was only able to sleep in a reclining position and that every three hours they would take turns helping Amelia into the kitchen to breathe the hot mist. She was improving, but she was extremely tired. They all agreed that the hospital would probably be the best place for her. Father Jonathan informed them that the hospital had just gotten a new emergency vehicle that looked like a wagon but had automobile parts, so it was horseless. He would inform the hospital to send it over to get Amelia. Catherine could ride in the emergency vehicle with her, and John could catch the trolley and meet them there.

At the hospital, Amelia was placed in a bed with a tent structure placed over her so that the steam would not escape. She was also given extra fluids to prevent dehydration. Lying under the tent was much more comfortable, and she was able to sleep much better. A lot of rest was what the doctor said she needed, and if she continued to improve, John could take her home in a few days. It was 9:00 p.m. when John and Catherine went back to John's house to get some rest. They didn't have a lot to say to each other because they had both been up all night and were exhausted.

Catherine went upstairs to Amelia's old room and fell asleep and John fell asleep on the sofa. The next morning, John dressed for work and when Catherine came downstairs, they went into the kitchen for tea and oatmeal. Catherine offered to stay at the hospital with Amelia while John worked.

Catherine and John had very little time alone while Amelia was in the hospital recuperating, and in their brief moments alone they talked mostly about Amelia, Catherine's job in the library, and sometimes John would talk a little about his parents and growing up. They were both cordial to each other, but it was obvious neither wanted to talk about the future.

Father Jonathan stopped John in the hallway when he came to visit Amelia and asked if he and John could have a little chat.

"In a couple of days it will be a new year, and soon you will speak to Catherine about your proposal. She will be sixteen in a couple of weeks," Father Jonathan said. "I have noticed the way you look at her and I do believe you are quite smitten with her," he continued.

John blushed and said, "You're quite right, she has certainly stolen my heart."

"What if you marry her and she decides she wants an annulment. Are you prepared for her answer?" Father Jonathan asked.

"I will support whatever choices she makes," answered John.

"Well then, perhaps now would be a good time to have a talk

with her before she goes back to the orphanage. Of course, she will need to keep it a secret so as not to disturb the other children. Let me know what she says," Father Jonathan said.

It was Thursday and the doctor was going to release Amelia the next day, so John needed to speak to Catherine before she went back to the orphanage. That evening, John and Catherine left the hospital around 6:00 p.m. Catherine thought John was acting a bit strange, but assumed he just felt a lot of anxiety over Amelia's illness. John didn't take the usual way home and he stopped the buggy on the side of the street by the Tremont Hotel.

"I'm going to buy you a wonderful dinner in appreciation for all the help you have been," John said smiling at her.

"That sounds good to me but you don't owe me anything," Catherine answered.

John asked for a quiet table back in the corner and Catherine was touched by his gesture. He ordered steaks for both of them, hot tea for Catherine, and a glass of wine for himself. John had been practicing all day what he was going to say and he needed a glass of wine to steady his nerves.

"I have been talking to Father Jonathan about the possibility of you coming to live with Amelia and me," John said. Catherine sat motionless and listened "Since we are not blood relatives and not suitable to be adoptive parents, it was suggested that on your sixteenth birthday we, you and I, would marry and become man and wife," John continued. "Before you answer, I want you to know that I have spoken with Father Jonathan and he said that as long as we are celibate and do not have intimacy you could get an annulment on your eighteenth birthday, and be free to do as you please." Catherine looked down at her plate in silence and then looked at John.

"You would do that for me?" Catherine asked.

"I would be honored if you said yes," John replied. "I will put no pressure on you to do anything you don't want to, and you could enrol at Ball High School and get your diploma," John said. "I have spoken with Amelia and she loves you and would gladly have you be part of our family. There is one condition though: Father Jonathan does not want you to speak to anyone about our plans if you agree. On your sixteenth birthday you would move out of the orphanage and come live with us after a brief ceremony."

"Wow," said Catherine in a low voice. "I was not expecting a marriage proposal. I really don't know what to say. You and Amelia have been more than kind to me and I would not want to be a burden to you," Catherine continued to say. "Would you still take other women out while I am your wife?"

"Of course not," John said softly. "We would be man and wife and I would honor our marriage vows. I just don't want you to feel like you are committed to me for the rest of your life. I would never expect that,"

"What if I fall in love with you and don't want an annulment?" Catherine asked.

"I wasn't going to tell you this, Catherine, but I've fallen in love with you. I want to spend the rest of my life with you. But you are so young and you have so much to look forward to that I didn't want you to feel trapped. After we marry, you will stay in Amelia's old room and we will take it a day at a time," John answered. They sat looking at each other and then they slowly began to smile at each other.

"Alright, then," said Catherine, "I'll do it."

Catherine sat closer to John on the buggy ride home. I'm going to be Mrs. John Merit soon, she said to herself and she was never so happy. When they got back to the house she was hoping John would kiss her but he didn't. Before they went upstairs Catherine asked John a question, "Are you sure this is what you want, Mr. Merit?"

"Yes," said John. "And I know what you are thinking. You want me to kiss you and I'm not going to. It would excite me too much, and then one thing would lead to another. In order for this to work for you, Catherine, we have to remain celibate. A light kiss on the cheek or holding hands is all we can do. Good night," John said, and kissed her on the forehead.

When Catherine returned to the orphanage her excitement had diminished and in the reality of it all, she decided it was just an arrangement. They would marry, live in separate bedrooms, and after two years she could get an annulment and be free to marry someone else. It's a wonderful proposal, she thought, except she loved him and knew she would never leave unless he wanted her to. Catherine understood the rules, and she would try with all her heart to make it work.

CHAPTER 22

David Brooks detested the holidays. In his thirty-three years he had never received a gift, at least not one that was wrapped and put under a Christmas tree. When he was younger and worked in the circus, the working girls always gave him a lot of attention and bedded him without any charge during the holidays. Now, to him it was just another day. Tom always gave them a week off during Christmas and New Year's, without pay of course, so David always put out feelers that he was available to be a bouncer at one of the clubs. Walking home from the Grande on Christmas Eve, he decided to stroll down Post Office Street and check in at some of the bars there. He passed by two saloons but didn't stop. They were too stuffy and one of them was for men only. He knew he would be working but still wanted the chance to find an available woman or prostitute. He worked last year as a bouncer at Toulouse's Bar a couple of blocks from the Grande so he decided to stop in and see the owner. New Year's Day was on a Saturday, so he was hired to work Thursday, Friday and Saturday, New Year's Day. The pay was good, eight dollars and fifty cents per day. Last year, he worked eight hours, from 900 p.m. to 5:00a.m., and only got five to six hours sleep. He managed to have a little fun during the off hours.

David wanted some action but didn't want to find it in Galveston. In Houston nobody really knew him and he could blend in with the locals. David figured that there wouldn't be much going on Christmas Day and decided to take a later train out of Galveston and get there around 8:00 p.m. Christmas Day. The train station was fairly empty and few people were waiting in the depot. He figured he would catch a nap on the way and was glad the train would be half empty.

His usual seat was empty at the back of the train so he settled in and picked up a day-old newspaper. He was scanning through it when a man stopped and asked, "It's Brooks isn't it?" David looked up, eyeing the man. He looked familiar, but David couldn't remember where he had seen him.

"Yes," said David, "and you are...."

"Husky, from Galveston Police Department. We met a few weeks back. You were a witness to a murder," said Detective Husky. David tried to ignore him but Detective Husky took the seat across from him.

"I used to live in Houston," said Husky. "My wife and two kids are there visiting her sister and I just got off work for a couple of days so I'm joining them tonight." David tried to be polite but surely didn't want to spend the next hour and a half talking to a police detective. "You got family there?" asked Husky.

David shook his head no and said, "Just some friends. I don't have much family, at least not in Texas. If you don't mind, I've had a long day and I'm gonna try and get some shut eye," David said as he put the newspaper over his face and slumped back in his seat.

"Sure, sure, you go ahead," Husky said. David was irritated and closed his eyes for a while, hiding behind the newspaper. He could hear Husky's heavy breathing and every once in a while he let out a belch. David stood up and said he was going to the dining car for some coffee.

"Great idea," Husky said as he jumped up and followed David. Darn, thought David, now I'll never get away from him.

The two men sat down at a small table and ordered coffee. Husky pulled out a cigar and lit it and David rolled a cigarette and put it in his mouth. Husky leaned up with his match to light David's cigarette, and David sucked in.

"You know," said Husky, "the Negro who killed that young woman, Joseph March, was his name, I believe, well he maintained his innocence up until he died. He signed a suicide note that the chief wrote for him because he couldn't write. But I was wondering, how did you manage to knock him out and hardly get a scratch?"

David bit his lip and didn't look at Husky. "I already told your chief that he crabbed Mrs. Eastman first and pulled her into the alley. I knew he was a lot bigger than me, so I saw a pipe on the ground and picked it up. I guess I caught him by surprise," David said.

"Was that before or after he stuck Mrs. Eastman?"

David got confused and said, "Before, no, I mean it was after she was going down. It all happened so fast, and I thought the son-of-a bitch was going to kill me, so I hit him with the pipe."

"I see," said Husky, as he rubbed his chin with his hand.

David was relieved when the conductor finally announced that the Houston stop was coming up, so he put a dime on the table for the coffee and waited. David jumped off the train before it came to a complete stop and was half way down the street when Husky stepped off. Something ain't right about that man's story, thought Husky.

Sergeant Husky's brother-in-law, Jack Shaker, met him at the train station.

"The girls are home cooking up a storm," said Jack.

"Glad the train was on time, then, 'cause I could eat a horse," Husky said.

The two men had a lot in common. Jack Shaker had been with the Houston Police Department and worked the beat in the Fourth Ward for over six years. Sergeant Husky also had worked with the Houston Police Department for five years before going to Galveston. Husky had introduced Shaker to his wife's sister and they got married.

"So what's going on in your neck of the woods?" asked Husky.

"Just the usual; drunks, druggies, prostitution -- and in the last month we've had two sisters who were prostitutes get murdered."

"Is that right?" asked Husky.

"You know, funny thing, a few weeks ago we had a prostitute die from strangulation," said Husky. "What was your cause of death?"

"Same thing," Shaker replied. "And then there was a teenager who was hung from the ceiling by her step-dad who claims he came home and found her that way," Shaker went on to say. "Funny thing though, we found some fingerprints on a glass, that didn't belong to either the victim or her dad. He'll probably do the time for it though, seeing as how there were all sorts of restraints in both bedrooms." Shaker said.

"Lots of sick people in this world," said Husky. Shaker agreed.

David caught the trolley over to the Fourth Ward and headed over to Josie's place, where he figured he could get a free meal. Josie answered the door and she was glad to see he had survived his last episode where he had almost gotten killed. "Supper's on," said Josie as she motioned David in. There were two other girls and an old friend of Josie's seated at the dining room table. She introduced them to David and went into the kitchen to get another plate.

"Wow, Josie," said David, "I bet you've been cooking all day. It looks like a feast."

The entire dining room table was covered with food. Fried chicken, meatloaf, mashed potatoes, collard greens, black eye peas, corn bread, as well as corn on the cob. David loaded up his plate and complimented Josie on her cooking. He found out that the two girls sitting across from him worked for Josie and the man was a frequent sleeping companion of Josie's.

When they were through, one of the girls asked where he was staying and he told her he wasn't sure, since Josie already had a visitor.

"You can stay with me," she said. She was a cute little thing, David thought, probably just sixteen or seventeen years old. She was kind of mousey looking and her name was Deborah, Debbie for short.

David smiled at her and said teasingly, "I'm out of work for a few days and I'm kind of short on money, so I'm not sure I can afford you."

"Well," she said, "seeing as how it's Christmas, maybe Josie won't take her cut and I could give you a reduced price."

"David, why is it you are always taking my money?" Josie said, kidding.

"You always take care of me Josie, you know you're like my second mother," David teased.

Josie poured some whiskey for everyone after dinner and they talked some more. Afterward, Debbie got up and stretched. She took David's hand and said, "Great supper, Josie, but me and David have some unfinished business to take care of."

David got up to go, too, but not before he filled his glass again with Josie's whiskey. The two went down the hall.

"And here I was, thinking I was going to have to spend Christmas all alone," said Debbie. When they got inside Debbie's room, there were several candles burning and the room smelled like jasmine. They could hear some soft music playing from a canteen across the street and David was already feeling the moment. Debbie threw her shawl across a chair and began untying the front of her blouse. Her breasts were unusually large and David watched with pleasure. He walked over to where she was undressing and kissed her neck.

"Hmmm," Debbie sighed. "That's so nice."

David reached his hand around the back of her skirt to untie it and it fell to the floor. Debbie reached up and began putting small light kisses on his neck and he leaned down for more. Next, she unbuttoned David's pants and pulled them down below his knees. David stepped out of his pants and picked up Debbie. They were both caught up in the moment when the door opened and Irene, the other girl from dinner, came in and said, "May I join you?"

David looked up and grinned at her. He motioned her in and then sat Debbie on the bed. "Strip," David said harshly and she did. While they were waiting for Irene to take her clothes off David crawled in bed with Debbie and then Irene joined them. The three spent the night together.

David slept until 11:00 a.m. the next morning. When he woke up both girls were gone. Oh no, thought David, as he checked his pants pocket. His money was still there. He was relieved about that and smiled at himself thinking about the great sex he had had the night before. He went down to Josie's room in hopes of getting some breakfast. Josie let him in and asked how the night went.

"Couldn't have been better," joked David. "You've got some good girls there, Josie. Guess you taught then everything they needed to know." Josie smiled and agreed with David.

"I know I owe you some money, Josie, and I plan to pay you, but I am a little short right now. I will be getting a little extra cash as a bouncer for three days over New Year's and I will hold some back for you," David replied.

"That's all right; I know you are doing the best you can. All I ask is you don't hurt any of my girls." Josie said.

"You know I wouldn't do that," David answered. "But the girls are fine. Ask them next time you see them." Josie heated up some leftovers and David ate again before he kissed Josie on the cheek and left.

David decided to take a walk over to Vickie's old place. He wasn't sure why. She was a sweet little thing, David thought to himself. He was a half-block away when he saw the front door of Vickie's house open and two men come out. He ducked behind some hedges and watched. One of the men was Sergeant Husky, and he heard him call the other man in a police uniform, "Jack".

What the devil is he doing here? David wondered. He tried to listen to what they were saying.

"Poor little thing didn't stand a chance with her old man. He was a giant compared to her," Jack said. "I'm still baffled by the fingerprints on that other glass we found in this girl's bedroom. We found the same fingerprints on an empty glass of another hooker who had been murdered several weeks before. They looked fresh. Maybe this girl had had sex with the same man who killed the other whore. Whatever the case, it looks like her step-father had been molesting her for some time. One thing's for sure, there is another murderer still out there, and we have his fingerprints."

The two men walked up the street talking, but David could no longer hear their conversation. He began sweating and watched them as they turned the corner. Wow, he thought. I've got to be more careful. David wasn't sure what they meant by fingerprints. They certainly did not have his as far as he knew. They might be on the glasses he drank out of, but since they did not have a stamp of his fingerprints, he was safe.

Sergeant Husky and Officer Jack Shaker were straight arrows. Sure, they often looked the other way when they saw others in their department taking short cuts and accepting a few bribes, but they tried to stay honest. Fingerprinting of convicts was something new to both of them but they read books and tried to figure out ways to solve crimes faster. The Houston Police Department had just begun having an evidence locker where they filed things away. Galveston was still behind Houston in solving crimes and unless there were witnesses, most crimes, especially murders of prostitutes, went unnoticed. It was not a priority. Husky and Jack spent hours talking when they spent time together. They were like brothers and thought alike. Neither liked the way the murders were prioritized, especially in Houston, where there were so many that took place in the red light district.

Husky gave Jack an overview of Anne Eastman's case and how the mayor wanted it solved quickly. Husky still had reservations regarding Joseph March's innocence and told Jack that David Brooks' story didn't add up. They decided to stay in close contact and let the other know by wire if any more prostitutes were murdered, and the details surrounding them.

David went back to Josie's house to get another free meal and if he was lucky, another free night of sex. He would leave the next morning and go back to Galveston.

CHAPTER 23

Catherine tried to concentrate on her studies. She kept thinking about living with John and Amelia and the excitement of going to a real school made her giddy. It was hard not to tell Katy and Erika. They asked her a lot of questions when she came back from looking after Amelia, but she tried to make light of it and said she mostly sat and tried to keep Amelia's spirits up. They also asked if Mr. Merit had ever tried to kiss her and she blushed and said, "Only on my cheek." Catherine wasn't sure when John Merit was going to pick her up from the orphanage and the next week dragged by.

The next Sunday, Catherine prepared herself again in hopes that John was coming. She hadn't heard any news about Amelia and if she still wasn't well, John wouldn't be able to come. She looked out the window of her room toward the street and saw John in his buggy a half block away. She grabbed her bonnet and ran downstairs and knocked on Sister Margaret's door. When Sister Margaret opened the door, she said that Mr. Merit had come for her, and was it all right for her to leave? Sister Margaret said that she needed to visit with Mr. Merit first and that he should come in. John Merit was in Sister Margaret's office for close to a half hour. Catherine sat outside wringing her hands and wondering what they could possibly be talking about.

Finally, the door opened and John came out saying to Sister Margaret, "I certainly understand and appreciate your advice." John took Catherine's hand, pulling her up, and the two of them walked outside to the buggy.

"May I ask what Sister Margaret wanted?" Catherine asked John. John smiled at her and told her that she had been talking to Father Jonathan about their plans and wished only the best for them.

"They really like you and are sad to see you leave; they wanted to be sure you understood what you might be getting yourself into," John said.

"Getting myself into?" asked Catherine.

"Well," John said, "as an example, when you start the next semester next week at Ball High School, and you meet a more suitable and age-appropriate young man, you might become resentful and be sorry you married me."

Catherine sighed and thought for a moment. "I suppose anything can happen, but you need to remember that I, too, will have made a commitment. My studies and future education is what I am most concerned about and besides, no young naive boy could ever measure up to you, Mr. Merit. You have spoiled me."

John smiled at her, and at that moment he was sure he was doing the right thing.

He began filling Catherine in on the plans for the day. First, they were going over to Minnie Wyman's house to get her mother's trunk. After they picked up the trunk, they had an appointment at 2:30 with Father Jonathan as he wanted to talk to both of them together. Depending how long that took, if there was time they would go back to John's house, visit with Amelia, and drop off the trunk before taking her back to the orphanage.

They stopped at Minnie's house long enough to pick up the trunk and explain to her that John was going to keep the trunk at his house so Catherine could go through it. Minnie hugged Catherine for a long time before she let her go and sadly bid her a good-bye.

"What could Father Jonathan possibly want to talk to us about?" asked Catherine nervously.

"I think he just wants to be sure you are fully aware of your rights and that you are doing this for the right reasons," John said.

"Well, I'm not changing my mind. I've thought about this a long time and I really think my mother would approve," Catherine said boldly.

When they got to Father Jonathan's office his door was open and he motioned them in. There were two chairs across from Father Jonathan's desk and he asked them to have a seat. Catherine was fidgety and took a deep breath, sinking into one of the chairs. John shook Father Jonathan's hand and sat next to Catherine.

"Traditionally, I like to visit with the couple before they say their marriage vows and while your intentions may be honorable, I felt I needed to give you the church's view on your arrangement," said Father Jonathan. "Catherine, is it your understanding that once you are married, it will be in name only and that you will not cohabitate as man and wife?"

"Yes, Father," Catherine answered in a soft voice.

"And John Merit, is this your agreement as well?" Father Jonathan asked John.

"Yes, Father," John answered.

"Good, then it is understood that if you meet these conditions, on Catherine's eighteenth birthday, either of you may request an annulment from the church," Father Jonathan continued. "And you will both respect each other's wishes and not contest it." John and Catherine answered yes at the same time. "I know you both will take your vows seriously and abide by the rules of the Holy Catholic Church. I will expect both of you to come to confession often and will be available for counseling in the event either of you might need it."

"The second semester of Ball High School will begin on January 10th. You have my permission to pick Catherine up along with her things up on Saturday the 8th. I see no reason why you and Catherine cannot be married after mass on the 9th and she can enrol at Ball High School as Catherine Merit," Father Jonathan said, grinning widely.

John's jaw dropped and he said, "That's wonderful."

Catherine was so surprised she found it hard to speak. "I, I guess so," she finally said.

John and Catherine didn't say a whole lot on their way over to John's house. Catherine felt a bit awkward and she looked up at John. "It's not too late to change your mind, I'll understand," said Catherine.

"I've already made up my mind, but are you having second thoughts?" asked John. "No, I don't think so, it's just not how I envisioned married life would be," Catherine said softly. "Are you going to be all right with not having sex?" Catherine asked.

John was astonished that Catherine was so blunt. "Of course," said John. "Just don't make it hard for me. I'm human and I have needs, too. Sometimes, the way you look at me with those beautiful, wide brown eyes, I desire you, but I will do the best I can to keep my hands off of you. I just ask that you do the same.

Catherine smiled, knowing this would be her greatest challenge. She had never had sex, and like most girls her age wondered what it would be like giving herself to the man she loved. Every time she was with John he gave her goose bumps and there was a yearning inside her that escalated every time John touched her. She dreamed of having him and giving herself to him. Living in the same house and seeing him every day was really going to be hard. It's the only way, she thought. I have to do this. I want to be with him.

When they arrived at John's house, he carried the trunk upstairs and Catherine visited with Amelia in the living room. Catherine told Amelia about their visit with Father Jonathan and that they would get married the next Sunday. Amelia was excited for both of them and asked Catherine if she had something to wear.

"I'm not sure, would you help me go through my mother's trunk and see if there is something she had that I could wear?" Catherine asked Amelia.

John helped Amelia up the stairs and half way up he picked her up and carried her into her old bedroom. Amelia squealed with laughter as John sat her down on the bed.

Catherine opened the trunk and paused, remembering that when she and Minnie had packed it before she left, her mother's wedding dress was inside it. Amelia asked her if she was all right and Catherine shook her head yes.

"It's just all so surreal to me. My mum won't be here for my wedding," Catherine whispered.

"We don't have to do this right now," answered Amelia.

Catherine didn't answer; she began taking things out of the trunk. The newer clothes were on top and, as she unpacked them, she found several of her mother's favorite dresses she used to wear to church. All of them had been beautifully made by her mother. The last dress close to the bottom of the trunk was her mother's wedding dress. Catherine pulled it out and held it up, beaming at Amelia.

"I think I just found my wedding dress," said Catherine, smiling. "My mother was sixteen when she married my dad and it looks like my size."

Catherine took her dress off and pulled the beautiful lace dress over her slip. The dressed stopped just below her ankles. She backed up to Amelia for her to button the tiny buttons on the back. It was a perfect fit. Catherine reached down in the trunk and pulled out a small hat that had tiny pearls sewn around the rim and toile surrounded by lace cascading from one side. She placed it carefully on her head and used one of the hat pins to secure it.

"You look beautiful," Amelia gasped as she smiled with pleasure.

Catherine looked at her reflection in the stand-up floor length mirror and said, "My mum would want me to wear this." She looked at Amelia and asked if she thought John would like it.

"He will be completely mystified by your beauty," answered Amelia.

Catherine carefully took off the dress and hung it on a dress hanger that was also in the trunk and placed it in the closet so John wouldn't see it if he came in the room. After she hung the other things in the closet and put away a few of her mother's personal belongings, Catherine looked in the trunk and found some old letters in a leather pouch and some family photos she placed around her new room. This was her new home now and she was determined to make it work. Catherine opened one of the letters and read it. It was a letter from her grandmother to her mother right before her wedding day telling her that she would be honored if Anne would wear her wedding dress on her wedding day. Catherine held the letter to her breast and knew that her mother had saved the dress for her. It warmed Catherine's heart knowing the history of the dress.

"I'm afraid it's time for me to take you back to the orphanage," John said to Catherine. They went downstairs and Amelia hugged her and gave her a wink. They had just enough time to stop by the cemetery on the way, and then Catherine returned to the orphanage.

CHAPTER 24

David woke up in Debbie's room after a night of drinking and sex. He was tired and hungry so he stopped by Josie's to say good-bye. She fed him again and he left to catch the next train back to Galveston. Debbie tried to talk David into staying another night but he had had enough, at least with her. It was 2:00 p.m. on Monday when the train pulled up to the station.

Two hours later, David was back in Galveston. He stopped in at the Toulouse Bar to mingle with the crowd and have a drink. If he was going to take care of the riff-raff over the New Year's celebration he wanted to check out who the regulars were and who the troublemakers might be. It felt good to be back in Galveston. He had a bad feeling about running into Sergeant Husky and the other police officer, but he shook it off. They don't have anything on me, David thought, and if they try and mess with me I'll just have to protect myself. I can outrun that Sergeant Husky and, if he is not careful, he just might have an accident. There was a poker game going on in the back room of the Toulouse Bar and someone asked David to join them. He was short of cash, so he said no and left. The Toulouse Bar was quiet at this time of day and David grew bored hanging around.

David started walking over to the Strand to see if there might be some action there. He was getting anxious and could feel his adrenalin begin to rush. He stopped on the corner and waited. The sun was setting and he looked at the clock on the street corner. It read 6:30. China town was located just off the main drag, so David hopped a cable car and rode over to see what was going on. The streets were crawling with vendors selling incense, trinkets, and food. He could smell the dried chicken and duck hanging off the trellises of their carts and he decided to try one. It was tough, but tasty. The chattering of the Chinese language roared at every intersection. Out of the corner of David's eye, he noticed an attractive Chinese girl across the street just standing in a doorway with her arms crossed. She smiled at him and he crossed over and nodded his head.

"You want sex?" she asked.

"How much?" David asked.

"One dolla," she said.

David knew he was in unfamiliar territory and he had to be careful. "I'll give you fifty cents," David said.

The oriental looking girl opened the door and motioned David to come in. He was surprised when he saw an older woman standing in the living room holding her hand out. The young girl said something in Chinese and they spoke to each other for a minute. He had no clue what was said.

"Give my mother the money," said the young girl, "and follow me."

David did as he was told and followed the girl to a back room. There was a mat on the floor and a chair beside it. She took off her dress and stood naked, looking at him.

David could smell opium in the room and he breathed in a deep breath. He unbuttoned his pants and walked over to the girl. It was over in a matter of minutes. He collapsed on the mat beside her, breathing fast. She got up and put her dress back on.

"Hurry, out, out."

David buttoned his pants and watched her dress.

"Out," she repeated, pushing him.

He walked out and the old lady was still in the living room looking at him.

The girl said, "You leave now."

David left and was dumbfounded by what had just happened. Apparently, the parents used their own home to whore out their daughter and waited around while she took care of her customer. When David left, he looked over his shoulder.

"You come back again," she said. David shook his head and walked over to catch the trolley.

On his way back, he noticed a young black girl on a bicycle turn a corner so he decided to jump off the trolley and follow her. It was beginning to get dark now and he had to walk fast to keep up with her. She turned down an alley and hit a pot hole, causing her to lose control of her bicycle and it turned over on her. David walked up to her and said "You hurt?"

The young girl looked up at him and said she was all right. He looked around the dark alley and didn't see anyone. She couldn't have been more than sixteen. She tried to get up and David picked up the bicycle and moved it so she could get up. When she got up, David cupped his hand over her mouth and pulled her further into the darkened alley. He picked her up and carried her as she struggled, trying to get loose. David opened the door to what appeared to be an old greenhouse. He knocked over several pots getting her in the door and he sat her on a table while she continued to struggle. She managed to free herself long enough to bite David's hand and he cursed. He grabbed her as she tried to get away and then put his hands around her neck and choked her. After a few minutes she collapsed. David moved quickly, and after he ended her precious life, he picked up the girl, carried her to the back corner and put her on the floor between some broken pots. He stood looking at her lifeless body. The hunt was over and he had conquered his prey. He felt alive again. David slipped out of the greenhouse, looking around to make sure there wasn't anyone close by. It was clear and he disappeared into the night.

Sergeant Husky was on duty when a Negro boy came running into the station.

"Come quick," he said. "Come quick. Someone just killed my sister." It was 10:00 p.m. when Husky looked at the clock. "She was supposed to come straight home and when she didn't, we went looking for her," said the boy.

"What's your name?" asked Sergeant Husky. "Terrance, Terrance Martin, sir," said the boy. "Hurry," the boy waved as he motioned to the door. Sergeant Husky waved to one of the other detectives to follow him.

They had to walk fast so they could keep up with Terrance and followed him about six blocks before he turned down a street. They continued to follow him and Terrance stopped several times so they could keep up with him. He finally motioned down an alley and took off. Husky and the other detective turned down the alley and saw a crowd of people holding lanterns.

They made their way through the crowd and heard a woman wailing at the top of her lungs.

"My angel, my angel, why, why?"

They finally made their way to the door of the greenhouse and saw a black woman bending over a young girl. They made their way over to the woman and gently got her up and walked her out of the greenhouse.

"Can someone tell us what happened?" asked Husky.

A Neegro man who identified himself as the uncle of the little girl told him that when Natasha didn't come home they went looking for her. When they found her bicycle in the alley, they got some lanterns to search the alley. The door to the greenhouse was halfway open so someone went in and saw her on the ground. Husky took one of the lanterns from someone and held it closer to the young girl. He saw blood coming from her mouth and her pantalets had been removed.

"Did anyone here see or hear anything?" asked Husky.

It was quiet and no one responded to his question.

"I didn't think so," Husky replied. Husky turned to the mother and said, "I'm sorry for your loss ma'am. Do you want to call the undertaker or shall we handle it?" He hated being so cold, but it was really out of his jurisdiction. It was unusual that the police department was even contacted. The blacks pretty much took care of their own. The uncle stepped forward and told Husky that the family would see to the burial.

It bothered Sergeant Husky that there was little they could do. Probably one of their own kind did it, he thought, maybe even the uncle. Since there were no witnesses there was little the police could do. The crime seemed strangely familiar, but it was far away from the red light district. He wondered if the murder could be related to the others. There was no way to know, so he decided to forget about it.

Catherine went about her usual chores after school on Tuesday. She noticed that Lillie Mae had not come in and there was laundry everywhere. She thought it was unusual, and wondered if Lillie Mae had taken ill. A few minutes later the caretaker, Mr. Jackson, came in and filled the tubs with water. "Where is Lillie Mae?" asked Catherine.

"She's in great distress," Jackson said. "Seems her oldest daughter was attacked last night and murdered." Jackson left out the part about the rape as he thought Catherine would be embarrassed.

"Oh no," Catherine said in disbelief. "Did they catch the person who did it?"

"No ma'am," said Jackson.

Catherine felt a knot in the pit of her stomach. She wanted to know more, but could sense Mr. Jackson's uneasiness talking about it. She felt terrible for Lillie Mae. Catherine put her sewing down and went over to help Jackson with the laundry. After he washed the clothes, Catherine took the basket of clothes outside to hang on the clothes line.

When the dinner bell rang, she went over to Mr. Jackson and said, "If you see Miss Lillie Mae, would you tell her that I will pray for her and her family?"

"Yes ma'am," Jackson replied.

Catherine felt ill just thinking about Lillie Mae losing her

daughter. She wished she could go to the funeral but knew that was out
of the question. If only she could just see John and talk to him. It
would only be a few more days and he would come for her.

That night Catherine dreamed she was back on the ship wearing
her mother's wedding dress and she was being chased by the man who
had attacked her on the ship. She woke up in a cold sweat, crying. One
of the girls went to get Sister Maria. "Shh, it's all right," she heard Sister Maria say. "You're just having a bad dream."

Catherine hugged her tightly and said she was fine now. Sister
Maria hesitated and reassured Catherine that everything would be all
right.

It was Thursday when Lillie Mae came back to work. Catherine
saw her earlier in the morning as she went into the laundry room. She
wanted to go to her but she had to go to her class and didn't want to get
in trouble for being late. The morning seemed to drag by and Catherine
could hardly concentrate on her studies. Before her last class, she
asked Sister Margaret if she could skip the class and go help Lillie Mae
with the laundry. Sister Margaret knew that Catherine was very fond of
Lillie Mae, and granted her request. When Catherine walked in, Lillie
Mae did not look up. She was busy scrubbing clothes so Catherine
walked over to her and touched her arm. Lillie Mae looked up, dried
her hands off and the two hugged each other tightly.

"I know nothing I could say would make you feel better," said
Catherine, "but I just want you to know I have had you in my prayers
and thoughts since I received the news."

"Ain't nothing nobody can do," Lillie Mae said., "The police
ain't no help and we'll never know who did it. Natasha was a good girl
and never hurt nobody. She had gone to the store for me. Some terrible person murdered my little girl and raped her." Lillie Mae fought
back the tears as she told Catherine what had taken place. Catherine
had not heard about the rape and she felt terrible for Lillie Mae.

"I wanted to go to her funeral, but I had no way to go," said
Catherine.

"We best git back to work," Lillie Mae said. "It keeps my mind occupied so I's don't cry."

Catherine wanted to tell Lillie Mae about her getting married next week but knew it was not a good time. Catherine helped her the rest of the day with the laundry, and soon it was 5:00 and time for dinner.

Friday was New Year's Eve, and all Catherine could think about was John Merit. It was quiet at the orphanage and the sisters tried hard to come up with things to occupy the children. There was a big parade in town, but there was no way to transport the eighty-plus children who lived at the orphanage. There was a light, misty rain outside and it was probably just as well, Catherine thought to herself. The waiting was unbearable for her. She sewed, read, and as always, talked with Katy and Erica. She wanted to tell them at some point about her upcoming marriage but wasn't sure how to explain it to them. She just might say that she was going to live with a relative but decided the truth was better. Once she was married she knew she would want to come back and visit with them and share her news about her marriage.

David Brooks was glad when he started working at the Toulouse Bar. He hated having idle time on his hands. As usual, there was nothing in the paper about the little black girl who had been murdered. He really wasn't worried, though. Except for Sergeant Husky, no one in the police department paid much attention to the black folks. There was a murder or two in the black community every week.

The Toulouse Bar was packed New Year's Eve. David had carefully strapped his ankle holster with his knife around his leg. He was determined not to take any crap from anyone. There was another guy named Larry who worked as a bouncer there full time.

"Just mingle through the crowd and make sure nobody walks their check. I'll be checking in with you from time to time throughout the night," Larry told David.

There was a small band playing the latest music but the dance floor was small and crowded. New Year's came and went and except for a few rowdy people every one was just having a good time. As 2:00 a.m. approached, the crowd had thinned out except for the prostitutes and drunks. A couple of men got into a fight over a woman, but David and Larry broke it up and kicked them out. All in all, the evening ended pretty well and David was glad he didn't have to use his knife. He didn't want another confrontation with Sergeant Husky. When his shift ended he was paid his eight dollars and fifty cents and he left to find a poker game. He was only able to steal a few drinks from the bar when no one was looking, so he needed a drink. After stopping to buy some more tobacco and some whiskey, he walked over to Fat Alley where he knew he could pick up a game of poker. It was the usual crowd. An empty seat came up and David sat down. After four rounds, David grew impatient over his repeated bad hands. Finally, he got a hand with two jacks and a pair of threes. Not great, he thought, but maybe he could bluff his way through it. After several raises David was into the pot for four dollars and fifty cents, and he needed badly to win. A full house beat him out and he threw in his cards, got up and left. He probably wouldn't have bid it up so high but he still had one more night to work at the Toulouse Bar and another night's pay. Saturday night was a slow night. He guessed that most of the crowd partied the night before. When it didn't pick up after midnight, the owner came over and game him a five dollar bill and told him they didn't need his services anymore. David was two weeks behind in his rent and it was going to take all he had in his pocket. He knew his best chance of getting some cash was to pick up a hooker later in the evening after she got through with her nightly work and had some cash in her purse.

David decided to take the back way around to the red light district and come up an alley so he wouldn't be seen. He kept his eyes fixed on his surroundings so he could avoid any crowds. He stopped halfway down an alley and waited in a back doorway. It wasn't long before he heard a man and woman turn down the alley.

"We can just take care of your business here," she said to the man. I need the money first." David watched as she took his money and put it in her purse. David waited while the man undid his drawers and pleasured himself. It was over in a matter of minutes. The man closed up his drawers and turned and ran down the alley into the street.

David moved fast. The hooker was adjusting her clothes and was still facing the building when David struck her on the head with a brick he had picked up. She fell to the ground and never saw David. He thought about raping her, but he heard voices, so he picked up her purse and ran down the alley taking the money out of her purse and throwing the purse into a trash can. When he got to the street he stopped and began walking slowly toward the trolley that was coming. David stuffed the money in his pocket. He would count it later when there weren't so many people around.

David pulled the lever for the next stop and got off the trolley. He walked the four blocks to his apartment and went upstairs. Fourteen dollars, David counted. Looks like she scored a big night, he thought to himself. He was feeling better already. He had a couple of drinks and two cigarettes and then went to bed.

CHAPTER 25

Sergeant Husky was not happy about coming in on Sunday morning after he had worked through the New Year's breaking up fights and calling the undertaker to pick up dead bodies. He was going through paperwork when one in particular caught his eye. Another prostitute was found in an alley just around the corner from Fat Alley. Usually it just got filed with all the other murders. This one was different because it listed her death as blunt force trauma to the head. Her purse was missing so they figured it was a robbery. Since she was a prostitute, there was no way to determine if the john she did in the alley was the murderer or if someone was lying in wait in the alley. Husky made a mental note of it and filed it away. He also went to the evidence room and did something he had never done before. He pulled out one of the first dead prostitute's file from the closed file evidence drawer and looked through it. The matches were still in a small brown envelope. Husky folded the paper down to the size of the matches and put them in his pocket. When he got back to his desk he scribbled a short note and put it along with the matches in an envelope and addressed it to Sgt. Jack Shaker, Fourth Ward, Houston Police Department. He placed the envelope in the outgoing mailbox for Monday's pickup.

CHAPTER 26

This was going to be the last Sunday Catherine was going to spend with John before they were married and she had knots in her stomach while she waited. She was hoping that he might take her somewhere special in anticipation of their wedding day. She was always ready early and she was waiting by the window looking out. It was relatively cool outside and she had grabbed her coat and bonnet holding it while she waited for John's arrival. After an hour, she sat down on the bed disappointedly and laid down looking at the ceiling. She must have fallen asleep because Katy came over to her and told her Sister Margaret needed to see her. It startled her at first, but she jumped up and went downstairs, meeting Sister Margaret in the hall. She handed Catherine another envelope with John's hand writing on the front.

Catherine walked down the hall to the laundry room and went in. She opened John's letter with her scissors and began to read.

My dearest Catherine:

Amelia is not having a good day today and while she assures me she will be just fine; I felt I needed to stay with her. I was in some special meetings at the bank yesterday and had to leave her alone. We are having some problems at the bank. Please understand this has nothing to do with you. I am saddened by the fact that I have to wait another week to see you, but Saturday will be here soon. I am look-ing forward to the day we will be together. Please have pa-tience with me.

> *My love,*
> *John Merit*

She read John's letter several times and was saddened by the fact that it would be another six days before she saw him. She reassured herself she was doing the right thing. After all, he did say he was looking forward to the day they would be together. She worried that his letter seemed to have some bad undertones. What kind of trouble would he be having at the bank? She wondered. What about Amelia, was she always going to come first? Catherine scolded herself for being angry with Amelia. She knew it wasn't her fault. Catherine grabbed a shirt from her mending basket and began sewing it. She had to stay busy or she would go crazy, she thought.

John Merit was sitting as his desk on Monday and the dismal news about the bank's financial condition was at the top of everyone's agenda. He had known the bank was in trouble for a couple of months now, but it appeared to be much worse than he anticipated. Even though Galveston was the second-richest city in the United States, the bank's president had made some bad investments and the examiners were mulling over the books in another room. John was most concerned about Catherine's trust account. As the trust officer of her account, he had seen early signs of mismanagement and took it upon himself to take small amounts in two thousand, four hundred fifty dollar increments and deposit them in another account he had set up at another bank. He would have preferred to move all of the funds but knew it would be noticed if it exceeded two thousand, five hundred dollars. So far he had moved all but four thousand dollars, and he knew every withdrawal was now being scrutinized by the examiners and he might get caught if he continued. He also had a savings account in his name and he had withdrawn five hundred dollars once every other week. He had only transferred two thousand of his five thousand dollars savings.

If the bank was able to hold out, he would have Catherine withdraw the rest of her funds the week she moved in with him. He was beginning to worry about his own future. If the bank filed bankruptcy, not only would all the money be held and seized subject to accounting, but he would most likely be without a job. He was worried and concerned that maybe he moved to quickly in asking Catherine to marry him. With Amelia's last illness and the four days she was in the hospital, he still owed the doctor and hospital eight hundred ninety-five dollars. He decided to get a cashier's check from his savings account and have it made out directly to the St. Mary's Hospital. Over the weekend, John updated his resume on his typewriter at home and made several copies. At noon on Monday, John mailed them to several of the larger banks in Galveston. He would follow up at the end of the week.

Shortly after John withdrew the eight hundred ninety-five dollars from the bank, he was called into the examiner's office.

"Come in, Mr. Merit," said the examiner. "It has been brought to our attention that you have made a sizable withdrawal, and we were curious why this amount at this time?"

"My sister is not well and she was recently in the hospital. She has been incurring a number of medical bills that I felt I needed to pay off. I am her only living relative, and I take care of her," John replied.

"I see," said the examiner. "I needed to follow through on this because we do not want to have a run on the bank. As you know, we suspect some foul play here and we will be looking at all of the bank's employees."

"I understand," John replied. "I would not want that to happen either. The money in my savings account is my money and I have a right to use it as I please," John said.

"That is true," said the examiner, "but you know things about this bank most of its customers are not aware of, and it would not look good if you depleted all of your funds at this time."

"Yes sir," John said and he went back to his office.

When John went to leave for lunch, he saw the bank president arguing with one of the examiners and he knew it was only a matter of time before the bank went under.

The rest of the week didn't get any better and John spent most of his time getting all of his records for the trust account in order. John was glad when the weekend came, even though he was apprehensive about picking Catherine up from the orphanage. He decided he didn't want to ruin her day by telling her he might be unemployed soon, so he would wait until after they were married.

With the two thousand dollars he had managed to move to another bank, it would take care of his living expenses for at least a year if Amelia did not have another illness. By then he felt he would find another job in Galveston. If worse came to worst he had connections in Houston and they would just have to relocate there.

CHAPTER 27

Catherine had all of her things neatly folded and in her small travel bag. She hugged Katy and Erika good-bye and promised them she would come back to visit soon. Catherine felt badly about taking her sewing machine and decided to leave it for the orphanage. She knew her mother would approve. Before she left, she gave two of the younger girls lessons on how to use it and told Sister Margaret she would be happy to come back and show others as time went on.

John picked Catherine up at 9:00 a.m. Saturday morning and all the children stood on the front porch and waved good-bye. Catherine was touched. She had only lived at the orphanage a little over four months and she admired all the sisters. She knew she would miss Katy and Erika and assured them they would always stay friends.

John and Catherine stopped for a few minutes at the cemetery and, as usual, brought a beautiful bouquet of flowers. On the way, John asked Catherine if she needed anything from the store and she told him she would need shampoo for her hair and some toiletries. They stopped at the mercantile and John visited with an old friend he ran into while Catherine shopped. She wasn't sure how much she could spend, so she only got the things she really needed most. John was waiting at the cashier's station when she finished and he paid for everything. She smiled at him and thanked him. John noticed that her shoes were badly scuffed and asked her if she had another pair. She shook her head no.

"One of the girls at the orphanage grew out of hers so I gave her

The Arrival

my other pair," Catherine said. John smiled and they walked down the street to a clothing and dry goods store. She tried on several pair of shoes before deciding on a pair of light tan shoes. They would compliment her mother's wedding dress, she thought to herself.

"You are much too generous, Mr. Merit," Catherine mused.

"Amelia told me you are going to wear your mother's wedding dress for our wedding tomorrow," John said.

Catherine answered, "Yes, it's a perfect fit."

"Well, unless you can think of anything else, I need to go home and check on Amelia," John said.

Amelia had lunch waiting when they got to the house. She looked like she was feeling much better and the two girls hugged each other. After John finished his lunch, he excused himself and said he needed to go into his office and do some work.

Catherine went upstairs and put her things away and sat on the bed looking around. She couldn't believe tomorrow was going to be her wedding day. She decided to pamper herself and take a long bath. She wanted to wash her hair with her new shampoo, too, so she set everything out she would need in the bathroom. It was over an hour before Catherine finished and she dressed in one of her mother's dresses. It was a little big on her, but in time she would take in a seam or two. She looked in the floor length mirror at her reflection. She was surprised when she saw herself. She must have grown an inch and her hair was longer. It was still wet even though she towel dried it, so she pulled it back and wrapped it in a figure eight and stuck some hair pins in it. She had found some small gold earrings in her mother's trunk and she screwed them to her ears. She took out her new shoes and put them on, approving her final look.

She heard the grandfather clock strike three o'clock as she came down the stairs. Amelia's door was closed, so she thought her to be taking a nap. She wandered through the living room onto a small, enclosed porch that John used as his study. His back was to her and she cleared her throat. John turned and looked at her.

"Wow, you look beautiful," he said.

Catherine walked over to his desk and asked what he was working on.

"Just some figures, nothing important," he lied.

"What would you like me to do now?" Catherine asked.

"What do you mean?" asked John.

"Well, I had chores to do at the orphanage and I want to do my part of the housework and cooking," she said.

John smiled and looked at her. "The lady who comes in to help Amelia does some of it and Amelia helps when she feels like it. I try to help her as much as I can, but I'm afraid the house needs some attention. I don't expect you to do it all, but we could sure use your help. Perhaps you and Amelia could get together and talk about it," John answered.

Catherine smiled and said, "I think we can do that."

Catherine sensed John wanted to go back to his work so she went into the kitchen to make some hot tea. She was at the kitchen table drinking her tea and looking at the newspaper when Amelia came in. Catherine got up and poured her a cup of tea.

"I guess John's in his study," said Amelia

Catherine answered yes and told her he was deep in thought.

"There's a lot of stuff happening at the bank and I'm not sure what it is. John doesn't seem to want to talk about it," Amelia said. "He's been under a lot of stress lately," she continued.

"Do you think I may be the cause of some of his stress?" asked Catherine.

"No," Amelia answered. "You're the best thing that has happened to him."

Catherine was pleased by her answer. The last thing she wanted to do was cause John any more additional stress.

"Would you like to help me?" Amelia asked

Catherine was delighted, and the two worked side by side making a meatloaf. "John's favorite," said Amelia. After dinner, Amelia announced that John always did the dishes and that she was going to take a bath and go to bed.

John got up and started putting water in the sink to wash the dishes. "If you still have work to do, I'll do the dishes," Catherine offered.

John smiled at her and said, "Why don't we do them together?" Catherine was relieved that he wanted to be with her. John washed the dishes and Catherine dried them. Just feeling his warm body next to hers gave her goose bumps. He looked so handsome with his sleeves rolled up and an apron on.

When they finished putting the dishes away, they walked into the living room and sat down. It seemed awkward at first, but John broke the silence. "Is everything to your liking?" he asked.

"Of course," Catherine said. "I slept in a room with eleven other girls and ate in a crowded dining hall; what's not to like?"

John smiled and then his mood changed. "Catherine, if I seem distant or uncaring, please understand that it's not you or your being here. There are a lot of things going on at the bank, which are complicated, and which I can't discuss. I just want you to be comfortable here. It's your home, too."

Catherine felt his agony and wanted to hug him, but thought better of it. No touching, she told herself.

"You remind me of my father. He worried a lot about our family, too. My mother would always reassure him that no matter what, we were a family and we could get through anything together," Catherine said. "I've lived through a lot of bad things, Mr. Merit, and I can't think of anything that would change my feelings for you."

"You are wise beyond your years, Miss Eastman," John said. He stopped for moment, thinking. "There is one more thing though, I have my mother's wedding band and I wanted to know if you would wear it?"

Catherine was already wearing her mother's wedding band on her right hand and she agreed. "Would you wear my father's wedding band?" she asked John.

"Nothing would please me more," he said.

The next morning they all slept in a little later and then got up and readied themselves for the big day. Catherine had wrapped the wedding veil in some tissue she had saved from her box of new shoes and put it in her knapsack. When she came down the stairs, she had put her long blue coat over her dress so John couldn't see what she was wearing. After a quick cup of tea and a muffin, the three left for mass at St. Mary's. When mass was over, she excused herself and went to an open room where she had seen a small mirror and placed her veil on her head and took off her coat. When she walked back in, Father Jonathan, John, and Amelia were waiting at the altar.

She was the most beautiful bride John had ever seen. Even Father Jonathan's mouth dropped open when he saw her. She had grown into a woman overnight. John and Catherine quietly listened as Father Jonathan gave his blessing and then they exchanged vows. They placed the rings on each other's fingers and Father Jonathan gave John permission to kiss the bride. Catherine looked up into John's eyes, not sure where he might give her a kiss. Will he kiss my cheek, my forehead, or a quick peck on my lips? She hesitated, waiting. John bent down and pulled her up to him and kissed her softly on her lips, lingering long enough for her to feel her heart skip several beats. She smiled at him when he released her and they stared into each other eyes, lingering again long enough for Father Jonathan to clear his throat indicating that the ceremony was over. John handed Father Jonathan an envelope with some cash tucked inside and thanked him for everything. Father Jonathan acknowledged John's gift, and on his way out he placed it in the offering box.

John had made reservations at Ritter's Restaurant. It was one of Galveston's finest restaurants, and the chef was famous for his seafood. They had invited Father Jonathan to come but he had an afternoon baptism he had to attend to.

The food was divine and everyone couldn't help but notice the new bride and groom. Catherine had taken off her veil, but she glowed like the North Star and John was handsome in his dark blue suit and matching blue and grey tie. Several people John knew came over to the table and congratulated them and wished them well. Catherine could hardly eat because she was so excited and asked the waiter if he could put it in a container for her to take home. All in all, Catherine couldn't have wished for a more beautiful day. The sun was shining, it was only fifty-five degrees outside and the wind was blowing slightly, filling the air with the fragrance of the bay. She was never happier and if her mother were there, it would have been the perfect day.

It was after three o'clock when they finally made it home. Amelia excused herself to take a nap and Catherine went upstairs to change. When she came downstairs she had put on another one of the dresses she had made for her mother. It looked all right she thought, a little bit too big, but she thought John would like it. She walked through the house and noticed John had laid his coat and tie on a chair and was in his study working. Trying to understand the inner workings of a man's thoughts, Catherine subconsciously excused him, and set about trying to find something to do. She went into the kitchen and found the dirty dishes from the morning's breakfast and filled the sink with warm soap and water. Once she had dried them, she opened the cabinet and put them away. Catherine had placed her leftover food from her lunch in the ice box and then set about looking for something light she could make for dinner. She came up with the idea that the leftover piece of fish was large enough to make a small pot of fish chowder. She found some chicken fat that she could use for the broth and took out some fresh vegetables to add to the pot. There was an ample serving of rice also in her take home container and she went about making the stew.

The aroma was inviting and wafted into John's study. It distracted him from his work so he got up to find Catherine in the kitchen.

"Do you ever stop?" asked John as he stood in the kitchen door.

"Idle hands make idle people, Mr. Merit," Catherine answered.

"I see," answered John teasingly. "It smells wonderful, may I help?"

"The soup needs to simmer for a while so I was going to stop and make myself some tea. Would you like some?"

"Sure," answered John.

"I told my secretary that I would be in a little late in the morning. I wanted to go with you to Ball High School and see that you are placed in the appropriate grade. Sister Margaret told me that you were educated well beyond the twelfth grade so I thought you might enrol as a senior the last semester," John suggested.

"That would be wonderful," Catherine answered. "I know I haven't mentioned this, but if I graduate early I would like to go to night school at the college next summer and take more math and science classes. That way I can be home with Amelia during the daytime and you could be here in the evenings with her while I go to class. Would that be all right?" Catherine asked.

"Of course," John answered and then asked Catherine what she would like to do with her education.

"I want to go to medical school. We're close enough to Galveston's medical school that I could take the trolley and be there in a few minutes," Catherine went on to say.

"Wow," John answered, "that's very ambitious. You know that it is predominately an all male school. I've only heard that a few women have even graduated from there."

"I know," Catherine answered. "If the studies are too hard for me, I'm sure I wouldn't have any trouble getting transferred to their nursing program."

"You'll make it," John responded. "I have all the confidence in you."

They all enjoyed Catherine's fish chowder and after visiting for a while and doing the dishes, they kissed each other on the cheek and bid good night. Catherine went upstairs and pushed the door shut, but it did not shut completely. She went about undressing. She was temporarily lost in the moment, humming to herself and taking off everything she had on.

John was already in his pajamas and was walking across the hall to the bathroom when he caught a glimpse of Catherine's naked body. He couldn't help himself from stopping, and watched her for a few minutes. His excitement grew and he closed his eyes, envisioning her in his bed waiting for him. Catherine sensed his presence and walked over and opened the door further and was standing in front of him naked. When John opened his eyes, she was staring at him intently.

"I, I'm sorry," John said. "You're just so beautiful." They stood looking at each other. John flushed with embarrassment, and Catherine grabbed his hand and pulled him to her.

They kissed passionately and Catherine could feel his manhood as he put his arms around her and picked her up. John kicked the door shut with his foot and picked up Catherine, carrying her over to her bed.

"Oh, Catherine," John moaned, "I want you so badly."

"I want you, too," Catherine said softly in his ear.

Catherine unbuttoned John's night shirt and began kissing his chest. They were caught up in a moment of need, kissing and exploring each other's bodies, hot with desire and a sensation inside them that was about to explode. John stopped for a brief moment, breathing heavily, and tried to bring himself back to reality and out of the moment.

"When was your last menstrual cycle?" John asked.

"About ten days ago," Catherine answered. "Why?"

John looked at her with a strange expression then he sat up. "It's not a good time. You could become pregnant," he answered. He got up and put his night shirt back on. "I'm so sorry, Catherine; you need to think this through. Once we have sex, you're committing to stay in this marriage for the rest of your life," he continued saying as he walked to the door.

Catherine was stunned by his abrupt dismissal. She had no idea what he meant when he said this wasn't a good time. She hadn't thought about getting pregnant, and when was a good time? She was so confused. She still had an aching feeling in the pit of her abdomen and she felt the wetness between her legs. She touched her vaginal area with the warmth penetrating down her leg. Catherine rolled over and sunk her head into the pillow crying softly. She woke up a few hours later shivering from the cold. Her body was still naked so she found her nightgown and put it on. She crawled under the cover and pulled the quilt up for more warmth. If she didn't have John soon she was going to go crazy, she thought to herself. John tossed and turned in his own bed most of the night. He ached to feel Catherine next to him and was torn between wanting and needing her, but they had made an agreement. It was going to be a long two years, he thought.

The next morning, John was cordial to Catherine at breakfast and they spoke very little on their walk over to the trolley. John thought it best to walk the two blocks to the trolley that would carry them to a stop one block away from the school. There were children of all ages catching the same trolley, and John felt it would be safe for Catherine to use this means of transportation. It also made a stop at the Rosenberg Library. After a brief talk with one of the counselors, Catherine enrolled as a senior taking accelerated math, science, English, history, and biology. The counselor warned Catherine she would be the only girl in most classes, but Catherine did not seem to mind.

John kissed Catherine on the cheek and left so she could go to her first class. He didn't get a lot of sleep the night before. He heard Catherine crying and wanted to go to her, but thought better of it. If they were going to make this work, he was the one who had to be strong. Catherine acted so maturely that John had forgotten she was still a virgin and perhaps her mother had not explained to Catherine about the consequences of having sex. He didn't feel comfortable asking Amelia to talk to her because Amelia had never been married. John decided it would be best if he could try and find the right moment to speak with Catherine about it.

When John made his way to his office, his secretary followed him in and closed the door behind her. She looked like she had seen a ghost.

"What's wrong?" John asked.

"You haven't heard? Mr. Fulton committed suicide during the night." Fulton was the bank's president.

"Oh, no," John said as he sunk into his chair.

"Everything is crazy around here," his secretary continued. "What's going to happen to us?" she asked John.

"I'm not sure," John answered.

John got up and went down to the conference room where several of the bank's shareholders were talking.

"Come in, John," one of them said. "I guess you heard about Fulton," the man continued.

The attorney for the bank informed John the bank was going under and that bankruptcy was their only alternative; Fulton had made some really bad decisions and compromised the funds.

"In other words, we can't pay our loans and we are heavily in debt. All of the employees will be given their notice to clear out their personal belongings at the end of the day."

The bank locked its doors and left customers screaming and shouting outside. They had obviously heard about the suicide and the bank's pending bankruptcy. They wanted their money, too, and John didn't blame them.

John briefly told his secretary what he had been told and that she needed to clear out her desk and leave out the back door. He proceeded into the safe deposit box area and opened his personal safe box first. He took everything out and put it in a paper bag he had saved in his desk. When he finished, John opened Catherine's and took out her things, placing them in another paper bag. John put everything in his briefcase, took out his key to the bank and placed it on his desk.

John could only imagine the turmoil that was taking place at the front of the bank and he didn't want to get involved with people shouting questions at him. He was no longer an employee of Galveston Island Community Bank and he didn't have any answers. John made his escape out the back door unnoticed, and walked home.

Amelia and the lady who came to the house during the week from 11:00 a.m. to 2:00 p.m. were just sitting down for a sandwich when John came in. The sitter had already heard the gossip and filled Amelia in with all the details. John put his briefcase down in his study and joined them in the kitchen.

"Is it true?" asked Amelia. John nodded his head, yes. Amelia asked John if he wanted a sandwich and John said he wasn't hungry. When the sitter finished her sandwich, she asked John if he needed her the rest of the day. John told her she could leave, but that she was still needed as he would be spending the next few weeks working in his study and looking for a job.

"You'll find something else," Amelia assured John.

"I know," John answered. "I'm glad it's over. I hate that Fulton stole from so many people and that he killed himself. It's been a rough two months and I'm looking forward to taking my time so I can find the right fit," John said.

"What about the money?" Amelia asked.

"By my calculations, I have enough money set aside for at least six to eight months."

Amelia was relieved. John went upstairs and changed into some old work clothes and came back into the kitchen where Amelia was cleaning up.

"I'm planning to lay low for a couple of days. Of course, I'll attend Fulton's funeral, but I really don't want to talk to anyone right now," John said. "The outside of the house needs a lot of attention and now that I have some free time, I'm going to take care of the things I've been putting off. I've neglected so much since Catherine came into our lives. Oh, Amelia, God, I love her so much."

Amelia shook her head with understanding and said, "I know you are trying to do what is best for Catherine, but I think you should give her a chance to tell you what she thinks is best for her. She loves you too, John," Amelia said.

"I know," John replied, "but I want her to be sure this isn't some temporary fancy and that she won't wake up some day regretting this and hating me."

John put on his overcoat and went out the back door.

CHAPTER 28

David Brooks was in Tom Gregory's office when someone came in and told them about the suicide of Galveston Island Community Bank's president and the pending bankruptcy. Tom owned a few shares of the bank's stock and had a small checking account there and was naturally concerned. The Grande Opera House had their accounts at another local bank, and Tom was relieved they hadn't opened one at the Galveston Island Community Bank. Tom left his office and told David he would be back later.

Tom caught the trolley across town and walked the few blocks to John Merit's house. The two men had gone through high school together and had been friends ever since. John was on a ladder hammering some nails into the facia board on his house when Tom hollered up to him. John came down and shook his hand.

"I guess you heard the news," John said to Tom.

"Yeah," said Tom, "but only in pieces." John filled Tom in on all the details including the fact that he, too, was now unemployed.

"You'll find something else, you're a smart man, John Merit," Tom assured him. John smiled and thanked him for the compliment.

"I got married yesterday," John said grinning at Tom.

"What! And you didn't invite me? Who's the lucky girl?" Tom asked.

"Catherine Eastman," John said smiling.

"Wow," said Tom, "I would never have guessed that."

"I only did it so she could live with Amelia and me and not have to stay at the orphanage. It's purely an arrangement. Father Jonathan has given us his blessing. If we don't consummate the marriage, she can ask for an annulment when she turns eighteen," John explained.

"You mean, it's a marriage with no sex?" Tom asked.

"Exactly," John answered.

"Have you lost your mind?" Tom asked. "I've seen her and she's lovely; how will you manage that?"

John answered, "It's a test. I'll admit it's difficult, but I'm doing it for her."

Tom thought for a minute and said, "You've just lost your job and you're committed to a life of celibacy?"

"Only until she turns eighteen," John assured Tom. "She wants to be a doctor and I don't want to chance her getting pregnant. If by her eighteenth birthday she wants to still be my wife, well, we'll just have to wait and see."

Tom shook his head thoughtfully. "Good luck," he said, and left.

When Tom got back to his office he filled David in on the details of what John Merit had told him.

"He married her?" David asked not believing what he heard.

"Yeah, she started Ball High School this morning," Tom told him. "Don't you have work to do?" Tom asked David.

David left Tom's office and went back to what he was doing earlier.

It was close to 3:15 p.m. and David told Tom he needed something at the hardware store. He walked over the corner of Avenue H & 22nd Street and stood across looking at the high school that Catherine was now attending. He took out his tobacco and rolled a cigarette and stuck it in his mouth. He didn't light it. The place was crawling with men and women picking up their children on foot and in buggies. He waited until he saw Catherine coming down the stairs of the school. She turned and headed west. He figured she was going over to catch the trolley. David was still across the street and took off on foot trying to beat her to the trolley stop. She got there first and boarded the trolley. It was full, so she had to stand and hold onto the strap. David pushed his way past several children and came up behind her. Catherine turned and she was standing face to face looking at David. He was grinning ear to ear at her.

"Fancy meeting you here," David said. Catherine cleared her throat and didn't know what to say. "Heard you and that banker, John Merit, got hitched yesterday. I heard he got fired from the bank this morning," David continued.

"That's not true," Catherine protested.

"Oh, I'm sorry; I guess you haven't heard about the bank president's suicide and the closing of the bank. They terminated everybody," David told her as his arm brushed her arm. Catherine felt sick to her stomach and she turned white. "Didn't mean to upset you, Miss Catherine," David teased. "How would you like to stop and I'll buy you a soda?" David asked.

"I'd rather be dead than be caught with the likes of you," Catherine said. Several people were looking at them now, and Catherine blushed. Her stop was coming up and she hoped David would not get off, too. She still had to walk home two blocks. Catherine exited at the front of the trolley and when it left, David was out on the street with her, having exited out the back of the trolley. She ignored him and began walking home. David grabbed her arm and turned her around. He was holding her so tight that she was sure it would leave a bruise.

"Listen to me, you little wench. You're just as cocky and stuck up as your mother and if you aren't careful, I may just have to take you over my knee and spank you," David said sternly. Catherine twisted her arm from his grasp and ran as fast as she could. She didn't want to turn around for fear he might be following her.

Catherine ran up the stairs to the front porch and was relieved the door was unlocked. She ran upstairs and into her room closing the door behind her. John was on a ladder beside the house when he heard the door slam. He looked at his watch and figured that it was Catherine arriving home from school. He got down off the ladder and went inside. He wanted to tell Catherine what had happened before she heard it from someone else.

John looked throughout the downstairs and when he didn't find her he went upstairs and knocked on her door. "Catherine," John called as he knocked. She didn't answer. John slowly opened the door, calling her name again. He heard Catherine crying softly and walked around the bed to the closet where she was crouched down on the floor, shaking and crying.

"Oh my God...Catherine, honey, what happened?" He bent down and sat beside her, pulling her into his arms. "Shhh, I'm here, sweetheart, please tell me what's wrong." She put her arms around his neck and couldn't stop crying. She was hyperventilating and John was at a loss of what to do.

"I'll be right back; I'm going to get you some water," John said.

"No!" Catherine screamed out. "Don't leave me, please don't ever leave me," she said in a whimper.

John picked Catherine up and carried her to the bathroom. Holding her in his arms he managed to run the water and put a wash cloth under it. John carried Catherine back to her room, closing the door with his foot and then laid her on the bed.

Catherine was holding him so tightly that he had to gently grab both of her arms from around his neck. He took the wash cloth and began wiping the tears from her cheek. Catherine couldn't look at him.

"Please, please, I need a few minutes to myself," she stammered.

"I'm not going to leave until you tell me what happened," John insisted. She looked away and rolled over, turning her back to him. John got up.

"All right," he said. "If you want me to leave, I will."

John went downstairs and into the kitchen where Amelia was making some hot tea.

"Something must have happened at school today. Catherine is upstairs crying and I can't seem to get her to tell me what happened," John told Amelia.

"Do you think someone told her about the bank?" Amelia asked John.

"Maybe," he said. "But I think it's more complex than that."

"Perhaps she will talk to me," Amelia suggested. John smiled at her and was relieved that Amelia offered. John carried Amelia upstairs and she slowly opened the door to Catherine's room.

"Catherine," she said softly, "John and I are worried about you. Do you want to talk?"

Catherine was still lying on the bed holding the wash cloth tightly up to her face and shook her head, yes. Amelia lay down on the bed beside her and began caressing her hair.

"Did something happen at school today?" Amelia asked Catherine.

"No," Catherine answered softly. "He was on the trolley," Catherine whispered.

"Who was on the trolley?" Amelia asked.

"David, David Brooks," Catherine answered. Slowly, Catherine began relaying her encounter with David Brooks to Amelia. "I don't want to tell John," Catherine said. "I'm afraid he will retaliate and he could get killed," she continued.

Amelia breathed out and said, "You poor darling; it will be all right. John is a sensible man. Once he gets over being angry he will find means other than fighting to keep him away from you. It's going to be all right, I promise," Amelia reassured her.

Amelia walked down stairs and relayed everything Catherine had told her to John, and he was infuriated. He went into his study and retrieved his gun from his bottom desk drawer.

"And what are you going to do with that?" Amelia asked. "Shoot him and leave your wife and me here to fend for ourselves? You could go to prison or worse, he could shoot you first," Amelia continued.

"She's right," Catherine said coming into the room. "Please put the gun away. I'll be more careful in the future."

John reluctantly put the gun back in the drawer and walked around the desk to Catherine. He took her in his arms and whispered, "I don't know what I would do if anything happened to you."

"I'm all right now," Catherine said. "I was just so scared and shook up. I really think the man is evil."

"I'm sorry you had to hear about the bank's problems and my termination from someone else," John whispered. Amelia quietly left the room. John took Catherine over to his office chair and he sat in it, pulling Catherine onto his lap. "I promise I won't do anything stupid. I'm going to see you get to school and back home safely every day, even if I have to do it myself," he promised.

Catherine hugged him and said, "I love you."

After dinner, John took Catherine into his study and opened his briefcase. He told her about taking everything out of the safe deposit boxes and that he had been moving small sums of money from her trust account and putting it in another bank.

"You may lose the rest of the money I wasn't able to transfer," he told her, "but there is still plenty left for you to go to college. Whatever you need, I will supplement."

Catherine understood about the money. She knew John had done all he could to protect her trust. "And what about you?" Catherine asked.

"I'll find another job. There are over twenty banks in Galveston and if I persevere, I'm sure someone will hire me," John answered. He smiled at her and grabbed her hand, pulling her close to him. "I love you, too," he said.

She smiled at him and put her hand on his face and used her thumb to outline his lips. He opened his mouth slightly and she moved her lips to his. He grabbed her tightly and picked her up and carried her upstairs. This time he opened the door to his bedroom, went in and closed it.

He pulled the covers back and laid Catherine on his bed. Oh, how he wanted her, needed her, wanted to protect her. She was everything to him. Catherine lay still while he undressed her and she watched as he undressed. He caressed her neck and kissed it, moving down the front of her bosoms. Her nipples hardened and welcomed his lips. She moved her hands through his hair and relaxed, enjoying his every touch. John's hand began softly stroking her thigh and she responded with a moan.

He carefully began caressing her and whispered, "Oh Catherine, you are so beautiful."

He moved his hand slowly over her abdomen and she responded pushing herself closer to him. She welcomed his touch as he fondled her and found the spot most vulnerable. She felt the unexpected pleasure of his touch and she had never in her life experienced anything so gratifying. Catherine was not sure how or where to touch John, so she began kissing him passionately and he kissed her back. Catherine pulled John closer to her, encouraging him to go farther but instead he took her hand and moved it down until she felt him. At first she was surprised and John sensed her reaction so he pulled away. He knew this was her first time and he didn't want to scare her. Catherine was mad at herself for becoming tense and she felt guilty.

I, I'm sorry," she said. "This is my first time and I'm not sure what to do."

John put his arms around Catherine and looked at her and said, "You don't have to be upset, Catherine, it will happen when you are ready. Every time we are together it will get easier." John started to get out of bed but Catherine pulled him back.

"Can we just try that again? I won't be afraid, I promise."

They explored each other's bodies in ways Catherine had never experienced. She was amazed and surprised when she experienced her first climax. She had never felt anything like this in her life. Was this supposed to happen? she wondered. She grinned up at John and pulled him to her and kissed him. John took Catherine's hand and placed it on him and he put his hand over hers showing her how to pleasure him. She obediently followed his every move and began caressing him and he came. They lay together quietly enjoying the tender moment and then John got up and walked into the bathroom naked and returned with a towel. He wiped Catherine's body clean and then threw the towel on the floor. John lay back down beside her and put his arm around her, pulling her closer to him. She rested her head on his shoulder and purred like a kitten, savoring every moment with this wonderful sweet man who was her husband. John pulled the covers up over them. Before he went to sleep John bent down and kissed her lightly on the forehead.

"You're stuck with me now," he said.

Catherine nuzzled closer and bit his ear tenderly. "I want to be stuck with you the rest of my life," Catherine responded.

John closed his eyes and smiled. It had been a troubling day for everyone and he wasn't sure what he was going to do about David Brooks, but for now, Catherine was his, and he couldn't have been happier.

John woke up early the next morning, showered and dressed in his best suit and tie. He felt invigorated and was ready to find a new job. Catherine was still asleep so he went downstairs and made coffee for him and a cup of hot tea for her. He put the cup and saucer, teapot, and tea bag on a tray and walked out the kitchen door, meeting Amelia in the living room. He gave her a sheepish grin and she smiled.

"Good for you, it was about time," Amelia mused.

John took the tray upstairs and nuzzled Catherine awake. She turned over and smiled at him. "For you," as he pointed to the tea. "Now get dressed, I'm seeing you to school today," John said. She tried to grab his arm but he stepped back and smiled at her. "Later," he smiled.

Catherine was dressed and ready to go in twenty minutes. She brought the tray downstairs and sat down with John and Amelia, filling her bowl with some oatmeal. They caught each other's eye and both turned away.

"You look mighty handsome today," Catherine teased.

"After I take you to school I'm going on some interviews," John said. "By the way, there was so much going on yesterday I forgot to ask you how your first day of school was," John asked.

"Oh, it went fine. I like my teachers. I have one study hall right before lunch and they have a wonderful library," Catherine answered.

Amelia told Catherine that she had made her a sack lunch and hoped she didn't mind a bagel and cream cheese sandwich.

"It's my favorite," Catherine answered and thanked her.

John accompanied Catherine to Ball High School and told her he would be waiting at 3:20p.m. when school was out. She tried to protest and assured John she would be okay, but he insisted. John watched her every move as she walked up the stairs. He felt guilty about the night before. They had gone too far and he knew it. There was no turning back now. He knew that it would be impossible to live in the same house with Catherine and not have her. She devoured him, which only made him want her more. It was still too early to start checking out future employment so he decided to go over to Tom's office and talk to him about David. Tom was walking up the sidewalk when John got off the trolley.

"Tom," he called. Tom turned around and walked over to John. "Have a cup of coffee with me?" John asked. The two started walking down the street to the corner drug store. They found an empty table and ordered coffee.

"So what's up?" Tom asked. John told Tom about Catherine's encounter with David Brooks and that David had threatened her."

"What time was that?" Tom asked.

"After school about 3:20 p.m. yesterday," John replied.

"David told me he needed to pick up something at the hardware store," Tom said. "What do you want me to do, fire him?" Tom asked

John.

"No, I'm not sure," John said. "If he thinks that Catherine or I had anything to do with his getting fired he might come after Catherine. I just wanted you to know what kind of man he is. Maybe keep a closer eye on him, especially in the afternoon," John continued.

"Even if I fired him for other reasons he could still come after her. I've been thinking about letting him go for some time now, but there's no telling what he might do," Tom commented and then said, "He's not reliable, and he drinks a lot." Tom and John agreed that the best thing to do was to let it go for now and not say anything.

John headed over to the Tremont Hotel. Many of the bank officers stopped there to talk banking and he thought it would be a place to start. He had several resumes in his briefcase in case one of them asked for it. John's hunch was right. There were several powerful men there, smoking cigars and having a round-table discussion about the cost of cotton seed.

John walked over and said, "Good morning, gentlemen." They invited him to sit and join them. The conversation changed quickly and they all wanted to know about the bank's demise. John smiled and said he had been informed by the bank's attorney not to say anything and was sorry he couldn't share any privileged information. They already knew that, but wanted to ask anyway. The conversation turned to the suicide of Fulton.

"Can you believe he just blew his brains out?" one of the men said.

John didn't reply. No matter what kind of trouble Fulton got himself into, he was a nice man and always treated John fairly.

"So, what are you going to do now?" asked someone.

"Not sure," John said, "I've had a few offers, but nothing I want to jump on." He didn't like to lie, but didn't want anyone to think he was a charity case.

"I heard you were instrumental in creating a trust department for Island Bank, is that right?" asked one of the more powerful bank officers.

"Yes," John said. "I spent a week in Houston and shadowed one of the larger bank's trust officers there after attending a three day seminar."

"What are you doing later today?" he asked.

"I have an appointment in thirty minutes but I'm free after that," John replied.

"Come see me at 1:00 p.m.," said the bank officer, and he gave John his card. John excused himself and said he had to leave for his appointment.

John smiled to himself as he walked back towards town. He made a couple of stops and dropped off his resume, visiting with some other fellow bankers along the way.

He picked up a newspaper at the news stand and leafed over to the obituaries. Fulton's funeral was tomorrow at 11:00 a.m. at the Presbyterian Church.

There was still ample time left and John knew he needed to face Father Jonathan. He caught the trolley and was at St. Mary's in a matter of minutes. Father Jonathan was in the confessional, and John decided this was as good a place as any. There were two people in front of him, so he went up to the altar and lit four candles, one for each of his parents, his deceased wife, and unborn child. When he finished with his prayer, he walked back to the confessional and waited his turn. When John entered the booth, Father Jonathan lifted the small door so he could hear John's confession.

"Bless me, Father, for I have sinned; my last confession was about three weeks ago," John prayed.

Father Jonathan said his usual prayer in Latin and then said, "What is your confession, John?"

John confessed about wanting to kill David Brooks and told him as simply as he could about his desires for Catherine and what they had done the night before.

"Since Catherine is your wife, your intimacy with her is acceptable; however, your intentions and promise to her to remain celibate have been jeopardized. If you continue, and you most likely will, the possibility of an annulment will not be possible. If there is nothing else, your penance is to say three Hail Mary's, The Act of Contrition and the Lord's Prayer. Bless you, my son." Father Jonathan closed the small door they were talking through and John left to say his prayers.

John always felt better after confession. He felt his soul had been cleansed and the sins flushed from his body. There was always the usual dread of having to confess to the priest your bad deeds, but once it was over, it was exhilarating. As a young boy, he really disliked going to confession because some of the other priests were harsher and made you feel like a criminal sometimes even with the smallest sin like lying to your mother or getting into a fight with a friend. Father Jonathan was much more sensitive and caring and often made it a point to be available for counseling if you continued to repeat the same sin over and over. John laughed to himself because since he had known Father Jonathan, he was more of a friend than a priest.

Still needing to kill some time, John walked over to the mercantile to see about getting Catherine a birthday present for her sixteenth birthday. He was thinking about getting her a new sewing machine. She loved to sew and he knew she missed not having one. While he was looking at several machines a salesman approached him and offered to help. After asking John some questions, he showed John a newer model that had just arrived. It was a Singer model 12K fiddle-bed with gold decorations that Catherine could use anywhere and it included some additional attachments. The cost was fourteen dollars and ninety-eight cents, which was a little more than John wanted to pay, but he bought it anyway. He asked them to hold it and he would pick it up the next day. That done, he stopped and ate a sandwich at the drug store and read the newspaper while he ate, waiting for time to pass so he could go to his next appointment.

Galveston Savings Bank was located a couple of blocks down from the Island Bank where John had previously been employed. It was a beautiful building with a Gothic influence. Rodger Trammel, the bank's president and the man John had met earlier at the Tremont lounge, showed him into his office. John handed Trammel his resume and Trammel looked at it closely.

"You're married; that's good," Trammel said. "We prefer our male employees to be married as it shows stability and character."

John smiled at his statement. There was a brief question and answer between the two men and then Trammel got up to show John around the bank.

"I still need to get approval from our board, but they usually approve most of the people I like to hire. You have a strong background with a financing degree, and that's more than some of us have," Trammel said. "The board meets on Monday so I can't say yes right now, but subject to their approval, I want you to restructure our trust department with a starting annual salary of eight thousand, five hundred dollars. If all goes well there will be frequent raises and bonuses, of course," Trammel continued.

John was pleased by his offer but wanted to think about it. He didn't want to sound like he was desperate.

"Let me know as soon as you can, as we meet in a few days," Trammel said. John shook his hand and told him he would drop by after the funeral the next day.

John was astounded by Trammel's offer. It was a thousand more a year than he was making before. He wanted to say yes on the spot, but thought better of it. He wanted Trammel to think he had other options, which he didn't at the moment. John looked at his watch and thought he had just enough time to pick up Catherine's birthday present and take it home before he met her after school.

CHAPTER 29

John made it back to Ball High School just as the final bell was ringing. He looked around and didn't see David Brooks anywhere and he felt relieved. He was excited to see Catherine and decided to wait until he got home so he could share the news with both Catherine and Amelia about his future job. He didn't want Amelia to feel left out now that Catherine was there. He sensed a little jealousy from Amelia.

It had been two years since his wife had passed and his relationship with his sister had grown a lot. She was dependent on John and now she had to share John with Catherine. Catherine was young, flirtatious, and beautiful, and he didn't want either of them to resent the other.

Catherine waved as she ran down the steps to meet John. They held hands and caught the trolley home. John took Catherine's knapsack and commented on how heavy it was. She told him she had a lot of homework and needed her books to study. John smiled and said he would be happy to help her if she needed tutoring. When they got home, John called Catherine and Amelia into his study and briefed them on his job offer. They were overjoyed by the news and hugged him.

"It's not a done deal yet; I have to wait for approval from the board, and I have to accept first. I'm meeting with the president again tomorrow after the funeral," John told them.

John was secretly glad that Catherine had homework to do.

Their intimacy was incredible the night before, but he was still concerned about the possibility of her getting pregnant and the less time they had alone together, the better. When supper was over and the kitchen cleaned up, Catherine spread her books out on the table and John went into his study. Amelia joined John in his study, asking him questions and telling him about her day.

"I'm really glad your arrangement has worked out and that Catherine is now your wife," Amelia hesitated before she finished her sentence, "but..."

"But what?" John asked softly. "Are you worried she might get pregnant?"

Amelia blushed and said, "Well I know you two love each other a lot and that possibility is there."

"I don't want her to get pregnant, either," John said. "She wants to finish high school and go to medical school and a baby would complicate everything, Amelia," John said, taking her hand, "I know it's just been the two of us for a while and having another woman in the house is a drastic change. Catherine wants this to work as much as we all do. Let's give it a chance. I don't want you to feel like the third wheel. Time will work everything out and I am going to make sure Catherine doesn't have an early pregnancy."

Amelia hugged John and went to her room, satisfied that John took time to discuss her feelings.

John was working on a draft of his will, which needed to be revised since his marriage to Catherine. He had taken several courses in law at business school and knew the general format. It was 9:30 p.m. when he looked at his watch. He went into the kitchen and found Catherine asleep with her head on top of one of her books at the kitchen table. He turned out the kitchen light and carried Catherine upstairs. She nuzzled into his shoulder.

"Where are you taking me?" she asked in a whisper.

"To bed," John answered.

"Mine or yours?" she asked sheepishly.

"Ours," John answered. Catherine was really tired and John helped her take off her clothes and put on her sleeping gown. He pulled back the covers and she crawled in. John readied himself for bed and when he got in, Catherine was sound asleep. John turned out the light and smiled to himself. He was the happiest he had been in a long time.

Catherine was up the next morning before John. She quietly dressed and went downstairs and made John some coffee and prepared a pot of oats. Amelia came in and Catherine prepared tea for both of them. John joined them for breakfast and complimented Catherine on her coffee making.

"John," Catherine said, "would it be all right if after school I went to the Rosenberg Library and looked some things up? I'll be home by 5:00."

"You don't want me to meet you?" John asked.

"No, I think I'll be fine. David Brooks just startled me the first time. If it happens again I will just ignore him and there will be lots of people around so I could always scream," Catherine assured him.

"If it happens again, we are going to the police," John answered. John knew the police would not do anything, but he wanted to put them on notice in the event he encountered a fight with Brooks. John reluctantly agreed to let Catherine go to the library but reminded her to keep up with the time.

After school, Catherine walked to the library. She kept her eyes open and frequently looked over her shoulder to see if David might be following her. She hated that he had that kind of control over her. She had found a small whistle in one of the drawers upstairs and put it in her purse. She was carrying it now. If she saw him, she would just blow the whistle and he would probably run away. Catherine had been to the library a couple of times with her mother and knew her way around fairly well. She looked around to see if anyone was looking and found her way to the biology section of the library. She scanned several of the shelves and her eyes stopped on a book that read: *Sexology*.

Catherine took it off the shelf and thumbed through it. She stopped at a picture of both the male and female human body and blushed. It diagrammed the sexual act between a man and woman showing how his penis would enter the woman's vagina and that once the sperm was released into the woman's vagina, the sperm would fertilize the eggs in the woman's ovaries. It went on to explain ovulation and at what times of the month the woman was most vulnerable to getting pregnant. So that's the process, she thought to herself, smiling. No wonder John was so concerned. Catherine took out her pencil and a piece of paper. She counted up the days on her fingers since her last period and wrote it down. She also took some notes from the book about what days were the safest. It went on to read that while following your body's calendar from month to month worked fairly well, the only guarantee from pregnancy was abstinence. John was right when he asked about her last period. She was right in the middle of her cycle and she could get pregnant. Catherine was relieved after she put the book away. When John didn't make love to her last night it bothered her, but now she knew. Education is a wonderful thing, and I can't wait to go to medical school, Catherine thought to herself.

Catherine checked out a couple of medical books to read in her spare time and she left the library. The clock on the street corner said 4:30 p.m. and there was more than enough time to get home. When she got off the trolley, she looked around to see if David Brooks was anywhere in site. She did not see him, so she walked home quickly and breathed a sigh of relief when she reached the front door.

When Catherine got home, she went into John's study and kissed his cheek. Amelia was in the kitchen preparing dinner and Catherine joined her. After washing her hands at the kitchen sink, she began setting the table. Amelia was really a good cook and the food was delicious. They visited for a while around the table and then Catherine and John did the dishes together. "

"Do you have homework?" John asked her.

"Some," she answered. "What about you?"

"A little," he said and smiled. "Meet you upstairs in an hour?" John whispered. Catherine's heart skipped a beat and she smiled and shook her head yes.

Catherine could hardly keep her mind on her studies but finished her homework in thirty minutes. She put her books away and quietly went upstairs to run the bath water and take a quick bath before meeting John in the bedroom. She had just gotten in the tub when there was a soft knock at the door.

"May I join you?" John asked with a sheepish grin as he stuck his head in the door. He was standing over her buck naked and she couldn't keep from grinning. Their eyes locked and John moved her to the middle of the tub, crawling in behind her and straddling her with his legs. She seemed so much smaller in the tub. John wrapped his arms around her and picked up the soap. He took the wash cloth and wet it, rubbing the soap and cloth together, and when the suds erupted he began washing Catherine's' breast. She lay her head back on his chest and felt his gentle hands touching her bosom. He began placing small kisses on her neck and she stretched her neck to the side wanting more. She felt his manhood come to life in the center of her lower back and she wanted to touch him, but couldn't. John moved his soapy hands lower and began caressing her, as she closed her eyes, drifting into a never, never land she had never experience before.

"Ahh, ahh," she moaned softly. "Ahh, John," she pleaded as she welcomed more. Her faint cries told John of her pleasure. He held her tight and she squeezed his hand. "You do such magical things to me," Catherine whispered to John.

Catherine turned around and got up on her knees facing John. She took the soap and cloth and began washing John, starting at the top by his neck and moving toward his back. She kissed him long and passionately and he pulled her closer, kissing her back. Afterwards, they lay in the tub holding each other, not saying anything until the water began to get cold.

John got out first and dried himself off. He pulled Catherine out and dried her off, too, and then he picked her up in his arms and he took her to his bed and crawled in beside her.

Catherine crawled under his arm, laying her head on his chest. "When I went to the library today I read a few pages in a book about sex," Catherine said. John looked down at her and didn't say anything. "I think I understand now what you meant about it not being a good time. It said that during your period and two days before your period were the safe zones. I don't want to get pregnant right now either, so if you don't mind making love to me while I am bleeding we can go all the way," Catherine said looking up at him. John bent down and kissed her on her hair.

"Sweetheart, I can just keep doing what we are doing. It's safer that way," John said.

"But I want to feel you inside me," she protested. "I want to do it the way we are supposed to."

John sighed and said, "Okay, just give me some notice, I'll need to rest up for it," he said kidding her and then he grinned.

John felt happier than he had ever been in his entire life. It surprised him at first when Catherine said she had read the books at the library about sex and having babies. He smiled to himself at the thought of it. Catherine was special and there was no doubt in his mind the she was meant to be his.

The next morning, John dressed in his suit and tie and accompanied Catherine to the trolley stop. It had not come yet so John waited next to Catherine with his arm around her. When they saw the trolley coming, John bent down to kiss Catherine and she held him close, not wanting the kiss to end.

"I love you, Mr. Merit, now and forever," Catherine whispered in his ear.

"My feelings exactly," John answered.

It was a brisk, cool day and John felt the walk over to the Presbyterian Church would be good for him. It was still early so he stopped in at a local diner to get warm and have coffee. He bought a paper and scanned through the newspaper and decided to look at the classifieds. Just curious, he thought, if the board didn't approve his hire, he needed to see what might be out there. There were several ads for banking positions in Houston, but relocating was not an option for him right now. Since Catherine wanted to go to medical school, it was important for them to stay in Galveston. John looked at his watch and it was 10:45 a.m., so he paid his tab and left. There were several people entering the church when he got there so he followed them in. The church was full and he found a place close to the back. The eulogy painted Fulton as a saint, a loving father and a smart business man. He agreed with some of it, but word on the street was that he had been embezzling the bank's money for over a year. He decided not to go to the cemetery and caught the trolley back into the banking district.

Rodger Trammel had not gone to the funeral. Even though he and Fulton knew each other, Trammel didn't approve of Fulton's business dealings. Trammel saw John come into the bank and walked out to greet him. They talked for a while and Trammel invited him to lunch. Trammel told John that he had polled all of the members of the board and they unanimously agreed to John's hire. They joined two of its members at the Tremont Hotel for lunch, and the deal was made. John was to start work the following Monday.

John was waiting outside Ball High School when the bell rang. He was excited about his new job, and the fact that his pay was only interrupted a few weeks didn't really hurt his pocketbook. John watched as Catherine came out of the building and stopped to look around. God, she was such a beautiful girl, and he was so lucky she was his, John thought. They really had not had a honeymoon to speak of and Catherine didn't seem to mind, but he wanted to do something special for her on her birthday. He wanted to talk to Amelia first, since it would mean leaving her alone overnight.

Catherine saw John and waved as she came down the stairs to join him. They caught the trolley home and walked the two blocks holding hands and cooing at one another. After dinner, Catherine started her homework and John motioned to Amelia to come into his study. He told Amelia his plan about surprising Catherine after school on her birthday by taking her to dinner and then a vaudeville show finishing off the evening by spending the night at the Tremont Hotel. Amelia had been feeling much better, and since Catherine and John would be in town and so close, she thought she could manage just fine alone. They decided to keep it a surprise and not say anything.

Friday, January 14th, Catherine woke up with a smile on her face and went downstairs for breakfast. John was already having coffee in the kitchen and she kissed him on the cheek. Amelia joined them for breakfast and they talked about everything except the fact that it was Catherine's birthday. In fact, the more she thought about it no one had even mentioned it since they got married. She noticed the date on the newspaper just to be sure, but there it was, January 14th, 1899. Catherine decided not to say anything and gathered up her books. John walked her to the trolley and kissed her good-bye. She waved back at him and tried to put on a happy face. When Catherine entered her homeroom, her teacher told her Happy Birthday. Oh well, she thought, I'll just go buy myself something tomorrow at the store. That will make me feel better.

John spent a good part of the day getting everything ready. He invited Amelia to help him select a new nightgown for Catherine and was surprised when Amelia selected a sheer pink silk sleeveless gown trimmed with lace and a matching robe. It was a bit pricey, but John wanted Catherine to feel special. Amelia selected some French perfume as her gift to Catherine, and John found a pair of matching slippers to finish it off. They had it all gift wrapped and sent over to the Tremont. After John saw Amelia home, he carefully packed an overnight bag for Catherine and one for himself. He caught the trolley over to the Tremont, stopped outside at the florist stand, and then checked in to the hotel. He had ordered the bridal suite. After getting the key, the bellman showed John to the room.

John stood in amazement as the bellman opened the door. It

was the most beautiful, lavish room he had ever seen. There was a fire burning in the fireplace and a small table with a white tablecloth and two chairs on either side. There was an ice bucket and two champagne glasses and a small vase of flowers. The presents he had purchased had already been delivered and were beautifully wrapped in pink with purple bows on top. John tipped the bellman and closed the door behind him. If John had figured right, Catherine's period would be starting any day now and he couldn't wait to feel her in his arms.

John quickly ran to catch the trolley to the school and was waiting anxiously when Catherine came out to meet him. He took her arm and they began walking away from their trolley stop.

"Aren't we..." Catherine stopped and then said, "Where are we going?"

John smiled at her and said, "I have something I want to show you." John took her knapsack and swung it over his shoulder.

"Come on," Catherine pleaded, "Just give me a hint." John smiled and shook his head no.

Catherine knew John had something up his sleeve and couldn't imagine what it was. Had he remembered her birthday, is that what this is all about? She thought. They were holding hands when they walked through the lobby of the Tremont. The bellman looked like a canary that had just stolen a worm and he couldn't take his eyes off Catherine. She was beaming and with John on her arm, they were a quite a handsome couple. Before John opened the door, he told Catherine to close her eyes. He swept Catherine up in his arms and carried her in the room.

"You can open them now," John said, "Happy Sixteenth Birthday, Catherine. I love you."

Catherine was overwhelmed, and she reached up and kissed John. "This is absolutely beautiful; I don't know what to say. Oh my wonderful husband, thank you, thank you, thank you. The suite is lovely. Oh my, it's more than lovely. I've never seen anything more beautiful."

John was pleased with himself and delighted Catherine was so happy. A bottle of champagne was in the wine bucket and John went over and popped the cork. "I realize you don't drink, but I thought a few sips in honor of this day were in order." He poured them each a half glass and they took a drink.

"Wow," she said, "This is divine." They both began to relax and John handed Amelia's present to her to open.

"Oh, I love this. I've never had my own French perfume. That was so thoughtful of Amelia." Catherine exclaimed.

"Before I give you the other presents from me, I wanted to ask you what you would prefer to do. We could go downstairs and have dinner and then go to a show at the Grande and then come back here and stay the night," John said.

"Or," Catherine teased, "we could stay in this beautiful suite and order room service and," she said grinning, "and fool around a bit?"

John smiled and said as he bowed, "Your wish is my command." Catherine walked over and loosened John's tie and took his jacket off.

"Don't you want to open your other presents first?" John asked.

"I am opening my present," Catherine said as she unbuttoned his shirt.

"I thought you might want to change into something more comfortable," John said. Catherine started taking off her dress and John stopped her. "My turn," he said. He walked her over by the bed and began undressing her. When he finished, he opened the larger box and took out her silk nightgown and put it over her head. He turned her around in front of the full length mirror. John had pulled out some of the pins from Catherine's hair, and it flowed over her shoulders and down her arm and back. "Look what a beautiful woman you've become, Mrs. Merit." Catherine watched John in the mirror as he began planting small sweet kisses on her neck and caressed her breast.

"The gown, I love it," Catherine whispered.

'You didn't really think I had forgotten your birthday, did you?" John asked

"I wasn't sure. I knew you had a lot on your mind," Catherine said.

"You're right; I've had you on my mind night and day," John whispered. They kissed each other on the lips and they were hungry for each other. John picked Catherine up, and holding her, he pulled back the covers on the bed and gently placed her in it. He picked up their champagne glasses and gave Catherine hers. They took several sips as they stared into each other's eyes. John finished undressing and Catherine watched with an eagerness and desire she had never felt before. Next John carefully removed Catherine's nightgown and threw it on the floor. They kissed and caressed each other, exploring and touching, wanting more as John and Catherine's bodies became one. Catherine received John's love with a passion and lust she had never experienced before. Their love for each other had no boundaries and for a brief moment they were in a dream where nothing mattered but the moment. They lay together a while, in the aftermath of euphoria. There were no regrets. They would be together forever.

They dozed off for a while and John woke up first. He went over and placed another log on the fire and poured himself another glass of champagne. John went into the bathroom and was surprised at how large the bathtub was. He turned on the faucets and began filling the tub. There were bottles of bath salts and candles placed around the outside of the tub. John lit the candles, threw some salts in the tub and went back and woke Catherine up. He picked her up and carried her to the bathroom, gently placing her in the tub. After retrieving their drinks, John joined Catherine and they soaked for a while and sipped their champagne.

"You really know how to spoil a lady," Catherine said.

"I couldn't think of anything else I'd rather do," John said. Catherine never had a chance to talk to her mother about sex, and she wondered if her mother and father had experienced the same passion with each other as she and John had. Love is so beautiful, she thought to herself.

John put his arms around Catherine and said, "I tried to be gentle. I hope I didn't hurt you."

"No, it was wonderful and I love you so much," Catherine said.

"How would you like to get dressed and we could go downstairs for dinner? They have a quartet playing in the lounge and we could dance later, just a suggestion. I packed you another dress and some toiletries," John said.

"That sounds wonderful," Catherine answered. They dressed and went downstairs where John ordered dinner for both of them. Catherine and John smiled tenderly at each other and for the moment, time stood still and they were lost in each other.

The next morning Catherine woke up before John and went to the bathroom. When she came back, she ordered tea and coffee and bagel to be brought up to the room. John woke up and saw her sitting in a chair, just staring at him. He got up and put on his underwear and went over to where she was sitting.

"Are you all right?" John asked.

"Just a little headache and I started my period," Catherine said.

"Well, I'm sorry for your headache, but I'm glad you started your period," John answered.

Catherine looked up at him and smiled. "I ordered breakfast to be sent up. I hope that was all right," Catherine teased.

"You can have and do anything you want, Catherine," John said. "I want this weekend to be the most memorable weekend you've ever had. I want to please you," John continued.

"It has been the most wonderful weekend of my life. You, John Merit, are my life. I would be nothing without you," Catherine replied.

When they returned home, Amelia was glad to see them. She had done all right by herself but didn't realize how empty and alone she felt being there without someone to talk to. Catherine went upstairs to put her things away and stood in the doorway overwhelmed and at a loss for words. The sewing machine John had bought her was already set up on the desk with a heart shaped note attached to it, "Happy Birthday, My Darling Catherine. I love you, John." John was standing behind her and walked up and put his arms around her waist. She wanted to cry for joy but willed herself not to. She turned and looked up at him and drew his head down so she could kiss him.

"You've already done so much and I've never been so happy," Catherine whispered.

CHAPTER 30

Several months had passed and the city of Galveston continued on a freight train path to prosperity. There was a lot of conversation about the city building a sea wall, but no one stepped up to the task or followed through. The city of Galveston was growing like wildfire, and so was Catherine and John's love for each other.

Catherine had maintained a 4.0 average and when she applied to the University of Texas Medical School, she was accepted pending her entrance exam. Catherine spent hours studying and when she took the test she scored in the top five percent. Before Catherine graduated, St, Mary's Hospital offered her an internship at the hospital and John and Amelia encouraged her to take it but only if it was during the day. Catherine had not had an encounter with David Brooks, but she often saw him lurking in doorways on her way home from school. She never mentioned it to John, but always walked home with her whistle in her hand.

David continued to make trips to Houston during breaks in the Grande's scheduled operas and entertainment events. He was able to keep himself occupied there by staying sometimes with Debbie one weekend and Irene the next. He had not made a kill since New Year's. Because David's desire for Catherine was unrelenting, he often stalked her and it became a game to him. Sometimes she noticed, but he was good at it and often used beards, hats and other paraphernalia from the costume department. Once when he had a beard, hat, and overcoat on, he was sitting next to her on the trolley. It pleased him that he could be so close to her and she never suspected it. With summer coming on, it was not going to be so easy. His beards, hats and overcoats had to be shed and he wasn't sure what his next move might be. School would be out and then he could make his plan.

David often scanned the want ads for another job. He was sick of Gregory always being on his back and the pay was pathetic. David stopped in the diner one morning and found a used newspaper; after ordering coffee, he turned to the classified section of the newspaper which said Jobs and Help Wanted. He scanned down and saw an ad for a funeral home. They needed someone who was trainable in the mortuary business. Someone who was good with his hands, could work irregular hours, and was strong. David decided to head over to Barker Bros. Funeral Home. He would deal with Gregory later.

David went into the men's bathroom at the diner and looked at himself. Sometimes he didn't shave, but today he had and he had on one of his better shirts. Clothes didn't mean much to him because he was more comfortable without them.

When he arrived at the funeral home, he was shown into the office of Simon Barker, the second generation of the Barkers. They hit it off really well and Barker was excited that David was in the theatre business and asked if he had ever used theatrical make-up. David lied and said, "Of course." He had seen the guys and girls put it on hundreds of times and it looked pretty easy, he thought to himself. They talked for over an hour, and Barker filled him in on the fact that he would also be taking care of the horses and carriages used to transport the dead and their families. Barker further informed him that he might be working some evenings and weekends but that when they were in between funerals and preparation of the bodies he didn't mind if David took off. He just needed to check in with Simon first. David was offered the position with a starting pay of fifteen dollars a week, including an incentive bonus at the end of the year. He wanted David to begin immediately and David agreed.

Gregory was angry and glad at the same time when David came into his office and quit. He was glad to be rid of him but a few days' notice would have been nice. Gregory wished him well as he didn't want to be on David's bad list.

David cut back on his drinking and decided he was going to do everything he could to get on the good side of his new boss. Besides, it offered him everything he needed to make Catherine his. David worked closely with the head mortician, Charles Selmer, and was especially interested in the use of formaldehyde and other chemicals used in embalming the bodies. He couldn't help but notice a bottle of chloroform, and Selmer warned David that if his nose came in direct contact with the chloroform, he would pass out. Selmer also told him that they rarely used it since their patients were already dead. Selmer had it because he bought it from a medicine man and thought it might come in handy one day. Selmer was a chemist at heart but couldn't make it into medical school, so he settled on being a mortician.

Once David was in the good graces of his new employer, they fitted him with a new shirt, suit, and tie to wear when he drove the hearse. He left it at the funeral home in a closet so he could change into it when needed. David liked his new look and admired himself in the mirror. He hated the tie, as it felt like a noose around his neck. That was a place he didn't want to go. David had access to the horses and the covered carriages. He couldn't have asked for more. He soaked up the entire medical and embalming procedures needed to further his new career and it surprised him that the corpses had no effect on him. Selmer even commented that most trainees got sick from the stench, and vomited. David was even good with the makeup. The first try at it, though, caused Barker to get upset.

"Davie," he said, she's not going on stage. Take some of that makeup off and make her look more natural."

His next attempt was better and even the family commented on how lovely their Aunt Sophie was. David was pleased with himself and his new image. He also wondered if Catherine might like his new appearance. Only time would tell.

It was summer now, and Catherine was beginning her new internship at St. Mary's hospital. She worked from 10:00 a.m. to 6:00 p.m. and often times she left early to stop at the library for books. Catherine learned how to give shots and she had an excellent bedside manner. The interns and doctors liked working with her, as she listened and took their direction well.

John's job at the bank was intense; it was up to him to bring structure and accountability to the Trust Department. He often worked late and frequently took work home so he could stay caught up. It was his job to look after over one hundred accounts and the files were a mess. He was told to work on the accounts in excess of twenty thousand dollars first and work down from there. Like every job he did, John applied logic first. He made an inventory of each trust's holdings on a balance sheet qualifying each investment by placing it under cash, stocks, insurance policies, etc. There was no uniformity on how the investments were originally kept. They were just put in a file with little accountability. It was monumental, but he approached it one at a time.

John's and Catherine's times together were few and far between. They both accepted the fact that abstinence was the best answer so that Catherine would not get pregnant, and limited their love making to once or twice a month. They maintained separate bedrooms and Catherine kept a calendar open on her dresser so John was privileged to check the dates. He always brought her flowers and left work early on their planned days. Amelia caught on to their routine, too and she smiled inside. She was glad they were so happy and tried to stay out of their way. When John brought flowers home, Amelia knew she would not only cook dinner, but take care of the cleanup. It was her way of giving them her approval. Their passion for each other was undeniable and they took their time with each other. There were soft kisses, caressing, foreplay and then the ultimate fireworks at the end. It wasn't the perfect life Catherine envisioned when they married, but it worked for them. She often thought of her mother and knew that her mother would be pleased that she had a loving family.

Most of the work at the funeral home took place from 9:00 a.m. to 5:00 p.m. Sometimes after work, David would have to go pick up bodies from the hospital or the city morgue, but he liked the irregular hours. He could park his horse-drawn carriage with a coffin in it outside the hospital and not be noticed. Many times when he picked up a body, he would see Catherine from a distance. If he ran late, he would just tell his boss that the body wasn't ready or that the papers were in the process of being signed.

He had some perks, too; he used the carriage for his own personal gratification. He would arrange to meet a hooker on his way back from the hospital and use the space between the coffin and the inner walls of the carriage that were lined in silk to pleasure himself with his pick of the day. He had his own traveling whorehouse, he laughed to himself.

It was not long before David figured out Catherine's routine. She had Wednesdays and Sundays off and sometimes she worked later on Wednesday evening, often not leaving before 8:00 p.m. David also looked around for a new place to live. Now that he had transportation he could check out some other digs. He found the perfect one.

It was Joseph March's old place. He met one of the heirs, who was attending a funeral at Barker's Funeral home and, during visitation, he learned about the old place. The man told him that the place was pretty run down but they preferred someone living there to keep the vandals out. David said he would take a look at it and let him know.

After work the next day, David asked Barker if he could saddle up one of the horses and take a look at the lodgings. It was only fifteen minutes at a steady gallop and it couldn't have been more perfect. The barn had a useable door that pushed open and closed so he could put a lock on it if he wanted to. There was a secure stable where he could keep a horse and unused tack and saddle. David had saved up a little money, so on his day off he bought a horse, a gun, and some chain, packed up what he needed from his apartment, and moved into the adjoining office that Joseph once used as his home inside the barn. Once he had Catherine in his captivity, he could chain her up during the day and then she would be all his at night. He smiled to himself, pleased with his accomplishments.

David waited patiently for the fall weather to set in. It infuriated him that he spent a lot of sleepless nights chasing away the riffraff that tried to invade the area on the beach behind his barn. He posted signs that read: Trespassers Will Be Shot, and after shooting his gun into the air to scare them away several times, they stopped coming.

Catherine started medical school in the fall and cut her work hours at the hospital to two evenings a week and Saturday. They tried to get her to work Sundays but that was her and John's time together and she refused to do it. She worked Wednesday and Friday evenings and used her breaks to study when she was at the hospital. At home, she always read a chapter or two ahead in case she couldn't study during breaks. Since she had not encountered David up close, she began to let her guard down. She had no idea he was now driving the funeral hearse and paid little attention to it when it was parked at the hospital. Tom Gregory did inform John that David was no longer employed with the Grande and that David told him he was moving to Houston to work for a funeral home. At least that was what David wanted Tom to think. Since David had begun work at the funeral home, he let his beard and moustache grow out and he thought he looked quite handsome. All the girls loved it and made a big deal out of it.

CHAPTER 31

It was getting close to Thanksgiving in the year 1899 and Galveston was alive and flourishing. Banking was a big business and the rich just kept getting richer. John had been given several promotions and was making a really good living. He secretly wished Catherine could be happy staying home and starting a family, but her desire to go to medical school was something he had accepted from the get go. She had turned sixteen earlier in the year and it went unsaid that there were no regrets. John knew Catherine loved him and would do anything he asked, maybe even give up her idea of being a doctor, but he would not consider asking her. He didn't want her to look back someday and have regrets. He loved her so much; he would even give his life for her if need be. Her happiness was his major focus, and even though he wanted children now, there was still plenty of time.

The medical school was out for a week during the Thanksgiving holidays and Catherine agreed to take some extra shifts at the hospital. She loved her work and admired the doctors she worked with. She couldn't help but think how fortunate she was to be married to a loving husband and work in a job she loved. She finished up her shift and made a few calls in the children's ward. Father Jonathan was there visiting, and he and Catherine talked for a while. Catherine finally looked at the clock and it was 7:15 p.m. She bid good-bye to Father Jonathan and decided to go out the back entrance since it cut off over a half block, making the walk to the trolley a little shorter.

She paid little attention to the hearse at the end of the street, even though it normally was parked closer to the morgue area when it picked up bodies. She had to walk right past it and didn't notice a large bearded man in an overcoat. He blocked her way, and when she tried to move around him, he grabbed hold of her and put something over her face. Catherine made an attempt to struggle but passed out within seconds.

David Brooks held the handkerchief he had soaked with chloroform on Catherine's face until she became limp. He opened the back end of the hearse and laid her to the side of the coffin. The hearse was wider than most carriages because it was equipped to carry two coffins at one time. David crawled in beside Catherine and placed a gag over her mouth, which he tied behind her head. He rolled her over on her stomach and tied her wrists securely and then he tied her legs. When he finished, he opened up the coffin and put her in it. The coffin was just a plain box with hinges to secure the lid and used only to transport bodies. It smelled of human decomposition even though there were air holes in several places for air to filter through it.

"Hey, is anybody in there?" someone asked knocking on the outside of the door.

Once David had secured the lid he opened the door and said, "What do you want?"

"Aren't you here to pick up a body?" a younger man dressed in hospital clothes asked.

"I already got one. I'll have to come back in the morning and get yours," David said.

The young man looked perplexed and scratched his head as David got up on the front of the wagon and gave the horse a command to go.

Catherine woke up after about ten minutes and was disoriented. The smell was disgusting and she tried to cough but couldn't. She tried to move, but her arms ached and she felt paralyzed. She didn't know where she was, and felt the coffin heaving up and down when they passed over the trolley rails. She thought at first it was a bad dream and tried to remember where she had been. Fear and anxiety flooded her body and she tried to scream but couldn't. She began to focus on her surroundings and realized she was in some kind of enclosure. When the carriage finally stopped she listened and waited. Was that a door opening, she wondered. A few minutes later the carriage lunged forward, went a short distance and stopped. She heard the sound of a horse and then the back door opened and she waited, not knowing what was going to happen next. Where was she, and who was out there? Catherine didn't move, and it surprised her when the latches opened and the coffin lid rose. It was dark and she couldn't make out who or what was there. Whoever it was, she felt the strength of his arms lift her out of the box and put her on the floor beside the box. The man jumped out the back and pulled her toward him, throwing her over his shoulder like a sack of potatoes. Catherine was petrified and she had never in her life been so scared. Was this another one of her nightmares? She willed herself to wake up. Her arms which were bound behind her back were throbbing and her mouth was dry from the gag. She was paralyzed with fear and she wandered if she would die tonight.

David knew the barn like the back of his hand. He had spent months setting up their little love nest and he felt his excitement grow as he laid Catherine down on a blanket. Catherine opened her eyes wide and looked directly into David's eyes.

"Hello princess, welcome to your new castle," David said as he grinned at her. Catherine struggled and tried to get up. David straddled her. His original plan was to bring her back to the barn and after securing her to a post he was going to take the carriage and horse back to the funeral home and then come back and have his way with her. David took the handkerchief filled with chloroform out of his pocket and put it over Catherine's face again and she passed out. He couldn't wait. He wanted her now and he decided to have her.

David hurriedly backed the horse and carriage out of the barn, closed and locked the door and left to go back to the funeral home.

Once there, he undid the tack and put the horse in its stable. He saddled up his horse and was about to leave when someone called his name.

"Get the body?" Charles Selmer asked.

"No," David answered. "After waiting for over an hour, they said to come back in the morning. I have to take care of some personal business tomorrow and I won't be in. Will you let Barker know?" Selmer wasn't happy about David not coming in because it meant he had to go get the body and prep it by himself. He started to say something to David but it was too late. He was gone.

Catherine woke up again and carefully listened for any kind of noise that might tell her where she was. She could smell the damp hay around her and she could hear the buzzing of flies. Her arms were aching and she tried to move them but realized she was tied to something. The cold damp barn made her shiver and she tried to lunge forward, but soon discovered that it was pointless. She felt cramping in her lower abdomen and she began to cry. After a while she stopped. Her mouth was dry from the gag and she moved her head from side to side trying to dislodge it. Then she remembered. The man she had seen earlier looking into her eyes was David Brooks.   Where was he now? She had no idea how much time had passed.

Catherine thought of her mother and wondered if David had caused her death. Then she thought of John and she closed her eyes tightly. How could she ever face John again? She couldn't stop the tears and then she heard the door to the barn slide open. Her fear escalated. Had he come back to kill her? She wondered. She began to tremble.

David took the saddle off his horse and Catherine heard the horse lapping up some water. A few minutes later she heard the stall door close and footsteps coming up to her. Catherine closed her eyes and pretended to sleep. David took out a bottle of whiskey, opened it and chugalugged several large gulps. He stood looking down at her, pleased with himself that everything he had planned had finally come together.

"Oh, Catherine, you really are beautiful." He slapped her cheek hard and it jerked her head. Catherine opened her eyes. "I've waited a long time for you."

David pulled down her gag and Catherine started to scream. David clinched his hand over her mouth to muffle her and with his other hand put the gag back in her mouth.

David took a cigarette out of his shirt pocket and lit it. He took in a deep drag as Catherine watched him intently. David took it out of his mouth and lowered it down to her neck. She could feel the heat as he waved it slowly over her, letting some of the hot embers fall onto her neck. It felt like tiny bee stings and Catherine tried to flinch. "You scream again and I'll put it out on your lower neck. The skin is thin there and will cause you a lot of pain, not to mention the scaring." Catherine tried to swallow but couldn't. David cautioned her again. "Even though there is nobody around for miles, I'll burn you. Understood?" Catherine tried to moved her head yes, but David knew she would be quiet. He was purposely trying to scare her. He really wanted to kiss her and he wanted the gag off. David slowly took off the gag and Catherine's mouth was so dry she could hardly get a syllable out.

"Why?" Catherine whispered.

David smiled and said, "Because I can."

David put his hands under Catherine's head and pulled her up to his mouth   kissing her. She closed her eyes trying to block out what was happening to her. She thought of John and how sweet his love making was. She tried to escape the moment by thinking of their first night together in bed, and then David released her mouth and she panted for air. The taste of the cheep whiskey made her sick at her stomach and she wanted to throw up, but didn't. David pulled her hair hard and she cried out.

David was breathing hard and his beard was scratching her face each time he kissed her. He was on top of her now and the pain was excruciating and she willed herself to die. Why had he chosen her?

Was he the one who killed her mother? If she didn't do what he wanted, would he kill her, too? So many things were racing through her mind and she prayed it would end soon.

Catherine had never felt such pain and horror. She was in hell, she convinced herself. And the devil was having his way with her. She knew that if by some chance she survived this, she would never be able to face her husband. The indignity of what was happening to her would never be erased from her mind. David fell asleep for a while and then got up and finished his bottle of whiskey and then opened another. He was beginning to slur his words and Catherine begged him to untie her. He continued drinking and ignored her. The night seemed endless and she prayed he would just end her life.

Every part of Catherine's body was aching from the trauma he had caused her, and she told David she needed to go to the bathroom. "Hell, I ain't got no bathroom," he laughed. Catherine was crying softly. "I'll untie you and walk you out to the water," he said.

David untied her arms and he got up and reached for her. He continued drinking from his bottle and he was wavering. It was hard for Catherine to get up because the pain was excruciating, but she finally managed to stand. Her wrists were burning from the ropes he had bound her with and she felt dizzy and weak. She tried to close her dress around her, but she stopped when he grabbed her arm and they went over to the door. He had a tight grip on her but he opened the door with one hand and they walked out towards the water.

"You try and do something stupid, I'll beat you up really bad," David said.

Catherine felt the sand under her bare feet. David slipped on something and they both fell. She waited for a moment for him to get up first, but he didn't. He had passed out. She managed to slowly release herself from his grip and got up. The sound of the water coming to shore was like music to her ears. She saw the white foam on the top of the waves as it gushed into the shore and the half moon gave her just enough light to see the bay. Catherine took off running and when she reached the water she looked up to find the North Star. She had no idea where she was going and decided to head to the East. She ran along the shore as the waves rolled in around her feet. Stumbling occasionally, she would get herself back up and will herself to run farther. She was gasping for breath when she stopped and turned back to see if he followed her. She saw nothing. She began slowly walking up the beach. The sun had just begun sneaking up, offering enough daylight for her to see. Catherine could make out two buildings and as she got closer she recognized the upstairs balconies of St. Mary's orphanage. She fell to the ground, finding it hard to make her body move any further. She struggled and, half crawling and half walking, Catherine made her way to the gate.

The sisters at the orphanage were just beginning to get up and sometimes they would walk outside to sit in a quiet place and say their rosary. This morning was no different. Sister Maria was sitting on one of the steps saying the Hail Mary when she first heard the sound. She stopped praying and listened.

"Help me," she heard a small voice cry.

Sister Maria got up slowly and then heard someone crying. She rushed over to the gate and opened it. When she looked down, there was a girl with her face in her hands crouched on the ground.

Sister Maria asked, "What on earth has happened to you, my child?"

Catherine looked up at her and grabbed for Sister Maria. They held each other and Sister Maria tried to console her. When she saw Catherine's bloody face and burn marks on her neck, she answered her own question. Another sister came out to help and together they took her up on the porch. Sister Margaret came out and told the other sister to get the horse and food wagon and bring it around to the back. She would take Catherine to the hospital herself. It was a half hour before the children would wake and Sister Margaret did not want the children to be frightened by Catherine's appearance.

The three sisters picked Catherine up and put her in the back of the wagon and covered her with a blanket.

Sister Margaret flashed a whip in the air and the horse leaped forward at a steady gait. They were at the hospital in less than twenty minutes and she pulled to the back where she hoped she might find someone to help her. There were two nurses walking up to the back door when they heard the wagon and looked around.

"Help me," Sister Margaret shouted to them.

Father Jonathan was outside Catherine's room when he saw John walking fast toward him. "I need to talk to you before you go in," Father Jonathan told him. They walked over to a small office and went in. "She's alive," Father Jonathan said as he slowly filled John in on what little Catherine was able to tell him. "The police have been notified and have sent out a search party for David Brooks."

"I want to see her," John said.

"There's more," Father Jonathan hesitated, and then continued. "She's been badly abused and has bruises on her face and neck. He has broken her spirit,"

John's face went white and he put his hands over his face and cried. He felt empty and his heart ached for Catherine's pain.

After a few minutes, he went over to a wash bowl and poured some water in it and splashed it on his face. After he dried off he turned to Father Jonathan and said, "I'm ready."

Catherine was in a semi-private room but she was alone except for a nurse checking her pulse. John walked over and stood beside her. Catherine was looking the other way staring out the window. John tried not to gasp when she turned to him. He took her hand and kissed it. Tears welled up in Catherine's eyes and she looked away. John sat in a chair beside her bed and he held her hand, not sure what he should say. After a while Catherine opened her mouth to speak but nothing came out. There was a glass with some ice chips sitting on the tray beside her and John took a spoon and put some ice in her mouth. Catherine waited for the ice to melt and she swallowed.

"I'm so sorry this happened," she said.

"Shhh, we'll talk when you feel better. I'm here and I will never leave you. Try and get some sleep," John answered.

When David woke up on the beach, there were four policemen with guns aimed straight at his head. The sun was already up and he had to squint his eyes to see their faces. They helped him get up and chained his hands behind him. "What's going on?" David asked. He was only wearing his shirt.

"Go find his pants," Sergeant Husky ordered one of the officers. They helped David into his pants and put him into a police wagon. Even though Sergeant Husky had previously searched the barn, he went back inside. Husky saw where the blanket was and the rope that had apparently been used to tie her up. Catherine's partial clothing had blood on it, and lying on top was an empty whisky bottle. Husky figured David got so drunk he passed out and that was how Catherine managed to escape. If Husky wasn't so straight he would have hung David from the rafters himself.

Catherine slept for eight hours straight and John was sitting beside her when she woke up. For a few minutes, she looked up and gave him an innocent smile thinking they were home. She raised her head and looked around.

"Where am I?" She asked John.

She seemed to be incoherent and demanded that John explain why she was in the hospital. John told her she had been in an accident and not to worry, that she would be all right. He was surprised that she couldn't remember what had happened, and relieved that her memory had been erased by the trauma.

Later, John visited with the doctor, who told him it was not uncommon for people to have short term memory losses when they experienced trauma. John knew deep down that this might be a temporary fix and that at some point they would have to address what happened. He decided to take it one day at a time. For now, Catherine was safe, but would she ever get over the indignity of the rape? John wondered.

The next day, John went to city hall to talk to the public prosecutor. David was still in custody and he knew Catherine would be expected to file charges as soon as she was up to it. John did not receive the news very well. David had informed them that he and Catherine had been having an affair and that Catherine had willingly gone with him back to the barn. He admitted to getting drunk and that things had gotten a little out of hand but she was okay and he hadn't killed her. John pounded his fist on the prosecutor's desk and said loudly, "That's a lie."

The prosecutor said he didn't believe David's story either, but was Catherine willing to go through a lengthy trial and have her name tarnished by David's accusations? John couldn't believe what he was hearing.

"I have a suggestion," said the attorney. "I think I could convince the judge to send him to the penitentiary for three to five years. He will most likely be put with a chain gang outside Houston at Sugar Land. In the Texas heat on work detail chopping sugar cane, he won't last a summer.

John thought for a moment. "Catherine won't have to testify?" he asked.

"The judge will probably ask her a few questions in private and that will be it," answered the attorney.

David was not given much of a choice. Either he could face a lengthy trial and possibly face a hanging or take three years at the penitentiary and maybe get out in a year if he behaved himself. David chose the latter. He wasn't ready to die and figured he could stand just about anything for a year. David was shackled and a chain was clamped on both of his ankles. David and two deputies caught a stagecoach and headed toward Houston. After an hour and a half of hard riding over rough terrain, the stage stopped at what David thought was an outpost. He later learned that it was a prison farm just west of Sugar Land, Texas. David had heard that most prison farms had been abolished, but apparently Texas specifically depended on prison leasing to aid the sugar cane growers.

David was met by two other guards and taken to a large plantation about ten miles south of where he was dropped off. They turned
down a dirt road and he saw men chopping sugar cane on both sides of
the road. There must have been six or eight men on horseback holding
shotguns and a couple of men on the ground with whips. Most of the
convicts were black and he only saw one or two white men in the tradi-
tional striped camp uniform. He was screwed, David thought to himself. The lawyer and the judge lied to him when they told him he was
only facing a three year prison sentence. Nothing was said about being
leased out to some prison farm.

The sun was beginning to set and the prisoners were placed in
single file to march back to their living quarters at the plantation. The
plantation was run by a man everyone called Bear. There was a reason
for his name, as he stood over six feet four inches tall and was one-
quarter Indian. He ran a tight ship and was an expert with a whip.
Legend was that he could kill a man with his bare hands, thus the name
Bear. After a quick dinner of hash and a roll, David followed the group
into a structure that resembled a barn.

The conditions were filthy and the smell alone was worse than a
pig pen. He looked around for a bunk. There were rows and rows of
posts that had planks nailed to them for beds. He looked up and saw a
rat run across one of the beams. While David was walking around trying to find a place to sleep he saw a white man taking off his shirt and
the tattoos were a dead giveaway. It was Ivan, Vickie's step-dad from
Houston. Every man in the barn was staring at David, and he noticed
no one was talking. Finally, as he walked toward the rear of the building, a younger black man who couldn't have been more than sixteen
pointed to an empty bunk on the upper level. David hoisted himself up
on it and sat there for a while looking around. This was going to be his
new home now, and he shivered at the thought of spending the next
year here. The bunk was hard and the noise from the snoring convicts
kept David up most of the night.

The whistle blew at 5:00 a.m. and David followed everyone out to the outhouses. The stench was sickening but he didn't have a choice. He'd made his mind up last night he was going to get through this and when he got out, David would take revenge on the city attorney. He was going to slit the man's throat and then he would find Catherine again.

CHAPTER 32

Catherine stayed in the hospital for two days recuperating and getting her strength back. John had taken three days off from the bank and he apologized to Catherine after he took her home and had to go back to work. He felt guilty leaving her there with Amelia. She seemed to have no memory of what happed to her and he thought that it was probably best that she didn't. The judge and the prosecuting attorney had visited her while she was in the hospital and they asked him to leave the room, so he had no idea what Catherine had told them. He was glad that he could stay busy working. Catherine agreed to stay home and not return to medical school until the second semester. The professors said that as long as she passed her midterm examinations, she could stay in the same classes. John had stopped by the medical school and told them Catherine had pneumonia and had to stay in. It was a lie he told to many.

Catherine stayed in her room a lot. Her memory was beginning to come back and she stayed withdrawn. As long as John thought she couldn't remember what happened, it made it easier. She wasn't ready to discuss it with him, or anyone, for that matter. She tried to keep busy reading her textbooks and studying. Catherine and Amelia played some cribbage and a card game once in a while and Catherine put on a good front.

John and Catherine remained cordial to each other sleeping in their own beds. Occasionally John would hear her crying and he wept, too. He didn't know how to reach her. When he would try to touch her, she moved away from him. One night Catherine had a nightmare and her screaming woke John up. He ran into her room and slipped under the covers and cradled her in his arms.

"Shhh,'" he said. "I'm here and I will never leave you. I love you more than anything, please talk to me."

Catherine did not say anything and she put her arm over his and pulled it firmly around her body. Catherine didn't really know what to say. She shut her eyes tight, praying she wouldn't cry. How could John still love her? If John knew all the things David Brooks did to her, he would probably never want to touch her again. Their lives would never be the same.

Every day was a new challenge, but Catherine still had not said anything about the kidnapping. John had noticed that Catherine had quit writing on her calendar and wondered if she had forgotten about that, too.

Catherine passed her midterm semester exams with the third highest score and John told her how proud he was of her accomplishments. She smiled at him and he thought she was going to kiss him, but she didn't. Catherine and Amelia decorated the Christmas tree and planned their Christmas dinner together. Catherine had not left the house except on the day John took her to school to take her exams. He offered to take her shopping or go to the cemetery, but she made excuses.

On Christmas morning, John gave Catherine a beautiful heart-shaped locket and Amelia a gold bracelet. John was surprised when Catherine handed him a present. It was a beautiful grey, blue, and maroon scarf she had knitted. He told her he loved it and kissed her on the cheek. It was the first time she did not shy away. He was making progress, he thought, and he smiled at her. John tried to be patient with Catherine. He felt guilty that he did not protect her. He was her husband and it was his job to protect her and he had failed. John had no idea how to console her or make her feel better. She ignored every kind gesture he did. He decided that if Catherine was going to put a wall between them, he would just have to be patient. Deep down, though, John knew in his heart that the hurt was too deep. David Brooks had broken her spirit and ruined her life, and John wished he could have just killed him.

Catherine went back to school the second week in January and for the first time since her ordeal, she felt human again. She knew she had become a recluse and she felt guilty that she was so unresponsive to John. She wondered if she could ever be intimate with him again without reliving the whole ordeal she experience with David. She wished that she couldn't remember anything, but the problem was that she did remember everything. Catherine checked her calendar that evening when she got home. She noticed that she had not marked her last period and when she thought back and looked at November's calendar, she had stopped bleeding seven days before David took her. She had not had a period since. Perhaps the trauma of it all interrupted her cycle. She pushed her stomach in; it was firm and a bit bloated. Catherine broke out in a sweat and her eyes started to tear. She looked at her calendar and counted up. It was six weeks from her last period. Five weeks since the rape. She sighed and convinced herself not to think the worst. She would probably start in the next day or two.

Two weeks later Catherine woke up sick at her stomach and she raced to the bathroom and threw up. She sat on the floor for a few minutes and threw up again. The door was partially open and John watched her. A few minutes later Catherine heard the front door slam. Catherine rolled over on the floor and cried.

John stood outside without a coat on. It was misty rain and he stood there looking up at the second story bathroom. He wanted to run, hide, kill David Brooks for what he did but it would not change anything. John went back inside the house and ran up the stairs. Catherine was lying on the floor crying and he picked her up and took her in his room and closed the door. He sat on the bed cradling her in his arms.

"There is nothing that bastard could do to you that would make me stop loving you, Catherine," John said as he kissed her tears.

"I, I'm pregnant," she whispered.

"I know," John said. "I know, and we will get through this together, baby. It's not your fault, and you have to stop blaming yourself."

"Don't you have to go to work?" Catherine asked John.

"It's Saturday," John answered. He held her tight and Catherine kissed him. For the first time in months Catherine felt close to John again, and she wanted him so much. Their kissing grew more intense and she moved John's hand down between her legs.

"Are you sure you want to do this?" John asked.

Catherine answered him back with a passionate kiss. John wanted more than anything to be intimate with Catherine, but decided to move slow and give her time. He began caressing her and she relaxed and accepted the pleasure she was receiving. She pulled him down on her and received him fully and completely. She knew she had satisfied John and tried to act as though he had pleased her too. Catherine knew in time it would happen again and she didn't want John to be disappointed. It was another lie she would have to live with. John fell asleep with Catherine in his arms and she lay there wondering how John would be able to watch her belly grow with another man's child...David's bastard child.

After a short nap, John woke up first and watched Catherine sleep. She looked so innocent and he loved her so much. Then he remembered, and his shoulders began to tighten and he felt like someone had hit him in his gut. Catherine was with child and it wasn't his. John knew what he had to do. When the time came and Catherine began to show, they would act like the perfectly happy couple everyone would expect them to be.

Catherine went to the doctor the next week and it was confirmed that she was pregnant. She knew most of the doctors and chose the one she admired and trusted the most. He was also the doctor who had treated her while she was in the hospital. Dr. Alan Copeland had attended the medical school in Galveston and had been a resident at St. Mary's Hospital for eight years. He was in his mid thirties, heavy-set, and he had a sweet disposition. Catherine liked Dr. Copeland a lot and he encouraged her to stay in medical school.

"This world needs more female doctors in it," he told Catherine once. "You'll make a good one...you know more about medicine than most graduates."

John and Catherine had decided not to say anything to Amelia about the baby and John knew when he got home from work and looked at Catherine's face, that it was confirmed. Catherine said she wasn't feeling very well and went upstairs. John followed her into her room. Catherine was facing the other way when John walked in. He knew she was crying and he went over and put his arms around her.

"Catherine," John said tenderly, "What happened to you happened to both of us. We're in this together. This is our baby, yours and mine, now. We will love it as our own." Catherine turned and hugged him tightly and they stood for a while holding each other.

CHAPTER 33

David's first week was worse than hell itself. To make matters worse he was shaking and throwing up and he felt like he had a constant hangover.

"It's all that damn liquor you been drinkin. Its poison and when you don't got it, it begins to leave your insides and it's a living hell," said a sixteen-year-old boy. His name was Jasper and when David asked him why he was there, he said, "They says I stole some lunch money from a white boy when I was at the store. But that ain't true. I saw a dollar on the floor and when I picked it up and tried to hand it to him he pointed a finger at me and said I stole it." David shook his head.

The whistle blew and the men lined up, waiting for the guards to count them off in squads of twenty and get their assignments. David threw up again and a guard came by and told him to breathe through his mouth, that it might help.

Brady was one of the more laid back guards and did what he could to help the men make it through each hellacious day. He had been managing chain gangs for five years now and didn't believe in whipping and battering the convicts like most of the other guards. He believed that if they learned to respect you they would work harder and maybe you might not get killed if one of them became angry enough to try something stupid like that. David decided he was going to try and get on the good side of Brady.

Every day was the same. At least one Negro a week tried to escape and was shot. There was always another new one to take his
place. The guards insisted that talking after hours was to be kept to a
minimum. They didn't want the prisoners forming any alliances with
each other and causing problems. There were whispers throughout the
night but you couldn't really hear what anyone was saying. The barn
doors were shut and locked every night and David wondered what they
did in the summers when the Texas sun would make the barn a living
inferno inside. He had a lot of time to think and if he wasn't thinking
about survival, he was thinking of Catherine.

All the prisoners in the camp had only one name. David's was
simply "Brooks." If a new prisoner came in and had a similar name, he
was given a name like Butch or Pothead.

One guy was called Engine because he had a strong voice similar to a train engine. It didn't really matter to David what his name
was. All he wanted to do was get through his sentence and get the hell
out.

Brady liked David because he said yes sir and no sir and he did
what he was told. Once David got through his addiction to alcohol, he
knew he could stand just about anything. The first month was really
rough but he wasn't ready to die yet.

Brady called David aside one day and said, "Brooks, do you
know anything about gardening?"

"Yes, sir," David said.

"The plantation owner needs someone to work around his house
and take care of his wife's garden. Think you're up to it?" asked
Brady.

David said, "yes, sir."

The next day Brooks was told to move to a smaller group that
was headed for the plantation. Brooks looked at the other three men.
One was Ivan, plus Jasper and another Negro by the name of Rooster.
They would be accompanied by one guard on horseback carrying a pair
of six guns and a shotgun. They walked three miles to the plantation

followed by the guard on horseback. The plantation was owned by a shipping magnate by the name of Peter Esquire, Jr. who had moved to the south from New York. He knew nothing about running a plantation, so he hired the best.

Jasper was assigned to the kitchen to do the dirty jobs the maids didn't want to do. It seemed Mrs. Esquire liked the help she had and brought three ladies, a butler, and a cook from New York with her when they moved. They were a bit too proper for the south and didn't like mingling with the rest of the black slaves that did the laundry and other less desirable duties like carrying out the piss pots. The plantation had no indoor plumbing and most likely if Mrs. Esquire had known that when her husband moved the family down here, she would have protested.

Brooks, Ivan and Rooster were showed to a small piece of rocky land that was quartered off and marked with stakes. It was their job to get it ready, as Mrs. Esquire wanted to plant a fresh garden. They spent days picking up rocks and putting them in a pile. Ivan was larger than the other two men so he was harnessed like a mule and Brooks and Rooster took turns pushing the plow while Ivan pulled.

The only saving grace was that the food they got to eat at dinner time was usually the leftovers from the family supper the night before. At the end of the day the three men and the guard made their three-mile walk back to the barn. Mrs. Esquire took a liking to Jasper and he was moved into the slave quarters located just outside the main house.

Catherine sensed that John was trying really hard to find acceptance of everything that had happened. Catherine was struggling inside to come to terms with the fact that her life had been drastically changed. She asked John if he wanted her to quit school but he told her that was her decision to make and that once the baby came, someone would have to care for it. Catherine knew there were no easy answers. Of course when the baby came, she would have to stay home and take care of it. She wouldn't expect Amelia to, and Amelia certainly wasn't capable.

Catherine wasn't quite two and a half months pregnant when she woke up one morning and started bleeding. She had a really bad backache and decided it would be a good idea to go by the hospital first to see Dr. Copeland and be just a little late for her second class at the medical school. She didn't say anything to John when he left for work. She knew he would be worried and she didn't want him to miss any more work. Since Dr. Copeland was busy making his rounds, he asked Catherine to wait in one of the examination rooms.

"I'm afraid you've miscarried," Dr. Copeland said. "The body has a way of absorbing most of the tissue, but I think we can take care of what's left and make sure an infection doesn't set in. This may be a bit uncomfortable," Dr. Copeland said as he probed inside of Catherine's uterus. Catherine heard him put something in a metal bowl and hand it to his nurse. Catherine grimaced at the sharp pain and felt violated by the procedure, but she knew it was necessary.

"Would you like me to put in a call to your husband at his bank?" Dr. Copeland asked.

"No," Catherine said. "I'm not hurting too badly and I don't want him to worry."

"All right, then, you just stay here and rest for an hour or so and I'll check back with you in between patients," Dr. Copeland said.

That's it? Catherine thought, the baby's gone? Catherine was covered in a sheet when someone knocked and Father Jonathan stuck his head in the door. He walked over to Catherine and put his hand on her forehead like he was checking for a fever.

"Our God works in mysterious ways, Catherine. I'm sorry for the loss of your unborn child but perhaps this is best. You and John can make a fresh start. Time heals a lot of things." Catherine smiled at him but didn't answer.

Dr. Copeland didn't come back until almost noon and Catherine had fallen asleep. "You are going to be just fine and you and John can have a dozen more children, if you want them," Dr. Copeland said. "You can leave when you feel up to it. You'll probably continue bleeding for four or five more days and then there will be a down time while your body tries to heal. If you and John don't want any children right now it would be best if you used a contraceptive or just abstain, and once your monthly cycle is normal, just go back to doing what you were doing," Dr. Copeland said and left Catherine alone again.

Catherine sat up and got off the exam table. It was hard for her to come to terms with the fact that she had lost her first child. Even though she had gotten pregnant by a mad man, the baby was half hers. She felt a little dizzy, so she held onto the table while she put the rest of her clothing back on. She felt weak but took in a deep breath and walked out of the hospital. It took Catherine fifteen minutes to walk to the trolley because she had to stop periodically to rest. She finally made it home and when she got there, Amelia and her caregiver were having lunch. Catherine excused herself saying she had a bad headache and went upstairs. She lay on the bed and cried. Would she ever feel right again? More importantly, would she really be able to have children?

John had clients at the bank most of the day. By the time he finished up his usual duties, it was almost 6:00 p.m. It was a clear, cool day and John thought the walk home might clear his head. By the time he got home, he had made a decision to ask Catherine to give up her schooling at the end of May and prepare for the arrival of the baby. By her and the doctor's calculations, the baby would arrive sometime in the middle of August.

When John got home, Amelia told John that Catherine had left school around noon and had come home with a bad headache. John knocked on Catherine's door and went in. "Honey, are you alright?" John asked. He walked over to the bed and sat down.

Catherine crawled up in his lap and said, "The baby's gone." John looked confused. "I miscarried."

"Are you all right?" John asked. Catherine shook her head yes, and told him that she had seen Dr. Copeland and that she would still be able to have children.

John hugged her and rocked her back and forth. Inwardly he was happy that they wouldn't have to face the challenge of bringing up an unwanted baby, but knew it would be hard on Catherine. "We will," John said. "We will have lots of children when you are ready."

John and Catherine spent a lot of time talking. They talked about everything except what happened the night she was abducted. He knew inside that Catherine remembered more than she let on, but figured it was her way of dealing with it.

They went back to their old routine of making love once or twice a month but the sadness never left Catherine's eyes. Catherine's spirit was broken and he knew that in a lifetime it would never heal.

Catherine finished her first year of medical school and went back to work at St. Mary's Hospital in June. John knew she loved working there, and with David Brooks in prison, she wouldn't have to be looking over her shoulder She seemed happier and every once in a while he could see a sparkle in her eye when she talked about saving a life or helping deliver a baby. But he knew the sparkle she once had in her eye with him was a thing of the past. Maybe that was supposed to happen, he thought. John had never experienced that same kind of passion with his first wife. When they had first married, they were intimate a lot in the first year but she never was into it like Catherine was when they first married. John's and Catherine's love-making had been special, and he missed that special bond they had experienced that first year. John was desperate to bring back the magic they once had, but he just didn't know how.

The Texas heat was beginning to set in and with the daylight lasting longer, it only meant more hours of hard labor. David, Ivan and Rooster continued to walk the three miles to the plantation every day and they had begun planting for the summer harvest. Jasper stayed at night with the other help in the old slave quarters. The garden was uphill from a spring-fed creek that they had dug out and dammed up with the rocks they had removed from the garden. Every day first thing, they spent hours filling buckets of water and carrying them up to water the crops. Their only salvation was that they could cool off from the Texas heat by dipping in the pool of water. Once the turnip greens, tomatoes, onions, cabbage and corn came in, the ground had to be tilled and made ready for the fall crop.

The summer heat played havoc with everyone. The creek started drying up, which meant they had to haul the water further in order to water the garden. Rooster was good with his hands and made a wheelbarrow so they could carry larger amounts of water farther and they wouldn't have to break their backs. The men didn't talk a lot and David had no intention in forming a bond with Ivan. David was still angry with Ivan's brutality towards Vickie but Ivan was oblivious since he had never met David before the prison farm.

David often thought of Catherine and the night he was with her. His hunger for sex was still there and he couldn't help but notice the women around the house. The guard was always no more than twenty feet away so it was impossible to have one.

The barn was opened up and aired out during the summer. The prisoners slept outside on the ground and each man was chained to the man next to him. They were chained in groups of five. David did some math in his head and figured he could petition the court for early release by next summer. He was sober now and he knew how to play the game. Most of the guards seemed to like him and he knew Brady would give him a good recommendation. It was just a matter of time and he had a lot of it.

David and his two prison mates had already left the camp and were about a mile out when there were several blasts of gun fire.

"Down on the ground," their guard yelled.

The three men fell to the ground.

"Hands over the back of your head, face down," the guard yelled and they complied.

David could see that the guard was nervous and he laid still, smelling the dirt coming up into his nostrils. There were more gun shots coming from their camp and the guard turned and looked back.

In that split second Rooster and Ivan jumped up and pulled the guard off his horse. Ivan grabbed his rifle and hit him over the head with the butt. They dug the keys out of the guard's pants pocket and undid their chains. Ivan mounted the horse but before he could take off, the guard pulled his six guns and shot him in the face. Rooster stood frozen looking up at the guard and the guard took aim at Rooster's heart and shot him. The guard pointed the gun at David, who lay frozen in the dirt.

"You wanna join them?" asked the guard.

"No, sir," David answered. "I wasn't in on their scheme, please don't shoot me," he begged.

The guard pulled the trigger back and shot a few inches from David's head and it was close enough to make his ears to ring . "You're not fit for living you coward. Now git your ass up and find a shovel," he told David. "Now dig three graves," he ordered.

It must have been a hundred degrees when David started digging. When he finished the first two graves, the guard told him to put the two men in the graves and cover them up. The guard motioned to the shovel and David picked it up and started digging. He thought seriously for a moment about hitting the guard over the head with the shovel but he saw a man riding up on a horse. It was Brady. Brady questioned the guard and then told him to take David back to the camp.

When David got back to camp, he found out that two guards and eight men had been killed. The prisoners had to go back in the fields and work and they only stopped once for a water break. They were not fed that day and they worked until sundown.

CHAPTER 34

Catherine loved being back at the hospital. The sisters, some of whom were nurses, and the doctors, called her Dr. Catherine. She was well respected and even though she still had three more years of medical school ahead of her, she was able to work hand in hand with the doctors. She was going to be eighteen in six months and she had the maturity of someone much older. No one at the hospital ever asked her about that night she had spent with David Brooks, but it haunted her like a ghost. It crept into her life at the most unexpected times. Once, a man who looked similar to David Brooks had been shot and brought into the hospital. Catherine froze when the doctor asked her to assist him. She often experienced crazy dreams, and the one she dreaded most was the one when David Brooks had both her mother and her tied up, and David raped her mother, forcing Catherine to watch. She grew accustomed to getting very little sleep and the nights that she slept with John were the worst. Catherine always had a nightmare afterwards and she would often leave John's bed and go back to her room so she wouldn't disturb him.

On several occasions, John would take Father Jonathan to lunch and would ask him for his counsel and prayers.

"Catherine is going through a difficult time right now and she is using her work as a means to deal with it," Father Jonathan told John. "You must be patient. Perhaps you should be more persistent with her. If Catherine were to get pregnant it would give her something else to think about instead of herself," Father Jonathan counseled. John thought seriously about what Father Jonathan said and told him that he might consider that.

After Catherine recovered from her miscarriage, she began attending mass with John and Amelia. Afterwards, the three would go somewhere for lunch and then go home. John usually went into his study, Amelia took a nap, and Catherine would go up to her room and study or sew.

That Sunday, John decided to change his routine. Catherine was putting on a simple housedress for comfort and John knocked and came into her room. Catherine smiled and asked what he wanted. John walked over to her and leaned over and kissed the back of her neck. He pulled the straps of her slip off and it fell to the ground. She didn't have anything on except her pantalets.

"I just miss what we used to have and I wanted to see you, feel you, and love you. Oh, Catherine, my body aches for you," John said in a whimper.

Catherine was stunned by John's aggressiveness and before she could say anything he had picked her up and put her on the bed. He was kissing her and taking his clothes off at the same time and then took off her pantalets.

"What if I get pregnant?" Catherine said in a whisper.

"Just let me have you for once, please," John begged. Catherine didn't know what to say but was submissive to his advances.

Catherine fought back the tears as the memory of her night with David took over. It did not take John long to give in to his desires. When it was over, John felt guilty and apologized. Catherine didn't say anything. She felt violated, even though she didn't resist. She knew men had physical desires that every wife was expected to meet, but John had never made her feel like it was her duty until today. John got up and dressed and left the room without saying anything else.

John had begun making it a habit of coming into Catherine's bed when he felt like it and one night after he had made love to her, she said, "You want me to get pregnant, don't you?"

"I want you to be my wife again. I can't change what has happened to you and I thought maybe if we had a baby it would make you stop thinking about yourself. There are two of us in this marriage," John answered back.

"I'm sorry I've been so selfish," Catherine answered. "If there are two of us in this marriage, why can't I have a say as to when I want to get pregnant?" Catherine had surprised herself. She had never had an argument with John and now she was snapping back at him.

Not knowing what to say, Catherine got up and put on her robe and went downstairs. A short time later, John went downstairs and found Catherine in the kitchen. She was waiting on the kettle to boil to make hot tea. John sat down across from her.

"You are right," John said. "I should have discussed it with you first and I am so sorry. Please forgive me." Catherine didn't answer. The kettle started to scream and Catherine picked it up off the stove and made two cups of tea. "I never knew I could love someone so much that it would cloud my judgment. You are everything to me, and I promise I will never ever hurt you like this again," John said.

Catherine touched John's hand and looked into his eyes. There were tears and he looked away.

"You were right," Catherine replied. "I have been thinking about myself. I thought that by throwing myself into my studies and my work it would all go away. I realize now that I have only been putting a wall between us. You are everything to me, and I love you so much," Catherine continued. Catherine got up and went to John. He held her in his lap and they hugged each other for a long time.

"Why don't we just forget about the calendar and let it be God's decision," Catherine said. "I know you want children, and so do I. I want to be your wife first, and I am not going to let my selfish desires be the cause of our problems. I love you, John Merit, and the past is behind us now."

John and Catherine finished their tea and John carried Catherine up to her room and put her in bed.   He turned to leave and Catherine grabbed his hand.

"Sleep in my bed tonight, please," she said and smiled up at him.

They fell asleep in each other's arms, and for the first time in months Catherine slept through the night.

Galveston had moved into a new century and the new U S. Census boasted that Galveston had grown at a rate of almost thirty percent, indicating that it was the fastest growing city in the South.   Thousands of immigrants were arriving weekly.   There were more and more automobiles and the telephone company had begun installing phone lines in many residential areas.   John had applied earlier in the year for a new phone and was relieved when his was installed.   They would be on a party line with four other neighbors.   Having a phone accessible if Amelia got sick or if he needed to call home when he had to work late gave him both comfort and security.   It was new-found freedom for John.   It meant that he wouldn't have to stay at home on Saturdays all day with Amelia and since Catherine worked most Saturdays, John decided that he would begin swimming Saturday mornings at the YMCA. He left the YMCA phone number and his work number by the phone in his study in case of any emergencies.   He also called home frequently just to let Amelia know his whereabouts and to ask if she needed anything.   Catherine used the phone to call and let John know when she was leaving the hospital to come home.

Catherine and John's relationship began to slowly mend.   They both worked hard at it.   After church one Sunday, John suggested that they all go to the beach.   Amelia was not up to it and told John he could check on her in the middle of the afternoon around 3:30 after her nap. Catherine and John were excited and made a picnic lunch.   The day was beautiful and the beach was not too terribly crowded.   They laughed and played in the water like two children and snuggled on their blanket like two teenagers.   It was a wonderful day and they had rented a large umbrella to lie under.   It was almost 4:00 p.m. when John got to a phone and called Amelia. She said everything was fine and that she was making soup for supper.

"No set time," she said. "You can have it whenever." Amelia laughed.

Catherine and John stayed until almost 6:00 and then went home. It was almost like old times, Catherine thought. She was slowly beginning to forget about the terrible night with David Brooks and looked forward to hers and John's love-making. There was only one thing haunting her now. She and John had stopped looking at the calendar and their love-making was more spontaneous. Why hadn't she gotten pregnant? She wondered to herself.

Catherine was looking forward to starting medical school in September. In a way, she was glad that she hadn't gotten pregnant. If she waited another month, then she would be able to finish her second year before the baby came. She smiled and was happy that a baby might be in their near future. Catherine was working at the hospital six full days a week, and she loved the people she worked with. The sisters were very supportive of her and she felt the doctors respected her too, even though she was a woman. If she did have a baby next summer, she would put her plans for medical school on hold and then just work part time at the hospital unless she could find a nanny. She would have to discuss that idea with John first. She loved him so much and she didn't want her dreams about becoming a doctor to come between her and John and their future.

John had already dressed for work on Friday morning when Catherine came downstairs. John had read on page three of the newspaper that there had been a terrible storm south of Florida and it was following a north-westerly route across the Gulf of Mexico. John and Catherine got into a discussion about storms and Catherine told John about the storm they had had in Sandgate and how it had washed out some of the roads, causing her father's and brother's deaths. Catherine asked John about the storms he had been through and he told her about a horrific storm in August of 1886, which destroyed the town of Indianola, Texas, about 150 miles south of Galveston, Texas. Catherine inquired about tropical storms in Galveston, and John said most people were not too concerned about them.

CHAPTER 35

On Saturday, September 8, 1900, Catherine was up early and made oatmeal for John before he left to go swimming at the YMCA. She scanned the paper for any news about the tropical storm and found a short article about the storm traveling in a more westerly direction and that it would most likely come through the Gulf and then turn northwest across Louisiana. Catherine put the paper down and opened the front door. Yesterday, the paper said the storm would go north across Florida, today it said it would go north across Louisiana. It hadn't turned north yet. What if it didn't? She wondered. What if it didn't turn north until it hit Texas? Catherine looked up at the sky. Rain clouds had drifted in and the wind had picked up. She went back into the house.

"Oh, there you are," said John.

"I went to look at the sky," Catherine answered.

"Why?" asked John.

"The storm that was in the paper yesterday had not turned yet and I was just wondering what we would do if the storm hit Galveston," Catherine said. She pointed at the article.

John read it and said, "I'll keep an eye out. If the wind picks up by noon, I'll put the storm shutters over the windows."

"But what about rising water?" Catherine said. "Sometimes when we had storms in Sandgate the waves would reach half way up the cliffs. There are no cliffs in Galveston. It's basically flat."

"That's why the houses closest to the beach are on eight- and ten-foot. stilts." John said, and kissed her good-bye.

They were not aware that several inches of seawater had already covered streets up to four blocks in from the beach on the Gulf side of the city, and the waves were getting higher.

Catherine couldn't help but worry about a potential storm. Before she left, she asked Amelia if she would be all right until John got home at noon.

"Of course, why wouldn't I be?" Amelia asked.

"Well, it looks like we might get some wind and rain and I just want you to be safe," Catherine answered. Catherine grabbed her umbrella and before she left she wrote down a phone number on a pad beside the phone. It was the number for the hospital and the floor she would be working on.

"I left you my phone number so you can call me if you need something," Catherine told Amelia and then she left.

It was already 8:40 a.m. when Catherine left the house. The wind had picked up quite a bit and the sprinkles of rain seemed to be surrounding her umbrella causing her face and her dress to get wet. She wondered why the rain came so intermittently and from different directions. She was glad she had not missed her trolley and made it to work on time. She didn't really know why, but something was nagging at her insides and she couldn't put a finger on it. Catherine's thoughts turned to John and she was glad he was getting out more and doing something he enjoyed. He was the most understanding and loving man, and she couldn't imagine life with anyone else. She had worked hard at putting her brutal attack by David Brooks behind her, and her life was beginning to have more meaning. John was so sweet and loving and she admired his patience.

When Catherine arrived at the hospital, she went to her locker to put on her laboratory coat. Her clothing was damp but she didn't mind. It was really warm inside the building and she hoped it would cool her off. She overheard several of the sisters discussing the weather and she tried to hear what they were saying, but only heard bits and pieces. Catherine was called to one of the rooms by Dr. Copeland and she forgot about the weather.

John finished his swim and then gathered with several other men at a diner across from the YMCA. They had heard from several people that the water had begun rising and that the people closest to the beach might feel more secure if they moved their families inland toward the city. John hated to admit it, but maybe Catherine's concern about the weather had some merit. He decided to head home and take the necessary precautions and board up the windows. It was close to 11:00 a.m. when he got home. He had not brought an umbrella but he didn't mind the rain. Amelia was glad to see him and said several of her friends had called and suggested that they seek a more secure place to ride out the storm. John could feel Amelia's concern so he told her to pack up the things she needed and he would take her to St. Mary's Hospital where Catherine was. "You can stay in one of the waiting rooms," John said.

Both John and Amelia put on their raincoats, and after walking part of the way to the trolley, Amelia kept getting caught up in her skirt so John picked her up and carried her the last block.

They finally made it to the hospital and John went to find Catherine. After Catherine and John got Amelia settled, John said he was going back home to board up the windows. Catherine was surprised that he was going back. "It won't take that long and if I don't do it, the damage could be really bad," John explained. "I'll call and leave word for you when I get through," he assured her.

It had begun raining on the night of September 7, 1900, in Sugar Land. The prisoners moved into the shabby barn that was supposed to be their shelter. The barn doors were left open so each prisoner was chained to the prisoner who was closest to him in groups of five and six. There were at least a dozen leaks in the roof and the rain water dripped onto several of the bunks causing those prisoners to sleep on the wet ground. David's was one of those bunks. He was chained with three others in a dry corner uphill from the running water, so his ground was still dry. The wind howled and the rain hitting the tin roof sounded like fire crackers going off. Sleep only came in small intervals and when one convict moved, the other men moved in the same direction. It was a terrible night and they welcomed dawn gladly.

The wind and rain had let up and hard, damp rolls were passed out for their breakfast. There had been some wind damage to the main plantation house the night before, so David and another, black, convict, called Rabbit because he had big pointed ears, were told to go with a guard and make the necessary repairs. The three-mile walk took longer than usual because of the muddy, wet ground. At one point the guard's horse slipped and the guard almost fell off but they recovered and continued the walk. It was hard to know what time it was when they got there because the sky was covered by thick black clouds and it had begun to rain again. David and Rabbit spent the first hour recovering the boards and roof shingles that had blown off the big house. David figured it was getting close to noon because he was getting really hungry. The guard blew his whistle just as the dinner bell rang, and motioned the two men to follow him. They walked to the back of the house where they were each given a plate of food. The three men walked over to the slave quarters and sat under the porch eating their meal. The slave quarters were about five hundred feet from the main house. They were almost through eating when someone came out of the main house and yelled, "tornado coming," and the dinner bell rang again.

Rabbit and David stood and looked in the direction of where they were pointing and saw a large, black, funnel cloud. David figured it was about three-quarters of a mile away. He saw the family and the help running outside and opening a storm door. Everyone walked through the open doors and disappeared under ground. Jasper was the last man standing by the open shelter and he was holding the door open. He waved for the three men to come. The guard slapped his horse and it ran off. He grabbed a set of chains and told Rabbit and David to hold out their hands so he could chain them to the porch.

Rabbit held out his hands and when the guard went to put the chains on him, David jumped the guard and knocked his head into the post. He gave his neck a violent twist and the guard went down. Jasper stood watching and David gave him a quick salute. Rabbit took off running away from the tornado. David thought better and ran toward the lower end of the dried creek bed and followed it in a south-easterly direction. He turned and saw that the tornado was gaining ground on him and he ran as hard and fast as he could in the mud and rain until he came to a small bridge and dove under it. Debris and limbs were flying all around him. David inched up between the two railroad ties that were holding the bridge and wrapped his arms around the smallest one, locking his arms together. The wind was like a locomotive traveling through his head, and he closed his eyes to keep the splinters and debris from hitting his eyes. It seemed to last forever but it was over in a matter of minutes. David continued to hold on for dear life, not sure if the eye of the tornado had already passed. He was alive and he had never been so terrified and then it began to tear away at him again. The eye had passed over him, and the worst had not yet come. The second hit was unimaginable, lifting David from his refuge and tearing away at every limb of his body. It was over and David knew it. His last thoughts were of Catherine.

The tornado had torn off the front of the second floor gallery of the plantation house and had destroyed the slave quarters. The family and the help were safe. The guard was found over a mile away, as was Rabbit. Both were dead from what everyone assumed were injuries caused by the tornado. Jasper never told anyone any different. David's body was never found, and he was also presumed dead.

CHAPTER 36

John splashed through several inches of water on his way back home. He pulled the storm shutters and boards out of the store room and began putting them on the lower floor of the house. The rain was beating down hard on his face and it felt like small nails stinging him. When he finished the lower floor, he retrieved the ladder and began putting the wood over the windows at the back of the house, which faced the Gulf. When he crawled up the ladder and looked toward the Gulf, he saw huge waves crashing over the beach. He worked quickly and when he got down from the ladder, he felt water coming into his shoes. The wind was picking up and he had four windows on the front of the house that he had not boarded up yet.

Catherine hadn't stopped to look at the time until she took the pulse of one of the patients. It was 12:30 p.m. She hadn't had lunch yet and she needed to check on Amelia, so when she finished she went to the second floor waiting room to see her. Catherine was surprised at the number of people in the room. There must have been at least twenty people, including some children. Amelia was still in the chair John had left her in. Catherine walked over to Amelia and helped her gather her things.

"Come with me," said Catherine, "I'll find you someplace that is not so crowded and I'll get you some lunch."

Catherine scanned the room and did not see John. Amelia asked if Catherine had heard from John, and Catherine told her she would call the house once she had Amelia settled. There was a staff lounge area at the end of the hall and Catherine took Amelia there. The room had a couple of beds for the staff to use when they worked the night shift. Amelia told Catherine that Father Jonathan had brought her some lunch earlier and that she was concerned about John, so Catherine went to make the call. The phone rang a dozen times and there was no answer. Either John was on his way back to the hospital or he was still putting up the storm shutters. Catherine asked Amelia how long it usually took John to put the storm shutters over the windows and she told her about one to two hours. Catherine did not want to worry Amelia, so she smiled and said he was probably on his way back now.

It was 2:30 p.m. and more and more families were arriving at St. Mary's. Father Jonathan and the sisters were trying to make the families as comfortable as possible and many had to sit on the floor. All the rooms were full with people who had been hurt by flying debris or other related injuries from the wind and storm. The emergency room doctors and nurses were busy treating cuts and some broken limbs of children who had fallen playing in the ankle-deep water.

Catherine tried calling John again, and was told by the operator that all phone lines were out because of downed telephone poles. Catherine walked up to the third floor and went to the far back corner window to look out. She was horrified at what she saw. The waves had crashed over the road along the beach and the first three streets where the houses sat were all underwater. There was hardly a standing structure along the beach, and the streets had disappeared. She looked out to the area where their house stood but the rain was so heavy it was hard to see that far. Catherine next went to the other side of the building and looked out toward the wharf. Boats were cradling back and forth and it looked as if some of the boats were now on one of the streets that was also under water.

Catherine hurried down the three flights of stairs to the first floor and found herself in several inches of water. People were everywhere looking for shelter. She saw Father Jonathan and asked whether he had seen John come in, but he shook his head no. Catherine was beside herself and started to run out the front door but Father Jonathan stopped her.

"The trolley is no longer running," he said.

Tears welled up in Catherine's eyes.

"Perhaps he decided to wait it out at your home," Father Jonathan said. A nurse stopped and told Catherine that one of the doctors needed her in the emergency room.

Maybe John hurt himself and is in the emergency room, Catherine thought to herself.

She ran sloshing in the water and when she got there she looked around but didn't see John.

"We have to move all the patients upstairs. The water is rising much too quickly," said one of the interns.

It was tedious and difficult trying to move the patients on stretchers up the stairs. Catherine carried babies and small children upstairs and placed them in the wards where the sisters were looking after them. Parents followed carrying their own children.

After everyone had been evacuated from the first floor, Catherine raced up to the third floor again and looked out. There were no streets. Crates, boxes and debris floated in random directions and then Catherine saw a lifeless dog floating. Shortly after that, she saw a large object that looked like man's clothing over a box and she realized that it was a man and he was dead. Catherine almost fainted from the thought that it could have been John, but it wasn't.

John finished putting up the storm shutters and other boards over the windows and went inside to clean up. His house stood four feet off the ground on large posts and he had to wade in over two feet of water to get to his front door. He left the ladder where he had last worked. When he got inside, he quickly went upstairs and took off all his clothing and threw all of it in the bathtub. John put on some old slacks and a work shirt and found his old rain boots in the back of the closet. He went back downstairs and went into his study to call Catherine. When he picked up the phone, it was dead. He hadn't eaten since breakfast except for the coffee and donut he had at the diner and thought it best to grab something before he left. John grabbed two slices of bread, some cheese, and a couple of pieces of ham and put it between the bread, taking a bite immediately. He went to the closet and put on his rain coat holding his sandwich between his teeth. When John opened the front door he was stunned by what he saw. In the thirty minutes he had been in the house the water was beginning to flow over his small front porch and began seeping into his house. That meant it had risen a foot in thirty minutes.

He looked out and saw lumber and debris from someone's house flow past him. He closed the door quickly. There was no way he would be able to walk all the way to the hospital. The trolleys were run on electricity and he knew they most likely were not working. John put his sandwich on a side table and went through the kitchen to the back porch. He retrieved a lantern, some matches and his life jacket. He walked back through the living room, picked up his sandwich, and took another bite. He noticed that as he walked, water was sloshing under his feet. He went to the kitchen and turned on the water faucet. It spurted and spit out dark-colored water. John smelled it and it smelled of sewer. He opened the refrigerator and took out a jug of water and milk and put them on the counter. He took the pan that they used to rinse dishes in and he filled it with cheese, lunch meat, some leftover chicken and a loaf of bread. He gathered it all up and took it upstairs. When he came back down to get the lantern and life vest, he noticed the water was up a few more inches. John made many more trips downstairs carrying important items back upstairs. He gathered pictures, things from his office, personal items from Amelia's room, each time noticing the water getting higher and higher and the howling of the wind stronger. Before John made his last trip downstairs he lit the lantern and placed it at the top of the stairs. He looked at the clock on the mantel and it said 4:00 p.m. He knew Catherine and Amelia would be frantic with worry and he picked up the phone one more time to see if he could reach an operator.

The silence on the other end of the phone sent an urgent message to his brain. He might not get out of this alive. John put the receiver back on its cradle and he stood frozen, wondering what his next move should be. He was angry with himself for not leaving earlier and knew Amelia and Catherine would be frantic with worry. It was too late to make an escape out the door so he thought it best to wait it out here. His thoughts were rambling in so many directions. His biggest concern right now was that if the water continued to rise, even up to the second story, he would be trapped. By nailing the storm shutters and boards to the outside of the house he had created a tomb inside. The water was up past his rain boots so John took them off and wadded through the living room and through the kitchen. He kept his tools in a closet next to the back door and he managed to get the door open by pulling with all his strength. After it finally opened, John felt around looking for a crowbar.

It was getting really dark now. The electricity had stopped working several hours ago and the light from the lantern did not give off enough light where he had placed it. John's hand finally gripped the crowbar and he turned and wadded back to the stairs. For some reason he began to feel cold. He was wet from his waist down and he went upstairs to the bathroom again and took off his wet clothes, throwing them in the bathtub on top of the others. If he was ultimately going to have to swim for his life, he needed to dress accordingly. John carefully selected a long sleeve shirt and pants that would protect his arms and legs from getting scratched. He put on three pairs of socks. Shoes were not an option. John picked up the life vest and put it on, pulling it tightly around his chest. It was a little small but it would give him some relief if he had to swim out. John next moved from room to room upstairs carrying his lantern, looking for an obvious window to make his exit. He decided the window in the bathroom would be his best escape because it faced north away from the bay. The window was stuck, and he couldn't raise it. Using the crowbar, John loosened the siding around the window. Next he removed the glass. Water began leaking through the shutters over the opening. Now what? He thought to himself. He began thinking of Amelia and Catherine, taking his mind off his own crisis. John took the lantern and walked into Catherine's room. He imagined her lying naked on her bed, motioning him to join her, and his eyes filled with tears. He might not ever see her again. John walked over to Catherine's desk and sat down in her chair. He took out a piece of paper and began writing her a letter.

My dearest Catherine:

> *Not knowing what God has in mind for me and unsure if I will ever see you again; I wanted you to know that my life began when I met you. You have brought me peace and joy that not every man will receive and I thank you for choosing me to be your husband. You are with me always, in life and in death.*

> *I love you,*
> *John*

John carefully folded the note and picked up Catherine's powder jar from her dressing table. He opened it and poured the powder out on the floor and placed the note inside. He screwed the lid on tightly and sat it back on her dressing table. John was about to compose another note to Amelia when he heard a tremendous thud on the side of the house. When John stood up, his socks were soaked. He quickly went into the bathroom, opened the window, and jabbed a peep hole between two boards he used to cover the outside of the window. He tried to look out but only saw darkness. Was it time? he wondered. Should he escape now? If the room continued to fill with water, the house might collapse, or he could drown. John's common sense willed him to leave. With all his might, John pushed and prodded the outside boards loose. Water was rising up to his waist and he hoisted himself up on the seal of the window and sat on the ledge with his legs dangling out.

There was just enough light for John to see the immediate devastation of the damage the storm had birthed. Street car trestles and yards of beams and wire floated past him. Several of his neighbor's houses had disappeared and the ones that remained standing looked like they were floating. Some were wavering back and forth. Something floated towards John and hit his legs; it was a corpse, a woman. John shuddered and watched bewildered by the sight and was undecided whether to jump into the water or wait for some miracle to come along and save him. He had no choice. He heard a roaring sound and the walls of his house collapsed underneath him.

John grabbed for a piece of one of the boards he pried off from his house and pushed off, forcing his body to lie face down on the board. It wasn't wide enough for his body but was narrow enough for him to use his hands to push away anything he came in contact with. It was dark, cold, and the pounding rain drove nails of pain into his back.

John felt like he was moving in circles and he prayed silently for God to end this madness. There were cries of despair in the dark coming from every direction and he realized he was not alone. John put the side of his face down on the board that was his lifeline and he gripped the sides tightly so he would stay on. How long would this last? John thought, and then he began to pray that if it was his time, God would take him quickly. He was ready. Although he was not yet twenty-eight, God had blessed him with a wonderful, full life and he was grateful for that. John began thinking of Catherine and Amelia and found peace knowing they were probably safe at St. Mary's Hospital.

The powerful storm created winds traveling over 100-miles per hour at approximately 6:00 in the evening. Darkness covered the sky and the strong vigorous winds became a force to be reckoned with. Many of the townspeople were killed by flying debris and timbers trying to make their way to the north side of the city.

The houses along the beach were no longer sitting on their

foundations and had either floated away or collapsed into the raging water. St. Mary's Orphanage housed over ninety children and ten nuns. The large row of tall sandy dunes supported by the salt cedar trees in front of the buildings provided little protection from the southern Gulf. There was nothing they could do. The nuns prayed and had the children sing their favorite songs, including "Queen of the Waves." There was no mercy for their despair. The sisters moved all the orphans into the girls' dormitory because it was newer and they felt it would be stronger. The younger children cried and the sisters did their best to console them. The sisters' greatest concern was for the smaller children so they tied clothesline rope around the waist of the little ones, tying six- to eight-children at a time, and then securing it to one of the sisters.

The fatal tidal surge struck the south shore and slammed into the two buildings, causing the boys' empty dormitory to collapse first and then it was slowly carried away by flood waters. Everyone had been moved from the Chapel on the first floor of the girl's dormitory to the second floor when water began to fill the lower level. Almost every window had been shattered, forcing the wind and rain throughout the building. Panic and fear filled the tender hearts of all present.

The end was relatively quick as the building seemed to be lifted up by the hands of God off its foundation. The roof came crashing down on those inside, causing immediate destruction. Their precious lives had been engulfed by the bay and the orphanage was no more.

The hospital was packed to capacity with many who were injured and those who had lost their homes. There was shock on all of their faces, many crying and many just staring at the floor. Catherine met Father Jonathan in the hall and she asked if he had seen John. He shook his head, no. Catherine got up and went to check on Amelia, who was just as anguished as Catherine was.

"We have to stay strong," Catherine told her. "John is a survivor, and I know he will come."

Catherine wished she really felt that strong, but she didn't want to worry Amelia any more than she was. Catherine knew if she didn't eat something soon she would feel faint and she knew the hospital needed her help. She wasn't hungry, but she slipped back to her locker and took out the bag of food she had brought for her lunch. She stood by her locker and forced herself to eat the bagel and cheese sandwich she brought. She put an uneaten half back in her locker for later. It would be a long night. Catherine could hear the demonic howling of the wind and felt an agony deep in her gut. Please, John, please come to me, she prayed. Catherine returned to the makeshift emergency room on the second floor and assisted the doctors. There were numerous injuries, broken limbs, cuts and bruises, and some had head trauma. She worked tirelessly throughout the night.

John's nightmare left him clutching a small board that his life depended on. The malignant storm was showing no mercy. Sections of roofs and dead animals bumped into him and one by one, children, women, and men, some black, some white. The storm's tyranny on the city did not discriminate. Whatever was in its path was consumed by the jaws of the mountainous waves. John seemed to drift in and out of sleep once the wind died down. His adrenalin kept him alert most of the night, but exhaustion set in and he must have fallen asleep. When he woke up he was trapped in a tangled wreckage of wood, telephone lines and fences. He heard moans and cries of other stranded, hopeless people, and prayed again for God to put an end to his misery. The intense blackness of the night seemed to last forever. There was a terrible chill in the air and John's growing pangs of hunger reminded him that he may have already had his last meal. John's past pierced his mind and he could see his first wife and unborn child, as well as his deceased parents. Was this it? He wondered. Is this the end? John's anguished body, weak, bruised and cut, simply drifted off to sleep again.

Thousands of Galvestonians were swallowed up throughout the night. Families taking shelter in their own homes drowned as their homes were ripped to pieces and carried away, their mutilated and mangled bodies lost in the darkness. Some went adrift as the waves retired back to the waters of the Gulf, never to be seen again. Houses and buildings were no longer there. Only the remnants of what once was.

Sunday morning's dawn shed a new light over the darkened corners of the city. The lone weary monster of a hurricane had proudly and cruelly played out its role, devastating whatever was in its path. What it had missed, the flood waters of the Gulf powerfully, and with malice, devoured in seconds. Those who survived had not slept the night before and nothing could have prepared them for this day of horror. They had come face-to-face with death in every shape imaginable. There were no streets and no houses. There were only piles of lumber and debris. The few houses and buildings, including St Mary's Hospital that had withstood the disaster were badly damaged. You could not walk very far without stepping over the dead. There were layers of slime that seemed to be breeding in the streets and often there would be a body that was naked. Their clothing had been ripped from their bodies.

Catherine, the doctors, nurses, priests, nuns and staff worked diligently throughout the night caring for everyone and doing what they could to minister to those who had lost loved ones. Catherine worked tirelessly to minister aid to the fallen victims and devastated families, and did so without sleep.

Dawn had broken and the fury of the night was over. Amelia had slept some but was hungry now. There was little food and worse, there was no drinking water. Catherine had only rested in small intervals and even when she was working, she was constantly looking at the door wishing John to come in. By last count over fifteen hundred residents had sought shelter at St. Mary's Hospital. The hospital's ground floor had flooded and numerous windows broken out, but everyone who sought shelter there survived.

It was late morning when word came that St. Mary's Orphanage had been destroyed along with all the orphans and sisters. There were three boys, however, who did survive by holding on to a tree. It was devastating news to the sisters and the priest. They were their family. The magnitude of their loss made them stop and reflect on their own lives. How could this have happened? There were no answers and all they could do was pray,

Catherine could hardly contain herself. Sister Maria and Sister Margaret were gone. All of them were now gone. It was unimaginable. Catherine could not hold it in any longer and she began to cry. It was difficult to comprehend what had just happened and she felt helpless and empty. Why, she asked herself, and she quietly prayed for their souls.

Every available building left standing in the city was now being used as a hospital. All of Galveston waited, hoping that help would come soon. The telegraph lines had been down since noon on Saturday and there was no phone service. Their only hope was that their lack of communication with the outside world would be noticed and someone would send help.

John woke up and lifted up his head, trying to get his bearings. It had stopped raining and when he tried to move his arm, it seemed to be stuck. Was he alive? he wondered. After the horrific ghouls of the night, John wasn't sure. He was lying on his stomach and something was on top of his left arm. He looked at it and tried to move his fingers. He turned and looked back over his shoulder, trying to figure out where he was and if anyone else was nearby.

"Help! Help!" John cried out.

His arm was hurting and that was a good thing, he thought. His fingers seemed to have feeling also. When John made an attempt to get up, the pile of debris shifted and several pieces of wood crashed down on him.

"Is anyone there?" cried John. He looked up and then down. The size of the lumber pile he was partially buried under was only about six feet high and he figured that he was somewhere in the middle. He cried out one more time. The life jacket he had been wearing was also caught on something that prohibited him from moving very far.

"Hello," shouted a strange voice.

John looked in the direction of the voice and saw two men coming. Both men worked carefully and diligently, moving some of the upper debris away from John so it wouldn't fall down on him. They worked for over thirty minutes before they could get to the large timber that had imprisoned John's arm.

Once he was free, John was able to stand on his own. He was weak and a bit disoriented, but he was alive. He didn't remember, but sometime during the night the timber fell on his left arm and broke it in two places.

"You're lucky to be alive," said one of the men.

"Do you have someplace you can go?" the other asked.

"Yes," John answered. "My wife is an intern at the St Mary's Hospital, and I want to go there if you can point me in the direction."

They pointed in the direction they had come and told John they were going to search for more survivors if he could manage on his own. John shook their hands and thanked them.

Maneuvering over all the mess and debris was difficult, but John managed to figure out where the street was and then realized he was only about six blocks from where his house used to be. John found an apron in the street and used it to make a sling for his arm. It was getting extremely painful but he knew he had to get to Catherine. He hoped and prayed the hospital was still standing. John stopped suddenly and felt sick to his stomach when he saw a small boy's lifeless body lying face up with his eyes open. His badly damaged body was naked and had come to rest next to a storm drain. In all his life, John had never faced such emotional trauma. He thought of Catherine and felt empathy for her when she suffered her brutal attack; the fear and anxiety that she must have felt when she thought she was going to die. How could he have not understood? He wanted, no needed, to find her. He was nothing without her. It took John over an hour to make his way through the rubble and torn city. The hospital was still standing. The wooden buildings that were beside it were gone, but the brick building that was the main hospital was still there.

Catherine was on the third floor and walked over to the window to look out. She had done this countless times, searching through the streets, watching closely when she saw movement. Families were carrying the dead, mothers and fathers were weeping over their lost loved ones. She felt their pain. Catherine had suffered loss. Her own family was gone and now she had to face the fact that her husband may be gone.

She almost walked back to continue her work when something caught her eye. A block or so away she saw a man with a slight limp and there was a white apron around his neck that he was using for a sling. She concentrated on his movements. Could it be John? Catherine took off running and took the steps two at a time, almost falling. Several peopled asked her where she was going but she didn't stop to answer them.

When she got outside, she saw nothing and wondered if it was just an illusion. Catherine couldn't remember what direction the man was coming from, so she waited. She walked around debris to get to the middle of the street to get a better view. She saw nothing. Tears began to fill her eyes as she tried to face the fact that John was gone. She picked up the bottom of her laboratory coat and tried to dry her tears away. When she finished and looked up, she saw him. Battered, dirty, and shaken, John was standing twenty feet away from her with a faint smile on his face.

"John!" she screamed, and ran to him.

John melted to his knees and Catherine threw her arms around him and kissed him. They both were crying and John's face was buried in Catherine's breast. They were together and both had survived.

John got up and Catherine helped him walk to the hospital. They stopped by to see Amelia who was equally as glad to see her brother had made it though the storm and then Catherine took him into the emergency room to set his arm. He was badly dehydrated, so she gave John some fluids and told him to lie still. She also took some disinfectant and used it to clean his arm and then his face and hands. His hair and body were caked with dirt and filth and she helped him undress and put some hospital clothing on him.

Father Jonathan came by to check on John and was delighted it was just a broken arm. When Catherine finished setting John's arm and putting a plaster cast on it, a nurse called Catherine to assist another patient but Catherine did not want to go. She couldn't leave John, not now.

"You go, Catherine, I'll be here when you are through. I could use some sleep," he said and gave her a slight smile. Catherine bent down and kissed him.

"I'll be back," she said. "I love you."

She stood motionless for a moment, just staring at him, and was thankful he was not seriously hurt. Catherine was exhausted and had not slept for more than thirty minutes since her arrival Saturday morning. She was working on adrenalin and she willed herself to work. After she finished with her patient, she went to her locker and retrieved the bagel and cheese she had not eaten. She had had a glass of milk earlier and some stale crackers, so she took the food to John along with a bottle of orange juice she had gotten from the staff's break area. He had not fallen asleep, so he ate the bagel and drank the juice Catherine had brought him. Food was scarce now and that may be all they got for awhile. Catherine had John moved to the upper ward so that the emergency room bed he was occupying could be used as it had been intended. Later that afternoon Catherine crawled into the bed beside John and fell fast asleep.

The destructive path of the storm and its offspring of wind and soaring waters destroyed over thirty-five hundred houses and hundreds of institutions and buildings. An estimated six thousand men, women, and children also lost their lives. The only communication with the mainland was by boat. All three of the railroad bridges and the wagon bridge had been destroyed. The pumping station that supplied drinking water to Galveston from the artesian wells eighteen miles from the city ceased to work. There were a few cisterns that were still used around the city and the ones that were positioned high enough to escape contamination were the only sources available for immediate usage. Food that was stored in cans and jars was collected from grocery stores, hotels and businesses to feed the hungry. It would be two more days before any help was able to get through from the mainland. The businessmen gathered together quickly to maintain some order to their business and outside military was brought in to stop the scavengers and looting that had taken over the city. It would take weeks to dispose of the dead and because of the magnitude, the only solution was to burn the bodies.

CHAPTER 37

Several days after the storm it was clear to everyone that Galveston would never be the same. Those who survived and still had homes standing offered shelter to those who lost everything. Minnie Wyman and Professor Edward Gordon had also taken shelter at the hospital. Minnie's other boarder had moved away prior to the storm. Minnie found out that her house was still standing and had minimal damage because she had someone put her storm shutters up the day before the storm. It was a miracle, she thought. Her house was one of the older ones on the street and she had convinced herself that the house just had good bones. It was also closer to town. Minnie knew Catherine, Amelia, and John were all at the hospital, too, so invited them all to stay at her house. It would take a few days for everything to dry out but at least it was a roof over their heads. They gratefully accepted.

Catherine, John, Minnie, and Professor Gordon slowly walked the debris ridden streets to Minnie's house. Catherine had made arrangements for Amelia to stay with the sisters at the hospital until the streets were passable and she could ride in a wagon. The smell of human decomposition and burning was difficult to bear, but they had no choice. In time Catherine knew that it would eventually disappear.

The second floor of Minnie's house did not get flooded like the downstairs, and because the house had been built up six feet on stilts and then covered with facia board, it had already begun to dry. The furniture and bedding were only damp on the first floor, and the few rugs covering the wood floors were hung on the clothesline to dry.

Minnie found dry food in the cupboard and the ice box seal protected the food inside. She made some sandwiches and opened up some cans of corn and green beans which they welcomed even though they were room temperature. It was their first real meal in two days. Professor Gordon shared some of his clothing with John and it hung loosely on him. He didn't mind and was grateful to have something clean to wear.

They were told that the Grande Opera House suffered damage, but it would be restored. John's bank also made it through the storm and would reopen. They were grateful they had survived. Catherine wanted to spend the next few days with John before he had to go back to work so she arranged to get a few days off from the hospital. The medical school would open again in a few weeks and she would return to school.

Catherine and John stayed upstairs in her old room and Catherine was overcome by emotion when she thought about her mother and their happy times together. She looked at John, determined to be the wife he wanted her to be. Nothing would ever separate them, not David Brooks, not a storm, nothing. They settled into their new home, happy they were together. The past was behind them now. They had survived it all. John came to her as though he were reading her mind and kissed her sweetly and lovingly.

"My little Catherine, everything will be fine. We will start over," he said.

Catherine looked up at him and said, "I want to have lots of children with you, Mr. Merit."

AUTHORS NOTE:

This is the first book of the Indignities trilogy. The Aftermath and The Atonement will continue the life of Catherine Merit as she struggles to find her place in America. Each book is filled with romance, heartache and tragedy and will hold you in suspense in every chapter.

CPSIA information can be obtained
at www.ICGtesting.com
Printed in the USA
FFOW03n1800050914
7231FF